THE END OF THE RAINBOW

V.C. ANDREWS®

THE END OF THE RAINBOW

G.K. Hall & Co. • Chivers Press
Waterville, Maine USA   Bath, England

This Large Print edition is published by G.K. Hall & Co., USA and by Chivers Press, England.

Published in 2001 in the U.S. by arrangement with Pocket Books, a division of Simon & Schuster, Inc.

Published in 2001 in the U.K. by arrangement with Simon & Schuster UK Ltd.

U.S. Hardcover 0-7838-9512-7   (Core Series Edition)
U.K. Hardcover 0-7540-1694-3   (Windsor Large Print)
U.K. Softcover 0-7540-9098-1   (Paragon Large Print)

The text of this Large Print edition is unabridged.
Other aspects of the book may vary from the original edition.

Set in 16 pt. Plantin by Elena Picard.

Printed in the United States on permanent paper.

British Library Cataloguing-in-Publication Data available

Library of Congress Cataloging-in-Publication Data

Andrews, V. C. (Virginia C.)
    The end of the rainbow / V. C. Andrews.
        p. cm. — (Hudson family series ; bk. 4)
    ISBN 0-7838-9512-7 (lg. print : hc : alk. paper)
    1. Teenage girls — Fiction. 2. Mothers and daughters — Fiction.   3. Virginia — Fiction. I. Title.
PS3551.N454 E54 2001
    813'.54—dc21   2001026378

THE END OF THE RAINBOW

Prologue

On my sixteenth birthday, there wasn't a single cloud in the sky. An uninterrupted sea of baby blue was spread from one horizon to the other, and the warm breeze scented with hyacinths, lilacs and daffodils was as gentle as the flutter of air from a passing sparrow.

It was magic.

Twilight the day before, I had pushed Mommy in her wheelchair down the ramp and turned her toward the lake.

"There's one!" Mommy cried as soon as she caught sight of the first blackbird lifting from a tree branch in the surrounding forest and gliding over the water.

Then, as we often did, we held hands and closed our eyes and made our wishes. It was our special little secret ceremony, something we had begun doing together since I was four because it was something she said she had always done. She believed in the power of the lake and its surroundings.

"I started doing it almost as soon as I had arrived to live with your great-grandmother Hudson," she told me. "Before that the only body of water I had really spent any time near was what was in my bathtub. A place like this was perfect for my dreams and still is. I know it will be perfect for yours as well, Summer."

We both had wished for a wonderful tomorrow. I imagined a day when smiles would float down from Heaven itself, settling so deeply in the faces of all my relatives and friends that they would all forget every sad or troubling thought, every unhappy moment. Then we would all ring in my new year in harmony. Mommy believed we needed a dose of magic here and there to protect us, especially us.

I didn't disagree, for now I was well past the age when I wouldn't be permitted to hear about and learn about the tragedies and the mistakes that marked our family history. Mommy confessed that sometimes — perhaps even more often than sometimes — she truly believed there was a curse haunting her every step, her every breath. Even her every thought.

"Anyone else would probably have come to a point where she was unable to make another decision, Summer. My hands used to tremble on the steering wheel of my specially equipped van even when I approached an ordinary intersection and merely had to decide whether to go right or left.

Surely something terrible would occur if I made the wrong choice, I thought. The only reason why I didn't freeze up was because I kept hearing my adopted mother's voice urging me on and chiding me for being afraid," Mommy said. "That woman could face down Armageddon."

I could certainly understand Mommy's fear and often wondered if such a curse could be passed on to me. That was Mommy's worst worry, too.

"What if the strongest, biggest thing I gave you was my own bad luck?" Mommy suddenly said, as if she had read my mind.

"That's silly, Mommy," I told her, even though I wasn't sure. "There's no such thing as being destined to have bad luck. It's all just chance and no one's to blame. You couldn't be the cause of anyone's trouble," I insisted and did so with such vehemence she had to laugh and promise not to speak such dark thoughts to me again.

But, she would. She couldn't help it. She was carrying a sack full of guilt.

She was especially pursued by the memories of her stepsister, Beneatha, being murdered by gang members in Washington, D.C. — where Mommy first lived — and also troubling her was the car accident that had killed her half brother, my uncle Brody, who I never met. I saw his photograph and was well aware of how handsome he had been and how much promise his future had held for him. He died rushing home after visiting Mommy when she lived here all alone. Grandmother Megan, Mommy's real mother, suffered a terrible nervous breakdown after Uncle Brody's accident. She almost committed suicide.

Aunt Alison, Uncle Brody's sister, still harbored ill feeling toward Mommy, although lately she disguised it well and was at least civil when she was here, not that she was that often. Recently, she had gone through a nasty divorce, her husband accusing her of being an adulteress and not only with one other lover either! That, I wasn't told however. That I overheard.

In our house the walls don't keep secrets behind them too well.

Anyone would think Aunt Alison should feel sorry for Mommy. Not long after Brody's death, she had become a paraplegic when she was thrown from her horse. Then she had suffered horribly under the hands of her bizarre and mad Aunt Victoria, Grandmother Megan's sister. For a while Mommy was basically a prisoner in this house. She hated talking about it. She said it revived nightmares, but Mommy believed that she had been punished for bringing all this bad luck. She actually thought she deserved it, and if it wasn't for my father, Austin, who had become her physical therapist, she might have succeeded in doing away with herself in this very lake we now serenely gazed upon.

We had filled this lake with tears enough, it seemed to me. It was time for smiles and laughter and sunshine, and if it took my birth and my birthdays to make that strong and stronger, I was happy to do it.

From where we looked out over the lake to make our wishes, we could see Uncle Roy, Mommy's stepbrother, repairing a window shutter on his house. After he had left the army, Mommy had asked him to work for her and Grandmother Megan's real estate and construction development company. He became a job foreman and soon began dating my nanny, Glenda Robinson, who was an unwed mother with a child only a year older than I was at the time, a boy named Harley. When Uncle Roy proposed to Glenda and she agreed to marry him, Mommy decided they should build their home on our property.

"I have all this land, Roy," she told him, "land that's no use to me. I'm not going to grow cotton or tobacco. This isn't Tara," she joked.

From what she told me, I understood Uncle Roy wasn't so eager to do it. She had to get my father to talk him into it. Uncle Roy had his reasons, which according to Mommy, stemmed from his stubborn pride. Later, I would learn there were other reasons, perhaps more important and deeper reasons, the sort that start somewhere near the bottom of your very soul and make themselves heard almost daily.

Mommy loved to describe the dramatic scenes from her past for me, deepening her voice to imitate Uncle Roy's. Sometimes I laughed; sometimes, I listened in complete wonder, mesmerized by her ability to get me to see it all happening right before me. After all, Mommy had attended a prestigious London school of drama and had almost become an actress.

"Roy still wasn't going to build his house here," she had told me. "I accused him of being afraid to marry a white woman and live on the same estate with a white man who married an African American woman.

" 'You're half white,' your uncle Roy reminded me.

" 'Well,' I countered, 'a hundred and fifty years ago I'd still be a slave, Roy Arnold. Don't try to make me feel any less or any better than you. If Mama Latisha heard such talk, she'd whip you good for it,' I told him, waving my skinny little finger in his face for a change. He had to shake his head and laugh. And then he had to give in and build the house," she told me.

A year after he married Glenda, they had a baby girl, whom they named Latisha after Uncle Roy's mother and Mommy's adopted mother. She was a pretty child, but just after she had turned three, she developed leukemia; she went so fast, the doctors nearly didn't have time to tell them there was little hope.

It almost destroyed Aunt Glenda. She nearly lost her faith. But then rather than hate God for it, she became very religious. Harley once told me his mother believed children were punished for the sins of their parents. After little Latisha's death, Aunt Glenda believed if she didn't become righteous, her daughter would suffer even more in the hereafter. It absorbed her full being now, and from the way he said it, I knew he was in mourning too, but not only for his sister. He mourned that he had also lost his mother to the tragedy and left his upbringing more or less to my uncle Roy.

"You'd never know I'm an only child now," he told me. "My mother acts as if Latisha is still with us, only out there, sleeping under the stars. Sometimes, she acts as if she hears her. She keeps all her things out, even washes and irons her clothes. It drives both me and Roy crazy."

The worst kind of sibling rivalry was being forced to compete with your dead sister for your mother's attention, I thought.

They buried Latisha on the grounds of the estate, close to their house. Uncle Roy put up a pretty fence and gate around her grave and tombstone. Aunt Glenda had turned it into a sacred site and a day didn't pass when she wasn't over there praying at her lost little daughter's tombstone. I looked out my window at night and often saw a lone candle burning, Glenda's silhouette forming under the stars or under an overcast sky. Once I even saw her out there in the rain and lightning, holding her umbrella, unconcerned about the lightning flashing around her.

"A mother never lets go," Mommy told me when we discussed the things Harley told me, "even if she has to put her hand through fire."

I was too young at the time of Latisha's death, but years later, I would hear Mommy mutter to herself that she had once again brought bad luck to someone.

"I should have let Roy live far away from me, just as he had wanted," she moaned.

No one got angrier at her for saying things like that than Uncle Roy. His eyes would redden like an electric stove range; he would swell up his shoulders, which made him look even wider and taller, and then he would deepen his voice to chastise her and forbid her from saying such things.

"You're the one Mama would whip for saying that," he assured her, his long, thick right forefinger pointed at her face like an arrow.

No one wanted to be around an angry Uncle Roy, least of all his stepson Harley. These days Harley was in trouble at school and with his friends so often, Uncle Roy's brow was practically frozen with deep wrinkles and thick rolls from his constant scowling.

"The Lord left me a strange burden," I overheard Uncle Roy tell Mommy more than once. "He took my chance to be a daddy away from me when He took Latisha, but He left me with a father's responsibilities for a boy I never fathered. You talk about curses being put on you. I don't think I've done anything to deserve this burden, but I've got it."

"Mama used to say it's not for us to decide whether or not what the Lord does is right or wrong, Roy."

"Yeah. That don't seem right either," he told her.

It saddened me to hear such things. I couldn't

help but think of Harley. It's hard, I thought, hard to be unwanted. I knew it made Mommy sad, too.

No one knew better than she did what that meant.

And I hoped and prayed it was something I'd never have to learn.

1

Happy Birthday, Summer

It seemed as if a rainbow had burst over our house and grounds. I knew that Daddy had been secretly planning some surprises, but I was not prepared for all that he had done. The moment the morning sun nudged my eyes open, I heard the gentle tinkling notes of "Happy Birthday to You." With sleepy eyes I gazed at a precious and dazzling merry-go-round spinning a menagerie of animals around a ballerina who danced at its center.

"I hope you always wake with a smile like that, Summer," Daddy said.

I looked up and saw Daddy standing there. His face was glowing almost as much as mine. I had his turquoise eyes, but Mommy's ebony hair and a complexion a few shades lighter so anyone could see that I had also clearly inherited Daddy's freckles, especially at the crests of my cheeks.

"Happy birthday, sweetheart," he said and

leaned over to kiss me on the cheek.

Mommy watched from her wheelchair on the opposite side of my bed. For a moment she looked so distant, almost as though she was on the outside of a great glass bubble set around me. I knew she was having one of those Evil Eye thoughts, those fears that whenever she was too happy, something terrible would happen. She seemed to realize it herself and brightened quickly into a smile. I rose to hug her.

"What were the two of you doing?" I cried as the merry-go-round continued. "Sitting here waiting for me to wake up? How long have you been here?"

"We were watching you all night," Daddy joked. "We took turns, didn't we, Rain?"

"Practically," Mommy said. "Your crazy father has been acting as if this was more his birthday than yours." She jokingly put on a look of disapproval. "More and more these days, he acts like a sixteen-year-old."

"You never lose the child within you entirely," Daddy assured us. "I want to blow out candles on my ninetieth birthday and unwrap presents. Don't forget to arrange for that, you two," he ordered, sounding like it was just around the corner.

Mommy shook her head and smiled at me as if the two of us were allies forced to tolerate another foolish man. Daddy could never be a foolish man to me, never, ever, I thought.

"It's a beautiful merry-go-round," I said as it stopped.

"That," my mother said, "is not even the tip of the iceberg. Look out the window," she urged me.

My room overlooked the lake. Grandmother Megan told me it had once been her room, and Mommy said she used it when she had first arrived. Now, she and Daddy used what was Grandmother Hudson's room, only they had changed the decor and replaced all the furniture. The bathroom had been updated to provide for Mommy's special needs.

In the beginning Mommy didn't want to make dramatic changes in the house. She said she felt an obligation to Grandmother Hudson's memory to keep it close to how it had been, but in time rugs wore, walls had to be repainted, fixtures replaced, appliances changed, and Daddy brought in a decorator to give it all what they called a more eclectic style.

The hallways still had the spirit of the nineteenth century with some Federal antiques, like a White and Dogswell clock that hung across from a circular mirror of that period. Mommy was very proud of all the antiques left by my Grandmother Hudson. Mommy had loved her very much, so much that I was jealous and wished I had been able to know her, too.

Grandfather Hudson's office was the same as it had always been, but much of the rest of the house — the living room, the kitchen, my bedroom and Daddy and Mommy's — had been modernized with lighter colors and softer fabrics. Recently my parents had redone the maid's quarters, covering the floor with a thick white shag rug and replacing what had been a hospital bed with a queen-size cherry wood one; this pleased Mrs. Geary very much.

After Glenda had married Uncle Roy and she and Harley had moved out of the main house, Mommy and Daddy hired Mrs. Geary through an agency. She was in her early forties at the time and had come from Ireland to live and work in America when she was in her late twenties. Now streaked with gray, her hair had once been almost as red as Daddy's. She had been working for her distant American relatives who she said treated her as badly as Cinderella's stepmother treated Cinderella.

"There was no respect. Everything I did was simply expected, too. Not an ounce of gratitude! I was glad to get out of there," she told me.

Daddy said he liked her because she had an inner strength and confidence he thought would make her an asset in a household where the mistress was disabled. Mommy and she took to each other immediately, and by now it was impossible for me to think of her as anything less than a member of our family. She was often a second mother to me, ordering me to dress more warmly or eat better. She even had something to say about where I would go and with whom I would go. A mother hen didn't hover over an egg as much as Mrs. Geary hovered over me as I grew up under both her and Mommy's wings.

"I spent almost as much time and energy as

your mother keeping you growing healthy and strong, and I'm not about to see my investment go sour," she told me if I complained. She loved to find words and expressions to avoid expressing her true feelings for me. It was as if she believed that the moment you told someone you loved her, you lost her. I would learn that her own early childhood and teenage years were filled with enough loss to make her think this way.

Nevertheless, I teased her whenever I could, especially about her endless ongoing romance with Clarence Lynch, the librarian at the municipal library. Like her, he was in his late fifties. They had been seeing each other socially for as long as I could remember.

Once, when I asked her why she had never married him, her reply was, "Why would I want to ruin a perfectly good relationship?"

It confused me, of course, and I ran to Mommy with questions. She simply smiled and said, "Summer, not everyone fits so neatly into the little boxes society has created. As long as they're happy, why ask them to change?"

In Mommy's mind, and I now think mine too, happiness and health were two sides of the same coin, the most important and valuable coin. People who were happy had more hope of being healthy; of course, people who were healthy were happy. Smiles and laughter were the best medications for the illnesses of the spirit.

No one illustrated this better than Daddy, I thought. He loved Mommy and me so much and was so happy that anyone could see him and feel him radiating with warmth and well-being. He was still a highly respected physical therapist who had assumed his uncle's therapy business and then had created a chain of unique health clubs that combined regular exercise with therapeutic programs. They were known as rejuvenation clubs; their theme was that through exercise and meditation aging could be slowed down and even in some cases reversed. National health and exercise magazines had even featured Daddy in articles. I was very proud of him and so was Mommy.

Yes, happiness and health were truly the twin sisters my family had adopted to live beside me. They nurtured wisdom and wove a protective wall around our house. Nothing terrible from the outside could hurt us, I thought. But what I also knew was trouble loomed nearby in Uncle Roy's sad and dour world, and it also came riding into our fortress in the form of a Trojan horse named Alison, my Aunt Alison.

"People who don't like themselves can't like anyone else," Mommy once told me. "Your aunt Alison hates herself. She just doesn't know it or want to know it. I feel more pity for her than I do anger, and you will, too," Mommy predicted.

Aunt Alison, as well as Grandmother Megan and my stepgrandfather Grant Randolph would all be here today for my birthday party.

Now in the morning light, I stood by the window and parted the curtains as Mommy had directed. For a moment I thought I was still

21

dreaming. My mouth hung open.

All of the trees below had been strewn with bright colored ribbons. Many branches had balloons tied to them and they were all dancing to the rhythms of the breezes. Tables covered with green and red and yellow paper tablecloths were all set up on the lawn, and a dance floor was being laid out as I watched. There was even a small stage for musicians.

Daddy had kept my party arrangements a big secret and had obviously paid people extra to come quietly on the grounds very early in the morning, before the sun was even up, to begin constructing it all.

"Your father was out there in the dark with a flashlight hanging balloons," Mommy told me.

"I thought it would be more fun to wake up to it than see it happening days before," he commented from behind.

I still had trouble finding my voice. Finally, I shook my head and shrieked with joy.

"It's . . . beautiful!"

I rushed into his arms to kiss him and then hugged and kissed Mommy who couldn't stop laughing at my excitement.

"Is your father crazy or not?"

"NO!" I cried. "He's wonderful!"

"You see," Daddy said, "at least I have one woman in this house who sees sense in the things I do."

"You poor outnumbered man," Mommy teased.

"Well, you should have heard Mrs. Geary mumbling how it was all too much of this or too much of that and how even happy shocks can be damaging to a young, impressionable spirit."

"Don't make fun of her," Mommy softly chided.

"Make fun of her? It's everyone else who's making fun of me. All right. I've got some small matters to look after, such as the parking arrangements. I don't want any of Summer's teenager friends driving their cars over the flowers," Daddy said and left.

Mommy shook her head and smiled after him. Would I ever find anyone I loved as much and who loved me as much as my parents loved each other? They were living proof that there really was such a thing as soul mates.

"You'd better get yourself dressed and come down to breakfast," she said turning back to me and starting away.

"I'm too excited to eat, Mommy."

"If you don't, Mrs. Geary will single-handedly rip every balloon off every tree and pack up the tables and chairs," she warned. We laughed.

I hugged her again.

"Happy, happy birthday, Summer. All your birthdays have been special to me because it was truly a miracle for us to have you," she said softly, "but I know how special this one is for you."

"Thank you, Mommy."

I knew how true that was, how difficult my birth was for her and how they had decided not to try to have any more children and test their good luck.

"I'll see you downstairs," she said and continued to wheel herself out to the chair elevator that would take her down the stairs and to the wheelchair below.

Never in my life had my mother ever stood on her own beside me. Never had we walked side by side or ran together. Never had we gone strolling through department stores or down streets to window-shop.

When I was old enough to push her, I thought it was fun. After all, I was a little girl moving my mother along. But somewhere along the way, I turned to watch other mothers and daughters walking through malls, and I looked at Mommy's face and saw the longing and the sadness and no longer did I feel excited or amused by it.

Was that what growing older meant? I wondered. Losing all your illusions?

If that was so, why were any of us so happy and so willing to blow out the candles?

Mrs. Geary milled about the breakfast table longer than she had to, studying me eat as if my consumption of food was part of some important experiment.

"It's a big day," she preached when I complained about being given too much. "Big days require bigger fortification. I know what's going to happen out there after the festivities start. You won't eat a thing and you'll be going, going, going

24

— draining and draining that wisp of a willow of a body of yours. That's when sickness comes knocking on the door anticipating a big fat welcome."

Mommy looked down at her dish of grapefruit slices, hiding her smile.

"I'm not a wisp of a willow," I protested.

After all, I was five feet four and nearly one hundred and fifteen pounds. Mommy told me I had a figure like hers once was, although I didn't need to be told. I saw the pictures of her when she was in acting school in London. In all of the photographs, she looked like someone just caught the moment after a wonderful new experience or sight. Her face glowed. There was no better compliment for me than to be compared to Mommy.

Mrs. Geary always came in the backdoor with her flatteries, especially about my looks and figure.

"Nature plays a trick on young girls," she informed me. "Before you have a woman's mind, you get a woman's body. It's like putting a diamond necklace around the neck of a four-year-old girl. She has no idea why everyone, especially grownups, are staring at her and she doesn't know yet how to wear it or carry it."

"Young people are different today," I insisted when she made these speeches at me. "We're far more sophisticated than young people were when you were my age."

"Oh please," she cried, slapping her hand over her forehead. It was her favorite dramatic gesture.

I actually heard the sharp crack of her palm on her skin. "More sophisticated? You have more teenage pregnancies, more children in trouble with drugs, more car accidents, more runaways.

"When I was your age, the only pregnant girl in the village was a girl raped by her idiot step-brother."

"Mommy!" I'd moan in desperation.

"She's only trying to give you good advice, honey," Mommy said, but she gave Mrs. Geary a look that said, "Enough."

"I'll eat at my party," I promised. "Daddy's having them make all my favorite things."

That was a mistake. I knew it the moment the words slipped past my lips. Daddy had hired caterers even though Mrs. Geary said she would prepare all the food. He insisted it was an unfair burden to place on her, but she countered with a surprising admission that preparing the food for my birthday was a special pleasure for her. In the end she was given the responsibility for the birthday cake.

She grunted at my statement and shook her head. Occasionally, Mrs. Geary would go to a stylist to have her hair cut and shaped, but most of the time, she wore it pinned back in a severe bun. For my party, however, she had surprised us all by having it cut and trimmed in a French style. She had pretty green eyes and a small nose and mouth but a chin that disappeared too quickly. At five feet seven, she was somewhat portly with heavy arms and a robust bosom. She did have a very soft complexion with not even a sign of an impending wrinkle, something she ascribed to keeping makeup and rough soap off her skin.

"Manufactured food," she muttered with disdain. "It'll have a mass-produced taste."

"Now, Mrs. Geary," Mommy gently chastised. "You know it's not manufactured food."

Mrs. Geary bit down on her lower lip, shook her head and went into the kitchen. Mommy smiled at me and said Mrs. Geary would be fine.

I gobbled down the remainder of my breakfast, too excited to sit a moment longer.

Daddy was outside working with the grounds people to be sure everything was set up the way he wanted it to be. A little more than two dozen of my girlfriends from the Dogwood School for Girls and almost twenty boys from our sister school, Sweet William, would be attending as well as some of my teachers and, of course, my family and Mrs. Geary's Mr. Lynch.

I didn't think of myself as going steady with anyone, but I was seeing Chase Taylor more than anyone else. I had gone on dates with him the last four weekends in a row, and it only took two consecutive dates with the same boy for the girls in my school to have someone practically engaged. I knew almost all my girlfriends envied me. Chase was handsome in a classic way with his perfect nose and sensual lips. He had eyes that could have been the inspiration for the blue sky on a perfect spring day. Daddy approved of him because he was very athletic, six feet two with what Daddy called football shoulders and a swimmer's waist. The truth was he played halfback on the football team and was the record holder for Sweet William's freestyle stroke. He was even thinking of trying out for the Olympics.

Chase's father, Guy Taylor, was one of the area's most successful attorneys. Their house was almost as big as ours, but their property wasn't as nice. Chase told me that his mother coveted ours.

"She wants whatever someone else has," he remarked with a frankness I hadn't expected. "So my father works harder and harder. He says it takes an ambitious woman to make a man a success. Are you ambitious, Summer?"

"I don't think I'm overly ambitious," I told him. "It's not good to be too ambitious. Mrs. Geary says, 'Men would be angels and angels would be gods.' It's a quote from some playwright."

He laughed.

"How lucky you are to have so wise a maid," he said. I didn't like the way he said maid and told him firmly that Mrs. Geary was more than a servant in our house. My flare of anger didn't frighten him.

He smiled at me and said when I got angry, my eyes were the most exciting jewels he had ever seen. I blushed and he kissed me. I thought, maybe Mrs. Geary was right after all about a young girl burdened with a woman's body. Feelings went off like alarms through my breasts and down into my thighs. We kissed again and again, each kiss longer and longer; when we touched our tongues on our most recent date, I had to scream at myself to stop him from pulling down the zipper on my Capri pants.

"Don't you want to?" he whispered in my ear. We had parked off the road to my house after going to the movies.

"Yes," I said, "and no."

"Teasing me?"

"Teasing myself," I said. "So let's stop before I break out in pimples."

He laughed.

"Who told you that would happen, Mrs. Geary?"

"No one. I made it up," I said. My sense of humor kept him smiling even though I knew he was frustrated. I was too, but I'd die before confessing it.

If he asks me out again, I'll know he really cares for me. If not, I thought, I've been lucky. That was something Mommy taught me.

Maybe I wasn't such a little girl. Maybe turning sixteen was an understatement. Maybe I was old and wise for my age and all the things Mrs. Geary thought and feared about teenagers today simply didn't apply to me. Maybe I was too arrogant.

Maybes hovered everywhere, bouncing about me like the balloons tied to all the trees.

I ran down Mommy's ramp in front of the house and joined Daddy at the tables. The party was being organized like a camp event. All my guests had been encouraged to bring their bathing suits. Four years ago, Daddy had gotten Uncle Roy to construct a raft which they placed at the center of the lake. We had pedal boats and two kayaks as well as two rowboats. The lake had catfish and bass. However, Uncle Roy complained that fishing in it was like dipping your hook into a goldfish bowl. He said there was no challenge.

He was over by the dance floor making sure it was laid down properly. I looked about, expecting to see Harley, too, but he wasn't anywhere in sight.

"Hi, Uncle Roy," I called approaching. He turned from the floor where he was kneeling and looked up at me.

"Hey, Princess. Happy birthday." He had been calling me Princess for as long as I could remember. Once, when I walked in on a conversation Uncle Roy was having with Mommy, I heard him wistfully say, 'She could have been my daughter.' I had no idea what he had meant at the time, but I knew he meant me.

"Thank you, Uncle Roy."

"The way some of you kids dance these days, this thing could splinter up in minutes," he complained. "I told them I wanted thicker boards."

"It'll be fine, Uncle Roy," I assured him.

"Umm," he said skeptically and stood up.

When I was younger, Mommy often described how safe and secure she would feel when she walked in the streets of Washington, D.C., holding Uncle Roy's hand. It wasn't merely his size, his muscles, his large hands that surely swallowed hers in a gulp of fingers that gave her this security. Uncle Roy had an aura of power about him, a danger that came from his sleeping rages, I thought. Although no one could ever be as sweet and loving to me as he was — with the exception of Mommy and Daddy, of course — I always sensed the tension and blood-red anger lurking just below the surface of his every smile, his every word, his every glance and look.

Even Chase remarked to me one day that my uncle reminded him of a secret service agent or something.

"He looks at me like he expects I might try to assassinate you. He makes me nervous. Man, I wouldn't want to face him in some dark alley."

"He's a pussycat," I said even though I secretly agreed.

Mommy told me Uncle Roy was so hard and distrusting because of all the disappointments in his life.

I didn't really understand what was the biggest, not yet, but soon enough I would.

It would be another gift from time and age, the sort you wished remained wrapped and left under the Christmas tree forever and ever.

"Where's Harley?" I asked Uncle Roy.

He did what he always did whenever Harley's name was mentioned. He tightened his lips and lifted his shoulders as if he was preparing to receive a blow to his head.

"Thinking up some crime or misdemeanor," he replied.

"Uncle Roy," I said smiling.

"I don't know. He didn't come down to break-

31

fast, which isn't unusual. That boy sleeps more than he's awake and especially sleeps late on weekends. Soon, he won't be able to; soon, he'll have to work for a living," he said with relish.

Uncle Roy was referring to the fact that Harley, if he passed his finals, would graduate high school this year. He attended the public school. Unfortunately, Harley had been in trouble at school most of his senior-high years. He had been suspended three times and almost expelled for fighting. He had been accused of vandalism and stealing, but that couldn't be proven.

Harley was far from being an unintelligent boy, and he was even far from being lazy, especially when he was doing something he liked. He had artistic abilities. He liked to draw, but mostly buildings and bridges. Mrs. Longo, his art teacher, wanted him to pursue a career in architecture, but Harley acted as if that was the same as telling him to pursue becoming a NASA astronaut.

Uncle Roy wanted him to enlist in the army, even though his own experience with it had been a failure. He had been court-martialed for going AWOL right after Mommy had fallen from the horse and become a paraplegic. He was in Germany at the time, and he wanted to come right home to her; but he had violated a leave once before and he was on probation. As a result he received a dishonorable discharge after serving some time in a military prison, which was something Harley threw back at him whenever they got into a bad shouting match.

It amazed me how fearless Harley could be whenever he had to face Uncle Roy. Harley was a slim, six-foot tall, dark-complexioned boy with hazel eyes spotted with green. He wasn't as handsome as Chase, but he had a certain look that reminded my girlfriends of Kevin Bacon, especially when he smiled with disdain or mockery, which he often did these days. He made fun of all the boys at Sweet William, even Chase, calling them and my girlfriends "mushy kids," because of their privileged lives, their money, their sports cars and clothes and what he termed their "fluffy thoughts."

He refused to categorize me the same way, however, claiming I was somehow different even though I came from a family with money and attended the same private school.

"Why am I different?" I asked him.

"You just are," he insisted.

"Why? I do everything they do, don't I? Few of them have more than I have."

"You just are," he repeated.

"Why?"

"Because I say so," he finally blurted and walked away from me.

He could be the most infuriating boy I knew, and yet . . . yet there were times when I caught him looking at me with different eyes, softer eyes, almost childlike and loving eyes.

It was all so confusing.

That was why I sometimes thought that Mrs.

Geary might be right about my being too young for the jewels of womanhood I was blessed with.

I looked toward Uncle Roy's house. I was disappointed. I had hoped Harley would be almost as excited about my party as I was and would be out here by now.

"Maybe I'll go see if he's at breakfast," I said.

"Don't waste your time," Uncle Roy advised. "Hey!" he screamed at one of the workmen. "You're putting that in wrong. It's a tongue and groove."

He walked away and I started for his house. Uncle Roy had built a modest sized two-story home with a light gray siding and Wedgwood blue shutters. It had a good sized front porch because he said he had always wanted a house that had a porch on which he could put a rocking chair and watch the world go by. He got his wish, but there wasn't much world to watch go by here except for the birds, rabbits, deer and occasional fox. With any main highway a good distance away, there were no sounds of traffic either. A car horn was as distant as the honk of a goose going north in summer.

Uncle Roy claimed he had always hated city life anyway, and when he had lived in Washington, D.C., he had gotten so he could walk in the streets and shut out everything. He did look like a man who could pull down shades and curtains and turn his eyes inward to watch his own visions and dreams stream by.

Above their front door, Aunt Glenda had hung

a bronze crucifix. Once a week, she brought out a stepladder and polished it. The front door was open, but the screen door was closed. I knocked softly on it and then called to her. I could hear her recording of gospel songs which was something she played while she worked in the kitchen or cleaned. She obviously didn't hear me, so I opened the door and stepped into the house.

There was always some redolent aroma of something she was cooking or baking. Today, I smelled the bacon she had made for breakfast. I called to her again and then looked into the small living room. She had turned it into a shrine to Latisha. There were pictures of her everywhere, on the mantel above the fireplace as well as on the tables and on the walls. Spaced between them were different religious items, pictures of saints, cathedrals, and icons of Christ. Usually, there were candles lit, although there were none lit this morning. The room itself had a dark decor, furniture made from cherry wood, oak and walnut with a wood floor and area rugs. Mommy and Daddy had bought them a beautiful grandfather clock as a house gift, but no one bothered to wind it and have it run.

"Every day now is the same as the one before it," I once heard Uncle Roy tell Daddy when Daddy had asked about the clock. "Especially for Glenda. Why bother with time?"

There was no one in the dining room so I went down the hallway to the kitchen. The music was playing on a small CD player, but Aunt Glenda was nowhere in sight. However, I saw through the pantry and back door that she was out hanging wash on a clothesline. She liked it better than a dryer because she said the clothing smelled sweeter from the scents of flowers in the air. As usual, she was wearing a faded housecoat and slippers. Her dark brown hair streaked with prematurely gray strands was down to her shoulders, and I could see from the way her mouth moved that she was either talking to herself or saying some prayer to her dead daughter.

I retreated to the stairway and listened for some sounds from above to indicate Harley was up. All I heard was the faint drip, drip of a bathroom faucet.

"Harley," I called. "Are you awake?"

"No," he immediately shouted back.

It made me smile.

"Talking in your sleep again?"

"Yes," he said. "Don't wake me up."

"It's late, Harley."

I started up the stairs. Harley and I hadn't grown up exactly like a brother and a sister, but we had spent so many of our young years together, I sometimes thought of him that way. Lately, if I suggested it, it seemed to bother him, so I stopped.

"Are you decent?" I called from the top of the stairway. There was just a short hallway to the right that passed his bedroom and what had been Latisha's nursery; there was an equally short hallway to the left that led to Uncle Roy and Aunt

Glenda's bedroom and a bathroom across from that. The windows on both ends were small, and the wood paneling was dark. Even with the bright day, it looked like a tunnel.

"Am I decent? Depends who you ask," Harley replied.

I laughed and stepped up to his bedroom doorway. He was still in bed, lying on his stomach, the pillow over his head to block out the sunshine, the blanket down to his waist. I knew from other times that he liked to sleep in his underwear.

Harley's room was half the size of mine. He had a very nice dark maple-wood bed, matching dressers and a desk Uncle Roy had actually built himself that was set to the right of his two bedroom windows. There were papers scattered in a disorganized fashion over it, two books opened and face down and a small pile of notebooks beside that. I could see his line drawings in one of the notebooks. Beside it was a book entitled, *American Houses.* As usual, his socks were on the floor beside the bed where he had thrown them and where he had dropped his shoes. His jeans were draped over his desk chair and the dark blue shirt he had worn yesterday was crumpled on the top of his dresser.

Unlike my room and the rooms of most of the young people our age, Harley's had no posters on its walls. He favored some rock bands, but interestingly enough he really enjoyed softer music, even Barry Manilow, although he never let anyone but me know. It was as if he believed that the moment some of his friends found out he was sensitive, he would lose face or worse yet, be challenged and teased and more vulnerable.

"I was hoping you would be up and out by now, or at least at breakfast," I told him.

He didn't turn, but I could see his eyes close as if he had a terrible headache. When he sighed, his entire body lifted and fell. Finally, he turned, dropped his head back to his pillow, put his hands behind his head and looked at me.

"Roy," he began, "came in here and laid down the law last night. The bottom line was that I should be sure to make myself invisible, not annoy anyone and not embarrass him or you or the family. He makes it sound as if a wild animal like me doesn't belong in the company of you civilized folks. It doesn't exactly fill me with enthusiasm. Believe me, he'd much rather I didn't come out."

"That's not true and anyway, I would much rather you did," I tossed back at him. "This is my special day, Harley Arnold, and you had better come out. You put on your nicest clothes, too," I ordered.

He laughed.

"My nicest clothes are what your mushy kid friends knock around in."

"That's not so either. I know what you have and what you don't," I told him and went right to his closet. "You should learn how to hang up your pants and your shirts properly. Look at this mess."

"Yes, Mother."

"Never mind being a smarty pants," I said

38

plucking the light blue shirt I liked to see him wear and a pair of slacks. "After we go swimming, come home and put this on," I instructed. "Wear those loafers with it and a pair of blue socks. And shave! And don't tell me you don't have any aftershave," I quickly inserted. "I bought it for you on your birthday, and I know you still have plenty."

"Why do you want me there anyway? You have your friends," he said sullenly. "You've got your Chase Taylor and his mushy buddies."

"You can call Chase a lot of things, Harley, but really, I don't think he's mushy."

Harley turned a dark shade of crimson.

"Yeah, I guess you would know," he muttered.

"Besides," I said ignoring his remark, "you know you're my most important friend, Harley. My birthday party wouldn't be a birthday party without you. So stop it!"

He looked instantly remorseful, turned and gazed out the window.

"From all that noise, it sounds like two birthdays are being set up out there."

"Wait until you see all that Daddy has done," I told him. "The trees have grown balloons."

He laughed.

"And Mrs. Geary has made a birthday cake to die for."

He nodded, looked down for a moment and then let his lips fold into a soft smile.

"What?" I asked expecting something that would most likely put me in a pout.

"Remember that time when — before the guests arrived — I put my fingers in your birthday cake and pretended they were your candles and Roy nearly exploded? I thought his eyes were going to pop out of his head on little springs." He laughed.

"Sometimes I think you do bad things just to get him angry, Harley."

"No. Me?"

"You know you're hurting your mother too when you get him upset."

His smile disappeared.

"She's beyond being hurt," he said. "You've got to be able to see and smell and feel to know when you're in pain, and she's beyond that."

"That's not true, Harley."

"It's true. Okay," he said. "I'll rise, but I'm not sure I will shine."

I stepped closer to his bed and seized his hair. He looked up surprised.

"You'll rise and you'll shine and you'll help make this the best birthday of my life, or else," I said shaking him a little harder than he anticipated.

"Ow," he cried reaching for my hand. He held my wrist a moment and looked up at me.

"You still haven't had the decency to wish me a happy birthday, Harley Arnold."

I let go of his hair, but he held my wrist.

"Happy birthday, Summer," he said and sat up, pulling me closer so he could kiss me on the cheek. His lips were very close to mine, so close that when he began to pull back, he grazed them with his mouth.

For a small moment, our eyes locked, and then I rubbed my cheek.

"Shave," I ordered.

My heart was thumping. He let go of my wrist.

"And get dressed and come out to help," I continued.

He just stared up at me, his shoulders gleaming in the sunlight that now poured through his windows.

"Okay," he said, his voice breaking, not reaching more than a whisper. He recovered quickly and gave me one of his impish smiles. "Your majesty," he added.

He started to get out of bed. I couldn't recall exactly when I had become self-conscious about his seeing me half-dressed, but he never seemed to care about my seeing him, even now. Maybe that was just something peculiar about boys, I thought, or maybe it was simply because of the way he and I had been brought up together.

Whatever the reason, it made me catch my breath in my throat.

I didn't leave so much as run away.

2

The Party Begins

The musicians arrived well before the guests and began to tune up just as Harley stepped out of his house. He was wearing the same pair of jeans and shirt he had worn yesterday, and he hadn't brushed his hair so that strands floated down his forehead and over his eyes. Uncle Roy was always after him to get a shorter haircut and often threatened to cut it himself if he didn't. It didn't go that far, but there were times when it almost had.

"If he ever tries it," Harley growled, "he'll regret the day he was born."

Every birthday lately, I wished for two big things: Mommy being able to walk again and Harley getting along with Uncle Roy. Neither seemed possible.

"You ain't coming to this party looking like that," Uncle Roy told him as he walked up from the house.

"I'm going to change after we all go swimming. Isn't that what happens first?" he asked turning to me.

"Yes," I said.

"Lucky for the lake or he wouldn't take a bath," Uncle Roy told Daddy.

Harley's face turned white instead of red. White anger was the worst sort.

"C'mon," I said before their hot words could spark a big fire. "Help me bring out the party favors and put them on the tables."

Harley looked like the roar of rage was making him deaf to any other sound, so I lunged for his hand and pulled him toward the garage where Daddy had the favors in boxes.

"Hey," Harley cried. "Take it easy."

"We don't have all that much time," I said. "They'll all start to arrive soon."

"Right, and we can't disappoint the gang." He looked back at Daddy and Uncle Roy, his eyes still red with fury. "He's always got to say something nasty," Harley complained.

"He means well though," I said.

"Yeah, like a rattlesnake does you a favor by biting you. I can't imagine what made my mother want to marry him, but I guess when you're unwed with a kid, you can't be so choosy. You take the first offer, even if it's from a man who has a prison record."

"He doesn't have a prison record, Harley."

"Sure he does. Military prison is just as serious."

"Well, none of that mattered to your mother. They must have been in love, Harley, and they still are."

He blew air through his lips as if my words were tiny flies annoying him.

"Well, Mommy tells me they were," I insisted. "She said they just seemed to gravitate toward each other. She told me, they took long walks and talked and fell in love just the way people do."

We entered the garage and I pointed to the cartons on our left. He didn't move. Instead, he gave me that curious look, his eyes laughing but his lips stiffly tucked in at the corners.

"What?"

"And how are people supposed to fall in love, Summer?" he asked. "What is there, a formula or something? Because if there is, I'd sure like to know it."

"No, there's no formula. Don't be silly," I said.

"I'm not being silly," he asserted. "Tell me. Really," he said folding his arms across his chest. "What do you think happened to them and what happens to anyone? Do bells go off? What?"

When I didn't respond, he added, "Is that what's happened to you and Chase Taylor?"

"Stop it, Harley."

"Stop what?"

"Teasing me, making fun of everything I say."

"I'm not," he protested, his arms out. "I really want to know." The sardonic smile left his face. "Don't you believe me when I say I wonder about

44

my mother and him all the time now? These days they barely speak to each other, and it's not just because of what happened to Latisha and the way my mother is with her religious stuff. If I didn't ask a question or burp at breakfast, it would be as if we were all in a silent movie.

"They never go anywhere, no dates, no restaurants, no movies. They don't talk about taking a vacation like your parents do. Your mother's in a wheelchair, and she does more than my mother these days. It's just as much Roy's fault as it is hers."

"Why is it you never call him daddy or dad or father, ever, Harley?"

"Because . . . he's not my father. My father is out there," he said waving at the door, "somewhere out there, and I'm not even a passing thought in his head. How do you have a kid and not even be a little curious about him, not care at all?"

"Well, Roy cares about you. He officially adopted you, didn't he?"

"Big deal," he said. "Who asked him to?"

"He tries to be a good father. He works hard to support you and your mother and he built a nice house and . . ."

"Forget it, Summer. You'll never understand," he said lowering his head.

"Why?"

"Because you're too . . ."

"What?" I demanded, my own anger rising like boiled milk. If he dares to say I'm too young, I thought, I'll . . .

"Nice," he said instead.

"What?"

"You trust everyone. I don't even trust myself," he said.

He went to the cartons and began piling them in his arms.

"What's that mean? I'm too nice? You're right, Harley. I don't understand. Why does my being trusting make it impossible to understand my uncle and you and your mother?"

"Let's not talk about it today, Summer," he pleaded. "It's your special day. I'll help with what's left to be done, and then I'll go home and wait until it's time to go swimming, and then I'll go in and I'll put on the clothes you picked out, and I'll sit quietly with my hair neatly brushed and eat and . . ."

"And dance and have fun," I insisted.

"Okay," he said. "Put one more carton on top."

"That's too many. Take those. I'll get the rest."

"Why is it everyone is so bossy here?" he moaned and started out.

I piled up the remaining cartons and followed him. Sometimes, Harley could make me feel just like a wire about to snap. I wished I could just scream and scream until the feeling was gone.

When we got to the tables, we opened the cartons and started to put the favors on the tables. Beside the printed napkins, cups and plates,

Daddy had a company make a pocket makeup mirror for the girls with the date of my birthday on the top; T-shirts with a picture of the lake and today's date under it; and a pen and pencil set for everyone with my dates on them as well.

"Not bad," Harley said as he unloaded the cartons. "It pays to be a friend of Summer Clarke. All the mushy kids will be in their glory."

"I told you to tell me who you wanted to invite from your school, Harley," I reminded him. "It's not my fault you didn't give Mommy and me any names and addresses."

"Right."

"Well, didn't I ask you?"

"Look, Summer, anyone I'm friendly with, Roy thinks is one step away from the gas chamber."

"Even the girls?" I pondered.

He looked at me a moment and then went back to setting out the favors.

"Harley?"

"The girls I talk to don't belong here," he said.

"What's that supposed to mean?"

"There's nobody I know who's good enough," he replied.

"Harley, don't make me sound stuck-up. You could have invited anyone you wanted, isn't that so? Well, isn't it?"

"Let it go, Summer. Please," he begged. I actually saw tears in his eyes.

"Okay, I'm sorry. I just wanted to be sure you had a good time."

"I'll have a good time. I'll have a good time. If I

don't, Roy will see that I'm turned into horse meat."

"Harley."

"I'm kidding."

"I don't want you to have a good time because Uncle Roy ordered you to. I want you to have a good time because it's my birthday and . . ."

He fell to his knees and clasped his hands.

"Please, your majesty. Mercy," he begged.

"Oh stop it, you idiot." I pushed his head and he fell over laughing.

We both turned as a large black Mercedes drove up. I knew it was one of my best friends, Amber Simon, a dark brunette who was a little on the heavy side, but with beautiful almond eyes and a sweet disposition. She had a crush on Harley, and I think he sensed it every time she came over and spent any time with him. I tried to be a match-maker, telling him that if she had someone take interest in her, she would gain self-confidence, lose weight and stop eating out of frustration. His answer was that her parents should just lock her in a room. He admitted that she was nicer than most of my friends and even admitted she had a pretty face hidden under those "mushy cheeks," but he didn't show any real interest.

Amber still had hopes.

She got out and called to us. Harley leaped to his feet.

"I'd better go put on my bathing suit and help get the boats and stuff set up," he said. "I prom- ised your father I would take care of that."

"At least say hello to her first, Harley."

He cupped his hands and screamed, "HELLO!"

Then he gave me his impish, Kevin Bacon smirk and headed back to his house, sauntering past Uncle Roy and Daddy without so much as glancing at them. They stopped talking and watched him go by, Uncle Roy shaking his head.

My heart felt heavy for Harley.

It was as if a cloud always hung above him, always casting a shadow over him, always threatening cold rain.

Even today.

Even on my birthday.

"Where's Harley going?" Amber asked, looking after him with disappointment. "He's coming to the party, isn't he?" she asked, her voice tinted with fear.

"Yes. He's just going to put on his bathing suit. He wants to get the boats, kayaks and the pedal boats set up for everyone."

"Oh."

"You brought your suit, right?"

"I hate what I look like in a bathing suit," she complained immediately.

"Didn't you bring it?"

"Yes," she admitted, swinging her bag toward me, "but I'm not putting it on."

"Of course you are," I insisted. "C'mon," I said taking her back to my house. "Let's talk before the others get here, and don't you dare do anything to make me unhappy today, Amber," I warned.

She rolled her eyes, looked after Harley once more and then followed me inside.

Mommy was just wheeling herself down the hallway and turned to greet us as we entered.

"Hi, Mrs. Clarke," Amber said. She went to her quickly and kissed her on the cheek.

That was what I liked the most about Amber. She wasn't only oblivious to the fact that Mommy was half African American, she also was uninhibited about her being in a wheelchair. Most of my other girlfriends weren't as generous or as comfortable around Mommy as Amber was.

"Hi, Amber. How's your mother doing?"

Amber's mother had recently been operated on to have her gallbladder removed. The doctors had told her it was so bad it could burst and rushed her into the operating room. Amber was in school at the time, and her father sent for her. Like me, she was an only child and very close to her parents.

"She's fine, thank you, Mrs. Clarke."

"I'm glad to hear it," Mommy said, even though she didn't see Mrs. Simon much. Amber's family was one of those southern aristocratic families who could trace their roots back to the early colonial days and let everyone know it.

"This is going to be a fun day," Amber predicted. Mommy beamed at me.

"I bet, and I'm sure you two have some plotting and conspiring to do with all these boys coming over," she added.

Amber laughed and followed me up the stairs to my room.

"Your mother is such a cool lady. It's almost as if she has fun with us or through us," Amber said.

"She's my mother, my sister and my best friend all rolled into one," I told her.

She smiled.

"I wish my mother was that way," she said, and then she snapped to attention and dug into her cloth bag to produce a small, attractively wrapped box.

"Happy birthday, Summer. I wanted to be the first to give you a present," she said.

"Thank you, Amber."

I peeled off the wrapping paper neatly and opened the box. It was a gold charm bracelet with sixteen candles.

"It's beautiful. Thank you, so much," I said and we hugged. "I'm going to wear it to the party," I declared and put it on. I held up my wrist and shook the charms.

"It's beautiful. Look how dazzling it is when it catches the sunlight."

"I wonder what Chase is going to give you," she said. "I bet it'll be something very expensive, a lot more expensive than my gift, something extra special, too."

"It'll be expensive, but more than likely his mother will have bought it."

"Why? Wouldn't he want to be the one to choose it? Wouldn't he want it to be something very special, something that represents his love for you? His mother can't do that."

"I haven't known Chase that long," I said shrugging, "but I can tell those things aren't that important to him."

"But he does love you, doesn't he?" she pursued.

"I don't know if I would call it love yet, Amber."

Her comment threw me back to my early conversation with Harley.

"Why not?" she asked with a grimace, as if I was bursting some bubble.

"We've only been seeing each other a little more than a month. Don't you think love should take a little more time and be a lot more extraordinary?" I asked.

"I guess," she said.

"I mean, some of our friends fall in and out of love as easily as they put on a new pair of jeans."

She laughed, but then grew serious again.

"I think it has to be love when you just can't think of anyone else, when you feel special just being near him, when you tremble if he simply grazes your arm or your shoulder and when you're afraid you'll say something wrong or look unattractive and lose any hope of winning him. That's love, isn't it?"

I knew she was referring to how she felt around Harley, and I also knew he had nowhere near the same feelings about her. Maybe the most painful thing in the world was loving someone who would never love you. You had to compensate and tell yourself that it just wasn't meant to be, that there was such a thing as soul mates and yours was yet to be discovered.

But that was hard to do.

Very hard to do.

"Well, isn't it?" Amber pursued.

"If that's not love, it certainly sounds like it's just around the corner," I offered and started to flip through my bathing suits to decide which one I would wear.

"I wish I could own a real bikini," I said, "but neither my mother nor my father would tolerate my buying and wearing one. They'd die if they saw me wearing what Catlin Stoffer wears and will probably wear today," I predicted.

"Watch out for her. She likes to steal boyfriends. It's a thing with her. It makes her feel superior."

"Who told you that?" I asked smiling.

"Gail Solt. You know she stole Neil Roland away and then dumped him a week later. Why else would she do it? She'll be after Chase for sure just to prove she can do it," Amber warned me.

"If he's so easy to win away from me, than good riddance," I said, holding up my neon green two-piece.

"Wouldn't it just break your heart?" she cried.

I thought a moment.

"No. I guess according to your definition, I don't love him then," I added.

She looked shocked at my indifference.

"Do you love someone else?" she asked.

"Why do I have to love anyone yet? I want to do

things — travel, learn, experience a lot before I give away my heart, Amber. Don't be so worried about it. You'll find someone to love and love you, I'm sure."

"I don't know," she said gazing at herself in the mirror. "I wish I had your confidence."

"You will," I said, but she shook her head.

"No," she decided. "You're special, Summer. That's why all the boys want to be with you. I bet even Harley wishes he wasn't like a relative."

"Well he is in my mind and I am in his," I said sharply, maybe too sharply. She looked hurt. I didn't mean to be critical of her. I didn't even know why I was so adamant about it. I smiled to restore our good mood. "So, you're free to win his heart."

"How can I do that?" she cried. "There are a lot of prettier girls coming here today."

"Just be sincere with him. He loves honesty."

She thought a moment and then nodded.

"Then I do have a chance," she said, "because not one girl coming knows what honesty means."

We laughed and changed into our bathing suits. Cars were arriving. We could hear them honking their horns. The music had even begun. A rain of festivity was falling over my beautiful home.

"My party! It's starting!" I cried looking out of the window at what seemed now to be truly Mommy's magic place.

"Happy birthday," Amber screeched and we held hands and hurried down the stairs to burst on the developing gala.

Harley was down at the dock setting up the boats and kayaks. He glanced back at the arriving guests and then dove into the water and started to swim to the raft, showing how little he cared to meet any of my friends.

I nudged Amber.

"Now's your chance. You can have him all to yourself. Just go swim out to the raft," I said.

She looked horrified.

"What if he swims away before I get there?"

"The lake is magical," I said. "You'll look like a mermaid to him."

"I'll look like a baby whale!" she moaned, glancing at her abundant breasts and wide hips.

"Take a chance. Nothing ever happens unless you do," I told her and went to greet my other guests.

Chase arrived with four of his buddies. He looked so handsome in his khaki pans and blue oxford shirt. Chase always had a tan. His friends teased him, calling him George Hamilton, Jr. I knew his mother had a tanning salon in their home, and he often used it, too.

Mommy came out of the house with Mrs. Geary right behind her and moments later, Grandmother Megan arrived in a limousine with Grandfather Grant and aunt Alison. Grandfather Grant was wearing a light blue sports jacket, black cravat and white pants. He did look dapper. Grandmother Megan had a designer skirt suit. Her hair looked a shade darker than usual. Alison wore a loose-fitting Empire-waist dress with a very low V-neck, so her bosom practically spilled out. I was sure it was the subject of discussion all the way from the airport.

Daddy's parents and Aunt Heather Sue arrived soon after. Aunt Heather Sue was married to an airline pilot who flew for American and was working today. She told me immediately how sorry he was not to be able to attend my party. I saw Aunt Glenda coming from the house, walking slowly, her head down, her arms folded. She had put on a pretty blouse and skirt, but her hair was still down, loose and somewhat unkempt. Uncle Roy's eyes grew small and troubled. He whispered something to her and then took her to meet the others.

The last guest to arrive was Mrs. Geary's Mr. Lynch, whom she immediately chastised for coming late.

"A librarian especially should know what it means to be on time," I heard her say. He apologized and hurried to greet me and hand me a gift.

All of the family and the adults sat in one section where they could watch the rest of us go boating and swimming. My presents were piled in a corner by the dance floor. Daddy had arranged for the boys to change in the garage, using the bathroom there. The girls would go into the house.

"C'mon," Chase said after he took off his pants, shirt and shoes. He was already wearing his bathing suit underneath.

"Where?"

He seized my hand to pull me away from everyone. "Let's grab a rowboat and be alone for a few minutes. I know what it's like to have a party in your honor. I've had a few," he bragged.

Of course, the boys all let out a howl to tease us. My girlfriends smiled knowingly, as if they had each been in a rowboat with Chase Taylor and knew what would inevitably happen. Nothing much could really happen, I thought. We were always in full view of the family and guests.

As we stepped into the boat, I looked out at the raft and saw Harley sitting on its edge, watching. Amber was sitting beside him. Even from this distance, I could see she was looking terrified.

Chase didn't see them until he began to row and turned the boat.

"What's Hardly up to?" Chase asked. He knew how much it bothered Harley when he called him that, and he knew I hated it.

"Don't call him that," I snapped.

"Why? It fits him. He's hardly this and hardly that," he replied laughing.

"When you have so much, it's doubly terrible to make fun of those who haven't enough, Chase."

"Okay, okay. I'm sorry. It's your birthday. I won't say or do a thing to make a moment unpleasant," he promised.

He rowed gracefully, his muscles making it look effortless for us to glide through the water as if we were sliding over glass. I could see how everyone was still watching us.

"Maybe later, we can go someplace where we don't have an audience, huh? Then I can wish you a happy birthday properly," Chase said.

"And what exactly does 'properly' mean?"

"You're sixteen today!"

"So?"

"Hey, let's have a few surprises, huh?" he teased. He did have such a handsome face with the straightest, whitest teeth, and those eyes just seemed to pick up all the colors around us and twirl them back at me. Any girl would have to have a heart of stone not to be dazzled.

"Now that you're getting along in years, I guess you're old enough to experience real lovemaking," he half kidded.

"How many girls have you said that to, Chase Taylor?"

He smiled. *"Moi?"* He put on a hurt look. "Never. You're the first," he asserted.

"If love lies could make your nose grow, you'd bump it ten minutes before the rest of you arrived anywhere," I said and he laughed so hard, he had to rest the oars.

"I really enjoy the way you put things, Summer. You're lying about your age, you know. You must have been sixteen years ago. No one could be as sharp as you and be only sixteen."

"Keep those compliments coming," I said. He actually turned a shade crimson.

"I'm not just handing you a line. I believe it. Really," he insisted.

He let the boat drift and then moved over so he

was sitting on the floor at my feet.

"They can't see me down here," he said in a conspiratorial tone and leaned over to kiss my toes.

"Stop it," I squealed, but he held onto my foot at the heel and touched the bottom at the arch with the tip of his tongue. It took me by complete surprise, but it sent a warm, electric surge up my leg.

"Stop, they can see you."

"No, they can't. Just keep looking like you're talking. Nod your head. Go on," he suggested. His hand moved up the side of my leg to my thigh. Then he got on his knees and looked back at the shore, reaching over with his other hand to touch the water as his right hand reached my inner thigh. I stopped it there.

"Don't, Chase."

"Just trying to give you something special," he whispered. "It's fun while they're all looking at us. They can't see. C'mon," he said pushing up against my hand. "I'll make you feel good."

I swallowed down a throat lump, feeling a wave of heat wash over me.

"Don't," I said a lot more firmly. "It's hot. Let's go swimming."

Without any further warning, I stood up and then dove off the boat into the lake. He looked both shocked and disappointed. I started toward the raft.

"Hey!" he called. "What are you doing?"

"Try to catch me," I called back. He sat on the

bench and dug the oars into the water, turning the boat and starting in my direction. I jabbed my hands in deeply and took long, graceful strokes, swimming better than ever. Finally, Chase gave up the rowing and dove in after me, putting on his Olympic-style speed. I just reached the ladder of the raft when he caught me and held me at the waist, keeping me from going up the ladder.

I screamed as he pulled me off. The moment I went under the water, his hands moved up from my waist and over my breasts, nearly lifting my top away. I shot up and spit the water out.

"Stop," I said and climbed up the ladder. I immediately adjusted my top.

Harley was lying back, his hands behind his head. Amber was sitting on the edge where she had been before. Harley had one eye open, watching me.

Some of the others started to swim for the raft as Chase followed me.

"And what are you two up to?" Chase asked in a wry voice and with a lusty smile. "And don't tell me hardly anything."

I glared furiously at him.

Amber blushed right down to her cleavage.

"We were just waiting here for you with our hearts pounding," Harley said. He turned slowly to look up at Chase.

"Something has to make it pound," Chase said. Harley didn't respond. Amber looked away and Chase took the opportunity to grab her at the waist and toss her off the raft. She screamed as she hit the water.

"Why did you do that?" I cried, feeling sorry for her. I knew how insecure she was already. Now she would feel so stupid and embarrassed because it had happened right in front of Harley, I thought.

Before I could stop him, Harley turned and kicked at Chase's legs, hitting them at the calves and sending Chase forward, where he lost his balance and fell off the raft. Some of the kids swimming toward us laughed and teased Chase, who came up sputtering. He swam around to the ladder and pushed Amber out of his way.

"Don't start anything," I cried as he came charging up.

"I'm not starting anything," he said. "I'm finishing."

He lunged at Harley and the two of them wrestled on the raft, each trying to force the other off the edge. I screamed. On shore, Uncle Roy and Daddy came to the edge of the water and started shouting in our direction. I saw Mommy wheel herself around the table toward them. Aunt Glenda kept her head down.

Neither Harley nor Chase would stop. Chase was stronger and finally got Harley almost to the raft's edge. Rather than go over, Harley bit Chase's hand, forcing him to release his grip. Then he lowered his head and hit Chase in the stomach with his shoulder, sending him backward, where he sat down hard and nearly fell over the edge, just catching himself from falling into the water.

"You bastard!" Chase cried.

"Stop!" I screamed as loudly as I could. Harley glanced at me and then dove off the raft and started for shore. Chase regained his balance, pulled himself upright on the raft and looked at his hand.

"Jesus, that animal bit me. Look," he said showing me his hand. The skin had been broken and there was a line of blood. "I'll have to get a tetanus shot. Who knows what diseases are in him?"

The other kids arrived, everyone shocked at the sight of Chase's wound.

"You provoked him," I said. "Now look at the mess."

I dove into the water and started for shore. Amber followed. I swam as quickly as I could, but I didn't get there in time to stop Uncle Roy from taking a swing at Harley, slapping him across the side of his head. I heard his shouted order at Harley to get home. Harley hovered a moment and then spun around and walked away quickly.

"Harley!" I screamed. He didn't look back.

"Roy, you were too hard on him," Mommy complained, wheeling herself up beside him and Daddy.

"It's the only thing he understands," Uncle Roy told her.

"You know that's not true, Roy. You of all people should know what it's like to have a father who doesn't hesitate to get physical."

"Yeah," Uncle Roy said. He looked at me standing in the water. "Sorry about this, Princess. I gave him a good lecture this morning, but it didn't help."

"It wasn't only his fault, Uncle Roy."

"It's never only his fault, but somehow he's always in the middle of something."

He turned and walked back to the tables. All the laughter and happy talk, even the music suddenly seemed frozen in the air.

I looked at Mommy who forced a smile back at me.

"Let it go for now," she said. "It's not the time for this sort of talk."

I nodded, glanced at Amber who had come up beside me and looked almost as heartbroken.

Then we both looked after Harley who had reached the house and gone inside, letting the screen door snap behind him like the door of a prison cell.

Daddy told the musicians to start playing again. The caterer's staff began to go around to the adults to serve them champagne and wine. I heard a loud peal of laughter coming from Aunt Alison's lips.

Chase came wading out of the water, holding his hand up dramatically so that the blood could drip down the side of his palm, making it look far worse. I could hear the gasps. Daddy went to him immediately and then took him to the house to get some antiseptic on the wound and bandage it.

It takes only a few seconds sometimes, a few moments, to turn the world from a day of rainbows to a day of thunder and storms.

Where was the lake's magic when I had needed it the most? I thought mournfully.

3

Into the Night

Despite the incident between Harley and Chase, the party was wonderful. Chase milked sympathy from all the girls and even some of his buddies when he emerged from the house with an impressive bandage on his hand. I knew Daddy would do as good a job as any doctor.

Daddy rang a cowbell to indicate we should all get out of our bathing suits, dress and come to the tables where a sumptuous lunch consisting of lobster, shrimp, roast beef and turkey dishes was served family style. Mrs. Geary complained there was enough food to feed a small village in Ireland.

"Just what's left over will do," she muttered to Mommy, but clearly well in Daddy's range of hearing. He and Mommy exchanged smiles.

While we ate, the band played and most of my friends got up to dance. Chase made it seem like he was enduring great pain in his hand just to ensure that I would have a good time. At one point Aunt Alison came over and fawned all over him. She deliberately leaned so far over the table that all the boys could feast their eyes on the sight of her breasts, exposed nearly to the nipples. I saw the boys peering and then looking at each other, some even reddening.

"Look at this poor boy's hand. You've got to protect him better," she told me.

The others at the table laughed.

"He's pretty good at protecting himself, Aunt Alison," I said, glaring at him and the way he was sucking up all her attention.

"Men are not as strong as they make out to be, Summer," she lectured, directing herself mostly at my girlfriends, who listened wide-eyed. "They need us more than they care to admit. They need us to tell them when they're making fools of themselves, especially.

"You've got to keep the reins firmly on your boyfriends, girls, or they'll go kicking and banging into everything. You know I'm right, don't you?" she asked them. Some of them nodded. Some laughed nervously. Amber looked shocked for me and kept glancing my way.

Aunt Alison turned back to Chase.

"The only reason to fight, honey, is to protect your lady. You don't want to do anything to spoil that handsome face of yours, do you?"

"No ma'am," Chase said, gloating.

"You won't forget my good advice, will you, sweet thing?" she asked him.

Chase never skipped a beat. "No ma'am," he said, winking at his buddies, "I won't forget a thing about you."

I saw their smiles and their laughter. Aunt Alison didn't see what a fool she was making of herself. She thought she was the cat's meow and sauntered back to the adults' table.

"Wow!" Chase said, dabbing his forehead with a napkin. "If I had an aunt like that, I'd really look forward to Thanksgiving."

Everyone laughed but Amber and me. I knew Aunt Alison had already had too much champagne and I knew my grandmother Megan and my grandfather Grant thought so, too, but she was hard to stop once she got started. Minutes later she was on the dance floor with two of Chase's buddies, moving so suggestively, she could have been in an X-rated club.

Finally, Grandfather Grant got her to sit down, only that turned her bitter and sarcastic, which only made them more uncomfortable. Mommy often told me she was their burden for life. Now I understood.

The highlight of the party was Mrs. Geary's birthday cake. She had Mr. Lynch help her bring it out. It really was a spectacular sight, all candy-pink and in tiers like a wedding cake. She insisted on cutting the pieces herself. Everything about cooking and serving was an art to her, but the extra tender loving care she put into it all warmed my heart.

"Happy birthday, dear," she told me when she

handed me the first piece. I hugged and kissed her, which embarrassed her, but pleased her, too.

After the cake I opened presents, looking toward Harley's house occasionally. I saw the present with his name on it and I didn't open it. I put it aside. Only Mommy seemed to catch my action, smiling and nodding.

I was really surprised at the gift Uncle Roy and Aunt Glenda had bought me. Uncle Roy had chosen a very expensive pearl necklace with a gold heart locket at the center. In it he had placed his and my mother's pictures. I was overwhelmed by the gift, of course, but the idea of having a locket with Mommy's picture and Uncle Roy's and not Daddy's beside it struck me as odd. When Mommy saw it, her smile stopped just before it completely formed, but her eyes darkened a bit. She glanced at Uncle Roy, who was staring at me and smiling.

"It's very beautiful, honey," she said quickly. "Roy, you shouldn't have spent so much."

Uncle Roy pressed his lips together and nodded.

"It's my pleasure. I mean, our pleasure," he replied. "Happy birthday again, Princess."

"Princess?" Chase whispered in my ear. "I knew I should be at your feet, licking your toes."

"Stop it," I warned him, but he laughed and promised he would tickle my toes with the tip of his tongue.

After I opened all the gifts, the dancing continued into the early evening. When the first stars appeared in the twilight sky, some of my friends began to leave. Everyone said they had the best time. No one even made a passing reference to the incident with Harley and Chase.

"How about we go for that ride now so I can give you my special present?" Chase asked me.

"I can't," I said. "I can't leave the family and I'm tired anyway, Chase."

"You're kidding. They won't care. They'd understand. It's your special day and night, Summer. You want me to ask your father's permission? I'll do it," he offered.

"No."

"Why not?" he snapped angrily. He hated ever being disappointed because in his world it happened so rarely. He stared at me, waiting for a response. "You're not mad at me for what happened on the raft with Hardly Do Good, are you?"

"You did start it, Chase, when you threw Amber off the raft, and I told you I don't like you calling him that."

"I was just having some fun. He didn't have to go be Mr. Macho Man and then bite me. Why are you taking his side anyway? You saw it all."

"I'm not taking any side."

"Yes you are. You like him, don't you? And I don't mean as a cousin only." He jumped at my hesitation. "I'm right, aren't I?"

"Stop it, Chase."

"That's it," he said. "That's sick. It's like all the jokes they make about people marrying their sisters."

"He's not really related to me," I moaned, "so stop that."

He nodded.

"Are you going out with me now or not?" he asked in the tone of an ultimatum.

"I told you I have to stay with my family. I want to stay with them," I added. "It's only right. My grandparents have come far to be here and they're leaving early in the morning."

"Fine," he said. He looked over at the others. "Maybe I'll make it up to Amber."

"What do you mean?"

"I'll show her a good time to make up for embarrassing her. Consider it another birthday present to you," he said, and swaggered toward her.

"Chase, don't!" I cried. He stopped and looked back, smiling.

"Coming with me or not?"

"You bastard," I muttered, and turned away from him. My heart was pounding.

When I turned around again, he was talking to Amber. She looked at me and then at him. He had underestimated his charm and power when it was confronted by our friendship. She shook her head and walked away from him and I let out a trapped hot breath.

Even more frustrated and angry now, he did what Amber had predicted he might. He headed for Catlin Stoffer, who had been flirting with everyone, especially him.

"You won't believe what Chase just asked me," Amber said.

"You don't have to tell me. I know what he asked. He's angry because I refused to go off with him," I said. "I'm glad you had sense enough to refuse him, too."

We both watched him walk toward his car with Catlin.

"They deserve each other," I said.

Amber looked sorry for me.

"To break up with your boyfriend today of all days," she moaned.

"It's all right. Cupid gave me a birthday present, too. He shot Chase's poison arrow at someone else."

Amber laughed and then looked sadly toward Harley's house.

"I feel bad for him. If I hadn't screamed and carried on, he might not have gotten into the fight and into trouble. Tell him I'm sorry," she said.

"I have a feeling he would have gotten into a fight with Chase no matter what, Amber. Don't blame yourself," I said. "And don't worry about Harley blaming you."

We hugged and she left with the others. I decided I would bring Harley a piece of my birthday cake and open his present with him beside me.

"Where are you going, honey?" Daddy asked me when I put a piece of the cake on a plate and started toward Uncle Roy's house.

"I'm bringing Harley a piece of my cake, Daddy."

"Maybe you better wait until tomorrow, sweetheart."

"I'd rather do it tonight, Daddy. I'll be right back," I said.

The rest of our family had gone into the house. Daddy looked at me with worry in his eyes.

"Don't get too involved in this," he warned. "He's got to work out his problems with his parents himself, Summer. You don't want to get in between."

"He's not a bad person, Daddy."

Daddy didn't look like he wanted to agree.

"He's not!" I insisted.

"Okay. Come right back, and if they're having a discussion, leave them be," he ordered.

"I will," I promised, picked up my present from Harley and started for the house.

I knocked on the screen door and waited. It was very quiet, but I thought I could hear Aunt Glenda crying softly. I knocked again and finally Uncle Roy came out to greet me.

"Princess? What's up? How come you're not with the family?"

"I wanted to bring Harley a piece of my birthday cake, Uncle Roy. Can I see him, please?"

"I'm afraid not," he said.

"Please, Uncle Roy. I won't be able to sleep if I don't see him."

He hesitated and then he looked at me and shook his head.

"He's not here," he said.

"What?"

"He's done it again," he said. "Added insult to injury."

"What has he done?"

"He's run away."

Everyone looked up when I entered my house, but only Mommy immediately saw that I was only seconds away from bursting into a flood of hysterical tears. I still had the plate with the piece of birthday cake in my hand and my present from Harley under my arm.

"What is it, Summer?" she asked, wheeling toward me.

"Harley's run away," I said. I felt the trembling in my chin.

"That poor woman," Grandmother Megan said. "To lose one child and then have this constant trouble with her other child."

She gazed across the room at Aunt Alison, who had fallen asleep in the oversize cushion chair. Everyone, especially Grandfather Grant, was thinking the same thing. Who knew better than Grandmother Megan what it was like to lose a child and be burdened with another's bad behavior?

"He'll be back," Mommy said, but I turned away quickly to hide the first errant tear and then ran for the stairway, not looking back once as I pounded up the stairs and into my room. There, I threw myself on my bed and buried my face in my pillow to stop any more tears.

Moments later, I heard the whirring sound of Mommy's elevator chair and I felt even more terrible. I had caused her to go through the big effort

73

it took to transfer herself and come up here. She did it faster than usual and was knocking on my door in minutes.

"Come in," I said, turning and flicking the tears from my cheeks.

The door opened and she wheeled herself in, closing it behind her.

"I'm so sorry you're upset on this birthday, honey. Please, don't be," she said.

I nodded, took a deep breath and looked at her.

"Why does Harley have to be so . . . so unhappy?" I asked her.

She smiled.

"He's not as unhappy as he is afraid," she said.

"Afraid? Harley? I don't think he's afraid of anything. That's his problem."

"No," she insisted, wheeling closer to my bed. "I know exactly what he's feeling. He's afraid because he sees himself in a world in which he thinks he doesn't belong. Can you imagine what it was like for me to come here when I was just a senior in high school after having lived in the projects in Washington, D.C., a ghetto world where drugs and crime were so rampant, you could look out the front window and think you were watching television news.

"It's easier when you're younger and you have a chance to adjust, but to be dumped into another world entirely with little or no preparation . . ."

"Why did your adopted mother keep the secret about your birth so long?"

"Oh, I think she hoped I would never find out,

74

but her husband was a hard man, in and out of trouble, losing jobs, irresponsible, and he revealed it all in a drunken rage one day. She had no choice. I cried a lot when I found out she wasn't really my mother."

"I'd die if that happened to me," I said.

"I guess I nearly did, but she was a tough little lady. After Beneatha's death, my Mama was determined to save me from that world. She confronted Grandmother Megan to insist she take on her responsibilities, which meant, to take me back. Of course, as you know, she was very, very sick, but it was like her to keep that a secret as well. She knew I would never leave her if I knew the truth."

"It must have broken her heart to see you go live with someone else."

"Both our hearts, but she never shed a tear in front of me. I'm sure she cried privately," she said sighing and growing silent for a moment.

"Anyway," she continued, "when I came here, Grandmother Hudson was not what you kids would call a happy camper. She was like a tyrant with her rules and threats, but I surprised her, I guess. I did so well in school and shocked her with my good behavior. Soon, she was confiding more in me than she was in her own daughters. Eventually, she needed me as much as I needed her, which was what made her sacrifice so great."

"What sacrifice?"

"Arranging for me to go live in England with her sister so I could attend a prestigious school for the performing arts. Just as we had gotten to know and love each other, she was in effect giving me up. The last time I saw her was when she said goodbye to me on our front steps. I often wonder if she would have lived longer had I remained here."

She was quiet a long moment and then smiled.

"But, if we dwell on the past, we're prisoners of it," she said. "The good thing was I gained self-confidence and realized who I really was. She gave me more than just my name; she gave me my identity, my sense of self.

"That's what has to happen to Harley. Despite the bravado he puts on, he's a very frightened young man. He doesn't know where he belongs yet."

"Why is Uncle Roy so mean to him then, Mommy?"

"That's another story," she said.

"Please, tell me, Mommy."

"I wish you could go to sleep with a head full of cotton candy tonight, honey."

"I can't. Please, tell me," I begged her. "I'm not a child anymore."

"No, I guess you're not." She looked down a moment and then took a deep breath and began.

"Years ago, when Roy and I discovered we weren't really brother and sister, he confessed his love for me. He wanted us to be man and wife. He carried that hope with him even after he had joined the army. Despite the fact that we didn't share blood, I couldn't think of him as anyone but

76

my brother. I tried, but I couldn't. It was a big disappointment for him. He always blamed cruel Fate and not me. He was devastated when he discovered I had married your father, but you were already born and he realized it was meant to be.

"I was happy when he started to court Glenda. I thought maybe he had gotten over it. I think he was well on his way, too, when tragedy struck and they lost Latisha. I never doubted that if he had her, he would be a better father for Harley as well.

"So don't judge him too harshly. He's still trying to find himself, too, trying to find some peace. Aunt Glenda is almost another child for him to take care of these days."

"I don't know why we're all in such a rush to get older," I said, pursing my lips. "We never knew how good we had it when we were just six or seven."

Mommy laughed.

"I mean it. When I was little, everything looked magical out there, just the way I hoped it would be today, but when you get older, you have to see reality and be mature and there goes all your pretty dreams."

"That's true, honey, but you're on your way to becoming a beautiful, intelligent young woman, and there's a different sort of magic waiting for you now, a magic you'll create in your own way."

"How can you say all that, Mommy, you of all people, considering what happened to you?"

"I have blessings. I have you to watch grow up. I'd rather be here in a wheelchair than not here at all. Yes, I lost my opportunities and my dreams, but they were quickly replaced with new ones, different ones. I guess happiness comes in different packages, honey, and when we think it can only come in one, we are a little blind."

I smiled at her. She was truly the strongest woman I knew. Everyone else would look at her and think handicapped, think she was only someone to be pitied.

"I just wanted my wonderful day to be wonderful for everyone," I moaned.

"Harley will be back and he'll find himself," she assured me. "I'd better get back downstairs."

I hugged and kissed her and then wheeled her out and helped her get into the elevator chair.

"Daddy put all your presents in the office," she said. "Take them up when you're ready. Oh, and a present arrived from England for you, from Grandpa Ward."

"Did it? He never forgets me. I can't wait to see him again," I said.

Mommy had located her real father when she had gone to England. He had left America years ago and had become a college professor. We had been to London twice to visit, and he had been here for Mommy's wedding and once with his wife Leanna and their children after Mommy had married. He had married a pretty English lady who was a poet and quite nice. I often felt our family was a little United Nations in and of itself.

"I look forward to seeing him, too," Mommy said.

I watched her descend and then I went back to my room and changed. I was going to go downstairs and sit with everyone until they decided to leave for their hotel, but when I gazed out my window and saw the party decorations gone and all the tables and chairs folded and taken away, along with the dance floor and small stage, I felt sad again.

It had all come and gone so fast, I thought.

I pressed my face to the window and stared down at the lake.

Suddenly, a silhouette took shape on the dock.

It was Harley.

He had come back, and he looked like he was sitting there and gazing up at my window.

In seconds practically, I grabbed the present he had given me and was down the stairs and out the door, hoping he wasn't just a wishful thought.

"Hey," I said walking toward him quickly.

"Hey."

He looked down at the water and then at me.

"Where did you go? I went to your house and Uncle Roy said you had run away," I said stepping up to the dock.

"I did, but I turned back as usual. One of these days, I won't," he swore.

"Aunt Glenda's very upset. I heard her crying when I went to the house."

He grunted.

"How do you know she was crying for me?"

"Well, you had run away, or at least that was what she believed."

"She probably still doesn't even know it," he said. He lowered himself back on the dock and put his hands behind his head to look up at the stars. "I guess everyone hates me now, too, huh? I nearly ruined your party."

"Wrong," I said. "But Amber feels bad. She thinks she was responsible because she screamed so much when Chase threw her in."

He laughed. Then he turned to me, just realizing.

"How come you're not off somewhere still celebrating with him?"

"We sort of parted company," I said.

"Parted company? You mean for good?"

"Yes," I said.

"Because of me?"

"No. I mean, that was part of it, but there was more reason to break up with him."

"Like what?"

"He's too . . ."

"Mushy?"

I laughed.

"Maybe," I said. "Some boys wear their self-confidence like a nice suit of clothes. It makes them look better, but in Chase's case, it's like he's wearing a flag wrapped around himself, the flag of Chase Taylor, and he wants everyone to stand and pledge allegiance, especially girls."

Harley's smile deepened and widened. He continued to look up at the sky.

80

"How serious did you get with him?"

"What do you mean?"

"You know what I mean," he said.

"You're a nosy one," I teased.

"You told me about your other boyfriends."

"Yes, when I was twelve."

"Fourteen," he corrected.

"Whereas you never tell me anything about your girlfriends," I countered.

"There's nothing to tell. The longest I've gone with anyone is four hours, to a movie and after or what-ever."

"Why is that, Harley? There's never, ever been anyone you liked enough to want to be with longer?"

He was silent and then he sat up and looked toward his house.

"I shouldn't have come back," he said. "I should have had the guts to keep going."

"You had to come back, at least for your mother. You're wrong about her. She needs you, too. Everyone would have been very, very upset."

"Right."

"They would!"

He turned to me.

"You too?"

"Of course. If I didn't see you out here, I would have been up all night, worrying about you," I confessed.

In the light of the stars, I saw his soft smile and his eyes twinkle. Then he looked toward the driveway.

"I have this dream lately, one I haven't told anyone, not that there's anyone to tell," he said.

"There's me."

"I know. That's why I'm telling you."

"Okay."

I waited quietly, fighting impatience while he obviously worked at building his courage. It made me so curious and excited, it filled my stomach with jumping beans.

"I have this dream that I find my real father, and he's a great guy who's sorry he never knew me."

"Has your mother ever said anything more about him recently, Harley?"

"Very, very little more than what she has already told me. He was a construction worker, a carpenter who worked on the rebuilding of the city hall."

"She still hasn't told you his full name?"

"Whenever I ask, she says you don't want to know a man who deserted us. Once, I said maybe he didn't know you were pregnant, but she claims he knew for sure. Then she clams up and refuses to talk any more about him. I haven't even tried to ask her anything about him in a long time, maybe a year, but the dream keeps coming back.

"I keep thinking that maybe, maybe if I found out where he was, he would be interested in me and maybe help me and maybe I wouldn't be such a loser, at least not to him. I know I am to everyone else."

"You're not a loser to me, Harley."

"I will be," he insisted.

"No, you won't. You're going to bear down and study for your finals and pass all your tests so you can graduate. Then you're going to try to be an architect, just like your art teacher told you."

"Sure," he said.

"I'll help you study."

"You will?"

"If you promise to try, really try. Will you?"

"I might," he said. "Just to prove Roy wrong," he added with a smile.

"Uncle Roy doesn't want you to be a failure, Harley. He's just afraid."

"Roy? Afraid? That's the only man alive whose shadow stays a few extra feet back."

I laughed.

"I don't fault him for that," Harley continued. "You want to know something else I haven't told you? I used to really idolize Roy, really look up to him. There was nothing I wanted more than being as strong and as feared as he is. I always thought it was better to have people afraid of you. That's why I worked beside him on construction. I thought I had to become as tough and as hard and I'd be all right.

"One time, I saw him lift a grown man with one arm and nearly choke him to death. He wagged him about like a rag doll before he put the guy down."

"Why did he do that?"

"He heard the man call him a dirty name. I bet every time that 'cracker' used a dirty name like that, he recalled nearly being hung in Roy's powerful hand and it choked him up," Harley said smiling. "He's got strength inside him that even he doesn't realize."

"Sometimes, you sound like you still idolize him, Harley."

"I don't want to idolize anyone. People let you down all the time. My motto is believe in no one but yourself," he declared.

"I won't let you down, Harley."

"You will, but you won't be able to help it, Summer. That's the only difference," he predicted.

For a long moment, neither of us spoke. Then I looked at the present in my hand.

"I saved opening this until I could do it with you," I said.

"Oh. It's nothing like the gifts you got from everyone else," he warned. "You shouldn't make a big deal of it."

"I don't care what it is, Harley. It's a big deal to me and don't tell me what to make important and unimportant in my life," I snapped.

He laughed.

"Okay. I'm sorry. And people accuse me of having a temper."

Carefully, I peeled away the gift wrapping paper. It was a thin flat box. I lifted the top. There wasn't much light, but the glow of the stars gave me enough to see a line drawing.

"What is this?"

I studied it, tilting it so I could see every detail. In moments I realized it was a picture of me and

Mommy holding hands and gazing out over the lake. A black-bird was just over the center. Long ago, I had told Harley about this special wishing ceremony of ours, but I never thought he would remember how important it was to me.

"You drew this?"

"I watched you and Rain do that a few times after you had told me about it. I guess it's not great, but you can get the idea at least."

"Great? It's more than great. Harley, this is wonderful. You have such a talent."

"I can do a little," he reluctantly admitted.

"Stop it, Harley Arnold. Stop making yourself sound like nobody. This is the best picture . . ."

My throat closed and opened with the ache in my heart.

"Oh Harley," I cried, the tears streaking down my cheeks freely. "It's the best gift of all!"

I threw my arms around him and hugged him and then kissed his cheek, but held onto him. He had his arms at my waist and for a moment, as if we had just opened a door, we stared into each other's eyes, neither retreating from what seemed to be the inevitable kiss, the soft meeting of our lips, the surrender of our selves in a caress so gentle and yet so complete, I felt my heart soar. For a long moment after we parted, I kept my eyes closed as if that would keep his lips on mine and lock the memory forever in my heart.

"I gotta go," he said quickly and jumped to his feet.

"Harley."

"I'd better get back and face the music," he said.

As if he had to flee from his true feelings, he rushed away, practically running.

Then he stopped, turned, and waved.

"Happy birthday," he cried.

"Thank you."

He walked on. Moments later, he passed through a shadow and appeared on his front porch. I saw him hesitate, open the door, and disappear inside.

Finally.

I took a breath.

4

The Oak Tree

Every morning since he had bought himself his motorcycle, Harley would be right behind Daddy and me as Daddy drove off to take me to the Dogwood School for Girls. Sometimes, Harley would be a little late in getting started, but he always managed to catch up to us before we made the turn at Spring Creek Road. We would go left and he would go right to the public school. Often, I would turn and wave, and he would lift his right hand, his face forward as if he had eyes at the side of his head or somehow could sense when I would look back to say so long for the day. I'd watch him disappear around the turn.

Almost the moment Harley bought the motorcycle with his savings and brought it home, Daddy made me promise in front of Mommy, practically keeping my hand on a stack of Bibles, that I would not ride behind Harley on his motorcycle. I suppose it wasn't very difficult to understand why they lived in such fear of any accidents. I remember how careful Daddy was teaching me how to ride a bicycle and how restrictive he and Mommy were about where I could ride it. Even though most of my friends were permitted to ride on the highway (some even riding from their homes to Dogwood), I had to remain on the property or ride in the park with Daddy.

Just as Mommy had ridden horses in equestrian class at Dogwood, so did I; I was told that I was a very good rider. Some of my girlfriends had their own horses and often I was invited to go on rides. I knew how nervous that made both my parents, considering what had happened to Mommy; somehow, Mommy swallowed the lump of terror in her throat, closed her eyes and said okay. Even so, I knew she was sitting on pins and needles until I came home safe and sound.

Weighing on her mind beside the fact that she had been so terribly injured in a horseback riding accident was her continual fear that the shadow of bad luck still hovered in the corner of our family's destiny, waiting for another opportunity to harm us. I could never forget the time when I was only five and I tripped while running down the stairs. I rolled and rolled, knocking my head against the steps. Mommy was so scared for a moment she couldn't find her voice. I sat up dazed, more frightened than injured, but she had me taken to the doctor nevertheless. It had always been like that for me: more panic than necessary whenever I cut or bruised myself, had a cold or the flu. Considering all that, it was not unexpected for my parents to be filled with terror the moment Harley showed up with his spiffy new cycle.

Harley was so proud of it. He had taken most of the money he had earned working with Uncle Roy on construction jobs and working for Daddy cutting grass or doing odd jobs around the property; then shopped and shopped until he found the motorcycle he wanted and could afford. Uncle Roy didn't give him permission to buy it, but Harley somehow managed to get Aunt Glenda to agree and cosign an insurance policy. Uncle Roy swore he wouldn't pay a penny to maintain the motorcycle or pay for gas. From time to time during the year, Harley worked weekends at a roadside diner busing tables just to make enough to keep up his motorcycle and give himself some spending money. I guess he always had a sense of independence, but it really took shape when he reached the age of fourteen. He had that air of maturity about him, that self-confidence boys don't achieve until they are either nearly finished with college or out in the working world.

His independence made me nervous because I began to sense Harley's increasing detachment from his family. Too often he acted and lived like a tenant in his own home, a tenant who knew that the day was soon coming when he would pack up and leave for good. Uncle Roy still considered him to be a burden and Aunt Glenda wasn't taking enough interest in him. The only time

Aunt Glenda went shopping to buy him any clothes or any of the things he needed was when Mommy practically forced her to come along with her.

Aunt Glenda hated being in public ever since the death of Latisha. It was as if she thought everyone was looking at her and somehow blaming her for her daughter's horrible illness. Mommy was afraid that deep inside her heart, Aunt Glenda really did feel responsible for Latisha's death. There were enough religious and bigoted fanatics out there to tell her that she had defied some moral rule by marrying an African American and having a child with him. I never thought God would be angry about something like that, certainly not if the two people really loved and cherished each other. Also, I thought it was just terrible that they believed God would take out his wrath on an innocent little girl.

"They don't think of it that way, honey," Mommy told me. "It restores their hate and their ugly thinking — that's all they care about really. I'm just worried about Glenda," she said, and she tried in so many ways to draw her back into social activities.

Aunt Glenda's reluctance was too strong, however. Time did not heal her; it thickened and widened her scar, so that she became more and more withdrawn, even from concerns and activities that involved her son. Eventually, it was really up to Harley to get things for himself. On occasion, most often when I or Mommy and I were willing to go along with him, Uncle Roy took Harley to buy things Harley needed, but that was so rare, I could count the times on my hands.

And so Harley hardened and became further and further insulated. Sometimes, when I looked out my bedroom window and saw him strutting across the grounds, he did look like a trespasser. Uncle Roy forbade him to smoke; so he did it secretly, standing behind the garage or off in a wooded area — just to be defiant, I thought.

When Harley was just a little boy, Uncle Roy made him keep his room and his things neat and organized as if he was sleeping in a military barracks. Harley often told me about Uncle Roy's sudden, unexpected inspections. To this day he wouldn't permit Harley to have a lock on his door. Up until last year, he was still running his inspections occasionally. If he found a pack of cigarettes or the bed sloppily made or clothes strewn about — as I had found them the morning of my birthday — he would rant and rave and then issue some punishment. Now, I thought Harley was being deliberately messy, just to show Uncle Roy that all his effort, all his growls and penalties were wasted efforts. The purchase of his motorcycle was the crowning moment in all this.

My parents didn't know that Harley was going to buy a motorcycle. Only Aunt Glenda had any indication, apparently, and she hadn't said anything to anyone about it, not even to Uncle Roy. We all heard him drive in with it. Daddy had just gotten home from work. I was the first person

Harley wanted to see his motorcycle. He came right to the door to call me out. Of course, he wanted to take me for a ride immediately, and I did almost get on behind him, but Mommy had come to the front door and screamed, "NO!"

We both looked back at her and saw such abject terror on her face, neither of us could speak or move for a moment.

"It's too dangerous," she said in a calmer tone of voice. Daddy came up beside her and then down to me and Harley.

"Any passenger you take on this," he told Harley, "has to wear a helmet."

"Oh," Harley said; the next day he bought an extra helmet to carry for passengers. He thought that Daddy might permit me to ride with him now, but that night Daddy and Mommy had made me make a promise.

I felt terrible telling Harley. The light of excitement, all the pride drained from his eyes.

"It's just because it's me," he muttered. "Everyone here thinks I'm going to destroy the world."

He shot off, nearly spilling himself at the foot of the driveway before I could offer any other explanation. It did no good to shout after him. There was too much noise. I heard him revving his engine and speeding down the back road; my heart pounded, fearing he would have a bad accident and everyone's predictions for him would be satisfied. Probably because he believed everyone was looking to get him or blame him for something all the time, he was really a very careful driver, keeping within the speed limits. There was never a complaint about him and soon, the sight of him on his motorcycle became nothing unusual. I, of course, was still prohibited from riding along with him.

Anyway, the next school day after my birthday party, Harley wasn't right behind us. I kept looking back for him and was surprised when we had reached the turn and he still hadn't appeared. I hadn't seen him all day, the day before. Daddy's parents were there for a late lunch; although we had invited Aunt Glenda and Uncle Roy, they didn't come. Uncle Roy called with the usual excuse: Aunt Glenda had a very bad headache.

Just after dinner that night, I walked over to Uncle Roy and Aunt Glenda's house to talk to Harley about when and how I would help him study for his upcoming final exams. Uncle Roy was sitting in his rocker, but hardly moving. He was in the shadows, and I didn't realize he was there until I was almost at the front steps.

"Hi, Uncle Roy," I said. "How's Aunt Glenda now?"

"She fell asleep," he said.

There wasn't much starlight because of some overcast, so I could barely see his face.

"Is Harley around? I wanted to talk to him about his schoolwork," I said.

"He went to sleep, too," Uncle Roy said.

"So early?"

"When all you do mostly is sleep and eat and

ride around on your motorcycle, it's not sur-prising," he muttered.

"Would you please tell him I'll see him to-morrow after school then, Uncle Roy?"

"I'll tell him," he said.

"Thanks for helping with my party yesterday," I continued.

"Oh you're more than welcome, Princess."

"Good night," I said.

"Good night," he replied, still well in the shadows. It was almost as if I was talking to a ghost.

When I returned from school that Monday, I hurried to change into a pair of jeans and a more casual blouse and sneakers. Then I shot out of the house and hurried to see Harley. I saw the motor-cycle was there beside the garage where he kept it covered with a piece of canvas. He had told me Uncle Roy wouldn't permit him to keep it in the garage, which was all right with him because he was afraid Uncle Roy might accidentally on pur-pose run it over.

I knocked on the door and Aunt Glenda ap-peared, wiping her hands on her apron.

"Oh, hi, Summer dear."

"Hi, Aunt Glenda," I said. She opened the door for me and stepped back, smiling.

"You had such a nice party and so many nice presents. It was just the sort of sweet sixteen party I wish Latisha would have had."

"It was wonderful, Aunt Glenda."

She stared at me a moment, her smile frozen,

but her eyes starting to darken with a troubled thought.

"Is Harley home?"

"Harley?"

She looked about as if she was flustered for a moment, as if the question was so unexpected she didn't think she could answer it correctly.

"Oh, yes," she said. "I think so anyway," she added.

"Is he in his room?"

"His room? Yes," she said. "That's it. He's in his room."

"I'll go see him, then," I said nodding toward the stairway. She smiled.

"I've got some potatoes up for mashing," she said. "Roy just loves my mashed potatoes."

"They are good," I agreed, which brought back her smile.

She nodded and started back toward the kitchen. I watched her a moment and then went up the stairs. I called to Harley. His door was closed. He didn't answer or open it so I knocked softly.

"Harley?"

There was still no answer. I turned the knob softly and opened the door as gently as I could. When I looked in, I saw him in bed, face down. Why was he sleeping this time of the day I wondered. I waited, but he didn't turn or move.

"Harley?" I still waited. I knew he had to have heard me. I knew he didn't sleep that soundly.

"Go away, Summer," he finally said.

"What? Why? Are you sick?"

"Yeah, I'm sick," he said. "Get outta here before you catch something."

"What's the matter? Maybe you should see a doctor."

"Yeah, a doctor," he said and followed it with a short grunting laugh.

"Well, what's wrong with you, Harley? Didn't you go to school today?"

"No," he said, "and I'm not bothering going back either. Just go home, will you."

"Harley Arnold, you better talk to me."

He sighed deeply. I stood there, waiting, my heart starting to thump like a jackhammer. What was wrong with him? Why this radical change?

"Harley?"

He turned slowly and pulled himself into a sitting position. I felt my heart stop and start as I gasped. His right eye was black and blue and there was an ugly swelling just under it.

"What happened?" I cried.

"I walked into a door," he said.

"Harley! Tell me!"

He looked down, took a deep breath and then began.

"When I came home after your party, Roy and I had a bad argument. I lost my temper and swung a chair at him. He dodged it and I went head over heels and slammed my face into the bottom of the chair. I nearly knocked myself out."

"Are you telling the truth, Harley? He didn't hit you?"

"I wish he had," he said. "How do you think I feel having done this to myself? Instead, he scooped me up, threw me over his shoulder, carried me up to my room where he slapped me down in this bed and then went and got me a piece of steak. Little good it did, huh?"

"You look terrible," I said, unable to hide the truth.

"I know. That's why I didn't brush my teeth and my hair and go off to school."

"You've got to go back to school, and you can't wait for this to heal, Harley. There aren't many days left for classes."

"What difference will it make?"

"I thought we had decided I would help you pass your finals. I thought we made a decision about it and that was that. You promised you would try if I helped you, Harley Arnold," I scolded. "You can't just give up because you hurt yourself. You can still see out of that eye, can't you?"

"Yes," he said.

"Then you can read and write and you can study. Now, I'm going home. You're getting up, getting dressed, gathering your books and coming over in . . ." I looked at my watch. "In twenty minutes. We'll put in two hours."

"Two hours!"

"Two hours and not a minute less." I turned and walked to the door. "And," I said turning, "brush your teeth and your hair."

He started to smile and then groaned with the pain.

97

"Maybe you finally learned something about that temper of yours," I said. And then I added, "But I doubt it."

I closed the door behind me, let out a breath and then smiled to myself and hurried down the stairs. A little less than twenty minutes later, Harley was at my front door, his books under his right arm, his hair neatly brushed back.

"Do I meet inspection?" he asked.

"We'll see," I said. "We'll use the office." I had already told Mommy and Daddy that Harley was coming over to study. They were in the family room watching television. I had warned them about Harley's black eye. I gave them Harley's explanation, but they both looked skeptical. Mommy tried not to have too much of a reaction when she saw him, but the sight of his swollen cheek widened her eyes anyway.

"Hi," he said and they nodded, speechless.

"What did you tell them?" he asked as we walked away.

"Exactly what you told me."

"They look like they don't believe it."

I stopped.

"Who would?" I asked and he laughed.

We went to the office and began to review his social studies material first. We worked the same time all the remainder of the week, then we expanded our study hours as the final exam dates approached. Daddy was worried I was spending too much time helping Harley and not enough on my own work, but I assured him I wasn't.

What I discovered was if Harley really did concentrate on something, he could grasp it rather quickly. In the beginning Daddy looked in on us occasionally. Whenever he did, Harley glanced at me with that sardonic smirk on his face. I ignored it until Mrs. Geary started appearing, ostensibly to clean something or find something.

"A little paranoia floating through this house?" Harley asked.

I couldn't think of any excuses so I just ignored his remark, but for the last two days before finals, I decided we would study in my room. There, I closed the door.

When we were little, growing up together, Harley was in my room from time to time, but over the last five years or so, he was rarely there. In fact, I couldn't recall the last time. After he entered, he just stood looking around at everything, drinking it all in as if he wanted to lock it forever and ever in his memory, memorize each and every detail. He smiled when he saw that I had put the picture he had drawn for me as a birthday present right over my bed.

"What?"

"Didn't anyone complain about your putting that up?"

"No, and besides, this is my room and I'm proud of that picture and want it as prominent as can be," I said.

I saw how his eyes warmed.

"You can have the desk chair," I said and sat on my bed. We were down to my dictating a mock exam for him and his answering the questions. I flipped through his books and papers, sprawling out comfortably, and began.

I was wearing a skirt and a blouse and had my hair down. Harley hovered over his paper and started, but periodically he turned and looked at me. While he worked I read some of my own material, so I didn't know how long he was looking at me. Soon, I began to feel his eyes on me. I looked up quickly and saw how he was staring.

What I hadn't realized was my top three blouse buttons had come undone and with the angle I was at, I guess I was revealing as much of my bosom as I might had I been lying there in my swimming suit. I didn't want to be so obvious about it, and I didn't want him to feel he had been caught doing something he shouldn't, but I sat up quickly and pressed my palm against my blouse.

"What?" I finally asked. "You can't be done already?"

"It was easier downstairs being interrupted," he said.

"Why?"

"I was afraid to do anything but concentrate on the schoolwork."

"So?"

He looked at the closed bedroom door and then at me.

"What?" I demanded.

"I can't look at you in here and not want to kiss you," he said without hesitation.

For a moment I thought I had lost the power of

speech. I tried to swallow, but couldn't. He shrugged and stood up.

"Maybe if I get that over with, I can concentrate," he said in a very matter-of-fact tone of voice; then he casually stepped over to the bed and leaned down to take my shoulders in his hands and bring his lips to mine. I was too shocked even to utter a note of resistance. It was a long, warm kiss. When his lips left mine, my eyes were still closed.

As soon as I opened them, he kissed me again. Then he stepped back as I caught my breath.

"Okay," he said. "I feel better." He walked back to his seat, looked at his papers and turned to me. "I missed the end of the last question, number ten."

He lifted his pen, and waited.

"Number ten?" he repeated.

I guess I looked like I was in a state of shock.

"What? Oh, yes, that was about *Macbeth*."

I flipped through the pages of notes while he waited. Every time I glanced at him, he had that soft, happy smile on his lips. Finally, I found the question and repeated it. He nodded and turned back to the paper.

I felt my cheeks because it seemed to me they were on fire.

Then I quickly buttoned my blouse and finally managed to swallow and take a deep breath.

After he left, I stayed up as long as I could to study for my own tests, but before I went to sleep, I stood naked at my window and looked out over the lake toward his house, toward the lit window I knew was his and felt as if his eyes were on me.

His kiss was still on my lips when I laid my head on my pillow.

I fell asleep only when I sank into a deeper place within myself, a cozy place where accidents never happened, where people never got angry at each other, where no one cried and where, if it ever rained, it rained softly, each drop full of sweetness and light and always afterward, followed by a rainbow.

Two days later, we both began our final exams.

Harley passed all of his tests. Even Uncle Roy was impressed and could only say, "Yeah, sure," when Daddy proposed they take us out to celebrate our good grades and Harley's graduation.

Mommy decided she was going to help Aunt Glenda prepare for the festivities. I brought Mommy over to their house so she could talk to her about buying some new clothes. As usual, the whole idea of getting out in public and doing all these things put an icy look of fear on Glenda's face, but Mommy spoke softly and quietly, had a cup of tea with her, assured her she would go along with her to all the department stores, and finally left with Glenda's agreement to do so. Mommy gently pointed out that Harley deserved her being excited for him.

"He's accomplished a great deal, Glenda. He needs to see you smiling proudly at him graduation day."

I thought Aunt Glenda was going to cry. Her

eyes filled with tears, but she sucked in her breath and nodded. Then she looked out the rear window in the kitchen toward Latisha's grave.

"It could have been wonderful for all of us," she said.

"It will be for Harley," Mommy emphasized.

I was so proud of her that day, proud of how she could handle someone as fragile as Aunt Glenda. Where did Mommy get all her wisdom? I wondered. So much of her adult life was spent confined to the wheelchair and to her therapies. She could have had the most cosmopolitan life, traveled, met all sorts of wonderful people, yet she didn't waste away at home wallowing in self-pity. She kept the light brightly lit inside her and held off the darkness.

Because of Mommy's influence, Aunt Glenda even went to a beauty parlor and had her hair cut and styled and her nails done. They stopped at the cosmetic counter in the department store and the beautician on duty performed a makeover right then and there to show Aunt Glenda some of the possibilities. After she and Mommy settled on a new dress and matching shoes with a matching purse, Aunt Glenda did look as if her youth and beauty had been resurrected.

No one was more impressed than Uncle Roy. I know it caused him to think about himself as well; without any fanfare, he went out the next day and bought himself some new clothes, too. When Harley saw what was happening, he looked astounded, but instead of being happy, he seemed even more worried. I went over to see him while he was cleaning and polishing his motorcycle.

"Did you see how pretty your mother is in her new hairdo?" I asked.

He nodded and kept working.

"Daddy told us about Uncle Roy's new suit. He went to the same tailor to get fitted. Isn't it wonderful?"

He didn't speak, but concentrated on some small part as if the whole world depended on it being spotless.

"Harley Arnold, you could at least give me one of your famous grunts," I said.

He stopped, looked at me and then stood up.

"It just makes me nervous," he finally admitted and after having done so, began to walk toward the lake.

"Why?" I asked running after him.

"I'm graduating, big deal. After the pomp and circumstance and all the cheers, what happens next? I haven't even applied to go to a college or do anything else. I haven't even enlisted in the army.

"We'll go to the ceremony, go out to eat with your parents, and then come home to . . . to nothing," he said. "My mother will hang up her new dress and put away her new shoes and purse and Roy will do the same with his suit. All it will be is . . . is some interruption."

"You've got to stop that," I insisted. I actually stomped my foot, which brought a surprised smile to his lips. "You've got to stop looking on the dark side of everything. Wrong, wrong, wrong. This is not some hiccup in your dreary life, Harley Arnold. You've achieved something and now you're going to do bigger and better things.

"You march right into the guidance office on Monday and talk to Mr. Springer. There are lots of schools that will still consider you for their freshman class."

"Yeah, and who's going to pay for that?"

"I bet if you get accepted, Uncle Roy will see to it. And you know you'll make good money working with him again this summer. You always do."

"Right," he said skeptically.

"You've got to try, Harley. You've got to seize the opportunity."

"Me? In college?"

"A few weeks back, you would have laughed at your passing all your finals and graduating, right? Well?" I pursued when he didn't respond.

"I guess so."

"Well, then, guess again and guess for bigger and better things," I insisted.

His smile widened.

"You're amazing, Summer. You're like that old oak tree that was hit by lightning years ago," he said nodding at the tree. "It grew new branches and kept going, hooking onto every ray of sunshine. I bet every depressed blade of grass or wild flower basks in its glory and gets up some hope."

"Call me an old tree, anything, as long as you don't give up," I said.

He laughed and then grew serious again.

"What do I do when you're gone?" he asked.

Every summer for the last four, I attended music camp in Williamsburg where I studied piano and the clarinet, attended ensemble sessions and participated in the school's orchestra. It was a small school with only fifty students, the girls on one side of a dormitory and the boys on the other. It was only a six-week program, but very concentrated. Mommy and Daddy usually visited on the weekends. At the end of the session, we performed a program for our parents, friends and relatives, and many local citizens attended because the school had such a good reputation.

The school provided for social activities as well, had a pool, ran movies twice a week and socials once a week at which students attending the school took turns providing the music for any dancing. There was a very comfortable, modern dormitory facility with two students assigned to each room. For the last two years, I had the same roommate, a girl a year older than I was. Her name was Judy Foster and she was from Richmond, Kentucky. She was a very serious music student, somewhat on the prudish side. I always felt that things cooled considerably between us the moment she fixed her eyes on my mother and realized I was part African-American. Fortunately, last year was her last and I would have a new roommate this year.

"Maybe you can come visit me," I suggested to

Harley. He never had before. "I know it's far and . . ."

"Really? You'd like that?"

"Sure," I said. "But only if you promise you'll try to do something meaningful with your life and not drift off like so many boys these days," I said sounding wise and mature.

"Aye, aye, Miss Oak Tree."

We both laughed and he suggested we go for a row.

"I'll do all the work," he promised. "You can just lie back and soak it up."

After we pushed off, I did just that. For a while neither of us spoke. The late afternoon sun was just falling below the tree line so that there were long, deep and cool shadows on the lake. With a soft, but continuous breeze it was truly refreshing.

"So," Harley said, "when you graduate what are you going to do?"

"I think I want to continue with music, and if I'm good enough, maybe someday work for an orchestra and maybe perform at places like Lincoln Center in New York. I'll try to get into a good music college."

"You'll get into anywhere you want," he said.

"Oh, are you trying to be Mr. Oak Tree now?" I countered and he laughed. Then he put up the oars so we would just drift. Sparrows and robins began to appear, looking for dinner in the twilight. Occasionally, one of the fish Uncle Roy called trained bass came close to the surface as if it were expecting bread crumbs.

Harley leaned over and looked at the floor of the rowboat.

"When I was about twelve, I think, I suddenly worried that you and I were really cousins," he began. "For some reason it never occurred to me before."

"Why would that worry you?"

"I was old enough to realize that if we were cousins, we couldn't be boyfriend and girlfriend."

"You never told me that."

"I was too bashful. I'm still too bashful. I'm not telling you now," he said still looking down. "I'm telling the floor of the boat."

I laughed and leaned over to push his head so he would look up. He did so slowly and our eyes fixed on each other.

"Then, I thought, we're too much like relatives anyway and that's why you never look at me like you look at a Chase Taylor. And then, I thought, we're just like your mother and Roy and maybe that's the family curse you tell me your mother fears."

"We're not like that, Harley. We've been to-gether a long time, but we weren't brought up to think we were brother and sister. It's a lot dif-ferent; if you heard the way Mommy described those days, you'd understand why. Don't think that," I said.

"I don't want to," he replied smiling. "That's for sure." He paused. "Another confession," he began. "When I saw you and Chase in this boat on your birthday, I was so jealous, I could hardly breathe. That was why I pushed him off the raft and started the fight. It wasn't to defend Amber's honor or anything."

"I think I knew that," I said.

"Does it make you mad?"

I looked away. The truth was it didn't. The truth was it was thrilling to have two boys clash over me, but I also knew it was wrong and could be ugly, too.

"I like it that you care, but I don't like you getting into trouble," I finally said.

We heard a car horn and saw Daddy had driven up. He got out and stood there looking at us. I waved and Harley took up the oars and started to turn the boat back toward the dock. Daddy stood there, waiting for me.

"Thanks for the ride," I said as he helped me up and out.

"It was too short," Harley said.

"There'll be other rides," I promised. He smiled.

"Right, Mrs. Oak Tree."

"See you later, Mr. Oak Tree."

I ran to greet Daddy. After he kissed me, he looked toward Harley. His eyes were dark, troubled for a moment.

"Everything all right?" he asked.

"Everything's wonderful, Daddy."

"Harley's got some big decisions to make about his life now," he said still looking after him.

"I know. We talked about that. He's going to see about getting into a school. You know how talented he is with his construction art, and how he is interested in planning buildings and bridges and things. He could be good at it, Daddy. He really could!"

"Okay, honey."

"Maybe you can help him, too, Daddy."

"I'll certainly try," he said. "Just be careful about one thing, honey. Be careful about your investment in people. Too often, we are disappointed in our relationships," he advised. "You've got to be secure about yourself first. Get your feet well planted before you lean in one direction or another. That way you won't fall on your face. You understand what I mean?" he asked, his eyes scrutinizing my face carefully.

"Yes, Daddy, I do." I smiled. "You want me to be like Mr. Oak Tree."

"Oak Tree?" He looked out at it. "Oh. Yes, that's it. That's it exactly," he said. Then he put his arm around me as we walked to the house.

The next day was Harley's graduation ceremony. He never looked more handsome, and Aunt Glenda and Uncle Roy were so impressive in their new clothes and styled hair, they attracted a lot more attention. Mommy and I held hands, especially when the graduates paraded in and onto the stage. After the speeches, the principal began to call out the traditional awards. I was sitting there, feeling a little sorry for Harley; I thought he would be almost invisible throughout all this.

And then came the best surprise of all. His art

teacher had chosen him for the art award. Harley looked so shocked, he didn't rise and had to have his name called twice. It brought some laughter. I gazed at Aunt Glenda. Her face beamed and Uncle Roy looked genuinely impressed. He glanced at Mommy who smiled at him. He was too stunned to get up and take a picture, so Daddy moved quickly and snapped it.

Afterward, Uncle Roy shook Harley's hand so hard, I thought he might have broken his arm. Some of the men he knew from work were congratulating him, too, and he was basking in it. All of us took turns hugging and kissing Harley. Afterward, as we headed out to the cars and to the restaurant for our celebration, Harley hung back with me.

"I've got you to thank for all this, Summer," he said.

"You thank yourself. You did it," I replied.

We had a wonderful dinner. I couldn't remember a time when we all looked more like a family. Aunt Glenda seemed truly overwhelmed with happiness she hadn't experienced for years and years. For a few hours in time, she was able to put aside her great sorrow.

On Monday, Harley did what he had promised and went to see the guidance counselor to make out some late admission applications. Two days later, Daddy and I packed the van with my things for the trip to my music camp. Harley had already begun working with Uncle Roy on a project we were doing for the county government.

When the time came for us to leave, I lagged behind, expecting Harley would come along to say goodbye. He had promised he would, even though he had gotten up hours earlier and gone to work. It looked like he wasn't coming, however. We were about to leave, and I couldn't make Mommy wait in the van. I was very disappointed when we started away.

But just as we got to the turn, I heard the sound of his motorcycle and moments later, he was there. Daddy pulled over so I could hop out to say goodbye.

"Make it quick, honey," he said.

"Sorry," Harley said. "I was in the middle of something I just couldn't stop."

"It's okay. I'm glad you made it even for a few seconds."

"I'll miss you."

"Just keep talking to Mr. Oak Tree," I said. I glanced back at the van. Daddy was watching us in the side mirror.

Instinctively, I grabbed Harley's hand and pulled him toward me, away from Daddy's line of vision. I gave Harley a quick, but firm goodbye kiss.

He smiled and I hurried back into the van.

We started away and Harley followed behind for a few moments before pulling ahead and then off to the left.

Holding that hand up as always.

Knowing more than ever that I'd be waiting for it.

5

Soul Mates

The Pelham School of Music ran its summer program from a complex of buildings just outside the city of Williamsburg. The school itself was named after Peter Pelham, who came to America in 1726 and spent a number of years in Boston, where he studied music and became the organist at Trinity Church. The orientation brochure for the school told us that Pelham moved to Williamsburg around 1750. He was the organist at Bruton Parish Church, taught young women at the time to play the harpsichord and spinet, and was the musical director when *The Beggar's Opera* was first performed in the city.

Although our teachers and counselors tried to keep a sense of decorum and history about us while we attended the Pelham School, the dormitory quickly revealed that a little over four dozen modern teenagers had become the residents. Rock and movie posters, as well as some humorous posters, were instantly slapped over the austere walls. Despite our study of classical music, the sounds of rock, country and pop came flowing out of windows and doors.

Everywhere else on the campus, things were prim and proper. We had a dress code at class. Boys had to wear slacks and white shirts with ties; girls wore black ankle-length skirts and white blouses, but no pants outfits and certainly no shorts. Once we ended the formal class day about five p.m., we could put on casual clothing; however, there was still a standard enforced in the cafeteria. After dinner, everyone could be as sloppy as he or she wished and it was not unusual to see us in old sweatshirts and jeans walking barefoot through the hallways.

We had a strict curfew of ten p.m. on weekdays and eleven p.m. on weekends. At those hours all radios, CD players and television sets had to be turned off. You could keep the lights on in your room as long as you wanted, but early to bed was strongly advised since breakfast began at six-thirty and ended at seven-thirty with the first class starting at eight.

On weekends, the pool was open, but bikinis and thong suits were absolutely forbidden. Our counselors and administrators referred to their own liability whenever anyone offered the slightest challenge or complaint.

"While you are here in our house," Doctor Richard Greenleaf began his opening talk to all the arriving students at orientation, "you have to obey our rules. We have made a pact with your families to become your surrogate parents while you are here under our wing. We have to have an absolutely no-tolerance policy when it concerns our safety codes. To illustrate how serious this is, I will read from the orientation document you were all given when you arrived — just to be sure there are no misunderstandings."

He adjusted his glasses and then lowered his voice to sound even more austere.

"There will be absolutely no smoking in the dormitory at any time. Just like on an airplane, anyone who tampers with one of our smoke detectors will be immediately dismissed and prosecuted. No alcoholic beverages of any sort can be on this campus. No illegal drugs can even be mentioned, much less brought onto this campus. It goes without saying that an incidence of vandalism or disrespect toward our property will be considered a very serious affront to the school. Anyone who violates a curfew or fails to have proper permission slips completed before leaving the campus will be asked to leave the campus permanently. Proper classroom decorum is paramount.

"We are all here for one main purpose, and that's to further our development and progress with our musical talents and education. Everything else is secondary. You are here because your families were willing to finance this pursuit. They have faith and expectations and we intend to do the best we can to justify that faith and succeed with those expectations.

"You have one of the most qualified and talented faculties in the country, state-of-the-art studios and five-star facilities. Enjoy yourselves, but work hard, very hard and help make this the most successful summer of music yet."

There was light applause, most of it coming from the parents and relatives who had accompanied the students to the school. Afterward, a lunch was held and we were all introduced to members of the faculty. My piano teacher, Professor Littleton, had returned, which made me happy. He was a very pleasant man with light gray hair, bushy eyebrows and rosy cheeks. He had the warmest eyes and great patience with students, always making us believe we could do better. He made us believe it was in us to reach a little further.

For a while I thought I wasn't going to have a roommate. A girl named Sarah Burnside from Richmond, Kentucky, was assigned to be my roommate, but somehow she had missed the opening program and lunch. While I was unpacking and organizing my things hours later, I heard a loud bang just outside my door and froze for a moment. I was alone. Mommy and Daddy were long gone so they could be home by dinner. Mommy hated prolonged goodbyes anyway, and Daddy thought it was best to just do what had to be done and go before a single tear could escape a single eye. He nearly succeeded, but Mommy was flicking them off her face like flies at our parting.

The door jerked open and a short — maybe four foot ten — girl with light brown curly hair nearly fell into the room over her large suitcase and her trombone case. She wore a bright, flower print one-piece dress that looked like it could double for a tent, a pair of blue sandals and no socks, along with a turquoise shell necklace that nearly reached her waist and one matching shell earring on her right ear. She wore white lipstick that looked like candle wax, and she had a splatter of freckles running down from each temple. Otherwise, her face was sweet and soft with very small, dainty features in perfect proportion, and her very prettily shaped brown eyes were the color of fresh walnut shells.

"Sorry," she said. She paused and looked around the room. "Good, it's big."

I thought anything would be a big room to her, even a walk-in closet.

"Hi," I said. "I'm Summer Clarke."

"I know. You know I'm Sarah Burnside, right?"

"I do now," I said smiling. "Why are you so late? You missed orientation."

"My mother," she said with a grimace, "can never get her act together. When you look up disorganized in the dictionary, her face is next to the definition. If she didn't have my great-aunt Margaret taking care of her business books, she would be closed ages ago."

"What does your mother do?"

"She has the Full-Moon Café, a very popular place in Richmond, Kentucky."

"Is she here?" I asked looking past her into the hallway and wondering why no one had helped Sarah with her things.

"No. She had to start for the airport because she's almost late for her flight home as it is."

Sarah lifted her suitcase with two hands. It was almost as big as she was. I jumped to help her and we put it on her bed. Then she brought in her trombone and closed the door.

"What's yours?" she asked.

"Mine?"

"Instrument?"

"Oh. I play the clarinet and the piano."

"I have enough trouble with one. This is my first time here," she added.

"I know. I've been coming here for four years and I've never seen you."

"Four years! You must be like Kenny G by now."

"No," I said laughing. "Hardly."

She shrugged.

"My coming here was my mother's idea. She wants me to absorb more culture," she declared with the back of her hand over her forehead and speaking in an exaggeratedly proper tone of voice. "Since her divorce, she's very concerned that no one gets the opportunity to say she's not doing a good job bringing me up."

"Oh," I said, just learning her parents were divorced. "I'm sorry."

"It's all right. It's one of those civilized divorces. My father comes around and gives her advice on the café from time to time. He works for a food distributor and my mother's café is actually one of his biggest accounts."

"Why did they divorce?"

"No one reason in particular," she replied with a shrug. "One day, they decided they had made a big mistake when they had said, 'til death do us part.' We all sat in the living room and had a sensible conversation and concluded that leaving it up to death was losing control of your life."

"We?"

"My parents have always included me in their decisions. They believe that a family should be the best example of a democracy, especially since every decision affects me as well as it does them. That's been going on since I was about three."

"Three? How could you help them decide anything at three?"

She shrugged.

"They believe in instinct, I guess, and paid attention to my moans, groans and smiles."

She unlocked her suitcase. Everything in it had simply been thrown in with very little organization: her toiletries were packed right alongside her undergarments, her blouses, skirts and socks, shoes and sneakers. None of those clothes were folded, but she had carefully packed her jeans.

"Do you realize you're wearing only one earring?" I asked.

She slapped her hand over her ears and grimaced in pain.

"Oh no. It must have fallen off when I went down to baggage. I'm sure I had it on the plane. Oh well, as my mother says whenever she makes a mistake, maybe I'll start a new fad: one earring only." To illustrate she meant it, she didn't take the remaining earring off.

I watched her unpack and put her things in the drawers just as sloppily as she had put them in the suitcase.

"How old are you?" I asked.

"Fifteen. What about you?"

"I'm just sixteen."

"What are the boys like here?" she followed without looking at me.

"Most of them are very nice," I said.

"How nice?" She turned and looked at me. I wasn't sure what that meant. "Are they too nice? I hate boys who are too nice; they make you work harder at getting something going."

"Something going?"

"A romance or something very hot. Didn't you ever go with anyone here?"

"No," I said. "To dances, but nothing very serious developed."

"Oh boy," she said shaking her head and finishing her unpacking. "Just as I feared."

"What?" I asked.

She turned and lifted her arms.

"Culture is no fun."

There was nothing shy about Sarah Burnside, I quickly decided. When I introduced her to people, she began to talk to them as if she had known them for years and years, and she didn't have the slightest inhibition about sharing her opinions about things or offering her opinions about what they were wearing. She had her own words for some things, too, especially things that displeased or annoyed her. If it was a minor annoyance, she called it Spewch; if it was something absolutely horrible to her, she labeled it Pewch. Our food was merely spewch, but many of our rules fell into the category of pewch.

"We should organize a protest committee and demand a meeting with Herr Director, Professor Greenleaf," she declared.

When Courtney Bryer told her we weren't here long enough for any of it to matter, Sarah responded with a vehement declaration that "Even an hour in a totalitarian state is too long! Just because we're studying music, it doesn't mean we have to give up basic human rights."

Most everyone simply stared at her; then when she wasn't looking, wagged their heads at me in sympathy. After all, she was my roommate.

As it turned out, Sarah talked about rebellion, but did nothing to foster it. She was going in four different directions at the same time most of the time, but when she finally sat and began to take her lessons and play, she turned out to be very talented and bright. Our teachers actually enjoyed her. She was capable of saying outrageous things, raising eyebrows and cracking serious faces into soft smiles, but as soon as the mouthpiece reached her lips, it all went away and beautiful music flowed.

She was immediately put into the senior orchestra and was gobbled up by the jazz ensemble. Although she was truly a character, she became popular and loved to move about the cafeteria bursting in on one clique or another to offer her flagrant opinions about anything and everything. Sometimes, I had the feeling she liked to shock or enrage other students just for the fun of it.

Our room quickly began to resemble a split-screen television picture. My side was neat, clean, organized. Hers had drawers half open with clothes spilling over the edges, clothes on chairs or even the floor; her bed was usually unmade and something was always hanging on her closet door, usually a slip or a blouse. Mrs. Bernard, our dorm headmistress, came by often and expressed her displeasure. Sarah would nod her head as if she was really paying attention and concerned, criticizing herself even more harshly, but the moment Mrs. Bernard stepped out, she exclaimed a loud "Pewch" and returned to her sloppy ways.

Her mother had provided her with some acceptable skirts and blouses; however she only had large-heeled and large-soled shoes that made her look comical walking from the dorm to classes or the auditorium. She looked like she was on stilts. I suppose everyone accepted it because it gave her another few inches of height.

She liked to talk herself to sleep every night, so I learned a great deal about her family whether I wanted to or not. I learned that her mother had given birth to her and that her parents had lived together with her for nearly three years before they actually married.

"If they hadn't, they wouldn't have had any significant legal expenses when they divorced," she told me. "I'm never going to get married. I'm going to live with four or five different men, in succession of course, and then live alone in Paris or London."

"You don't want to have a family?" I asked her.

"I might have a family or I might not, but if I do, I won't give up my independence. It's very important to have your independence," she lectured. "Don't become a Mrs. Somebody and lose yourself in your husband. We've been liberated from all that. Men have to accept us as equals or not at all."

"I think you can be equals and still have a family," I told her. "And I don't think you have to give up your identity to be a mother and a wife."

She was silent. I had the feeling that she would rather not speak than say anything that might offend me. I also felt that she often sounded like someone who didn't really and truly believe in what she was saying. In fact, I thought that sometimes she wanted to believe the exact opposite.

"Are you still a virgin?" she followed that night.

"What? Yes," I said quickly.

"A lot of girls these days want to be virgins until they actually marry," she said sounding like it was a wild, new idea. "And not just because of all the sexually transmitted diseases. They just think it's important. Is that why you're a virgin?"

"I suppose it is," I said. "I think there are some things that should be kept sacred or special."

She was silent again. I was afraid to ask her if she was a virgin, but she offered the answer.

"My mother keeps telling me to be sure I'm careful, to be sure I'm careful about not getting pregnant or sick, as if that's the only thing that matters."

"It is important," I said.

"Pewtch," she said and surprised me by adding, "The only thing that matters is that you really care for the person you're with, that you want to do it with him more than anyone else, ever. That's all that's mattered to me whenever I've done it."

"But you said you're going to have five love affairs."

"So? You can love more than one person like that, can't you?"

"I don't know," I said. "No," I concluded after another moment, "I don't think so. My parents were meant for each other and no one else. I believe in soul mates."

She was silent for a long moment again. Then she turned to me and stared so long and hard, I had to ask, "What?"

"You have to be especially lucky to have only one love forever and ever," she declared. "I don't feel I am or will be. I guess I'm more like my mother than I care to admit."

It was the saddest moment we had together. I

thought she was going to cry, but she turned over in bed instead and stopped talking.

After nearly a week had passed, Harley called me. We had phones in our rooms, but at exactly ten p.m., they were shut down. Anyone who needed us for an emergency or something after that would have to call Mrs. Bernard directly.

"How's it going, Mrs. Oak Tree?" I heard.

"Harley!"

"I thought I'd surprise you and call."

"I'm glad you did. I could die waiting for you to write a letter. How's everyone?"

"The same," he said. "Roy's terrorizing his construction crew. My mother is humming hymns in her sleep. I saw your mother yesterday after I came home from work. She was down at the lake. We had a nice talk," he said. "She told me things about her youth I never knew."

"I miss everyone already."

"Everyone?"

"Especially you, Harley. When can you visit? I have to get special permission to go off campus, and I don't expect Mommy and Daddy would want me to ride off on your motorcycle here if I can't there," I added quickly. I didn't want him to be disappointed.

"That's all right. I wouldn't want to do anything but see you anyway. How's the weekend after next sound?" he offered. "I won't have to work that weekend."

"It sounds wonderful."

"I'll be there by noon Saturday."

"Good. You can have lunch at the cafeteria with me. The food isn't anything special, but you'll enjoy meeting everyone and . . ."

"Isn't there an oak tree we can sit under? I'll stop and buy us some sandwiches and cans of soda."

"Yes, there is."

"All I want to do is spend some time with you, Summer," he said.

"Okay."

"How's your new roommate?"

"Interesting," I said. "You will at least have to meet her."

He was silent a moment.

"This place isn't the same without you," he finally said. "Even the birds are complaining."

I laughed.

"I sent out all my applications," he continued. "Lot of good it will do."

"Don't you be pessimistic," I warned him.

"Okay," he said. "I'll be a dreamer as long as I can include you. Can I?"

"Of course you can," I said. It sounded too formal, too much like giving him permission to include me on some paperwork. I regretted my tone immediately.

"What about if I just dream about you?" he pursued.

"We might meet then," I said. "I'll have the same dream, only about you."

I could almost hear him smile.

"I'll call you again before I come up," he promised.

Sarah came in from a late jazz session just as I cradled the phone and sat on my bed.

"Why so wan and pale, fair lover?" she asked.

"What?"

"It's from a famous poem. You look like you just lost your best friend."

"No, I just heard from Harley, and it's made me a little homesick."

"Oh, your noncousin cousin," she said. I had told her some of my family history.

I looked up at her.

"That's not the look of homesick. That's the look of love," she declared. "And you know what that means?"

"What?"

"You'll have to decide if he's the one and only. When is he coming here?"

"The weekend after next," I said.

"Fine. Leave it up to me. I'll tell you after only ten minutes with him. I have a built-in soul mate detector," she quipped.

"Pewch," I cried at her and she laughed.

As crazy as it seemed and even though we were so different that we could be extraterrestrials to each other, I was growing to like her a lot.

The weekend before Harley was coming happened to be the weekend of our first school dance. Sarah was in the band playing for it. The preparations for the dance were simple. The school cafeteria personnel provided a selection of food and desserts, and there were some decorations: signs welcoming us all to our summer session, some large musical notes and bars that were cut out of big pieces of construction paper and hung from the ceiling along with some streams of crepe paper. The ballroom always had large portraits of great composers on the walls as well.

I knew most of the boys at the school from previous years. There was no one who had drawn any particular interest from me, but still, going to a dance was something to look forward to, especially after so many days of concentrated work. Sarah had been telling me about a boy she thought was very handsome. His name was Duncan Fields and he played the trumpet in their jazz ensemble. I had noticed him in the cafeteria and on the campus. He was a new student and apparently already very popular from the way some of the girls were fawning over him.

No one could deny he was good looking. He had rich, dark brown wavy hair with strikingly blue eyes and a firm, strong mouth. Even from across the cafeteria, I could see how confidently he smiled and spoke. There was something regal about his posture, although I didn't think he was arrogant.

He had glanced at me a few times in the hallways and while crossing the campus, always flashing that movie star smile with teeth that glittered like tiny mirrors catching the sunlight. However, I didn't think anything special of it because he seemed to look at almost every girl in the school the same way. In my heart of hearts, I thought he was a dream, but not especially for me. It was almost as if he was already reserved for some glamorous destiny to live among the gods and goddesses of film and television and was just passing through the lower world of us mere mortals.

The night of the dance was particularly warm. It began somewhat overcast and the clouds seemed to put a lid on the day's heat, preventing it from escaping and keeping us in an oven. The dorms had air conditioners and so did the ballroom, but the humidity made everything sticky. I chose to wear a camisole peasant dress in a cool Hawaiian print. Mommy had told me it was perfect for casual events. Sarah wanted to look bohemian and did look cute in her black beret, gypsy skirt and off-shoulder blouse with some long silver earrings depicting astrological signs. This time she wore two earrings.

We entered the ballroom earlier than most of the other students because Sarah had to set up with the band. Duncan was already setting up and had started playing his trumpet. He glanced at me over his instrument and wiggling fingers, and I saw his eyes warm and smile. Then, he turned and blew a little of *Carnival of Venice*, which I knew to be a fairly difficult piece. Everyone stopped what he or she was doing to listen. After a few moments, he paused and shrugged as if that was nothing. Why make a big deal of it? He looked embarrassed by the attention he had drawn to himself.

"You're Burnsy's roommate, right?" he asked me, stepping down from the small stage that had been set up for the musicians.

"Burnsy?"

"That's what we call her."

"Oh. Sarah. Yes, we room together," I said.

"Clarinet?" he continued, pointing at me. I nodded. "You're pretty good. I heard you one afternoon."

"I'm adequate," I replied.

"Adequate?" He laughed. "Hardly that. You're a lot more than adequate," he said, his eyes drinking me in from foot to head and then back down quickly as he widened his smile. "The only disadvantage to my playing tonight is I won't have all that much time to get to meet people and dance. When I step off for a break, I'd like to dance with you," he said. "Would you save me a spot on your dance card?"

"I don't have a dance card," I said.

"You will," he predicted.

"I see you've introduced yourself to my roommate already," Sarah said finally noticing. She stepped up beside him. He wasn't much more than six feet tall, but when Sarah stood next to him, he looked like an NBA basketball player.

"Not really," Duncan said. "I don't know her name. Why don't you be nice and introduce us formally."

"Who wants to be nice?" Sarah quipped. Duncan raised his eyebrows and smiled. "All right, all right," Sarah said. "I'll introduce you formally. This is Summer Clarke and Summer, this is Duncan Fields."

"Hi," Duncan said. "I like your dress."

"Thank you."

Sarah jabbed him in the side with her elbow.

"Hey!" he protested, grimacing with pain.

"You didn't say anything about my dress. I thought you said I was the love of your life."

"You are," he declared, laughing.

"Yeah, right." She shook her head at me and returned to her place in the band.

"She's a barrel of laughs," he said. "Actually, she's one of the most talented trombone players for her age that I've played with, and I've been at a few of these music camps."

"I know she is."

"She likes you. She's always talking about you."

"Really? I was afraid we were too different to become friends," I said.

"You could probably become friends with anyone," he declared.

"How do you know that?" I challenged. I hated artificial compliments.

He laughed.

"A little bird told me," he replied. Then he grew serious and added, "When you've traveled a lot and met many different people, you get so you can tell pretty quickly who are the real people and who aren't."

I stared, unable to speak for a moment. His eyes were so strong, so sincere. He smiled and looked at the band.

"Got to get to work. See you later," Duncan told me, "if Burnsy doesn't kill me first."

I had to confess that I was surprised at how nice he was. Despite his good looks and talent, he didn't seem to be full of himself as did so many of the other boys here, yet he had a real sophisticated air about him.

I stood there for a while watching the musicians start to work out their program. Duncan was serious and professional about it. My presence didn't distract him.

After a few more minutes, I retreated to join the girls now streaming into the ballroom. So many of them were talking about Duncan. Bits and pieces fell around me. His father owned a computer manufacturing company in Delaware. He had two older brothers, one just graduating law school. His mother was a well-known socialite who served on national charity committees and was involved in raising campaign money for important Republican senators. They had a winter home in Palm Beach, Florida, as well as a mansion in Wilmington, Delaware. His parents usually spent most of their summers in Southern France and he had attended prestigious music schools in Europe. This was his first summer in a long time to be spent in America. He was one of the few boys on campus who had his own car and permission to go just about anywhere he wanted on his free time.

When the band began to play, the dancing started. Duncan moved rapidly to the forefront and at times, the whole school paused to listen to him. I saw many of my girlfriends swooning. For some reason it annoyed me, and when I gave it some thought, I think I was annoyed because they were all so obvious.

Before long, Duncan took his first break and disappointed some of the girls who had been eagerly anticipating his attention. Instead, he headed directly for me, joining me at the food table. Without asking, he took the plate from my hand and put it on a table.

"That can wait, can't it?" he asked.

"No," I said, but he laughed, ignored me, and took me onto the dance floor. With everyone watching us so closely, I couldn't very well be unwilling. He was a good dancer, too, and with the band playing so well, I let myself get into the music, maybe too much. Out of the corners of my eyes, I could see other boys nodding to each other with admiration and lustful smiles, and some of the girls glaring with enough envy to drown the whole female population in green sop.

"I like how you move in that dress," Duncan whispered. "You're practically a work of art."

"Thank you, I guess," I said and he laughed.

"It's a compliment, trust me," he said. Then he really put himself into the dancing.

We were both sweating visibly when the song ended.

"I guess their air conditioning isn't working so well in here," he said offering me his handkerchief. I thanked him and wiped my face. When I handed it back, he dabbed his own forehead. "It's probably cooler outside. Thanks for the dance," he said and returned to the stage to continue playing.

After the band took its break and sat down to have something to eat and drink, I joined Sarah.

"You guys sound great," I said.

"Thanks. You looked so hot out there before, dancing with Duncan. Everyone was envious, the girls of you, the boys of him."

I felt myself blush and glanced over at him. He looked at me across the table as if he was stealing a forbidden peek and quickly turned back to the girls who had surrounded him. He didn't make it a point to come over to talk to me afterward either; minutes later, he and the other band members were playing again. They played until the party came to an end this time. Our chaperones informed us it was curfew and the dance began to break up.

I glanced back at Duncan, who was putting his trumpet in its case and talking to Sarah. She laughed at something he had said, and then she quickly joined me at the door to return to our room.

"Have a good time?" she asked.

"It was fun."

I kept expecting him to say goodnight to me, but he continued talking music with the other band members.

If anything, his apparent restraint made me even more curious about Duncan Fields. He had seemed so interested in me at the beginning of the dance and we did have a good time when we danced, but after that, he hardly looked my way. I knew because I was continually looking at him and expecting the same.

"Did Duncan say anything about me?" I finally asked Sarah as we headed down our corridor.

"Uh-huh, but I told him you were going hot and heavy with someone from home who was coming to see you soon."

"Oh," I said.

She stopped and tilted her head.

"You sound disappointed. Should I have kept that a secret?"

"No," I said quickly. "You did the right thing."

She laughed.

"See?" she said. "See why I don't believe in soul mates?"

"I'm not upset," I insisted.

"Spewch," she muttered and plodded down to our room ahead of me.

I felt myself fuming inside, but it was more because of my comments and reactions than hers, I realized — that both confused and angered me. When I set my head down on my pillow a little later after we had put out the lights, I lay there with my eyes wide open. I was only sixteen, I told myself. Why should I feel so much guilt about having fun with another boy? I liked Harley. I liked him even more than I had realized, but maybe we were rushing into things. Was I absolutely a horrible person for even having these thoughts?

Tossing and turning in bed, I even groaned aloud and expected Sarah to wonder why, but she had fallen asleep quickly. I could hear her heavy, regular breathing. She had her back to me and was tightly folded under her blanket, hugging her pillow as if it were her favorite teddy bear.

Then I heard what sounded like hail hitting the window. I turned curiously. Our window looked out on the east end of the dorm. Beyond the lawn was a small wooded area. There was no moon, but the sky had cleared and offered enough starlight to throw a silvery glow on the dark campus. I stared a moment. Just as I was about to turn away and try to get to sleep, I saw his head silhouetted in the window and heard the gentle tap.

My heart stopped and started. I looked at Sarah, but she didn't budge an inch. He tapped again, and I rose out of my bed and went to the window, squatting down to open it.

"Hi," Duncan Fields said.

"What are you doing here?"

"Couldn't sleep so I thought I'd pay you a visit. Sarah awake?"

I looked back at her. She was still very quiet, unmoving except for her regular breathing.

"No."

"Good," he whispered. "I really enjoyed dancing with you. I didn't want to make a pig of myself and ask you again."

"That wouldn't have been making a pig of yourself," I said.

"Yeah, well, you know how gossip gets started

in places like this, and I know you have a serious relationship. Sarah told me."

"I'm not engaged or anything," I said so quickly I surprised myself.

"Oh. That's good. You mean I still might have a chance?"

"For what?"

"To win your heart," he said, his eyes glittering.

"It's not some kind of prize," I replied and he laughed.

"I like you," he said. "I hope you like me."

"I don't know you well enough to like or dislike you," I said.

"Well, I'll have to rectify that, if I can," he said. "Why don't you come out? We'll go for a walk or something and talk some more."

"What? You mean, crawl out the window?"

"That's what I did."

"No, that's . . ."

"Against the rules, I know. We don't have to get caught and it wouldn't be that long. C'mon," he urged. "It's beautiful out here."

"No," I said, but my heart began to pound with the thought of it.

"Aw, c'mon. You're a lot more sophisticated than most of these other girls. I can tell," he said. "You're not going to let some silly rule keep you locked up in there. It's not even midnight. If you and I were home, we'd probably be up on a weekend night like this, wouldn't we?"

"Yes, I suppose so," I admitted.

"So? C'mon. Just for a few minutes. I was

willing to risk my musical career for you. You could at least reciprocate," he added.

"Your musical career? Hardly," I said.

He stepped back and held out his hand.

I looked at Sarah again. She still hadn't moved. Could I do this? Should I? At the moment it seemed to be the most exciting thing I had ever contemplated.

"Wait a minute," I said and tiptoed to the closet to get my robe to put over my nightie. Then I slipped on my sandals and returned to the window. My heart was thumping so hard, I didn't think I had the strength to crawl out the window. I moved it farther up slowly, carefully, and then I hesitated.

"Where are we going?"

"For a walk. What's the big deal?"

I felt like I did have a good angel on my left shoulder and a bad angel on my right, both whispering frantically in my ears. My good angel said, "Don't do it. Why is this so important? If you want to see him, see him tomorrow. Why risk getting in serious trouble for a walk?" My bad angel said, "You're such a goody-goody. The worse thing you've ever done is watch MTV after two in the morning when your parents thought you were asleep. Grow up. You're sixteen. Stop acting like a child. Live a little and have some fun."

I took a breath and climbed out. He helped me by holding my waist and guiding me down to the grass. For a moment we both stood there in the shadows, his hands still on my waist, his face so

138

close to mine, I could feel his breath on my lips and cheeks. I stepped back.

"There, you did it," he said, "and you're still alive."

"I don't want to stay out too long."

"Me neither," he said. "I've got a dream that starts in about an hour, and it's a prize winner."

I started to laugh and he put his hand over my mouth.

"Shh," he said. "You want to get me into serious trouble?"

He looked back and then he guided me away from the dormitory and down the pathway that fanned out toward the main building.

"Where are we going?" I asked in a loud whisper.

"Where we'll be safe," he said. "My car."

It was like a small bird had woken suddenly in its nest and started to raise its wings to fly out just as a large, dark hand came down over it.

That's what my stomach felt like inside.

But I kept walking, excited and thrilled and yet so afraid and nervous, I didn't feel my legs taking me deeper and deeper into the shadows.

6

Deep into the Shadows

"Why are we going to your car?" I asked him.

"It's just down here in the parking lot reserved for guests," he replied as an answer. "I got it just before I came here so I didn't have much chance to show it off and besides," he said looking back and then around us, "it's better than taking a chance walking around here. I've got this great CD player in it with Bose speakers. Wait until you hear the great sound!"

"We'll attract more attention playing music, won't we?"

"Not if we play it low," he said. "You have your own car yet?"

"No."

"Just keep asking to use your parents' cars and soon enough you'll get your own," he advised.

"Is that how you got them to buy you yours?"

"Sorta."

"Sorta? What's that mean?"

He stopped and looked at me.

"Your father's not a lawyer, is he?"

"No, why?"

"Every girl I meet these days has a lawyer for a father," he replied.

"What's wrong with that?"

"Nothing's wrong with it," he said, "except sometimes they sound like lawyers the way they question every little thing I say or suggest and do."

"Oh." What a strange complaint, I thought.

"So, what does your father do?" he asked and started walking again.

"He owns and operates a chain of health clubs as well as a physical therapy business."

"No kidding. I figured you were in good shape for a reason," he said laughing. "Most of the girls here look like they're still growing out of puppy fat."

"They do not," I said. Suddenly he sounded so arrogant.

"There she is," he said, nodding at a spanking brand-new vehicle. I was surprised to see that it was a van. He reached into his pocket and produced a remote key.

"Watch this," he said and pushed a button on it.

The van's back door slid open and the lights went on.

"Hurry," he said, taking my arm and rushing me along, "before one of the corrections officers sees us."

"They're not that bad," I said, but he practically shoved me into the vehicle. Then he jumped in beside me. A moment later, the lights went off and the van door closed and locked in place.

"Safe," he declared and let out a sigh of relief. "Mr. Dickens, the dorm Nazi, can't see us from the dorm anyway. He goes around sniffing like a hound dog, hoping to catch the scent of smoke or something worse. Something better, I mean," Duncan quipped. "Did you want a cigarette? There's a pack in the glove compartment."

"No thanks, I don't smoke."

"That's right. Daddy's a health guru. I forgot."

"I wouldn't smoke anyway," I said.

"Even a joint?"

"Especially not a joint," I said. He raised his eyebrows skeptically.

"Right."

"I mean it," I said firmly.

"Good. I wouldn't want to get involved with a bad girl," he added, laughing.

"You can tease me all you want."

"Hey, I'm just having a little fun. That's why we're here, isn't it?"

I glanced at him and then looked toward the administration building.

"I don't want to stay here long," I said. "We're sure to be seen."

"Relax." He leaned back on his seat and closed his eyes. "Watch this."

He pushed a button on the door and the back of his seat started to level out until he was nearly prone.

"I sleep here sometimes," he told me. Then he

hit another button on his remote and the music started.

"Isn't that Ravel's *Boléro*?"

"Uh-huh. You ever see the movie *10*?"

"I don't think so."

"Oh it's in that movie and it's just great, perfect for the scene."

The *Boléro* began to build slowly, getting louder and louder. I gazed back toward the dorms. I wasn't feeling comfortable or titillated anymore. Duncan continued to lie there with his eyes closed.

"I thought we were just going for a short walk," I said.

"Relax. You're too uptight about everything." He took a deep breath and closed his eyes.

"You don't want to get into trouble, do you?"

"Whatever," he said. "I didn't want to come here this summer. My parents twisted my arm. Actually," he said lifting his head and turning to me, "I made them buy this van to bribe me. That's the sorta thing you tried to pin me down on before."

"Why was it so important to them for you to come here?"

"They like me to be occupied while they're off living it up in Europe," he said.

"So, why couldn't you go someplace else, maybe in Europe where you'd be closer to them? You did go there before, right?"

"The rumor mill grinds on," he muttered.

"Is that true or false?"

"See what I mean? You sound like a lawyer."

"I'm just confused. That's all. I don't mean to sound like I'm cross-examining you."

He laughed.

"Yes, yes, all right. I'll confess. I went to music school in France last summer," he replied, "but I didn't want to go back to the same place."

"Oh."

"Actually, I was not invited back," he admitted.

"What? Why not? You're so good."

"There was a misunderstanding about something, and I didn't want to put in all the energy it would take to straighten it out."

"Why not?"

"Forget about it," he said a bit more roughly than I expected. "I'm here now and with you," he added, sitting up as if he just realized it himself. "And there's no place else I'd rather be. I'm glad you came out with me. How do you like the van?"

"It's very nice," I said, "but I'm surprised. I thought you'd have . . ."

"Something more flashy? Other guys want those low to the road, high-performance sports cars. Not me. A car is a second home for me, and there's nothing shoddy about this. These are real leather seats. As you can see, the rear is great, roomy. I can get the whole jazz ensemble in here and perform on the road," he bragged and I laughed.

"Well, I said I was surprised, but I'm not saying it was a foolish choice."

"Right. I knew you'd think that. I could tell

144

right away that you were smarter than the other girls here."

"I am not," I said, not sure what he meant anyway. Smarter about what?

"Hey, you know what I have here? A video player and a small television set."

"Really?"

"Yes. Let me show you," he said.

"I really should get back, Duncan. Sarah will wake up and wonder where I am."

"She's out of it, exhausted. Don't worry about it. We'll go back in a minute."

He leaned forward to turn on his video deck and television, which were housed between the front two seats. I saw the glow of light.

"Relax, let your seat back a little," he urged.

Before I could react, he leaned over and pushed the button that lowered the back of my seat.

Something told me not to remain in the rear of the van, but instead to open the door and start back.

"Isn't this terrific? I mean, it's like a small apartment, my own apartment."

"It's great," I said.

"Try it. Lay back," he said.

"No, I'd rather . . ."

"Aw c'mon. Look at this," he said reaching behind his seat and producing a pillow. He put it on my side.

The music was getting louder. In the glow of the small television screen, I could see his wry smile. His eyes had turned into tiny bulbs.

"I want to go back," I said and reached for the door handle, but it didn't move. "Unlock it," I said.

"What's the rush? C'mon, relax," he insisted and reached around my waist to pull me toward him. He did it so roughly, I fell against him and he embraced me tighter and kissed me before I realized what was happening.

"Welcome to Duncan Fields' love boat," he announced.

I thought that was all there would be to it — just a big, silly joke; but he had other things in mind. When he didn't loosen his grip on me, birds of panic began to flap their wings hysterically in my chest and stomach.

"Let me go," I said.

"Don't you like it here? Just lay back. Give it a chance. You'll see how comfortable it is."

"I've got to get back, Duncan."

"Hold on," he insisted, now seizing my right wrist. His fingers tightened like handcuffs around my narrow bone.

"You're hurting me."

"Then relax, will you? You're the first girl I've asked to my van here, and there's a whole line who wished it was them."

"Then go knock on one of their windows," I said. "I want to go back now."

The music was getting louder and louder.

"You sure didn't dance like a girl who wants to go back now. Why do you have to be such a tease?"

"I'm not a tease. Dancing is one thing. This is another. Please let go of my wrist."

"You crawled out of that window pretty quickly and without much convincing," he continued.

"Now I realize I shouldn't have. I want to go back."

"No you don't. You think you do, but you really don't," he argued and then he kissed me on the neck, turning me more toward him as he did so.

"Duncan, stop."

"And you came out in your nightgown, too. Anything more under that?" he asked, slipping his hand into my robe and putting his palm squarely over my breast. "Nope. Just as I thought."

"Stop!" I cried. I tried to push him away with my legs, but he just reached down and under them, lifted his body, and pushed me underneath. When he dropped himself on me, I was pinned to the seat, which was now fully reclined.

His other hand began to pull away my robe and then went down to my thighs and lifted my nightgown.

"Duncan, what are you doing? Stop!" I screamed. He stopped my second scream by putting his lips over my mouth, where he kept them.

When he released my wrist, I tried to pound his head and push him off, but he was so heavy and so determined, my blows fell like fists of butter against him. He didn't flinch or cry out. He moaned and I felt him moving his left hand between us, undoing his pants.

"You're the first," he whispered. "The first in my love boat."

"Let me go. Stop it! Stop it!"

The shock of his hardness between my thighs took my breath away. I gasped, seemingly choking on air. I was in a terrible panic, fighting to breathe, and I think I passed in and out of consciousness within seconds because moments later, I felt him penetrating and pushing harder and harder into me. He raised my legs, sweeping away my ineffective attempts at any resistence.

I thought I was screaming, but I couldn't be sure because there was a thunderous roar in my ears. As it went on, I kept thinking, This isn't happening to me; it can't be happening. But of course, it was.

He cried out and I felt him stop almost immediately and collapse over me, his breathing hard and fast. The *Boléro* was in a crescendo. The music seemed to make the whole van vibrate, or was that just my body shuddering from the violation? I didn't move. I felt as though I had left myself and no longer had any control of my arms and legs. Slowly, he rose and sat up. I saw him brush back his hair and then he hit a button and the music stopped.

"It is really hot tonight. So humid. You ever been in New Orleans in the summer? I don't think it's much worse there than here tonight."

He sat quietly and I didn't move for fear I would shatter like some cracked piece of thin china. I watched him turn off the glowing small television set.

"I'm really thirsty," he said. "The next thing I'm going to do is have a refrigerator installed in here."

He fixed his clothing and then he looked at me.

"You'd better get back," he said. He hit the remote key again and the door slid open, the lights coming on. "C'mon." He reached for me, but I cried out.

"Get away from me!" I shouted and turned away.

"Suit yourself, but we've got to go," he said.

The car light resembled a harsh spotlight. My eyes felt like they were burning. I grimaced in pain, turned my body and spilled myself onto the parking lot in my effort to get out quickly. I heard him laughing as I got to my feet.

"Having trouble walking after being in Duncan Fields's love boat?" he asked. He started around the van toward me.

"Get away from me!" I cried and started running.

"Hey. You didn't even say thank you for a nice evening. Where's your manners?"

I heard his laugh behind me, which made me run faster. When I drew closer to the dorm, I slowed down to a walk. Until that moment I hadn't realized I was sobbing madly. My face was streaked and soaked with tears, which kept coming. I stood there, gasping. In a panic I looked back and saw him sauntering toward the dorm. He paused, looked toward me and then continued to go around to the boys' side, where he disappeared in the shadows.

Slowly now, I walked to my room. When I reached the window, I looked up at it as if it was the top of Mount Everest. I guess I was moaning and crying quite loudly now, for Sarah finally woke and came to the window. She gaped out at me.

"What are you doing out there?" she asked.

"Help me," I said.

"What?"

I reached up for her and she took my hand. I don't know where she found the strength, but somehow she lifted me off the ground enough for me to get a hold on the windowsill and continue until I was in the room. I fell forward into her arms, but slipped quickly to the floor where I sat and sobbed.

"What is it? What were you doing out there? Summer, talk to me," she begged. "You look terrible. What happened to you? Tell me!"

I took some deep breaths and pressed my hand to my heart to keep it from pounding right through my chest. Finally, I managed to get out the words.

"Duncan . . . came here and talked me into going for a walk with him."

"He did? When?"

"We . . . we went to his car. He wanted to show me his van," I said.

"And?"

"He got me into the backseat and . . ."

"And what?"

She was down on her knees now, looking right into my face, her hands on my shoulders. I started to cry hard again and she shook my body hard.

"What? What?"

"He raped me!" I screamed and fell forward into her arms where she held me and rocked me and stroked my hair, telling me it would be all right, to be calm. It would be all right.

I don't know how long we sat there, but I think I passed out and woke before Sarah got me to get up and lie on my bed. Then she sat beside me and held my hand.

"We've got to go get Mrs. Bernard," she said. "You can't let him get away with this."

"No," I cried, terrified. "How am I going to explain going out the window and going off with him?"

"You thought you were just going for a walk," she said.

"But it was still against the rules."

"Against the rules? Summer, you were just raped. Don't you think that's more important than some stupid dorm rule?"

My mind was so jumbled. I couldn't think; I couldn't think!

"Why did I go? Why did I go with him?"

"Not to be raped, I'm sure," she said. "I can't believe he did this. He seemed so nice. He's so good looking and talented. Why does he have to rape anyone?" she asked rhetorically, but the question hung in the air like an accusation. I could see how it might unfold, how what I was saying might be disbelieved. "The way some of those girls ogle him, he would just have to look at them to get them to go to the back of his van," she continued.

"Well, I'm not one of them," I said, my anger giving me some strength.

"I know that," she said. "It just doesn't make any sense." She shook her head. "I guess he's just crazy," she concluded.

She stood up and headed toward the door.

"I'll get Mrs. Bernard."

"My parents will be so upset," I said. "I'm afraid of what it will do to my mother. You know she's handicapped."

She paused, her hand on the door knob.

"Well, what do you want to do?"

"I don't know." I shook my head so hard that I felt a pain shoot through my neck. "I don't know what to do."

"Did he use protection?" she asked.

"What? Protection?"

"Yes. I'm sure you know what I mean? Did he do it in you?"

"Yes," I said, actually first realizing the implications.

"You've got to worry about that. How long since your last period?"

"How long?" I put my hands over my temples. I still couldn't think straight, couldn't remember. "Um, about a week or so, I think."

"*Or so* gets me nervous," Sarah said. She took a deep breath. "All right. Let's be logical about this.

Suppose you don't tell and you get pregnant. Then what? You say, oh, by the way a few weeks ago, Duncan Fields raped me?"

I looked at her and the dam of tears broke again. I sobbed so hard, my ribs ached. She tried to calm me down, but I all I did was get very nauseous and had to run to the bathroom to vomit in the toilet. Afterward, I was so exhausted, I could barely get to my feet.

"Too soon for morning sickness," Sarah said attempting to make some sort of joke.

"What would you do now?" I asked her.

"Sneak down the hallway to his room and put a pillow over his head and then sit on the pillow," she replied.

I smiled at the utter impossibility, and she hugged me again.

"I guess you don't have much of a choice," she added, sitting back on the bathroom floor with me. "If you keep it to yourself now, you'll never get anyone to believe you later."

I nodded.

"C'mon," she said standing and holding out her hand. "I'll go with you."

I took her hand and stood and then the two of us went out of our room and down the hall to Mrs. Bernard's quarters. Sarah knocked for me. She had to knock again, a little louder. Finally, Mrs. Bernard came to the door and looked out at us. Her face looked more wrinkled and creased than usual. She was struggling to focus and get awake.

"What's wrong?" she asked clutching her robe tightly closed and looking from me to Sarah and then back to me.

"Summer has something to tell you," Sarah said.

"What? So?" she followed. "I don't want to stand here in my doorway all night. What do you have to tell me at this late hour, Summer?"

"It's something terrible," Sarah replied for me, and Mrs. Bernard stepped back to let us in.

The arrival of the police on the campus went relatively unnoticed because they didn't flash any lights or sound any sirens. The black-and-white patrol car seemed to slip in and out of the shadows. Dr. Greenleaf had been called out, along with Mrs. Mariot, the president of the board of trustees. The lateness of the hour now made it all truly seem like a dream. As if to illustrate how important it was to keep all this discreet, no one spoke in a voice much above a loud whisper, not even the police. A policewoman had been brought along to speak with me and to take me to the hospital, explaining that I had to be examined.

"It's very important to establish as soon as possible that what you said happened did in fact occur."

Doctor Greenleaf explained that he would have to phone my parents immediately. That set off a whole new round of sobs for me. Daddy asked to speak with me and I went to the phone before

154

leaving for the hospital. He sounded so far off and so frightened.

"How are you, baby?" he asked.

"I'm okay," I said even though I felt so weak and terrified, I could barely stand. My throat was so tight, it hurt to speak, but I didn't want to put him and Mommy into a panic.

"We'll be starting out right away."

"I'm sorry, Daddy," I cried. "I'm sorry."

"Hey, don't you be sorry. No one's going to blame you for anything, sweetheart. You just do what they want you to do. I want that animal behind bars," he added, growing stronger with his anger. I could see him talking through clenched teeth.

"I don't want Mommy to get sick," I moaned.

"She'll be fine. She's stronger than I am," he assured me. "You just hold yourself together until we get there. Promise."

"Okay, Daddy."

"We'll be there soon," he said, his voice starting to crack with emotion.

I hung up quickly. The policewoman, Officer Wilson, had to hold me tightly and nearly carry me out the door to the police car for my trip to the hospital. Little did I know, this was but the start of a long nightmare.

By the time I was examined and returned to the dormitory, it was nearly morning. Sarah had fallen asleep but jumped up the second I entered the room. She took one look at me and almost burst into tears herself.

"Was it very bad?"

"Horrible," I said, "but the police have what they want."

"You look exhausted."

"I am, but I want to take a shower and get dressed. My parents will be here soon."

"Everyone's going to wonder where you are," she said.

"I know."

"I won't tell them anything. I'll just say you're not feeling well," she promised.

I nodded and went into the bathroom. I had barely toweled off and gotten dressed before Daddy and Mommy arrived. They both hugged me and held me. Daddy was right about Mommy: She looked stronger than he was. His anger and sadness for me made his eyes bloodshot and kept his lips trembling when he spoke. Mommy remained calm.

"Doctor Greenleaf asked us to meet him at his office as soon as you are ready, honey," she said.

"It was partly my fault, Mommy. I snuck out the window after curfew and went with him," I confessed. "I just wanted to go for a walk and talk."

"Okay, honey. Don't get yourself so upset over it that you won't be able to talk. Just tell everyone who has to know exactly what happened."

"How could this happen here?" Daddy cried, his arms out.

"Austin," Mommy said, her eyes big with reprimand.

He shook his head and stood by the window as if he was looking directly at the scene of the crime.

"Okay, Mommy," I said. "I'm ready."

"You want to get something to eat first, honey?"

"No," I said. "Let's just do what we have to do."

She nodded and Daddy pushed her wheelchair with me walking beside them. We got Mommy into the van and drove over to the administration building. One look at Mrs. Whittaker, Dr. Greenleaf's secretary, told me she knew the sordid details. She leaped up from her chair and told us she would tell Dr. Greenleaf we were there. Not a half-dozen seconds later, she was ushering us into his office. Mrs. Mariot was there as well as a short, plump, balding man. Mrs. Mariot was a tall, distinguished-looking woman in her early fifties with light brown hair. The plump man had a round face with watery dull brown eyes and a thick nose over thin lips, now stretched into a disgusted smirk.

Two chairs had been provided for us. Daddy wheeled Mommy up beside one of them, which put her between the man and us. Mrs. Mariot was on the other side, both of them now like bookends. Dr. Greenleaf leaned forward to place his elbows on his desk and put his hands together with the fingers in a cathedral.

"Mr. and Mrs. Clarke," he said, "this is Margaret Mariot, president of the board of trustees, and this is Stanley Haskins, the school's attorney."

Daddy nodded suspiciously at the two of them, and Mommy gave them a very small, quick smile.

"Well, now," Dr Greenleaf began, "we've got a very difficult situation here, which we must handle delicately and carefully so little or no more damage can be done to anyone concerned," he began.

"Handle?" Daddy said quickly. "There's only one person who's been damaged here, my daughter. I don't think handle is the right word."

"We realize that profoundly," Dr. Greenleaf said quickly, his eyes swinging from Mrs. Mariot to Mr. Haskins and back to Daddy.

"Has the animal been put in jail?" Daddy demanded.

"He's been taken to the police station for questioning, but the district attorney hasn't had him officially charged and arrested yet, Mr. Clarke," Mr. Haskins said.

"Why not?"

"It's a favor to us and to you."

"What?"

"Let's try to be as calm as we can under these difficult circumstances," Dr. Greenleaf pleaded.

"Calm. This is my daughter!" Daddy screamed at him.

Mommy, who had been watching Dr. Greenleaf squirm in his chair while he spoke, put her hand over Daddy's and looked at him.

"Let's let Dr. Greenleaf talk first, Austin."

"Thank you, Mrs. Clarke. I assure you, Summer's welfare is our primary concern here." He looked at Mrs. Mariot. "I think I speak for the entire board of trustees when I say that."

158

"He does," Mrs. Mariot said. "I'm here to confirm that."

Daddy sat back but didn't relax. Dr. Greenleaf glanced at Mr. Haskins.

"Mr. Haskins has had some experience in these matters. I think it's best we listen to what he has to tell us."

Stanley Haskins smiled, his face softening like putty as his lips stretched and contracted when he leaned forward toward us.

"What we have here is something popularly known as date rape," he began.

"She was hardly on a date," Daddy snapped.

Stanley Haskins stared at him, only his eyes betraying his discomfort. His soft smile lingered on those rubber band lips.

"Well, Mr. Clarke, I'm afraid what you and I used to call a date has changed. Any occurrence where the two parties willingly meet to enjoy each other's company would fall under that heading these days."

"Well, what's that matter?" Daddy charged.

"It will matter very much if this ever sees daylight in a courtroom," he replied calmly.

"If?"

"Let's begin with what we know. We've gathered some information that will help us here. There was a school dance earlier in the evening. Summer danced with Duncan Fields and they appeared to be getting along fine. One of our chaperones, Mr. Saunders, even had the impression they knew each other well, very well," he added glancing at me. "Did you get to know Duncan before the dance, Summer?" he asked me.

Mommy and Daddy both looked to me for my answer.

"No sir. Not really. I saw him on the campus, but we never spoke before the night of the dance."

"What if she knew him anyway?" Daddy asked. "We're talking about rape!"

"Can I play the devil's advocate here for a few minutes, Mr. Clarke, and maybe save you, your wife and daughter some terrible aggravation?"

Daddy glared at him.

"Please do, Mr. Haskins," Mommy said, her eyes small and penetrating.

Mr. Haskins directed himself more to her after that. He turned back to me.

"You met Duncan Fields for the first time at the dance, danced with him once, and then, when he came to your room, willingly crawled out your window, violating the school's rules, and went off with him with nothing more than your nightgown and robe on at the time?" he asked quickly.

"I just thought I was going for a walk," I said.

"So that's all true?"

"I was just going for a walk," I said more firmly.

"But you went with him into his van. Why?"

I glanced at Mommy. Tears were burning under my eyelids.

"He wanted to show me his new car."

"Couldn't you just look in it? Did you have to get into it?"

160

"He made the door open with his remote key and . . ."

"Why didn't you stop and return to the dorm?"

"He said he wanted to show me his music and . . . I didn't want to get in."

"But you did. Did he drag you in?"

"Well, he practically pushed me."

"But you got in willingly? You didn't scream, resist, did you? Well, did you?" he demanded.

"Not then," I said, my voice cracking, tears popping at the sides of my eyes.

"What are you talking about?" Daddy practically screamed at him. "How does any of that give him the right to rape my daughter?"

"I'm not saying it does, Mr. Clarke. However, remember, you're asking the district attorney to go forward and convince a jury that she was raped and didn't willingly have sexual relations with Duncan Fields."

Daddy's mouth opened and closed without a sound. Mr. Haskins turned back to me.

"The hospital report doesn't show any injuries, no traumas. Your clothes weren't torn."

"No injuries!" Daddy leaped to his feet. "What kind of a man are you? Do you have children?"

"Yes, Mr. Clarke, as a matter of fact, I have two daughters, one in her twenties and working on her masters in education and another just starting at the University of Boston. I worry about them all the time. I also have a son in high school, a senior, and I worry about him, too. I tell him how important it is to think ahead and whenever possible avoid even the appearance of impropriety, especially in today's litigious society where everyone runs to court for anything, even a loud burp."

"Sit down, Austin," Mommy said sharply.

Daddy glared at everyone and did what she wanted.

"What exactly is it you people want from us?" Mommy asked. "We get your point. It won't be easy. It will be nasty. This boy's family obviously has money, and they will have a good defense attorney."

"Exactly, Mrs. Clarke," Mr. Haskins said.

"And so?" Mommy pursued.

Mr. Haskins looked at Dr. Greenleaf and nodded slightly, which was obviously his cue to pick up their rehearsed scenario.

"We are all deeply disturbed and upset by this event, Mrs. Clarke. We recognize the school has certain responsibilities and liabilities."

"Right," Daddy said. "Whatever happened to that, 'we're your surrogate parents' line you used at orientation?"

"Yes, Mr. Clarke, exactly. We are sorry that we let you down on that score. Even if your daughter disobeyed our rules, we should still be vigilant about her welfare here, and Duncan Fields's welfare as well, for that matter.

"We've contacted his family and he's been expelled from Pelham, all his tuition naturally forfeited. As independent citizens, you can go see the district attorney later today, of course, and move forward as you see fit. We're hoping you might find an accommodation that is satisfactory to you. Anticipating other legal and civil difficulties, the school is prepared to offer you a monetary settlement should you be willing to keep this unfortunate incident out of the public eye, however."

"You mean you're offering us money to shut up and go away?" Daddy asked, his eyes wide.

"Compensation that you deserve," Dr. Greenleaf said glancing at Mrs. Mariot.

"There are many other students here and families who will be injured if this becomes a tabloid headline, Mr. and Mrs. Clarke," Mrs. Mariot said. "We have them to consider as well and the faculty and all the good things the school does and can do."

"You're offering us money?" Daddy repeated, nodding as if he had just received a sharp blow to his head.

"We're trying to do the best we can for everyone concerned," Dr. Greenleaf insisted. "You see that, don't you, Summer?" he asked me, smiling.

"Don't talk to her," Daddy ordered. "Don't do that." He rose and put his hands on Mommy's chair handles. Then he nodded to me and I got up and stood beside them. He looked from Mr. Haskins to Dr. Greenleaf and then Mrs. Mariot.

"I don't know where we're going to go with this right now. I know we're going directly over to the dormitory and get Summer's things together so we can get her out of here as quickly as possible.

"As for you, Mr. Haskins and your role as

devil's advocate . . . you might be right. Everything you're implying could happen in court. Maybe a jury would look at Summer and Duncan and think two spoiled rich kids were playing with fire and one got burnt. Why bother us with it?

"But how do you think the Duncan Fieldses of the world are born and nurtured? The rich and the privileged worry about their lily-white reputations and are willing to do anything to protect that, even if it means excusing and tolerating someone like Duncan Fields.

"We came here today expecting to find you people as disturbed and as outraged as we were. We actually believed that crap you spewed out about being responsible and concerned for our children's welfare.

"Instead, we find the three of you circling the wagons to protect yourselves and pretend you're only doing it to keep Summer and us from any further suffering. You'll give us some compensation from your insurance company, and you'll send Duncan Fields back out there unscathed really.

"But you know something, Mr. Haskins," Daddy said glaring down at him, "someday he or someone just like him will tempt your daughter. I hope that doesn't happen. I hope your children have wonderful, healthy and successful lives.

"But if it does or even almost does, I hope you'll think back to this morning and remember my daughter's face and all your fancy dancing.

"Then I hope you go look at yourself in the

mirror and see yourself for the first time.

"Thanks for your time," he concluded, turned Mommy's chair and wheeled us to the door. I lunged to open it and we left in a wake of silence.

Mommy reached up for my hand as we left the administration building.

"See why I married this man?" she asked me, smiling through her tears.

I bit down on my lip and held my breath to keep myself from crying.

I nodded.

We paused as we went out the front door and I looked around the beautiful campus.

"Let's get out of here," Daddy said, "before I smash something."

While he and I packed my things, Mommy rested in Mrs. Bernard's quarters, who made coffee and brought her something to eat. Daddy took my things out to the van and loaded them in. As he was doing so, Sarah arrived.

"What's happening?" she asked, her face full of worry and fear.

"I'm leaving the school. They've expelled Duncan, and they don't want any bad publicity. My parents are very angry. I can't stay here."

"Is Duncan in jail?"

"I don't know where he is. Daddy's going to deal with all that later."

"Oh," she said plopping on her bed. "I hate to see you go."

"I know. Let's stay friends," I said. "Please write me."

"Okay." She nodded and shrugged. "I'll miss you."

"Me too," I said.

We hugged and Daddy came to the door.

"All set," he said.

I introduced him to Sarah and then introduced her to Mommy.

"I'm sorry about all this," she told them.

"Thank you."

"You'll call me, won't you?" she asked me.

"Yes, of course, and write and everything," I said.

She followed us out to the van.

"The place is buzzing," she whispered, "but no one knows any details. They just know something's not right because Duncan didn't show up for his classes, nor for practice either, and his roommate saw him get into a police car."

I nodded.

"None of it will be a secret too much longer, despite what Dr. Greenleaf hopes," I said.

"I swear I won't be the one to gossip."

"I know. Take care of yourself," I said.

"You too."

I started to get into the van after Daddy had Mommy secure. Sarah stood there, watching.

She lifted her hand to wave goodbye as Daddy started the engine. Would we ever see each other again?

Sometimes, people do pass each other like trains in the night, glimpsing through the lit windows for a few fleeting seconds, capturing an

166

image, a word, a small memory and then going on, into their separate worlds, leaving only the echo to linger for a few moments before dying out like candle light and leaving only the darkness.

The school fell back behind me, the music drifting away in the wind.

"Are you all right, honey?" Mommy asked.

"Yes," I said, my voice so small, I thought it came from someone else, a girl half my age.

"You'll be fine," Daddy insisted, more to convince himself than me. "And I'm not finished with any of this yet. That's a promise," he pledged.

None of us spoke.

A deep silence fell over us and settled in our van with only the whir of the tires on the highway providing any sound at all.

That, and the quiet beating of my frightened heart.

7

Secrets in the Night

It was as if someone had died. Sorrow, anger, indignation and disgust knit themselves into a heavy blanket and draped themselves over us and everything in the house. Mrs. Geary was at the front door as soon as we pulled up to the ramp. Her face looked like the image in a stained glass window, an ancient moment of great sadness captured on the tip of an artist's brush and embedded forever and ever in the glass. She came out, clutching her hands against her breasts, waiting to set eyes on me to see how bruised I was emotionally and psychologically.

Daddy helped Mommy out of the van, and Mrs. Geary approached us.

"I've got some of my homemade tomato rice soup hot on the stove," she said looking toward me. She knew it was one of my favorites, especially the way she made it.

"We're all so tired. I don't think any of us has

much of an appetite," Mommy muttered as Daddy began to push her up the ramp.

"Something hot in your stomach's important at times like this," Mrs. Geary advised.

"She's right," Daddy said. "We'll get settled in and then have some late lunch."

Mrs. Geary put her arm around my shoulders. Never one to show her affection openly, she surprised me.

"Damn the devil," she said.

We all entered the house and then, after Mommy was set, Daddy returned to the van to get my things.

"Go rest for a while until Mrs. Geary gets some food together," Mommy advised me.

I nodded and went up to my room. For a moment I just stood there in the doorway looking around. Being brought back like this seemed like such a defeat. I felt so foolish. I should be at my piano lesson right now. What were my teachers told? Doctor Greenleaf surely made up some grand lie to keep it all secret.

I sprawled on my bed and stared up at the ceiling, thinking about it all.

Daddy interrupted my sad musings when he came by with my things.

"No rush in putting it all away," he said when he saw me lying so dejectedly on my bed.

"If only I hadn't gone out the window to be with him, Daddy."

"*If only* are two words I hate," he said. "What happens is *you* dwell on your own innocent actions and *he* gets a pass on his criminal actions. Stop doing that," he insisted.

My chin quivered. The sight of my sorrow and pain made him furious. His face hardened, his eyes radiating fury.

"I'm going to call Grandpa Grant," he decided. "He'll know what to do next."

Before I could say another syllable, he shot out of my room and pounded his way down the stairs to his office. My stepgrandfather was a very important and influential attorney now. He had been a U.S. attorney, worked for the Justice Department and knew presidents personally. Still, I couldn't help but feel more embarrassed about another person knowing, even family.

Mrs. Geary didn't wait for me to go down to lunch. She brought a tray up with a bowl of hot soup and crackers.

"Get some of this in you," she said.

I didn't want to be hungry. I wanted to starve myself, to somehow punish myself. I knew exactly what was going through Mommy's mind all day. This was another example of her bad luck, her curse falling on the people she loved, and it was all because of me, me!

"C'mon, dear, sit yourself up and get the soup down. You don't want to get yourself sick. I know you. You'll feel sorrier for making yourself more of a burden if that happens and then where will we be?"

She said the magic words, of course, knew the formula with which to get me to do the things she thought I should do. I sat up and she placed the tray on my lap and stood back to watch. I started to eat.

"It really was my fault, Mrs. Geary. I was so stupid to put myself into the situation."

"Now how would you know the evil in someone else's heart, dear, especially one of those boys from refined families?"

"Just because his parents are rich and influential people, it doesn't mean he's any better than anyone else," I said. "No one knows that better than I do now. I'm such a little idiot, trusting people."

"You're hardly more than a child. What are you supposed to be, a wise old lady? I know many a woman twice your age who's been a lot more foolish and trusting."

I kept eating, my self-pity turning more and more into anger at myself while Mrs. Geary ranted on.

"Next thing I'll hear is people who get robbed deserve it because they walked around without an army guarding them. Just because you leave a window slightly open or a door unlocked, it doesn't mean a thief has a right to your things, does it? You can't be expected to be so alert, so cautious. If we go about thinking the worst of everyone we meet, we'll never be at peace a minute," she said. Her eyes narrowed with suspicion. "Who put the blame on you?"

"Never mind," I said.

"Not your mama and papa, I know. Was it your

school people?" She shook her head at my silence. "A good girl's got a hard road to hoe almost any-where these days," she muttered and started to unpack my things for me.

"I can do that, Mrs. Geary," I said.

"I know you can. I just don't want to be idle a minute right now," she said.

I finally smiled. When you have people around you who love you as much as my parents and Mrs. Geary loved me, you realize that when something bad is done to you, it's truly done to them as well. We shared disappointments and pain, triumphs and happiness as if we were all one person.

I finished my soup and got myself out of bed. Instead of lying up here and moaning and groaning, I belonged downstairs comforting Mommy, I thought. However, when I descended, I didn't find her anywhere in the house. Daddy was in the office, talking on the phone. He just looked at me and turned his chair to indicate he wanted privacy.

I went out and saw Mommy at her usual place looking over the lake.

"Are you all right, Mommy?" I asked as I ap-proached. She looked up.

Her face was so pale, her eyes bloodshot. It put a hot flash of pain in my heart.

"You should go rest, honey," she said almost breathlessly.

"I'm all right, Mommy. You're getting yourself sick, though. I almost kept it all a secret just because I was afraid of this, and now I wish I had," I moaned.

"Oh no, honey. No, don't say that. You can't keep something like that a secret anyway. It would eat away at you something awful."

"You're sitting out here blaming yourself and your curse, right?"

She smiled and took a deep breath. Then she looked out at the lake and talked softly, almost as if she was really talking to herself.

"When I learned your grandmother Megan was my mother and she had been with an African American man in college, I wasn't only upset over the fact that Mama Latisha wasn't really my mother. I was also terribly afraid. Not only were there bigoted white people who said a child from a mixed racial relationship was an abomination, but there were bigoted black people who felt the same way.

"After I learned the truth, I guess I just expected trouble would be my lifelong companion, so when bad things happened to me or people I loved, I naturally felt responsible.

"Of course, the wise and intelligent part of me tells me that's all very foolish and just helps feed the hate and the racism that pollute our world."

She turned to me.

"When I heard what had happened to you, my heart just stopped and I almost didn't want it to start again. I've never told you the details about my stepsister's death because they were ugly, sordid details, and I didn't want to put any of the hideousness in your mind. Every parent wants to protect his or her child from unpleasant things. That's why we're so worried about what you see and do.

"But," she said, turning back toward the lake, "maybe that's wrong, Summer. Maybe that's very wrong. I should have told you more. I should have prepared you for the wolves out there. Instead, I lived under the illusion that our money and our idyllic world would put a shield around you and protect you wherever you were and whatever you did. Maybe it was my own desire to forget and stick my head in our golden sand. Maybe that's why I feel responsible. I should have known you can't hide from the evil around you. I should have known," she repeated and pounded her small fist into her lap.

"No," I muttered. "You can't blame yourself, Mommy."

"Yes," she insisted. "There's a lot I should have told you." She paused, looked down and then took a deep breath and looked up at me again.

"After my stepsister and I found out the truth about me, we became even more estranged. She had always resented the love Mama Latisha gave me and the attention I received, especially from Roy. She felt she was neglected and I was favored. The new knowledge was not relief for her. It threw salt in her wounds to learn that I wasn't even blood related; yet I was, in her eyes, loved more by her mother and her brother.

"She was always rebellious, angry. She got in

174

with a bad group, snuck away to a party where she was drugged and raped."

"Oh no."

"And they took pictures of her and tried to blackmail her with them, asking for money. We kept it a secret from my stepmother and from Uncle Roy. It was what Beneatha wanted and I went along with her because I wanted her to like me, to love me, so much.

"In the end we both walked into a trap, and I fled to get help. When I returned, she had been murdered.

"Roy was furious at me for not telling him what was going on, and despite what Mama said to me afterward, I knew she was disappointed in me, too, but no one hated me more than I hated my-self.

"Mama Latisha got me out of that world as quickly as she could, and I lived under the fantasy that evil waters didn't run in these privileged rivers and lakes. Eventually, I learned that it did, but often in more subtle ways. I should have spent all these last few years warning you, preparing you, but instead, I tried to make you into the girl I wished I could have been: pure, untouched, for-ever happy. How stupid."

"You warned me about things, Mama. We had good talks. It was my own stupidity."

"I should have made it more vivid for you, honey. It was my responsibility, my job and as you can see, I was more than well equipped to do it. I had all that bad experience, but I didn't make use

175

of it. I wasted it. I let it continue to harm me, harm us."

"Please don't do this, Mommy," I pleaded. "It will only make me feel worse about what I did, too."

She looked at me for a long moment and then she smiled and opened her arms.

I knelt down and fell into her lap where she held me for a while and stroked my hair just the way she used to when I was just a little girl.

"Okay, honey," she said. "I'll stop. We'll be all right."

She kissed me on the forehead and I sat back on the grass. A few moments later, we heard the sound of Harley's motorcycle. He shot up the drive and turned toward his house when he spotted us and brought his motorcycle to a sudden stop. For a moment he straddled it and looked our way, just to be sure he was seeing right.

"Oh no, Mommy. What will I tell Harley? He'll be so upset. There's no telling what he might do."

"Then don't tell him anything for now," she said quickly. "Tell him you got sick and we wanted you home for a few days."

Harley turned off the motorcycle and waved. I waved back and he started toward us. In my heart of hearts, I knew how difficult it was going to be for me to lie to Harley. Being so close for so many of our formative years, we knew all the little nuances in our gestures, looks and voices.

Aunt Alison, who was an expert liar and proud of it, once told me the best way to succeed with a lie is to first convince yourself it's true. Maybe I wouldn't have such a hard time doing so, I thought. I really was sick. In fact, I haven't often felt as sick as I did at the moment.

I rose and walked toward him.

"Hey, what are you doing here?"

"I had to come home for a while," I said.

"Why?"

"I got sick at school and my parents thought I should," I replied.

"What happened?"

"It's too disgusting to talk about," I said. That wasn't a lie.

"Summer," Mommy called as she turned toward the house, "don't stay out too long, honey."

"Okay," I said. "I'm still weak," I told Harley.

"Can I come over to see you later?" he asked quickly.

"Maybe you had better wait until tomorrow," I said giving him a quick smile and turning.

"I'm sorry you're sick," Harley called after me, "but I'm glad you're here," he added.

I closed my eyes and kept walking with my head down. I didn't look back until I was beside Mommy at the front door. He was still looking our way. Even at this distance, I could feel the suspicion in his eyes.

It's not lying that hurts so much, I thought. It's whom you lie to.

"Rain!" Daddy called from the door of the office as soon as we entered the house. Daddy never needed more than a syllable of rage to reveal how angry he was. "You'd better come down here a moment. I've just spoken with Grant."

I started along with Mommy.

"You should go back upstairs, honey," Daddy said.

Mommy paused, looked up at me and then back at Daddy.

"No, Austin," she said. "I want her to know it all, everything."

"Are you sure?" he asked, his voice full of admonition.

"Yes," she said firmly. "Never as sure as I am now," she added, and we went down the corridor together to join him in the office.

Mommy wheeled herself up in front of the desk, and I sat quickly beside her. Daddy was at the window, his hands behind his back. He shook his head and then he returned to the desk and faced us.

"Grant has had a long, frank conversation with the district attorney. Duncan Fields' attorney was at the police station almost minutes after they had brought him down for questioning, and from what Grant says the district attorney tells him, this Duncan Fields was like a seasoned criminal, cocky and well versed on his rights and how to conduct himself. A few phone calls to the right places revealed he has had some other similar incidents, but all of them were quashed."

"He did something at his last music school in France, didn't he, Daddy?" I asked.

"Yes. It seems so. You can just imagine the money that took to settle that one, being it was in a foreign country," he told Mommy.

"So, if he has this record —" she began. He held up his hand.

"I didn't say he had a record, Rain. All that the district attorney told Grant were things that were off-the-record. There's nothing written down, nothing that would come up in a search for his criminal history. In short, nothing admissible in a court of law."

Mommy shook her head.

"To get to the heart of this situation," Daddy continued, "Duncan claims that Summer invited him to come to her bedroom window, that she had made the rendezvous arrangements while they were dancing."

"That's a lie, a big fat lie!"

"Of course it is," Daddy said. "I don't think there's anyone, even his own attorney, who believes it, but it's his story. He said you wanted to come out and he told you that you and he would get into trouble, but you practically jumped into his arms. Then you begged him to show you his car. When you got there, you practically raped him, according to his side of the story. He's seventeen, you're sixteen. Both of you are legally minors, so we couldn't go after him on corrupting the morals of a minor."

"What are you saying, Austin?" Mommy asked.

"The short of it is the district attorney doesn't feel he could win a guilty verdict.

179

"However," Daddy said sitting hard on the desk chair and looking at the desk, "he told Grant he put on the best show he could muster, and he's gotten the Fieldses to agree to send Duncan to psychological counseling for at least a year."

"Psychological counseling," Mommy repeated, spitting it out like a sour apple.

"Grant says that under the circumstances, the way they were described to him, we're lucky to get that. Of course, the school did expel him, but he'll be in some other school within a week or so. Probably pretty far away, maybe in Europe again."

"How disgusting," Mommy muttered.

"There's more," Daddy said. "Haskins called and offered us twenty thousand dollars if we'll let it go and not drag the school into any civil suit. I had Grant call him back because I didn't want to speak to him and they've already raised it to forty-five thousand."

"I don't want to put Summer through any more of this, Austin," Mommy said.

"No, but I hate the thought of taking their money so I told Grant to tell them we'd agree if the money was donated to Women's Shelter in the Storm, the organization to protect and defend abused women."

"That's a very good idea," Mommy said. She looked at me. "Summer, we're talking about all this as if you didn't have a word to say."

"It's all right with me, Mommy," I said. "He's a liar though."

She nodded.

"Grant has told your mother," Daddy said to Mommy. "She wanted to come down to see Summer right away, but I thought we could use a few quiet days before we see anyone."

"That's wise, Austin."

"What if . . . something happens to me, Mommy?" I asked.

They were both quiet, both immediately understanding that I was worried about getting pregnant. The look on their faces revealed how much they didn't want to think about it.

"We'll have to wait to see, of course, but if it does, we'll deal with it then," Mommy said quickly.

Daddy lifted his fist and slammed it down so hard on the desk, I thought it might split into two pieces. Everything jumped, some things falling over. Mommy gasped and brought her hand to her throat.

"I can understand why some people are driven to murder," Daddy said, his lips so taut with rage that little white dots appeared in the corners, "or at least why so many people favor the death penalty."

"None of that is going to do you, me or Summer any good now, Austin. Please."

He nodded.

"I know. I wish there was more I could do for you, baby," he said to me.

"I know you've done and are doing all you can, Daddy."

"Let's all take a deep breath," Mommy said,

"and try to carry on with our lives. Maybe we'll all take a trip, go to the seashore or one of the islands," she suggested.

"Yeah," Daddy said. "Okay."

He rose and went back to the window. Mommy looked at me and then turned to leave the office.

"Oh," Daddy said, turning back to us, "I have some things to check at the health club office. I'll just be gone an hour or so," he said.

"Don't be too long, Austin. Mrs. Geary's working hard to make dinner extra special for us tonight."

"I'll be there. I'll even be hungry," he promised. He was smiling at us, but there were tears icing his eyes.

Mommy went to rest in the sitting room and I returned to my bedroom. I didn't cry anymore. I just sat by my window and looked out at the lake. I wondered how I would ever kiss another boy, hold his hand or permit him to embrace me. Would I shake and panic just at the thought of going on a date? Could time and a thousand bubble baths ever wash away the shock and the violation?

My dark thoughts were interrupted when I heard the doorbell ring. I rose and went to look down the stairway to see who it was. I was expecting it to be Harley, who I imagined had decided he couldn't wait to visit. Mrs. Geary was there opening the door. It was Uncle Roy.

"Is Mrs. Clarke downstairs?" he asked her.

"I'm here, Roy," Mommy said. "It's okay, Mrs.

Geary," she added and wheeled up to the sitting room doorway.

He waited until Mrs. Geary was gone and then turned quickly to Mommy.

"What happened to Summer? Why is she home from music school?" he asked with a firmness. I wondered what Mommy would say and lingered to listen.

"Come into the living room, Roy," she told him and he followed behind her.

I came down the stairs slowly and stopped midway when I could hear their voices. It wasn't just curiosity. I really wanted to see how Mommy was.

"There was an incident at the music school," she began. At first I thought Uncle Roy was speaking too low for me to hear, but it was just a long pause.

"What sort of an incident?"

"A very bad one involving a boy."

Mommy's voice began to crack. I rose, undecided about whether I should go back to my room or just run to her. I descended a few more steps and listened hard.

"Tell me about it," Uncle Roy said.

I could hear Mommy start to sob.

"Easy, Rain," Uncle Roy said in the most gentle, soft and caring voice I had ever heard him utter. "We've been through hard times together. We both know what it's like."

"I know, Roy." She paused and blurted, "She was raped. She went for what she thought would be an innocent walk with a boy after curfew hours, and he managed to get her into his car where he violated her."

"Damn," Uncle Roy said. "Did they get the boy?"

"Yes, but it's complicated, Roy."

"So he's getting away with it?" Uncle Roy quickly concluded. "Another rich boy getting away with something?"

Life was black and white to him. In his world people were either weak or strong, right or wrong, rich or poor. There was little room for compromise.

"We can't put her through any more pain, Roy. Austin is beside himself over it. I'm worried about him, too. I keep thinking it's all the curse, Roy."

"I know you would think that. You once told me we couldn't be man and wife because it would bring down all the wrath of God on our heads. You couldn't think of me as anything but your brother, even after . . ."

"Please, Roy," Mommy said.

I was holding my breath.

Even after what?

"I know, I know. I got to keep it all under lock and key in this heart of mine. I can't see how any worse could have happened to you, Rain. All right, where's this boy live?" he asked.

"He's gone by now, Roy, probably out of the country. You're right about it. His parents are wealthy people who just keep protecting him, getting him out of trouble. There's a curse for you."

"Their money keeps solving it though," Uncle Roy said bitterly.

"Not forever, Roy. It will come back on them someday."

"Yeah," he said skeptically. "Right. Never mind all that for now. How's she doing?"

"She's strong, Roy."

"She's your daughter. She got to be strong. She could have been mine, too," he said sadly. "Why does someone so good have to be hurt like this?" he raged.

I heard Mommy start to sob and then Uncle Roy go, "Easy, Rain, easy."

I was at the foot of the stairs now. I inched forward to the doorway and peered in to see Uncle Roy on his knees in front of Mommy, embracing her so firmly, she was pressed to him, her face on his shoulder. He stroked her hair and then he kissed her on the cheek, his lips pressed to her face and moving down closer and closer toward her lips until he kissed her there.

"Rain," he said still holding her, "if only we could have made more of that time in England and . . ."

Mommy opened her eyes and saw me standing there.

"Summer!" she cried.

I turned and ran to the front door.

"Summer, honey!"

I closed the door behind me and hurried down the steps and out of the reach of our front lights.

I rushed around the house and ended up in the gazebo, my heart thumping.

Why was I so upset and disturbed? I always believed in my heart that Uncle Roy was capable of being gentle and caring. He always spoke softly, lovingly to Mommy. It was the way a brother should be, wasn't it? Even though he wasn't a blood relation, he had grown up with her as his sister. A brother could hold and kiss his sister to comfort her, couldn't he?

But there was something more in the way he held her and kissed her, and what was he talking about? What had happened between them in England?

My whole world had gone topsy-turvy in minutes. It was as though everyone I knew wore masks, and the masks were falling away. I felt dizzy and weak and I had to lie down. My heart was still racing. Minutes later, I heard the door open and close. Uncle Roy came down the steps and started to call for me.

"Summer. Your mama wants you to come back inside. Summer, where are you?"

I didn't answer. I sat there, my blood racing, my pulse throbbing in my neck.

He called me again and then he started toward his own house, his head down. I sat back, my arms folded under my breasts and just stared down at the gazebo floor.

"I thought you were so sick," I heard. At first I thought I had imagined it.

When I turned, I saw no one for a moment or

two. Then Harley moved out of the shadows toward me.

"Harley? What are you doing out here?"

"I could ask you the same thing, Summer. What's going on? I saw you come running out of your house, then I heard Roy screaming for you," he continued as he approached the gazebo. He paused at the railing and waited.

My tongue seemed pasted to the roof of my mouth. It had gone on strike if I dared to utter another lie, I thought.

"I didn't come home because I was sick, Harley. Not exactly," I added.

He continued to stare. Then he nodded.

"I know," he said. "I felt that when you spoke to me before and then, when Roy learned you were back, I saw how concerned he quickly became. Are you going to tell me the truth?"

"Yes," I said, "but it's not easy to talk about it."

"Okay," he said. "I'll be patient."

He hopped over the railing and sat beside me.

"There's nothing you can do about it, Harley Arnold, so I don't want you rushing off on your motorcycle and make me feel terrible for telling you. I couldn't stand another troubled thought."

"Uh-huh," he said.

"I mean it. I want you to promise with all your heart and I want you to know that if you break your promise, I won't talk to you anymore or care about you or anything."

"Okay," he said.

"Okay, what? Do you promise?"

"I promise," he said with great reluctance.

"I did a bad thing. I went for a walk with a boy after curfew."

"That's it?" he asked quicky, grimacing.

"No," I said.

"What else?"

"I was more stupid. I let him talk me into looking at his new van and when I got into it . . ."

"What?" My silence filled in the blanks very quickly. "He did something to you?"

I nodded.

"Remember your promise," I warned him. Even in the darkness, I could see his rage building. I certainly could feel the heat of it.

"Well, what did they do? I mean the school, the police?"

"He was expelled from the school."

"And?"

"He's been sent to a year of counseling," I added.

"That's it? What's his name?"

"No one can do any more about it, Harley."

"What's your father doing about it?"

"He's done all he can and so has Grandpa Grant."

"You should have told me right away," he said. "Weren't you ever going to tell me?"

"Yes, I guess," I said. "It's not something I want to talk about, Harley."

Any indignation or disappointment he felt quickly disappeared.

"I'm sorry, Summer. I should be asking you how you are."

He reached for my hand and held it.

We sat there like that for a few long moments, neither of us talking.

"If there's anything I can do, you'll tell me, right?" he finally asked.

"Yes, thank you, Harley."

"Why did you run out of your house like that? Did Roy say something nasty to you, blame you or anything?" he demanded, ready to fight for my honor.

"No, no," I said. "Nothing like that."

"Then."

"I'm still very upset, Harley. Everything upsets me. Please understand."

"Sure," he said.

"I'd better go back inside," I said rising.

He stood up quickly.

"Thanks for trusting me," he said.

"Just remember your promise," I admonished.

He smiled.

"There's nothing you could ask of me that I wouldn't do for you, Summer."

"Thank you," I said.

I started to turn away and he put his arm around me and held me against him for a moment. It made me tense. I couldn't help feeling so ashamed, even though I knew I shouldn't.

"I've got to go," I whispered and hurried off the gazebo and toward the house.

"Good night," he called after me.

I didn't reply. The tears were choking my throat.

As I started up the stairs toward the front door, Daddy pulled into the driveway. He honked his horn and got out quickly.

"What are you doing outside?" he asked, hurrying to me.

"I just wanted to get some air, Daddy."

"Oh."

He put his arm around me.

"You all right?"

"Yes," I said.

"Hungry, too?"

I wasn't, but I nodded.

He kissed me on the cheek and we entered the house together.

Mommy was waiting in the hallway. She and I looked at each other.

"Summer?" she said.

"I'm okay," I said. "And hungry, too."

"Everything's ready," Mrs. Geary called from the dining room doorway.

Daddy kept his arm around my shoulders as we followed Mommy down the hallway.

The air was so thick with our troubled thoughts, it was hard to breathe, much less sit at the table and have a normal dinner. Daddy tried to get some conversation going by talking about the clubs and some personnel problems. Mommy listened but her eyes swung to me often as she searched my face for some hint about my feelings. I tried to avoid her gaze, which was enough to confirm her fears.

Afterward, I excused myself as quickly as I could and went upstairs to sleep. When I slipped under my blanket, I closed my eyes and in seconds, fell asleep.

I never heard anyone come up the stairs. Later, Daddy told me he had come up to look in on me a number of times. I awoke suddenly at nearly four in the morning. For a while I was very confused. There was a split second or two when I hoped and thought everything that had happened was just a nightmare. I hadn't even gone to music camp yet.

The illusion was short-lived, of course. I sat up, wiped my eyes and took a deep breath. I was very tired, but I didn't feel like falling back to sleep. Even though I had forced myself to eat Mrs. Geary's wonderful dinner, I was still hungry. I decided to go down and get a glass of milk and maybe have some bread and jelly.

The upstairs hall light was dim as was the downstairs hall light. The house itself was sleepy quiet, my parents' bedroom door closed. The carpeted steps kept my descent a secret. I made my way to the kitchen quickly and began to fix my snack. I was almost finished eating when I heard the distinct sound of Mommy's elevator chair. I sat there listening to the click of metal and then the soft sound of her wheelchair moving down the hallway.

She was in her nightgown, her hair down.

"I thought you might have gone down for something," she said smiling. "I haven't been able to sleep much. On and off all night," she continued. "Daddy took a sleeping pill and he's snoring away. Are you all right?"

"Yes."

"Would you pour me a glass of milk, too?"

I rose and quickly did it. She came to the breakfast table and I handed her the glass of milk. She sipped some and peered at me over the glass.

"Why did you run away from us like that earlier, honey?"

"I don't know," I said quickly.

"How long were you standing there?"

"A while."

She nodded, paused, drank some more of her milk and looked at me.

"Uncle Roy didn't want to live here so close to us, you know."

"Yes."

"I was so used to having him nearby, watching over me when I was younger. After he and Glenda married, I thought it was fine, everything would be fine. Sometimes, I think life is like a stream of water making its way over land and it runs into one obstacle and starts to flow in another direction. Once it gets moving again, it doesn't think about where it had been going.

"I guess that's just wishful thinking." She shook her head at my look of confusion. What did all that mean?

"I'm babbling. I'm tired," she said. "Sorry."

"No, it's all right, Mommy."

She looked at me hard.

"I don't want any more secrets between us, Summer. Whether I like it or not, you're a young woman now. You've handled this terrible situation very maturely, more maturely than I could have handled it at your age, even living where I was living and seeing the things I saw almost daily. I'm proud of you, honey."

I nodded and looked down.

"Summer?"

"Why were you kissing Uncle Roy like that?" I finally asked. "He was holding you so close and when he kissed you, you looked like you were kissing him back."

"I thought that was it," she said nodding. "Uncle Roy has been my big brother so long, I guess I can't stop being a little girl when he comforts or protects me."

"That wasn't a little girl's kiss, Mommy. He wasn't kissing you like a big brother kisses his little sister either."

She stared a moment, her eyes small.

"It's so complicated, honey, and it's late."

"I thought you didn't want any more secrets between us."

She sighed and shook her head.

"You have so much on your head tonight."

"One more thing won't matter," I insisted.

She smiled.

"You are stronger than I was," she concluded. She sat back, closing her eyes and grimacing for a moment as if the thoughts were already bringing her pain.

"After Uncle Roy found out the truth about my birth, he came to me and confessed that he had been hating and punishing himself for years because of the feelings he had for me, feelings he thought were unnatural.

"He was actually happy we weren't really related and he wanted me to feel the same way about him, understand?"

"Yes," I said.

"I couldn't, but he kept trying to get me to change. I loved him so much and hated the thought of his being so unhappy, that I did try. However, I couldn't change and he had to face that fact. He thought Fate had been cruel to him, to us.

"When he met Glenda, I was so happy because I thought that finally he would find happiness and learn to live with what had happened to us. As you know, he and Glenda have had their own share of tragedy. Your aunt Glenda is hard to live with. Roy has come to me often to cry about it.

"Sometimes, he falls back to the old wishes and dreams. I do my best to help him and help him try to make a life for himself and Glenda. Usually, I'm very good at it. Earlier tonight, I stumbled. It won't happen again, but I was weak, frightened for you and I just slipped."

"What did he mean when he talked about what happened in London?" I pursued.

She bit her lower lip and shook her head. Tears were in her eyes.

"Okay, Mommy," I said quickly. "I understand. I'm all right."

She smiled and we hugged.

"It's so good having a big girl to talk to, Summer. You're my best friend now."

"And you're mine, Mommy."

"Good," she said. "Want to go back to sleep?"

"Yes."

I put everything away and helped her into the elevator chair. She went up, into her chair and back to her bedroom, pausing at the door to smile at me.

"See you in the morning, honey," she said.

I went into my room and then went to the window and looked out over the lake toward Uncle Roy's house where he was in bed, maybe staring into the darkness, thinking about the strange turns and twists his life had taken.

Secrets hovered in all the shadows between our two houses. When the sun came up, they retreated into our hearts, waiting, hoping to be discovered, to be reborn in the light of day.

What great secret had been passed on to me?

What now waited in my heart?

8

Burying the Past

I felt like someone who had been holding her breath under water until I learned it was definite that I was not pregnant. What an added horror that would have been. Mommy looked just as relieved as I was. Daddy had become very quiet about all of it. He was like someone who had been forced to swallow sour milk and didn't want to talk about it or hear any references to it for fear it would make him sick again. He didn't want to hear anything more about the music school and was very happy that my stepgrandfather had taken care of all that had followed.

Mommy arranged for Ms. Lippincott, my regular piano teacher, to come to the house and work with me twice a week. I practiced the clarinet on my own whenever I had the urge. Daddy wanted me to go to work with him every day. He wanted me to help out at the office, but I wasn't ready for it. It was more comfortable to stay close to home, take walks and occasionally swim in our lake or go rowing.

Late afternoons, I sat with Mommy on the rear patio and we talked and did needlepoint together. One day seemed to flow into the next, all of us talking softly, moving about as if we didn't want to wake up the bitter memories sleeping at our feet.

Grandmother Megan and Grandfather Grant came to visit after my first full week home. I thought I was going to hate every moment of it. So did Mommy, because Grandmother Megan began her visit by acting as though I had died.

"You poor, poor child," she said as soon as she set eyes on me. "You poor little girl."

"She's hardly a little girl anymore, Mother," Mommy said. "And I don't mean because of what happened. She's sixteen and very mature and responsible."

Grandfather Grant went off with Daddy to the office and left us in the living room.

"Yes, yes, I know that. What did the doctor say?" Grandmother Megan asked Mommy.

"She said she was fine. There are no complications, if that's what you mean."

"*She?* You have a woman doctor for Summer?"

"Doctor Melrose. She's in with Doctor Stern, and Summer was more comfortable with her."

"Oh. Yes." She looked at me again with such pity that I thought she might start to cry any moment.

"I'm all right, Grandmother," I insisted, but her

expression of grief just grew deeper.

"I hate to see you lose your innocence so soon in your life, Summer," she continued and followed it with a long, dramatic sigh as she sat back and swung her eyes toward the window.

Mommy glanced at me and smirked.

"You weren't much older when you lost yours, Mother," she said.

Grandmother Megan stiffened quickly and looked at her.

"Even so, Rain, that was with my consent. It's hardly the same loss of innocence."

"There's no point in making her feel any worse than she feels about it, Mother."

"I know that. Don't you think I know that?" She paused and studied me. "You mustn't think about it anymore," she said. "You must pretend hard that it never happened, that it was just some bad dream. That's what I do when I'm faced with something unpleasant and it works if you really try hard. Lately," she continued, more to Mommy now than me, "that's all I do in regards to Alison. Do you know that last week she went out four times with four different men. When I commented about it, she told me she was window-shopping. Now what's that supposed to mean, window-shopping? How do you window-shop for men?"

"Why didn't you ask her?" Mommy inquired.

"And have her tell me? Thank you, no. No thank you. That girl enjoys shocking me. I don't want to hear about any of her exploits."

"She's just looking for attention. You've got to show her you're interested in her, Mother."

"What? How can you say that? Look at all I've bought her and all the opportunities I've provided for her. I've sent her on more trips than a travel agent takes, and I can't tell you how many times Grant has had to bail her out of one problem or another.

"She's simply ungrateful," Grandmother Megan concluded. "Spoiled and ungrateful."

"You can only blame yourself for that, Mother."

"Nonsense. Some girls are just . . . inclined to be spoiled. I wasn't spoiled, was I? And I had anything I wanted. My father thought the sun rose and set on my smiles and tears."

She looked at me again, shaking her head, her lips trembling.

"You poor, poor dear. Your first experience with a man should have been wonderful, romantic, something to cherish in your heart forever and ever. Forget it. Just forget it. You know what you should do?" she said, suddenly animated. "You should go out in the back and bury the memory. I've done that and it's always worked for me."

"Bury the memory?" I looked to Mommy, who only shrugged and shook her head. "How do you do that, Grandmother?"

"I'll show you," she said jumping up. "Get a piece of paper and a pen. Come on. Let's do it," she insisted.

"Mother, please. You're being ridiculous,"

Mommy chastised softly.

"I am not. Summer doesn't think I am. Do you, dear?"

"I . . ."

"Just get a sheet of paper and a pen," she said.

I glanced at Mother who raised her eyes toward the ceiling and then I rose, went into the kitchen and fetched the pad and pen that were always by the telephone.

"Good," she said when I brought them back. "Now sit right here," she said patting the chair next to the corner table. She put the pen and pad on the table. "Go on."

I did as she asked and looked up at her.

"Write down what happened as simply and as quickly as you can. Go ahead," she ordered.

"Mother," Mommy protested.

"Just be quiet for a moment, Rain. You don't know everything there is to know. I've learned some things with my added years."

"I don't really want to do this, Grandmother," I said.

"Of course you don't. It's painful, but it's like throwing up rotten food. You've got to get it out of you. Do it quickly. Go on, dear."

She stood over me, waiting, hovering like a grade school teacher insisting her student write the sentence over and over until she got it perfect.

I took a breath, thought a moment and then jotted down the most basic two-line description: *I went for a walk with a boy at school. He got me into his van and raped me.*

"Perfect," Grandmother Megan said. She tore the page out of the pad and folded it over and over until it was only an inch or so wide. She held it tightly in her clenched hand as if she had caught an annoying fly. "Now let's go get a shovel, find an out-of-the-way place out back and bury it as deeply as we can. Come along," she said energized by the plan.

"Everyone is going to think you're absolutely mad, Mother."

"It's not for everyone to know," she replied "Summer?"

Mother looked at me, her expression suddenly curious because of mine. I couldn't help wondering if it would work. Maybe there was some magic in it. Grandmother Megan was certainly an expert when it came to avoiding sadness.

"I can't stand this anymore. I'm going to see about Mrs. Geary making us some lunch," Mother said and started wheeling away from us

"Come along, dear," Grandmother Megan said putting her arm around my shoulders.

We walked out together.

"Now where are the ground tools kept these days?" she asked.

"Still in the shed by the garage," I said pointing. We headed for it and I located a spade.

"I know the exact spot to go to," she whispered.

She led me around the house and to the right, almost to the woods.

"I once buried a doll here," she told me. "I had dropped it and it cracked into two pieces. My fa-

ther had brought it back from a trip for me. It was so beautiful and precious. I cried so hard, I nearly cracked myself into pieces and then my father said I should give my doll a funeral. My sister Victoria thought it was absolutely ridiculous, but my father and I came out here. He dug the grave and we put the broken doll into the ground. Then he covered it and we said a prayer and I did feel better.

"Go on, dig your little grave and bury your horror," she ordered.

I glanced around. There was no one watching us outside, but when I looked at the house, I thought I saw Mommy peering out of the window in the kitchen nook. As quickly as I could, I dug a hole.

"Drop it in," she said handing me the folded paper.

I did so and then I covered it quickly. She stepped on the covered hole as if she was stamping down on an ugly insect.

"Stomp it," she commanded.

I stepped on it.

"Harder," she instructed. "Go on. Harder and harder."

I did so and I had the strangest feeling that I was crushing my nightmares.

"Harder," she chanted and then added, "die, die, die."

I muttered that, too.

"Okay," she said putting her hand on my shoulder. She smiled at me. "It's gone. You've rid

yourself of it. Don't you feel lighter, freer? Well? Don't you?"

"Yes," I said. Maybe it was crazy, but at the moment, I did.

We walked back to the shed to put away the spade and then returned to the house to have lunch. Not once during the remainder of that day was a word spoken about what we had done or what had happened to me. When I said goodbye to her after she had gotten into the limousine later, she looked out at me, smiled and said, "It's gone, all gone." She patted my hand and sounded just like Mommy did when I was little and she wanted to convince me my nightmare wouldn't return.

Then she and Grandfather Grant were driven off. After the limousine disappeared, I stood and gazed over our great property. Everything was plush, the trees thick with rich green leaves, the grass like carpet with all our summer flowers blooming. It looked full of life and cheerful, yet I had the distinct feeling that the grounds of this estate were peppered with little graves, all filled with Grandmother Megan's moments and memories of unhappiness and all gone from her mind.

Was it madness or was it great therapy?

Sometimes, we have to believe in a little magic, I thought. That's what I told Mommy when she brought it up later.

"My mother is absolutely bonkers," she said.

"Maybe."

"Don't tell me she convinced you that you can

bury bad times as easily as that."

"Wouldn't it be a nice thought, Mommy?" I asked. "A little magic?"

She stared at me and then shook her head and laughed.

"Maybe," she admitted. "Maybe that's what I finally found myself when I found your father and later, when we had you. I guess that's magic. Just the same," she said, "please don't tell anyone about your mad grandmother. It's too embarrassing."

I didn't say I would or I wouldn't. I did eventually tell Harley and when I told him, he didn't laugh at it. He looked envious and said, "One of these days, I'll ask her to help me bury a few things."

It wasn't hard to figure out what they would be, so I didn't ask. Most of our conversations were about good things these days or funny things. Harley visited with me as much as possible, doing his best to cheer me up. When he came over, he talked continuously as if he thought any small silences between us would drop me quickly back into the thick pool of sadness. In fact, he was over so often, I heard Uncle Roy outside the house one day begin to reprimand him for it.

"You're making a pest of yourself when those people need some peace," he told him.

For a few days after that, Harley did stay away. Then late one night I saw him silhouetted in the moonlight, walking along the bank of the lake. He stood staring at the water. He was there so long, I was sure something was wrong, so I slipped out of my room and down the stairs very quietly to join him.

"Why are you out here so late?" I asked as I drew closer. I had my arms folded under my breasts and wore my robe and slippers. Harley was still dressed in his jeans and black T-shirt. He glanced up at me and then looked toward his house.

"I couldn't sleep and finally gave up trying," he said.

"What's wrong?"

He didn't answer for a very long moment.

"Is Aunt Glenda all right?"

"No," he said sullenly.

"Why?"

I expected him to say something like the same old thing, but he didn't.

"You don't remember what today is then?" he asked, still not looking at me.

"Today?" I thought. "Oh," I finally said when I realized. "I'm sorry, I forgot."

It was the day Latisha had died. Maybe I didn't want to remember. Every year on the anniversary of her daughter's death, Aunt Glenda dressed in black and draped a funereal atmosphere over herself and anyone who came within a hundred yards of her.

"I wish I could forget, too," Harley replied sharply through clenched teeth. "Maybe I should rip out this page on the calendar and bury it someplace like you and your grandmother buried your bad memory. I doubt I could do it," he said and looked away as he continued.

"I was almost eight years old when she died, but I still had trouble understanding what death was. Latisha was often sick. I remember her being in the hospital a lot, but death was still something that happened only to old people. I think for days and days afterward, I kept expecting Roy and my mother would be bringing her home."

He laughed.

"I guess I thought if young people died, they died for only a little while. For them, death was nothing more than just another illness that they would get over. The doctor would make her better.

"My mother spent a good part of every night out there at her grave. I remember her telling Roy she thought Latisha might be frightened, all alone in the dark.

"He didn't have much patience for that and yelled at her for talking so foolish.

"Then she turned to her religion because it made her feel better about Latisha's going. She was in heaven with angels, so she wasn't alone and wasn't afraid. According to my mother, Latisha felt sorrier for us having to mourn her passing down here on earth.

"My mother would sit beside me at the dinner table and tell me all that, almost the way another Mother might read a fairy tale to her child.

"She broke open her Bible and read to me from it, and then told me all about Heaven. Roy couldn't stand it. He would get up and leave, sometimes without finishing his meal. My mother didn't notice or care, I guess. She had begun drifting away from both of us.

"You know what it's like waking up in the middle of a terrible thunder-and-lightning storm when you're just little and you call for your mother, but she's not there because she's more interested in being out at the gravesite of her dead daughter? I didn't get much comfort from Roy, I can tell you that. He would stick his head in my room and growl, 'Stop being a baby. Nothing's going to happen to you. Go to sleep.'

"I used to wonder if anything ever frightened him. Sometimes, I wanted to be like him because of that, and sometimes I hated him because of it."

He stopped talking and looked at me as if he had just realized I was standing there listening.

"Sorry I went off at the mouth like that," he said.

"Oh, that's okay, Harley. I wanted to listen."

"Here I am telling you my troubles. What a selfish SOB I am, huh?"

"No. Besides, I don't want to dote on my unfortunate experience," I said.

"Unfortunate? It was far from something haphazard or destined. That creep. I wish I knew his name. I wish I knew where he was. I'd wipe that smug smile off his face."

He stood so stiffly, his arms at his sides, his hands clenched.

"I know you would," I said, touching his

shoulder. "That's why I'm not telling you any-thing. You would just get into trouble, and how do you think I'd feel then?"

He was silent.

"I'd feel absolutely horrible, Harley."

He nodded, his body relaxing.

"Can I tell you something very private?" he asked.

"Of course. We've always trusted each other, haven't we?"

"Yeah, yeah," he said, just hating any reference I made to our being like brother and sister, if not close cousins. "I don't mean that keep-a-secret kid stuff."

"What do you mean, Harley?"

"I mean what I felt and thought when you told me what had happened to you. I know I should have been most upset about what he had done, but what bothered me the most is hearing you went for a walk with another boy at night. You thought you might have a nice summer romance, didn't you?" he asked in a very accusatory tone of voice.

"Harley Arnold," I said growing indignant, "I don't see how that's your business."

"Of course it is," he said. "I was hoping you and I would have had the summer romance, a summer romance that would have gone on into the fall and long after that," he blurted. "Sorry," he quickly added before I could speak. "Sorry I bothered you. Sorry I bother everybody," he muttered and started quickly away.

"Harley!" I called after him, but he kept walking. I felt the frustration raging inside me and stomped my foot, fuming.

And they say girls are hard to understand, I thought.

I went back into the house and up to my room where I stood by the window and looked for him in the darkness below. I didn't see him anywhere, and I was too tired to keep looking.

He didn't come by the next day, but the afternoon after that, Harley joined Mommy and me on the rear patio and just sat watching us do needlepoint. He said "Hi," and Mommy said "Hi" and smiled at him, but I just gave him a look and kept working. He and Mommy started to talk about the weather and then his work. He glanced at me occasionally, but I concentrated on my needlepoint. Finally, he said, he had heard from one of the colleges to which he had made a late application.

I looked up expectantly, but he didn't add anything.

"Well, Harley Arnold," I finally said, "don't just sit there keeping us guessing. What did they say?"

"They said I could come around and learn some stuff, if I wanted."

"What?"

"That's wonderful, Harley," Mommy said.

"Learn some stuff? What kind of an admission to college is that?"

He shrugged.

"Let's not make a big deal of it," he said. "It's

just one of those community colleges."

"It's still an opportunity, Harley," Mommy said. "Don't waste it."

He nodded and lowered his eyes for a moment like a subdued puppy. Then he looked up at me sharply and smiled. I couldn't help but laugh.

A moment later Uncle Roy came around the corner of the house and stopped, very surprised to see Harley sitting there.

"What are you doin' here now?" he demanded without saying hello to anyone.

Harley fidgeted in his chair.

"Nothing," he said.

"Nothing? You ain't supposed to be off the project this early."

"Jerry said he was finished with the Sheetrock for the day," Harley replied.

"So? What about Bob Matthews? I told you I wanted you with him as much as possible so you could learn more about electrical work. I spent all that time talking him into letting you be his apprentice. You'd get a lot more done than just sittin' here watchin' a couple of women do needlepoint. What are you goin' to be, a seamstress?"

Harley turned two shades of red, one darker than the other.

"He's not bothering us," Mommy said.

"That's a relief, but he's not on the job he's supposed to be on either."

Uncle Roy looked at me and then at Harley.

"You'll get docked a day for this," he told him.

"Big deal," Harley snapped. "It's coolie wages

anyway," he spat out, and got up to walk away.

"Those coolie wages pay your expenses, boy," Uncle Roy shouted after him.

Harley didn't look back, but I saw how his neck lifted as if he had been slapped on the back of his head.

"Mama always used to tell us you can get more with honey than with vinegar, Roy," Mommy said.

Uncle Roy grunted.

"She also said you give him an inch, he'll take a foot."

"She was talking about your father."

"Hmm," Uncle Roy said. He watched Harley a moment longer and then he turned back to us. "Anything you need, Rain?"

"No, we're fine, Roy. Thanks. How's Glenda? I haven't seen her out for a few days."

"It's that time of year," he replied.

Mommy put her needlework down and thought a moment.

"Oh, I forgot," she said.

"Yeah. Latisha died ten years ago day before yesterday."

"I should have remembered," Mommy said.

"Not with all you've had on your mind, Rain."

"Still, we should have remembered," Mommy insisted. "I'll go over to see her later."

"She'll just be sitting in the house, rocking and humming her hymns. She won't even know you're there most of the time," Uncle Roy said.

We heard Harley start up his motorcycle and

then head down the driveway.

"Where's he going?" Roy asked rhetorically. "Just like him to pick this time to be his usual troublemaker self."

"Maybe he's thinking about Latisha too, Roy."

"I doubt it."

"He is," I blurted. They both looked at me. "He was talking about her the night before last."

"Night before last? I don't remember that," Mommy said.

"You and Daddy were already asleep. I saw him wandering outside and went out to speak with him. He said he couldn't sleep because of the memories, Uncle Roy."

"Hmm," Uncle Roy said, his eyes dark with thought. "Just the same, he should be thinking more about his mother and not get himself into any trouble. I'll see you all later," he added. He waited for Mommy to smile and nod and then he walked away.

"Do you think things will ever be good between Harley and Uncle Roy, Mommy?" I asked.

"I don't know, dear. Uncle Roy has had a hard life, full of disappointments. He grew up in a very dangerous world and had two young girls to protect. In his mind he lost them both, and then he lost his daughter."

"Maybe if he and Harley had some mature conversations and Uncle Roy trusted him more with all that, they would get along better."

"Maybe, Summer, but that's between them. For now, we've got a full plate in this house," she said smiling. "I saw you received a letter from Grandpa Larry."

"Yes, he wants me to come visit again. He offered to buy the ticket."

"You haven't written to him and told him anything about . . ."

"No. Should I?"

"I don't want you to have to think about it, but I suppose he'll be disappointed that you didn't tell him. Being family means being part of the bad as well as the good."

"Okay," I said. "I'll write him tonight."

"Maybe you should go to England for the rest of the summer," Mommy thought aloud.

"I don't know, Mommy."

"Well, you don't do anything that makes you nervous, honey. When you're ready, you'll go," she said.

She returned to her needlepoint. I thought a moment and then I returned to mine.

We didn't speak for a long time, but we didn't need to say anything aloud. There was something between us, something we said with every movement, every breath, every glance and smile. How lucky I was to have her, I thought.

And then I thought about Harley, who was so alone. All his silences were deep and dark even when he sat in the same room with his mother and Uncle Roy.

In fact, all three of them were alone.

Two days later we had one of the worst heat

spells ever. The humidity reached close to ninety-eight percent and the temperatures went over a hundred. Nights did little to cool it down. There was such a drain on the electricity in the area that some places were experiencing brownouts. Even the animals were depressed. All the birds lingered on branches in the shade. I felt sorry for Harley and Uncle Roy out on their job. There were stories about roadworkers and other outdoor employees actually fainting from dehydration. Except for sitting in the house under a fan or in front of the cool air vents, the only relief was in the lake, which Daddy said was the warmest he had ever felt it.

As soon as he returned home from work, Harley was in the water. One afternoon, he didn't wait to change. He drove his motorcycle down to the dock and dove in, clothes and all. Mommy and I thought it was very funny, especially when he stepped out and emptied his shoes, but Uncle Roy thought he was just being stupid.

We did more night swimming than ever. I would come out about eight and usually find Harley was already at the raft or just floating near the dock. Except for the small light at the dock, we would have only the moonlight or starlight. On overcast, heavy nights, Mommy didn't want me to go too far out.

"Just wade and get yourself cooled down, honey."

It was too warm for her to stay outside and watch us, so Daddy would come out occasionally and check or take a dip himself. Uncle Roy rarely ever went swimming. If he did, he just dove in on the other end of the lake, closer to his house. When Harley was younger, Uncle Roy kept him on that side as much as he could, claiming he didn't want Harley to bother us, but Mommy made it crystal clear that he was never to make Harley feel like he didn't belong. Now, of course, Harley could swim the entire width of the lake, so it didn't matter much where he dove in.

That weekend my aunt Alison paid us a surprise visit. Often Grandmother Megan didn't know where she was or where she was going, so she never called Mommy to tell her. I had a piano lesson that Friday afternoon. The music made me melancholy because it and my lesson reminded me that I was missing so much by not being in the music school. It all seemed so unfair. I was positive Duncan wasn't experiencing any melancholy. He never wanted to be at the school in the first place. I had simply been a means to an end. He was probably laughing about it somewhere, telling new friends about this dumb girl who tried to get him into trouble.

Thinking about it actually made me angry enough to want to tell Harley everything, especially Duncan's name and address, and thus send Harley after him like a hound-dog to hunt him down and punish him or, at least, to wipe that smug, confident smile off his face.

The heat from my thoughts only exacerbated the discomfort I felt because of the hot spell. After my lessons, I ate a light dinner and then put on my bathing suit and marched down to the lake. At first, I thought Harley wasn't there. It was darker than usual, being there was no moon in the sky, but as my eyes grew accustomed to the night, I saw him lying on his back on the raft, slightly illuminated by the stars.

Coming across the lake from his house was some soft, religious music, hymn music without the words. Tonight it seemed appropriate. I knew Mommy would rather I not swim out to the raft on a night like this, so I called to Harley, but he was either asleep or simply didn't hear me. I couldn't imagine he would ignore me. I was frustrated enough to decide I would swim out to him. However, just as I started to go into the water, a pair of headlights washed away the darkness and threw a beam of light over the water as far as the raft.

Harley sat up, shading his eyes with his hand and looking toward the dock.

I waved and he waved back. Then I turned to see who it was and heard Aunt Alison's laugh. There was the slam of car doors, more laughter, followed by her calling my name.

I answered and waited as she came down to the dock, followed by a tall, lean man with hair so light blond that it looked nearly white. Aunt Alison dangled a cigarette from the corner of her mouth. She wore very short dark blue shorts and a blue halter.

"How's my favorite niece?" she cried.

"I'm okay, Aunt Alison. I didn't know you were coming."

"Neither did I, but we were only fifty miles away and I told Harper all about my family and this wonderful estate, didn't I, Harper?"

He laughed and drew a cigarette out of the pack in the top pocket of his short-sleeve shirt. His jeans were tight-legged, and he had a very narrow waist.

"Harper is a swimmer," she said. "He swam for the University of Virginia, didn't you, Harper?"

"Tried out," he said.

"It's the same thing," she quickly decided. She looked around. "So where is everyone? On a night like this, I half-expected my brother-in-law would be dipping my sister in the lake."

"Mommy can swim if she wants to," I said sharply. "It's good therapy for her."

"Sure it is. Like I told you, Harper, my half-sister is in a wheelchair. Fell off a horse. You ever fall off, Harper?" she asked him, her smile so full of lust I could see it glitter even in the dim starlight.

Harper smiled back and shuffled his right foot.

"Never had a horse buck more than I could handle," he replied, and they both laughed.

Then Aunt Alison looked out at the raft and squinted.

"Is that Harley out there?"

"Yes," I said.

"Oh. How has Harley been since your Sweet Sixteen?"

"Fine, just fine, Aunt Alison," I said.

"Damn, it is hot, Harper. We should have gone to the beach."

"Told you," her boyfriend said.

"We'll go tomorrow. Maybe," she teased. She leaned against him and kissed him on the neck. "He's a pretty one, isn't he, Summer?" she asked. "I found him wasting his time at some college kid hangout, didn't I, Harper?"

"Yes," he admitted.

"He fell in love with me the first minute, didn't you, Harper?"

"Head over heels," he agreed.

"No, head first," she said and they both laughed. Then she turned back to me. "So you're going swimming?"

"I was about to," I said.

"Harper? Care to show off your best stroke?"

"Sure," he said.

"Let's do it," she decided.

Of course, I expected she would take him into the house, introduce him to my parents, go to one of the guest rooms and change into a bathing suit. But right before me, she slipped off her shorts and began to undo her halter. Her boyfriend, excited by the impulsive action, fumbled at the button on his jeans. I was so shocked, I couldn't move for a moment.

"You're going in naked?" I asked.

"Skinny-dipping is the best — right, Harper?"

"Only way," he said.

My heart pounded. I looked toward the house

and then as Harper slipped off his pants, I moved into the water quickly and started to swim toward the raft. Fled toward it was more like it, I guess. I don't think I ever swam as fast or as hard. Harley came to the edge by the ladder and helped me up quickly. We could hear them splashing and laughing near the dock.

"What's going on?" he asked.

"Aunt Alison arrived with a boyfriend named Harper, and they both took off their clothes."

"You're kidding," Harley said gazing toward them. "They're naked?"

"Yes. She's so crazy."

I sprawled on the raft on my stomach and looked toward the dock. Harley sprawled beside me. Their laughter echoed over the water. We could see them embrace and fall into the water and then splash each other.

"They look like they're having fun," Harley said.

"Fun? That's so rude. He didn't care if I saw anything or not. He didn't wait for me to turn my back."

"Did you look?"

"No," I said sharply. "Of course not."

"A bunch from my public school go skinny-dipping at the creek," he said.

"Have you ever gone with them?"

His hesitation was as good as a confession.

"I just wanted to see what it would be like," he said. "I only went once. I don't really like those guys."

"What about the girls?" I immediately asked.

"Um . . . one or two of them might make the cover of *Car and Driver*," he said laughing.

I poked him.

"You're teasing, Harley Arnold. I bet you do have someone you never told me about."

"I do not," he insisted.

Before I could ask another question, he lifted his eyes from mine and said, "They're heading out here."

"Oh no."

I looked out and saw them swimming toward us.

"Let's just go back to the dock. We'll give them the raft," I decided.

"Now that's not being very polite," he said smiling.

I stood up.

"Are you coming with me or not?"

"Take it easy. I'm just teasing you," he said.

Suddenly, we heard my aunt Alison scream, only this time the scream was not a scream of fun and excitement. It sounded like a scream of desperation.

"What's going on?" Harley wondered aloud.

We watched as Harper stopped swimming.

"Did she go under?" Harley asked, amazed.

"Help!" we heard Harper cry.

Harley dove in and I followed. Just before I did, I heard another loud splash on my right. Both Harley and I swam as fast as we could. Harley was well ahead of me, but when I raised my head on my stroke, I saw another person silhouetted in the water. It was Uncle Roy. He was up and then under, and then I saw Aunt Alison's head bobbing as he dragged her back toward the dock. We reached Harper who was choking on some water and seemed to be struggling as well.

"Are you all right?" Harley asked him.

"Yeah, yeah," he said, catching his breath.

I swam past them, Harley and Harper followed. Uncle Roy reached shallow enough water to stop swimming and scoop Aunt Alison into his arms, carrying her toward the dock.

"Uncle Roy, is she all right?" I screamed.

"Go get your daddy," he called back to me.

As soon as my feet touched bottom, I waded in and then, without looking back, ran as fast as I could to the house. I went up the ramp instead of the stairs and practically tore off the front door lunging in.

"Daddy!" I screamed. *"Daddy, hurry!"*

He stepped out of the sitting room and looked at me, eyes wide.

"What?"

"It's Aunt Alison. She nearly drowned. Uncle Roy pulled her out to the dock. Hurry!"

Mommy wheeled up behind him and followed as quickly as she could. Daddy leaped over the railing instead of taking the stairs and ran toward the dock where Uncle Roy had Aunt Alison lying on her back.

"What happened, Summer?" Mommy asked.

"Aunt Alison drove up with some new boyfriend, and they decided to go skinny-dipping. I swam away to the raft to join Harley; they started to come out when suddenly she just went under."

"Oh no. She must have gotten a cramp. Wheel me down, quickly."

I pushed her toward the dock. Daddy was already involved in resuscitating her. He was breathing into her mouth, feeling for a pulse, then he began CPR. Her body seemed limp, her eyes shut. My heart was thumping so hard, I thought I would simply fold up on the ground. She looked dead.

Daddy never panicked. He just went through his steps methodically, never looking up, never speaking. Uncle Roy, fully clothed except for his shoes, stood by, drenched. Harper had his jeans draped over his private parts as he sat dumbly on the edge of the dock watching. Harley came over to stand beside Mommy and me.

"Austin?" Mommy finally called. He shook his head but kept working.

Finally, some water trickled out of the corners of Aunt Alison's mouth and that was followed by spasmodic coughing. Daddy looked up and nodded, smiling.

"Summer, give me your towel," he called and I hurriedly did so. He draped it over her and gradually helped her to catch her breath. Immediately, she turned her head and vomited. After that, she groaned and leaned against Daddy.

"Let's get her into the house," he said. He lifted

her carefully and carried her toward the house.

Uncle Roy looked at Harper.

"Get dressed," he ordered. "Didn't you see these two young people here?"

Harper moved as quickly as he could, abject terror in his face. I started to push Mommy up the path and Harley joined in to help me.

"I didn't know she was coming here," Mommy muttered. "It would have been just horrible, just horrible."

"Your father's terrific," Harley said. "Man, he never blinked. He was looking right into the face of death and telling him to get going."

I nodded and smiled at him.

"It was Uncle Roy who got her out in time though," I reminded him.

"Yeah," he said looking back at Uncle Roy, who stood hovering like a prison guard over Aunt Alison's boyfriend, Harper. "I didn't know he could swim like that. Lucky he was out there. Or," he said glancing at me, "maybe it wasn't luck. Maybe he's been out there more often than we know."

Mommy put her hand on mine and looked up at me.

I knew why.

Uncle Roy was always there, always looking out for her.

He was still looking out for her when he was watching over me.

I should be trembling, I thought. I should be so afraid after what had happened to me and what

223

had nearly happened to Aunt Alison.

But I wasn't.

I had all these men about me: Daddy, Uncle Roy, and Harley.

It was like having a warm blanket wrapped around you whenever you even thought about trembling.

Harley had to leave us at the door.

"I better get out of my wet suit," he said.

"Come back," I urged. He knew I meant I was still shaken up from it all and wanted company.

"Sure," he said smiling.

He shot off toward his house like a track star.

"I'm not even going to tell your grandmother Megan about this," Mommy said. Then she looked up at me, a smile around her eyes. "If I did, she'd only write it on a piece of paper and bury it in the backyard.

"One of these days, all those seeds of unhappiness are going to sprout into black trees with tears dangling instead of leaves," she added.

"How horrible," I said.

Mommy grew very serious.

"You don't bury your bad times and pretend they never happened, honey. You face them and you conquer them. Then you can bury them.

"That's what I've done," she said. "That's what I'll always do."

She said it as if she knew there was more to come.

9

The Lake's Victim

Aunt Alison never so much as said thank you to Uncle Roy. When she was resting comfortably, she cried that she was hungry and then, when she saw Daddy, she teased him instead of thanking him for his part in saving her life, too.

"I couldn't ask for a better mouth to give me mouth-to-mouth, Austin," she told him. "I feel a little sore here," she said indicating her breast, "where you pumped so hard. It probably would have been easier if I was flat chested."

Daddy never really blushed like other people. He got red only around the crest of his cheeks and around his eyes.

"It would have been easier if you hadn't gone swimming," Mommy commented for him.

We had put Aunt Alison in the guest bedroom. Mrs. Geary had brought up some hot chicken noodle soup for her, but she wouldn't take a spoonful. She insisted she needed something stronger and finally settled for a vodka and orange juice. After that, Daddy took Harper downstairs to give him something to eat and drink, while Mommy and I stayed with Aunt Alison.

"I guess I've embarrassed the family again," she told Mommy as soon as Daddy and Harper left.

"What were you thinking, Alison? How could you bring a man here to go nude swimming with Summer and Harley right there anyway? Roy's very upset, too."

"Roy's upset? He's not the one who almost drowned. And besides, what is he upset about? He's no angel."

"I wouldn't say anything unpleasant about Roy. If it wasn't for him, you most likely would have drowned. Apparently, your new boyfriend was incapable of acting quickly."

Aunt Alison pouted a few moments and then she shrugged and smiled at us.

"I didn't bring him along to be a lifeguard anyway. He's better at other things. Well, maybe just one thing," she added laughing. "How long am I supposed to lie here like this?"

"Austin says you've had a very traumatic experience. You don't realize what a toll it's taken on your body yet. He said you should go to sleep."

"Poo on that," Aunt Alison said sitting up and not caring that the blanket fell from her naked breasts.

"Cover yourself for godsakes, Alison. If you're not embarrassed, you might embarrass someone else," Mommy chided.

Aunt Alison smirked and looked at me.

"You don't look so terrible," she said. "For what happened to you, that is."

"Her pain is not on the outside, Alison."

"Oh, pain. Half the time that I've been with a man, it's been like a rape. Either I'm doing the raping or they are," she added with a laugh.

"If you think you're being clever and outrageous, you're not," Mommy said, her eyes small. "Summer is only sixteen."

"I was fourteen the first time I did it," she told me unabashedly. "I didn't enjoy it, of course. Too painful and the boy was a clod. I kept thinking if this is what I can expect, I'll be a nun."

She laughed and drank her vodka and orange juice. Then she took a deep breath and slipped down under the blanket, moaning like a kitten.

"Maybe Austin's right. Maybe I am more tired than I think."

"Of course he's right."

She looked at me again.

"Mother was so worried about her. She was never as worried about me," she told Mommy and pouted. "Poor little Summer this and poor little Summer that. It was coming out of my ears. I had to get away for a while, and that's when I found Harper. Umm," she said snuggling under the blanket, "what a find."

Mommy glanced at me and then looked at Alison who closed her eyes and seemed to fall asleep immediately. We both waited a few moments, then Mommy nodded and we started out as quietly as we could.

She moaned.

"Send Harper up, please," she muttered.

"You should just rest for a while, Alison."

"Rest, pest," she mocked.

Mommy shook her head and we continued out. Harley had arrived and was in the sitting room with Daddy and Harper, who still looked absolutely terrified.

"How is she doing now?" Daddy asked first.

"Unchanged," Mommy said, smirking. Daddy laughed. Harper raised his eyebrows with surprise and confusion. "She's asking for you, Harper, so you might as well go back up to her," Mommy told him.

"Oh. Sure," he said rising. "Well, thanks," he told Daddy and left.

"What a night," Daddy said.

"You were wonderful, Austin."

"I only did what I'm trained to do. Everyone should know some first aid, especially CPR," he said directing himself to Harley and me.

"I'd like to learn more," Harley said.

"I'll give you some quick lessons this week. Stop by when you get a chance," Daddy told him.

"Thanks."

"Where's Roy?" Daddy asked. "I bet he could use a stiff drink after all that."

"He's home. My mother's been . . . a lot more depressed than usual," Harley revealed.

"Oh?" Mommy said. "What do you mean,

Harley? What is she doing?"

"That's just it. She's not doing much. Sleeping mostly. Roy's been trying to get her to eat. She barely nibbles on anything."

"I'd better get over there tomorrow," Mommy said. "Maybe I can get her to do a little shopping with me."

Harley looked at the floor. I knew from the way he tightened his mouth and lowered his eyes that there was much more to tell, but he was too embarrassed or too frightened to talk about it, even with us.

"I'd better get home," he suddenly decided and stood.

"I'll walk halfway with you," I offered.

"Thanks," he mumbled. He looked at Mommy and Daddy, smiled and said good night.

We didn't speak until we were outside.

"I really thought she was dead, didn't you?" Harley asked.

"For a while, I did, but I kept telling myself Daddy would save her."

"Yeah, it's nice to have a father you can believe in and trust like that," Harley said.

"Uncle Roy was the big hero, Harley. Even Daddy says that," I reminded him. He nodded. "He came out of nowhere like Superman."

"That's Roy."

We walked quietly for a few moments, Harley keeping his head down.

"What else is wrong with Aunt Glenda, Harley?" I decided to ask.

He stopped, his hands dug so deeply into his pants' pockets, he looked like he would rip out the stitching. Even in the darkness, I could see the tears cloud his eyes, despite his grand attempts to prevent it. Harley was always afraid of revealing his emotions. I could remember him as a child, tightening his face into that inscrutable mask. There was a second level in the depth of his eyes that I had only recently learned to reach.

"She's been walking in her sleep," he disclosed. "And not only in the middle of the night. Almost whenever she falls asleep these days, she rises and does things."

"What kinds of things?"

"Looking after Latisha as if she was still there. I don't mean just caring for her clothes or seeing that the room is clean and going out to the grave. She's talking to her aloud and then she's . . ."

"What?"

"She sits in the rocking chair in Latisha's nursery and holds her arms as if Latisha was in them and sings lullabies to her. I woke up night before last and heard her singing. It was a little scary. I don't mean like ghost scary. It was frightening to listen to her doing something crazy like that.

"Next thing I hear is Roy urging her to come back to bed. She tells him she's got to get the baby back to sleep first, and he's talking to her as if he sees Latisha in her arms, too, saying, 'She's asleep, Glenda. Put her in her crib.'

"All sorts of memories came rushing back when

I heard this stuff. I thought I was still dreaming, in a nightmare, you know what I mean?"

"I can imagine."

"I got up and looked in on them. Roy was squatted down beside her, stroking her arm and talking softly, trying to get her to wake up, snap out of it, but she just wouldn't. Finally, he turns and sees me there. He just stared out at me. I never saw him look like that. He wasn't angry or sad. He was more like . . ."

"Like what, Harley?"

"More like he was afraid. Seeing fear in Roy's face made me turn to ice inside.

" 'What's wrong with her?' I asked him.

" 'Just go back to sleep,' he said. 'There's nothing you can do.'

" 'Ma!' I called to her anyway and she . . . she started to cry. She cried so hard, her body looked like it was going to shatter into pieces. Roy held onto her and she shook him, too. He waved me away and I went back into my room. It seemed like hours went by before I heard him leading her back to bed.

"She didn't get up in the morning to make us any breakfast. Roy did it. I looked in on her, but she was dead to the world. I was afraid to leave her. I wanted to call your mother, but Roy got angry and said Rain had enough troubles of her own. She didn't need his, too.

" 'It's not just your trouble,' I snapped at him. 'She's my mother.'

" 'Then don't cause her any worry,' was his response. Like what was happening might be my fault."

"I don't think he meant that, Harley."

"Yeah, well," he said, walking on, "he should have called your mother. Sometimes, I think he worries more about her than he does about my mother, his wife."

"No, I . . ."

"You don't hear what he says to us, Summer," Harley blurted, spinning on me. "What he says to my mother, I mean. As long as I can remember, he's compared her to your mother, made her feel she wasn't as pretty or as good. If my mother ever complained about anything, anything at all, his comeback was always, 'You should be glad you're not in a wheelchair, Glenda.' He's been holding up that picture of your mother for years and years, using it like a whip to keep my mother down like some caged animal."

He continued, imitating Uncle Roy.

" 'Why don't you take as good care of yourself as Rain does? She's a paraplegic, and she's still concerned about her hair, her face. She still takes care of her health and does what exercise she can.' Stuff like that."

"I never heard it," I said.

"No, he wouldn't do it in front of you or your mother or father."

"Maybe he thought it was good, that it would help," I suggested weakly.

He stopped again and smiled at me, but a wry smile.

"C'mon, Summer. You're smarter than I am, even though I'm a year older. You know Roy idolizes your mother. He doesn't just treat her like a stepsister. She just has to look at something she wants done and he's leaping to do it."

I looked away quickly.

"I'm not saying your mother doesn't deserve his devotion. She's done a lot for him, but I know there was a time when he thought he could be her husband."

"What?" I said spinning back to face him. "How do you know that?" I asked, astounded. He had never so much as suggested such a thing to me.

"I heard a conversation between them once when she was at the house visiting my mother. My mother was in the kitchen, and he thought I was upstairs.

"Your mother didn't encourage him or anything, but I never heard him whine like he did that day, moaning about cruel fate playing a dirty trick on them, making them think they were real brother and sister."

"I know," I admitted. "Mommy's told me about that, but that's over. That's long over."

"It's never over," Harley said. "When you fall so deeply in love with someone, it's like your heart's been scarred forever, Summer. You can do all sorts of things to distract yourself and try to forget, but every time you have an unoccupied moment in your thoughts, she'll come rushing back in like the tide."

"How do you know that?" I asked, impressed.

"I know because it happens to me with you," he confessed. "You're always asking me about other girls I've been with. Well, that's why it's never worked for me. I see you when I kiss them. You asked, so I'm telling you," he concluded.

I didn't know what to say. I just stared at him. He looked at me and then out at the lake.

"I've got to get home. See you tomorrow," he said and hurried off.

"Harley," I called.

He turned.

"What?"

"I hope you have a good night."

He laughed.

"Keep Alison out of the lake and we'll all get some rest," he said.

I watched him walk through the shadows toward his house, toward the deeper shadows that waited within. It filled me with such pangs of sadness; my own tears, hot and heavy, came flowing down my cheeks. As soon as I entered the house, I ran up to my room and closed my door.

When I looked at my bed, I was suddenly afraid to go to sleep, afraid of my own dreams.

I heard a peal of laughter coming from Aunt Alison's room so I went back to my door and peered out. She was dressed in her shorts and halter. She and Harper were headed for the stairway. I opened my door farther.

"Where are you going, Aunt Alison? Why aren't you resting, like Daddy told you?"

"Resting is for old people. We're heading for the beach. Harper has an uncle who owns a small hotel, and we called ahead and made arrangements to occupy the honeymoon suite."

"Honeymoon suite?"

She laughed and touched my cheek.

"Summer, honey, you don't have to be married to have a honeymoon."

Harper laughed harder.

"Does Mommy know you're leaving?" I asked.

"We're just going down to tell her. I know she'll be heartbroken," she said. Then she leaned closer to me. "Don't let that stupid incident at the music school ruin your sex life, and don't let my little escapade prevent you from going skinny-dipping with Harley. If I was your age, I'd go with him," she added, then laughed and started down the stairs.

I stepped back and closed my bedroom door.

Blood couldn't mean all that much, I thought. She shared some with Mommy, but they were as different as the spring and the fall. Yet, what she had said had titillated me in an unexpected way. It frightened me. What if I was more like her than I thought?

The demons that slept in her blood might be sleeping in mine; nudged, they, too, could rise to the surface like bubbles and make themselves snap and pop when I least expected it. Perhaps we had no one more to fear than ourselves. Maybe that's what frightened Uncle Roy.

And Harley.

And me.

I rushed myself into sleep like I had rushed into the relief of the lake, seeking to be soothed, seeking to forget.

Grandmother Megan buried secrets in the yard. The rest of us buried them in our hearts.

Who was better off?

I woke to the sound of a screaming ambulance siren. My first thought was Aunt Alison has done something else. I heard a great deal of commotion below in our house. For a moment I just sat there listening. Then I rose and went to the windows. The ambulance was making its way toward Uncle Roy's home, but what I saw was Uncle Roy, Daddy, Harley and two of our grounds workers standing in a small circle.

"What's going on?" I asked myself aloud and hurried to get into some clothes and down the stairs. "Mommy? Mrs. Geary?" I called at the foot of the stairway. There was only silence in response. More frightened than ever, I rushed outside and saw Mommy with Mrs. Geary standing beside her. Mommy was holding her hand and they were both looking across the lake. The ambulance had stopped and the paramedics were kneeling beside someone.

"Mommy!" I shouted and ran to them. "What's happening?"

"Oh honey, it's Glenda," she said. Her cheeks were streaked where tears had traveled and were still traveling.

"What? What happened?"

"We're not sure yet, Summer. Uncle Roy called for Daddy and then they called for the ambulance."

"That poor woman," Mrs. Geary muttered.

"Harley," I cried and started toward them.

"Summer, wait!"

"Oh no." I broke into a trot, not feeling my feet touch the ground.

As I drew closer, I saw that Harley had turned his back on everyone else and had his head down. Roy stood beside him talking to him, but Harley just kept shaking his head.

"Daddy!" I cried when I stopped running and broke into a fast walk.

The paramedics had Aunt Glenda on the stretcher and were lifting her to carry her to the ambulance, only . . . they had the sheet over all of her!

"Summer, don't go any farther," Daddy said and enveloped me in his arms and body to keep me from getting any closer.

"What happened to her?" I asked through my flood of tears.

"The lake finally claimed a victim," he said in response and turned as the doors of the ambulance were being closed.

"How?"

"Some time early in the morning, she rose quietly and went down and out of the house. In her nightgown, she walked into the lake. When Uncle Roy realized she was gone, he went running through the house and then he came out but couldn't find her. He spotted her in the lake, face down," Daddy said. Tears weren't coming from his eyes, but I knew he was crying inside. His voice cracked. He took deep breaths to keep his sobs contained.

After the paramedics closed the ambulance door, they stopped to talk to Uncle Roy, who listened and nodded. Harley, who had his back to us the whole time, broke away and just started to run toward the woods.

"Harley!" I screamed after him. He seemed to run faster.

I broke free of Daddy's arms.

"Let him alone for a while, Summer," Daddy urged.

"No, Daddy," I replied with firmness. "This is the worst time for him to be alone."

I started after Harley. Daddy didn't try to stop me or call me back anymore. I glanced at Uncle Roy. His tears had drawn streaks of salt down his cheeks and his chin. Harley disappeared into the woods, but I continued. When I reached the perimeter, I called for him. He didn't respond, but I continued after him. I could hear branches cracking ahead. I called and called and listened, but all I heard were more branches and sticks being smashed in his path.

The woods grew thicker and darker. When we were younger, Harley and I did come here often, but we never went too far into the forest. There were acres of it in this area of the surrounding terrain. We did have a favorite spot, a collection of large rocks near a stream that sometimes ran heavy and sometimes was practically dried up. We collected some of the more colorful polished stones, which we pretended were very valuable jewels. He seemed to be heading in that direction, so I plodded on, hopeful I'd catch up with him there.

At first I didn't see him. Then I caught sight of his sneakers and the bottom of his legs behind one of the larger rocks. I walked slowly around it and then stood there looking down at him. He wasn't crying. He was sitting on a rock, staring at the water and fingering a small branch nervously. He didn't look up, but he knew I was there.

"Harley," I said.

"Isn't it strange how water that we need to live can also be deadly. Look at it, how pretty it is rushing over those old jewels. Put your hand into it today, and it will feel so good, so cool. Then put more of yourself until you're completely in it and it will claim you and smother the life out of you.

"Do you think that's true of everything, Summer, everything that's pretty, that tempts you?"

"No," I said.

He nodded, a crazed smile on his lips.

"What happened to her, Harley? Why did she go swimming in her nightgown so early in the morning?"

"Swimming?" He laughed. "You think she went swimming?"

"I don't know. Daddy said Uncle Roy said . . ."

239

"She didn't go swimming. Who knows what she saw in the water? Maybe she saw Latisha calling her or maybe she looked out at the lake and thought this was a cool, beautiful way to get back with Latisha. Maybe she saw what had almost happened to your aunt Alison and it gave her ideas.

"My mother wasn't much of a swimmer, Summer. You know that. You could count on the fingers of one hand how many times you and I ever saw her go swimming. And she never swam anyway. She just waded."

He paused and looked down.

"Maybe she was walking in her sleep. I don't know. No one knows. They can only do what I'm doing, guess."

"What did Uncle Roy say?"

Harley didn't respond.

"Harley?"

"He said it was his fault for falling into such a damn deep sleep. He was exhausted from working all day and then spending all that effort and energy on your aunt Alison. So he didn't hear my mother get up and go off, but he still expected she would be in the house, maybe in Latisha's nursery pretending she was holding her or maybe downstairs making something for her to eat. When he didn't see her in the house, he thought she was up at the grave, and when he didn't see her there, he started to get worried and frightened. That was when he turned his eyes to the lake.

"His scream woke me," Harley said. "It was the

most god-awful scream, like an animal. I actually shook for a moment. Then I got up and pulled on my pants, grabbed a shirt — practically tripped and killed myself getting my feet into my sneakers — and ran out to see what was going on.

"By then he was pulling her in and then carrying her in his arms. 'Call Austin!' he shouted and I called your father. He was over here in minutes and tried the same CPR stuff on my mother, only it wasn't working so he told Roy to call the paramedics. You saw the rest, I guess."

I nodded and sat beside him.

"Maybe she's better off," he muttered.

"Oh Harley, don't say such a thing."

"I don't know what else to say. She wasn't getting any better; as you know, lately she got worse. But there used to be times when she would stop mourning, stop praying, stop thinking about Latisha for a while and look at me as though she really saw me."

He smiled.

"She had this look on her face sometimes, this look like she had just woken from a long, long sleep and realized I had grown up.

" 'You're going to be a handsome young man, Harley,' she would say. 'Your daddy was very handsome. Poisonous handsome,' she called it because all he had to do was smile at a woman and she would weaken in her knees. I'd beg her to tell me more about him, but she would shake her head and remember her religion. 'No, he was the devil. The devil can have a very pleasing face,' she told me. 'Don't think about him. I shouldn't have spoken like that. God forgive me,' she would say and go pray for a pardon.

"When she saw me like that, really saw me, she would talk to me like my mother should, asking me questions about school, about what I liked to do. It was a torment though, a torture that I grew to hate, Summer."

"Why?"

"Because she would soon return to her dark, depressing state of mind, and when I spoke to her, she would look at me as if I was just a dream. I stopped talking to her, stopped asking her questions, sometimes stopped seeing her. She became a ghost long before she drowned today, Summer. My mother died a long, long time ago. I've been an orphan longer than I care to remember," he said.

He tossed his little branch into the stream and we both watched the water carry it off.

"Oh, Harley, I'm so sorry. It's so terrible."

"Yeah," he said. "Terrible."

He leaned over and scooped some water into his palms.

"You happy now?" he screamed at it. "You satisfied? You've got her! You've got her!"

His face was so red, the veins in his neck straining and tightening against his skin. He looked like he might explode if I touched him, but I did.

"Harley."

Suddenly, he just started to cry, his whole body

shaking. I put my arm around his shoulder and he brought his head to mine and sobbed. I kissed his hair and held him tightly.

"Why did I sleep so deeply? Why didn't I hear her walking out?" he moaned through his tears.

"She was probably barefoot, gliding over that floor, Harley. You can't blame yourself for that, no more than Uncle Roy can blame himself."

"We should have been watching her more carefully. She wasn't right in the head. We should have expected something like this."

He sat up, grinding the tears out of his eyes with his balled fist. Then he nodded to himself and stood, his face filling with that stoic determination.

"C'mon," he said. "There's no point in trying to run away from it."

I rose and he let me take his hand. We didn't speak. We walked through the forest. Birds fluttered from branch to branch around us like a curious crowd of onlookers wondering about the intruders. When we stepped back into the sunlight, the ambulance was gone. There was no one standing about Harley's house.

"Maybe it was just a dream," I whispered.

"A dream we both had? Not a chance," Harley said walking faster.

"Where are you going?" I asked as we drew closer to his house.

"Up to my room, I guess."

"Why don't you come home with me and have a little breakfast or at least some coffee? Mommy would want you to, Harley."

"Not now," he said. "I've got to be by myself."

"Will you come in a while?"

"I don't know."

"If you don't, I'll come back for you, okay?"

He didn't answer. He walked to the front door and went in. I stood there for a moment and then folded my arms under my breasts and walked with my head down all the way back to my house, feeling so empty inside, I had to keep wondering myself if all this was really happening.

Mommy and Mrs. Geary were in the kitchen. Mommy was sipping some coffee. They both looked up quickly when I stepped in.

"How is he?" Mommy asked.

I shook my head and started to cry again. Mrs. Geary rushed over to embrace me and hold me.

"Did he tell you what happened?" Mommy asked and I described the events as Harley had related them to me.

"That poor woman," Mommy said.

"Where's Daddy?"

"He went with Uncle Roy to the hospital. There are many legal things to look after. Maybe you should have asked Harley to come here, honey," she said.

"I did. He wanted to be alone."

"I'll call him," Mommy promised, but I didn't think Harley would answer the phone and told her so.

When Daddy returned, he looked pale and tired. He knelt down to embrace Mommy, and they held each other for the longest time while I sat waiting. Then he sat and looked at both of us.

"Roy's pretty broken up, blames himself. He says he should have brought her to a doctor, maybe had her in some sort of clinic."

"She wouldn't have gone to a doctor, and she would have just died away from here, Austin."

"I told him that, but he insists this happened because he ignored too much."

"I'll go over there now," Mommy said.

Daddy nodded.

"I'll drive you."

"I want to go too, Daddy," I said.

"Okay, honey."

"You don't need to drive me, Austin. Summer will push me in the wheelchair. It's more trouble to get in and out of the van," she decided.

I wheeled Mommy out. Daddy said he would join us in a while after he made some business calls. He had some things to do for Roy as well.

A long time ago, Uncle Roy had built a small ramp at the rear of his front porch just for the times Mommy would visit. She wasn't there all that often, but he built it anyway. I came to realize that he had built it hoping she would come to visit more.

I knocked and called through the screen door. Uncle Roy told me to come in, not expecting Mommy was with me. He was sitting by himself in the living room. When he saw her, he got up quickly.

"Oh Roy, I'm so, so sorry," Mommy told him.

She reached up for him and he fell to his knees and buried his head in her lap as if he was a little boy. She stroked his hair. He didn't cry. He just held himself against her. She looked up at me.

"Why don't you put up some coffee and see about something to eat, honey?"

I nodded and moved quickly to the kitchen, glancing up the stairway toward Harley's room. The noise I made and the murmur of Mommy and Roy's voices caught his curiosity, and minutes later I turned to see him standing in the kitchen doorway.

"Mommy's here to visit," I said. "I've put up some coffee. How about something to eat? Toast and jam . . . cheese?"

"Whatever," Harley said. He dropped himself in a chair and stared at the table while I worked. As soon as the coffee was ready, I poured two cups. I knew Uncle Roy liked it black and Mommy liked a touch of milk.

"I'll just bring this to them," I told Harley. He looked up and nodded.

Halfway down the hallway, I heard Uncle Roy say, "I'm being punished, Rain. I'm being punished for still having so strong a feeling for you."

"Don't be foolish, Roy."

"God knows and God's punished me by taking my child and my wife," he insisted. "It's all my fault. All the tragedy and the misery is on my head."

"Stop it. That's stupid talk and you know it. I won't listen to it," Mommy said harshly.

"Mama knew. That was the real reason she was so eager to send you off to live here. She wanted you far away from me, and she thought if she got you firmly planted in this rich, white world, I'd have no place and no entry. She didn't anticipate all that happened and your bringing me here, but she knew and I knew she knew. I should have followed her secret wishes and forgotten you."

"Please, stop it, Roy. Please," Mommy pleaded.

"My fault," he muttered. "My fault."

I let out the hot breath I had been trapping in my lungs. Before I took a step forward, however, I turned and realized Harley was right behind me. He had been there the whole time, too, and had heard every word. His eyes fixed firmly on mine.

"Coffee's getting cold," he said.

I hurried ahead and brought them their coffee. Harley followed in slowly and Mommy took his hand and spoke to him softly, urging him to be strong.

"You want to keep thinking about your future, Harley, and work hard to do the things that would have made her proud."

He nodded and thanked her. I returned to the kitchen and prepared a tray of food. Afterward, everyone came into the dining room and ate something. Daddy arrived and he and Uncle Roy went off to discuss the funeral arrangements. Mommy insisted Harley come to our house for dinner. He said he would, but he didn't. When I called, he said he was just too tired and told me to thank Mommy.

The days before and around Aunt Glenda's funeral seemed to be days without hours and minutes, just a flow of time that made every moment seem exactly like the moment before and the moment after. It rained the day before the funeral, but cleared up that morning. All of the people who worked for Mommy and Grandmother Megan's company showed up at the church. The death had been ruled accidental, even though anyone who knew about Aunt Glenda knew it was the result of some form of madness.

Dressed in his suit and tie and standing beside Roy, Harley looked so much older. It was as if his mother's death had ripped him boldly out of his teenage years and dragged him kicking and screaming into the dark side of manhood. He didn't cry during the church service. He kept his face forward, his eyes fixed on his own thoughts, and he seemed to move in and out of consciousness as the congregation rose to sing a hymn and then sat and rose again. Finally, it ended.

Aunt Glenda, at Uncle Roy's insistence, was buried in the plot beside Latisha. She was finally back with the child she had lost. After the internment, we had food and drink prepared at our house. Harley was there, but very uncomfortable, just able to nod or mutter to all those who came to him to offer condolences. I sat beside him constantly and made him eat something.

Before it ended, he went home. I offered to walk with him, but he told me he just wanted to get home quickly and go to sleep. He promised he would call me in the morning. He did, very late, but we spent most of the day together, talking and going for a row. He agreed to come to dinner when my mother threatened to have Mrs. Geary cook it at his house if he didn't.

The following day Uncle Roy went back to work. He couldn't sit around and mourn anymore; he said that working would at least occupy his mind. Harley didn't go back with him. He remained home. I called, but he was very secretive about what he was doing, telling me he would call me later.

Later ran on and on into the late afternoon. Mommy had invited both him and Uncle Roy to dinner again, but Harley didn't come with him this time. Uncle Roy made excuses for him and said maybe it was better Harley had some time to himself.

"I'll try to get him back to work in a day or so," he promised.

I called after dinner, but Harley didn't answer the phone. I wanted to go over there to see why not. Mommy stopped me, however.

"Sometimes people need some space, honey. Give him a chance. He needs to grieve in his own way," she advised.

Reluctantly, I listened and went up to my room to read and watch television so I wouldn't think about him. It was difficult. I don't know how many times I went to the window to look across the lake at his house. He didn't have many rooms lit, and I wondered if he was even there. I hadn't heard the sound of his motorcycle, but I thought he might be walking or sitting down at the lake.

What could he be doing all day and all night? I wondered. I worried so much about him, I thought it would just be impossible for me to go to sleep. I tried, of course. I prepared for bed and slipped under my blanket, listening to the sounds in the house. Daddy and Mommy had come up hours ago and were in their room. The house had its usual creaks and groans in the summer wind, but I heard something different and listened very hard. It made my heart thump faster.

Footsteps in the hallway were barely audible, but I heard them and then, seconds later, I heard my bedroom doorknob turning and sat up to see Harley.

"Summer?" he called. "Are you awake?"

"Harley! What are you doing here?"

He didn't answer immediately. He stepped in and closed the door behind him. There was just enough light from the new moon coming through the window for me to see him hurry to my bed-side. He sat quickly.

"What is it?" I asked.

"I spent all day going through my mother's old things," he replied, "things she had buried in boxes in our attic closet. There were so many things I had never seen before, things from when she was young, letters and memories, ribbons and pictures of her family. I don't know why she never showed them, but she didn't."

"Oh," I said thinking it was a very natural thing

for him to have done. You want to hold onto the memory of someone you love. You would do anything that would help.

"Then, I found it," he announced excitedly.

"Found what?"

"My father's name. There was a letter he had written to her, explaining that he had to go on a job."

"What is his name?" I asked.

"Fletcher Victor. My real last name is Victor," he told me with great pride. It was as if he had discovered he came from royalty, but I guessed that discovering your real identity had to be as wonderful.

"Did you learn any more about him?" I asked.

"Yes," he said, "but not from the letters. I called Timmy Gross, this guy in my class who is a computer whiz. I'm practically the only one who ever talks to him in school. He talks about going on the Internet like some people used to talk about going to outer space. Anyway, I gave him my father's name, and he ran a search and guess what? He located him. A name like Fletcher Victor is kind of unique. There were twelve, but eight were easy to rule out. They were either too old or had never been out of their state. We narrowed it down to four and started on them.

"Finally, I reached one who was very quiet when I described myself and my mother. He listened and at the end of my little speech, he said, yes, he was my father."

"No!"

"Yes, he did and guess what else he did after I told him my mother was dead?"

"What?"

"He invited me to come to see him and maybe, if we got along, to live with him. He's in upstate New York, a place called Centerville."

"What are you going to do?"

"I want to go, at least to visit."

"What does Uncle Roy say?"

"I haven't told him. I'm not going to. He'll probably be happy to see me go anyway. Especially now," he added.

"I won't."

"I know and that's why I'm here."

"Why?"

"I want you to come with me, just for the visit," he said. "I'll need your opinion about everything and there's no one I trust more than I trust you," he added.

"Daddy would never let me," I said.

"You'll do what I'm going to do," he replied. "You'll leave a note and just go. Will you?" Before I could even think of an answer he followed with, "It means everything to me."

It was as if someone had poured ice water over me and then threw me into an oven.

"I need you to be with me for this," he whispered.

He said it with such desperation in his voice, I couldn't refuse him any more than I could refuse to breathe.

Impulsively, perhaps, perhaps madly, I said, "I'll go."

After he had left, my thunderous heart kept me up almost the remainder of the night.

What had I promised?

What would I do?

10

The Open Road

Late in the morning, Harley stopped by to tell me he was going to the bank to withdraw traveling money.

"I've put in most of my paycheck every week for college money," he explained.

"Then you shouldn't take it out, Harley."

"This is far more important to me, Summer. Besides, I heard your father and Roy talking about my mother's life insurance. There's money coming to me to be placed in a trust for my college expenses or whatever. I wish I never had to touch it," he added. "I'd like that money to be there until I have children of my own and they get it. If things work out with my real father . . ."

His voice drifted off along with his dream. In the bottom of my heart, I felt the icy trickle of warning. To put all your hopes in anyone or any one thing was always dangerous. Mommy had taught me that a long time ago, but I was afraid to say anything discouraging. Harley had emerged from his terrible sorrow and depression because of his discovery. It would be cruel to do anything to stop his climb back into the world of hope and happiness.

"Roy goes to bed about eleven-fifteen. I'll leave about eleven-thirty," he continued, "and I'll walk my cycle up to the garage where I'll wait for you. We'll walk it down to the road and then start it so there's no danger of anyone hearing us go.

"Bring one soft overnight bag of clothing and necessities, okay. We'll get anything else we need later. I should have enough money."

"I have some money in my room," I told him. "I've been throwing loose change and dollars in a drawer. I bet it's more than two hundred dollars."

"Terrific," Harley said. Then he looked at me, his face close to crumbling with happiness. "You're the nicest person I know, Summer. To be willing to do this with me, to be willing to risk everyone's anger, too, is much more than I deserve or should ask of you."

"I'm doing it because I want to do it, Harley."

"I know." He nodded. "Thanks," he said and left for the bank.

Mommy used to tell me I had a face like a storefront window. Anyone could take a good long look at me and see every thought on display, every feeling revealed. I wasn't good at deception; lies in my mouth were like fish out of water. Knowing that, I tried to avoid both her and Mrs. Geary most of the day. Fortunately, it was a day for a piano lesson, so that took up a good deal of time. Then I went up to my room and practiced my clarinet. Daddy had a great deal to do at the office and called to say he would be late for supper. Even with all I had to do and with all that was happening, the passage of time was like thick syrup being poured from a narrow bottle. Every time I looked at the clock, it seemed the hands were stuck in place.

Mommy made only one comment when she saw me going from one thing to another.

"You're fidgety today, Summer. Anything wrong?" she asked.

"No. Just trying to keep myself occupied," I told her.

"I know. Me too," she said. "I'm still thinking about having your father take us on a holiday. Maybe now, more than ever," she added, and went off to talk to Mrs. Geary about the dinner menu.

Of course, I hated being even slightly deceitful. I was in a conflict, a part of me wanting to please Harley and a part of me hating what I would do to Mommy and Daddy by sneaking off. I decided I had better spend a lot more time writing the note I was going to leave behind, so as to make sure I said everything right and made them understand why I had to go and why I hoped they would for-give me.

I sat at my desk and began, writing the first sen-tence and then disliking it and rewriting and re-writing, crumpling the paper four times before I decided I should just write everything simply and honestly. There was no way to disguise the reality of what I was about to do anyway.

Dear Mommy and Daddy,

A few days ago, Harley made a startling discovery. He learned who his real father is and where he is. He wants to go visit him, and he has asked me to go with him. I know he's very nervous about it, maybe even afraid of being disappointed. He needs me with him. The discovery and his new hopes have helped him cope with his great tragedy and sorrow, and I am so happy for him, I have agreed to go.

I know you will be upset about this. I know how much you worry about me, but I also believe you will be understanding and forgive me. I will call you as soon as we arrive and let you know where we are and what we are going to do.

Despite your own misfortune, Mommy, you have always been a giving person, and you have taught me to be the same way. No one is more compassionate than you, Daddy, so you should understand as well.

Love,
Summer

I folded it and put it in an envelope which I would leave at my place by the breakfast table. After that, I chose the things I would take and filled my best soft carry-on bag. Once all that was completed, I had nothing to do but wait. My stomach felt as if it was filled with bubbles popping. I tried reading; I tried watching television. Nothing stopped it. I heard Mommy and Daddy talking softly on their way to bed. Just hearing their voices made me feel more terrible about my secret trip with Harley. They were going to sleep at ease and in the morning, they would be filled with concern. Had I done a horrible thing? Would it be even more horrible to back out now? If so, Harley would be devastated.

I didn't think my legs would work when the time came to go downstairs. I was sure I would trip and make a racket. Somehow, I managed to glide over the floor and down the stairs, barely causing a creak. The whole house seemed to be holding its breath along with me. I paused in the entryway, looked back as if I was saying goodbye forever, and then slipped out the front door.

It was a partly overcast night with a large cloud blocking the moonlight, but I was able easily to see Harley standing in front of the garage. He looked as still as a dream. I took a deep breath and hurried to him.

"Hi," he said.

"Hi."

"Everything go all right?"

"I think so," I said glancing back.

"Okay. Let's go," he said, which turned my heart into a race car engine.

We walked through the shadows and down to the road. Once there, he handed me the extra helmet and showed me how to fasten it. Then we attached my carry-on bag to the rear of the motorcycle.

"Here we go," he said. "Just keep your arms around me if you want or hold onto the handles. I'll go slowly," he promised.

I couldn't speak. I nodded even though he wouldn't see it; then he started the engine, shifted, and we were off.

"Too windy?" he shouted back.

"No, it's fine," I said, but I put my head against him anyway. I closed my eyes, too.

Ordinarily this road was quiet even in the daytime. This late at night there was no one else on it. Every fifteen or twenty minutes, Harley would ask how I was doing.

Harley's plan was for us to get a good start, maybe riding for four or five hours, and then check into a motel and rest until midmorning. We would ride all the following day. He believed we would make it to the upstate New York village late in the afternoon or early in the evening. As it turned out, he was worrying too much about me and decided to stop after only three hours.

We found a relatively inexpensive motel off the highway just outside Baltimore, Maryland. Part of its neon sign was broken and the wood cladding on the units looked like it needed a complete refurbishing. There were only two other units occupied, but we were afraid we might have to ride quite a distance to find another place.

When I dismounted, I felt myself spin. Harley steadied me and laughed.

"A little different from horseback riding, huh?"

"I feel like I'm still moving," I said.

He got us a room with two double beds. It smelled musty and the lights were so weak they made the walls look even a paler yellow. The rug between the two beds was worn thin, the floor beneath peeked through. I was afraid the bed wasn't very clean either, but I was so tired that as soon as I took off my shoes and lay back on the pillow, I think I actually passed out.

The tension had been exhausting. All during our ride, I continually looked back, half-expecting that Daddy had discovered my note and rushed out after us. Of course, he had no idea which direction we were heading; nevertheless, every time I heard a car behind us or saw headlights, my heart stopped and started.

The moment I lay down, Harley went into the bathroom to take a shower. The sound of the water was the last thing I heard until sunlight through the worn-thin, dusty curtain washed over my face and snapped open my eyes.

For a moment I forgot where I was and what we had done. I lay there looking up, thinking and thinking, and then I turned and saw Harley had already risen and was in the bathroom shaving. He stepped out with a towel wrapped around his waist and laughed at me.

"You okay?"

"I don't know. How far did we get?"

"About a hundred and twenty miles, at most," he said. "We've got a big day ahead of us. It's about another three hundred and fifty miles."

I groaned and sat up. My inner thighs ached a little.

"Shower works, but you've got to play with the hot and cold even after you've stepped under it if someone else along the row here turns on theirs, I think. You get yourself up and started, and I'll do some reconnaissance and find us a decent place to have breakfast."

"Okay," I said and rose, feeling very groggy.

After my shower, I woke up. I ran a brush through my hair and got dressed quickly, glancing at my watch and realizing that hours ago, Mommy and Daddy had discovered my note. I didn't want to think about it, but I was sure by now Uncle Roy had been called and they were all meeting and discussing what to do. Harley came in as I was putting on my sneakers.

"We'll have to go about ten miles," he said. "No sense in coming back here."

"Who'd want to?" I complained.

He laughed.

"They ought to charge less when you have to share the room with roaches."

"Roaches?" I glanced around and then quickly picked up my bag and stepped out of the room.

I put on my helmet and we started away. What he had found was a roadside diner. Surprisingly, I was very hungry and ordered juice, blueberry pancakes and coffee. He just had some juice and cold cereal.

"I travel better on a light stomach," he explained.

261

"Does your father know when to expect us?" I asked him.

"Yeah. I gave him a good idea." He took out his map and showed me the remainder of the route we were going to take. Everywhere he could, he chose secondary roads. "We'll be less obvious."

"Why do you think we need to be?" I asked.

He smiled.

"You don't believe for one moment that your father and Roy haven't called the police, do you?"

"The police?"

"Sure."

"Does Roy know where we're going?"

"No, but they'll get a general alert or something going in every direction. Trust me," he said as if he had been a fugitive most of his life. "But don't worry about it," he assured me. "We'll get there."

"Did your father tell you much more about himself?"

"He told me he's a house painter and he's always been pretty busy. He said he has a woman living with him. Her name is Suze and she's Haitian. I guess he wanted me to know all that in case we arrived before he got home from work.

"The village is quite small, but he said we couldn't miss his house if we tried. It's an octagon, built back in 1869, a landmark there."

"Really?" After a beat I said, "What's an octagon house?"

He smiled and took out a pen. Then he spread a napkin between us on the table and drew a rough outline.

"It's exactly what it sounds like, an eight-sided house. His is two-story. They're very rare. Only a few thousand were originally built, mostly in New York, Massachusetts and the Midwest."

"You know so much about architecture, Harley. You've just got to do something with it and not waste your talent."

He shrugged.

"I can't pretend I knew all that, Summer. After I spoke with him, I looked it up in one of my books and learned about it. It was made popular by a man named Orson S. Fowler who claimed that it enclosed more floor space per linear foot of exterior wall than the usual square or rectangle. He said it was more efficient in building costs and prevented heat loss, increased sunlight and ventilation and eliminated dark and useless corners. I can't wait to see it," he added.

I stared at him. His eyes were lit with interest and excitement.

"I think it's just wonderful that you have such a passion for architecture, Harley."

He smiled.

"I'm really a passionate guy."

The waitress brought our food, and we started to eat. I didn't realize how hungry I was until it was set before me. Harley laughed at my gobbling.

"What? Oh. I look like a pig, huh?"

"No," he said. "I just enjoy watching everything you do, Summer."

I felt myself blush.

"Because you're with me, I don't feel afraid of anything," he added.

I nodded.

"But when we get there, Harley, I've got to call my parents."

"Sure," he said. "Let's get there though."

After we ate, we were back on the highways. It was still quite warm and humid, but I started to enjoy riding on the motorcycle as I became more and more accustomed to it, to the way Harley moved his body to make turns and shift gears. I soon felt as if we were attached, my body quickly reacting to every twist of his.

When we turned off the main highways, we passed many nice farmhouses and went through quaint villages. In some places, people took great notice and interest in us; in others, they barely glanced our way. I suppose it depended on how often motorcyclists went through their towns or passed their homes. We rode for hours and hours, stopping once to rest just outside of New York state near a wide stream of water. Harley found a shady spot under a sprawling old oak. We had decided to buy some sandwiches and cold drinks and turn our lunch into a picnic.

"Funny," he said sprawling on the grass and looking up at the sky, "back home, we hardly ever did anything like this. I don't mean barbeques and afternoon parties. I mean just you and me having lunch outside, maybe down by the lake. It feels good, relaxing."

I smiled and unwrapped our sandwiches,

handing him his. We both sat silently for a while, eating and looking at the water that rushed by over the rocks and around the bend.

"I keep wondering what I'm going to feel when I'm face to face with my father for the first time. Do you think we'll look like each other?"

"You'd have to look something like him."

"Yeah, but some people look so much like either their mother or their father. Amber looks like she was cloned from her mother, for example."

"What about me?"

"You look a lot like your mother, but you have your father's eyes and those little freckles," he added laughing. He turned serious for a moment and looked out at the water again. "I guess if someone's your flesh and blood, you've got to be a little alike. It won't be like meeting an ordinary stranger, right?"

"Hardly," I said, but he still looked very nervous about it.

"He wanted me to come. I guess he must have thought about me from time to time, right? He probably got involved in a whole new life and just didn't know how to come back. Maybe I've got a half brother or half sister out there. Maybe two of each!"

"You might," I said. "He didn't mention any other children though, did he?"

"No. But maybe he thought he shouldn't."

"You said Suze was his woman, but he didn't call her his wife."

"No, he didn't, but he could have been married

and divorced or . . . lost his wife. House painter," he muttered. "That figures, right? I mean that he does manual labor, works with his hands. I work with my hands."

"You're very intelligent too, Harley. You're not just some laborer."

He raised his eyebrows and shook his head at me.

"The only reason I graduated was because of your help, Summer."

"Still, you had to be the one to do it and you did and you're going to do more," I insisted.

He laughed and continued to eat. He looked up at some dark clouds on the horizon.

"I hope that storm keeps going the other way," he said. "We're making good time now. I'd hate to have it slow us down."

"Maybe we shouldn't rest too long then," I said as he lowered himself to the grass again and closed his eyes.

"Just a little longer," he said. "Just a little . . ."

I sat there, finishing my sandwich and drink. When I saw what looked like a blackbird on the other side of the stream, I couldn't help but think about Mommy and feel bad for her again.

"Harley?"

He didn't respond so I turned and looked at him. His breathing was regular; his eyes were closed. I was thinking about calling Mommy, but what if she started to cry? What would I do?

I rose and walked to the water. The gurgling sound was mesmerizing and the water itself looked so clear, fresh and cool, I felt like wading in it, baptizing myself in its natural goodness and washing away the darkness that had settled in me ever since Duncan Fields trapped me in his car.

Perhaps that was another reason why I was taking this trip with Harley. Perhaps I was running away as well and trying to leave behind the innocent and emotionally wounded girl who was just soaking herself in self-pity every day. I knew everyone was trying to help me, to get me to feel better, but it was impossible to look into Daddy's eyes or Mommy's or Mrs. Geary's and not see the sympathy and sorrow they felt for me. It was truly as if I had become a marked woman, stained forever. Ironically, it had been only Aunt Alison who left me feeling as if I had merely been scratched. But that wasn't a remedy for me either.

Years ago, it seemed, men and women treated sex and love like halves of the same wondrous experience, the most important experience of life, perhaps the very reason to be. Somehow, sex for people like Aunt Alison and Duncan Fields had become a game, a toy, a pleasure to be had and discarded at will. People used people merely to satisfy themselves, and love, love was forgotten or thought to be just another temporary thing that might or might not be there for us. Why think about it, put any effort into achieving it or finding it? First of all, that required personal sacrifice and actually caring for someone else more than you cared for yourself. Second, it took far too much trust and risk. You had to bare your soul to someone.

The Duncan Fieldses of the world thought they were very clever, I'm sure. They strutted through each day looking for conquests, building a bank account of satisfied lusts and thinking this was what made them wealthy, special, even desirable, but surely they were destined to wake up later in their lives and look around to discover they were all alone and their lives had been nothing much — a dream, streaming by like this water.

I looked ahead to where the stream turned and disappeared and wondered where it ended up. Was there some beautiful lake waiting? Did it have to rush over rough waterfalls first? Did it splinter and trickle off into smaller and smaller streams that eventually dried up? It wouldn't be dammed up here and kept. It would find a way around and follow its destiny.

It was what I had to do, what Harley had to do.

Somehow, deep inside herself, I was sure Mommy understood.

"Hey," Harley said coming up beside me. "Why did you let me fall asleep? If it wasn't for that nervy squirrel coming up close to me . . ."

"I thought you needed the rest," I said.

"Yeah, I got enough. C'mon. We'd better get going," he said.

He glanced at the water.

"It's beautiful and so peaceful," I said.

"I know. Maybe there's something like it waiting for us ahead," he said smiling.

"Maybe."

I followed him back to the motorcycle. We put

on our helmets and moments later, we were flying over the highway, neither of us trying to talk, the wind whistling by, the world around us flowing past so quickly, it resembled the very stream we had just left.

An hour into our ride, a state police patrol car came onto the highway and tracked behind us. Harley saw it in his mirror. I could feel his body tense up.

"Don't keep looking back at him," he shouted. "I'm going to take the next exit."

He did so and I held my breath. Would the policeman follow us off? Had Daddy and Uncle Roy done just what Harley had thought and called the police? How disappointing it would be for us to be turned back before Harley had met his real father at least, I thought. I didn't look back. We followed the ramp to an intersection and quickly turned left as if we knew exactly where we were going. Then we snuck a look and saw the patrol car had not followed. Both of us let out trapped breaths and Harley slowed down. He brought the motorcycle to a stop.

"I thought that was it for sure," he revealed. "I wasn't going to stop if he put on his bubble light. I would have tried to lose him."

"What will we do? What if he's waiting ahead because he realized who we might be?"

He took out his map and studied it a moment.

"We'll stay on this secondary road for a few miles. I'd say we're only a couple of hours away now, even with all the detours," he concluded.

He started off again. The homes we passed looked smaller, older. We didn't go through much of a village either. There was a garage, a quick-stop store and a small restaurant. After another fifteen minutes or so, a red pickup truck shot out of a gravel driveway just ahead of us, causing Harley to slow down quickly. He cursed under his breath. I could see two young men in the truck, the passenger wearing a baseball cap. They were going very slowly now, so Harley pulled out to pass and accelerated. As we went by, the driver leaned out and shouted. He was a thin man who looked like he was in his early thirties but prematurely balding. When he widened his smile, I could see he was missing some teeth on both sides.

I didn't understand what he shouted, but Harley ignored him and went even faster. I thought that was the end of it, but moments later, the truck was right behind us, dangerously close in fact. The driver started to lean on his horn.

"Harley!"

"I know. A couple of idiots," he said. Suddenly, he whipped to the left and slowed so the truck had to go by us. It continued on around the next turn and disappeared.

"What were they doing?"

"Just having their idea of some fun, I guess."

He kept our speed down. When we made the turn however, I didn't see them ahead of us.

"Where are they?"

Harley didn't respond. He sped up again. I held

tightly onto him. Then, out of a field of corn stalks, the truck came shooting onto the highway and fell right behind us again. Again, they drove up behind us, dangerously close and leaned on their horn. A few cars whizzed by in the other direction, but no one paid any attention to what was happening to us. We were now on a long stretch of what looked like an unpopulated area, just cornfields and woods.

My heart was pounding and I could see from the way he was holding himself that Harley was very worried, too. This time when Harley tried to pull into the left lane and slow down, they did the same.

"They'll cause an accident!" I screamed.

I knew Harley was afraid to stop. He tried to go faster, but they were able to keep up with us and I thought, with our not knowing the highway that well, it was even more dangerous to go faster. Now the wind was tearing at my skin. Our bags flapped madly.

"Harley!"

"Just hold on!" he cried. We were coming up to a sharper turn. Now, they were just pressing down on their horn continuously. I wanted to put my hands over my ears. The noise was deafening.

"They must be drunk or crazy," Harley shouted.

At the end of the turn was a gravel road into the field on the right. Harley made an instant decision. Without hitting the brakes because he was afraid of their truck smashing into us, he whipped to his right and into the gravel drive. They flew by us, but Harley lost control and we spun and then fell over, both fortunately landing in the grassy area where there were no rocks, but when I rolled, my left foot got caught and I felt it twist badly. The pain shot up my leg. I barely had time to scream.

The motorcycle stalled. Harley got to his feet as quickly as he could and I rolled over on my back and reached for my ankle.

"Summer, are you all right?" he cried dropping to his knees beside me.

I waited a moment, listening for the sound of any other pain announcing itself somewhere else on my body, but nothing else came. My ankle was enough, however. I groaned, the tears coming to my eyes.

"My ankle," I said.

He went right to it and pressed softly around the ankle bone.

"It doesn't feel broken," he said. "You probably twisted it badly."

"Who were those men?"

"Just two idiots out for some thrills at our expense," he said looking back at the road. We both listened for a moment, but thankfully heard no returning vehicle. "We'll have to get some ice on that ankle as soon as possible," Harley said. "You hurt anywhere else?"

"I don't think so."

"I'm sorry, Summer. Damn, I thought that was the best thing to do."

"It probably was. They wouldn't let you lose them any other way."

I started to sit up and he held me.

"What about your motorcycle?"

"I don't know," he said.

He went to it and stood it up, inspecting as much as he could.

"It doesn't look like anything's broken."

He tried starting it and after a few attempts, it did start and seem to run okay.

"I could go get some help," he suggested.

"Oh no, Harley. Don't leave me here," I cried. "I'll get back on."

"You sure?"

"Yes, absolutely," I said.

"Okay."

He helped me up. I stayed off my ankle and got back on the motorcycle.

"Maybe there's a hospital or something down here," he said.

"I'll be all right, Harley. I just need some ice and we'll get an Ace bandage to wrap it."

"Right, doc. I forgot you were an expert in first aid."

We started out again, both of us very anxious about what lay ahead. Were those men in the pickup truck waiting for us on another side road or driveway to continue harassing us? That fear kept my attention away from the continuous thump, thump, thump rising out of my ankle and reverberating up my spine. I took deep breaths and held onto Harley. He drove a little faster as he

273

became more confident; finally, we saw a garage on our left.

We pulled in. There was a soda machine, but no ice machine. Harley set the motorcycle so it would stand and told me to just sit tight while he went inside the garage. After a few minutes, he returned with a rag full of ice cubes.

"The guy had a refrigerator and gave me this when I told him what happened. He said he thinks he knows the idiots."

A man about forty or forty-five, stout, in a pair of gray coveralls stepped outside, wiping grease off his hands and looking our way.

Harley reached into his tool kit and came up with a roll of tape. He told me to hold the ice against my ankle while he taped around it and my leg until it remained there without my holding it.

"How's that?"

"Now who's the first aid doctor?" I asked, forcing a smile through my grimace of pain.

"It should keep the swelling down, right?"

"Right. I probably strained the tendons."

Harley went back to thank the garage mechanic and get some more information about the road ahead and our destination.

"He said we're only about an hour and ten minutes from Centerville, but I've got to get back on the main highway. We'll have to take our chances with the highway patrol."

"That's better than running into those idiots again, Harley."

"Right. Sorry," he said again.

"It wasn't your fault. You did great," I told him.

After we started out, the ice began to make my whole leg freeze. I took it as long as I could and then I had to tell him to pull off so I could take off the packet.

"It's swollen pretty good," he said studying my ankle. "Maybe it is broken."

"Let's just get there, Harley," I said. "I'll be all right once I can rest."

He nodded, worried, and we continued. The last fifteen minutes or so seemed to take forever, but finally we saw the sign announcing the village and we pulled off the highway and headed for Main Street.

"Do you know where to look?"

"Yes," he said.

It was one of those villages with a long main street and some side streets. All the stores were located in a row with some restaurants and small stores on some of the side streets. There was a fire station about midway and across from it was a police station and village hall. It looked like a train had once had Centerville as a stop. The tracks were gone, but the strip where they had been was still there about halfway down the main street.

Here and there we saw some pedestrians. The traffic was light. Some of the stores looked like they were closing already or had closed. The brightest window seemed to be a bar and grill called The Pit Stop.

"Mostly turn-of-the-century buildings," Harley said, nodding at the structures that leaned and looked tired. "Not much has been built here for over a hundred years except some of the homes we've passed."

It was a sleepy little town, a place the world forgot. Major highways had been built around it, keeping people away. Except for a lumber company on the way in, there was no sign of any major business or industry. Ghosts were probably chafing at the bit, waiting to claim it, I thought. It was certainly not a town young people would come back to after they had finished school or training. When the owners of these small stores and family businesses passed on, each would disappear like a blip on a radar screen. Even the memories would scatter in the wind.

Somehow it seemed the right place for Harley's real father to be, a place to escape to, to run from your past and join citizens who were long forgotten. Just as we reached the end of the main street, Harley slowed down and turned right on a side street. I thought he was going to his father's home, but he brought us to a stop in front of a shingle that read Doctor Richards, Family Practice. It didn't look like a doctor's office. It looked like someone's home: a two-story Queen Anne with a wide front porch, cement steps and a narrow, concrete-square walkway. There was a small lawn, some pretty bushes and flowers and what looked like a swinging chair on the right.

"We can come back afterward, Harley," I said.

"No. Let's look after that ankle first, Summer," he insisted.

"It might get us into trouble though," I moaned.

"We'll be fine. We're here. A little while longer won't matter," he insisted. "Just lean on me and keep off the foot," he said guiding me off the motorcycle.

He put his left arm around my waist and then literally lifted me and carried me down the walkway, up the stairs and to the front door. It was unlocked so we went right in and paused in the hallway. To the right was a small lobby, but there didn't seem to be anyone around. A moment later, however, a small woman, about fifty with a bundle of gray hair curled over her forehead and temples and big, round dark brown eyes, came out of a door in the rear. She was wearing a white dress. It wasn't exactly a nurse's uniform, but it was close.

"Oh, what happened to you?" she cried as if she knew us for years and years.

"Motorcycle accident," Harley said. "She's hurt her ankle and we want to be sure it's not broken."

"Of course, of course. Here," she said opening a door on her right into an examination room, "take her in and help her onto the table. I'll go get Doctor."

"That's a first," I said as Harley helped me in. "She didn't ask if we had health insurance first."

He laughed and helped me onto the examination table. We both looked around at the diplomas on the walls. He had gone to medical schools in New York City.

"Well, what do we have here?" a short, gray-haired man in the open doorway asked. He continued to chew on something he was eating, his soft full checks trembling with each bite. Even though his hair was all gray, cut short with a receding hairline that was beginning to show white scalp, his eyebrows had remained dark brown. He had a thick nose and a small mouth, but his face was friendly and pleasant, his eyes even a bit amused.

The woman who had greeted us stepped up beside him and then followed him into the room.

"I'm Doctor Richards and this is my wife, Anna," he said. "So, what happened?"

"We had an accident," Harley began. "Two guys in a pickup truck harassed us on my motorcycle, and I spilled on a gravel driveway trying to get away."

"Um-hmm," Doctor Richards said, nodding as if he had expected it or had it happen at least once a day.

"She's hurt her ankle," Harley continued.

Doctor Richards stood in front of me and looked down at my ankle and then at me.

"Hurts to beat the band, huh?"

"Yes sir," I said.

"Okay, just pull yourself back a bit more and let's get that foot up where I can see it. Got to get closer to things these days," he continued, smiling at Harley and then at me. Harley helped me back on the table until my foot was up. With very, very gentle fingers, the doctor undid the laces of my sneaker and took it off. He brought down the sock and peeled it away, his fingers barely touching my skin.

"Wiggle your toes for me," he asked and I did.

"Any pain?"

"Not much, a little," I said.

He studied my ankle.

"Did you land on it?"

"No, I rolled over on it, I think."

"I see," he said.

"We put some ice on it as soon as we could," Harley explained.

"Did you? Well, that was smart," the doctor said.

Very carefully, he began to examine my ankle, moving it every way and watching my face. He felt around it.

"Might be fractured, but I doubt it," he said. "Looks more like strained tendons."

"That's what she said," Harley remarked.

"Oh. You practice medicine, too, do you?" Doctor Richards asked with a smile.

"No sir."

"Her father is a therapist," Harley continued. "She knows a lot about first aid and stuff."

"Oh. That's good," Doctor Richards said nodding. "Good to have a little knowledge if you don't abuse it. However, there's also that business about a little knowledge being a dangerous thing. Too many people think they can hang out a shingle like mine these days. Bad for business," he added with a silent laugh. "Well, let's get some more cold packs on this and get it strapped up. You've got to stay off it for a while, maybe a week or so, maybe more.

"You all staying with someone here in town?" he asked.

Harley glanced at me quickly. Doctor Richards caught that.

"Or are you just passing through on your way to civilization?" he followed.

"No sir. We're visiting someone. Fletcher Victor," Harley said.

"Fletcher?" his wife Anna asked.

"That must be Buzz's real name," Doctor Richards told her.

She smirked as if he had said a very silly thing.

"I thought it was Ed. We know everyone here, of course, but the Victors are a family that keeps to themselves. Come to think of it, I don't recall ever asking Buzz what his real name is."

"He wouldn't volunteer it," Anna muttered. "I'm surprised he sent you over here," she added. "Why didn't he have that woman work her magic instead?"

"Woman?" Harley said.

"You haven't been there yet?" Doctor Richards asked.

"No sir. We came here as soon as I saw your shingle. We've just arrived."

"No better advertisement for a doctor than a shingle," Doctor Richards quipped. His wife just pulled her shoulders up, lifting her small bosom.

"Yes, well, let's fix you up," he told me.

When he was finished taping my ankle, he gave me some pills for the pain and a crutch.

"You can borrow this until you have to leave," he said. "How long you planning on staying?"

I looked at Harley.

"We're not quite sure yet, sir," he said.

"Okay. No problem."

"What kind of health insurance do you have?" Anna asked me.

I did have my family's medical card. Daddy insisted I always carry it in my wallet. I gave it to her. She turned it in her hands as if she wanted to be sure it was not fake.

"Do you need any money too?" Harley asked her.

"No, this is fine," she said. "I'll be right back." She went out.

"Let me look at that again tomorrow," Doctor Richards told me.

Harley and I thanked him. When Anna returned, she gave me a paper to sign and then gave me back my card.

"Use that crutch," Doctor Richards advised as we started out. Harley held onto me. We went back to the motorcycle and Harley worked the crutch over the bars and told me to keep the rest of it under my arm.

"I'll go very slowly and we don't have far to go," he said.

"What a sight I'll make. What a way to greet your father for the first time," I moaned, full of a thousand anxieties now that we were moments away. "What do you suppose the doctor's wife meant about that woman using magic?" I asked.

"Who knows, but we could use a little magic about now," Harley muttered.

How could I disagree with that?

11

Face-to-Face

When we turned down the street his real father lived on, I could feel how nervous Harley was. His body stiffened to stone. We pulled up in front of the odd-looking house and for a few moments just idled there, gazing at it.

The house was located at the end of the street on a cul de sac it didn't share with any other home. A tall chain-link fence marked the boundaries on either side. The fence didn't look like it belonged a thousand yards near such a home, much less a few hundred. It was the sort of fence found in an industrial area, not a residential one.

The grass desperately needed to be mowed. Dandelions and weeds were everywhere. The front of the house, although also in need of pruning, wasn't as unkempt. There was a row of rhododendron bushes on both sides of the front porch. A narrow sidewalk constructed from field-stone was bordered with bushes about knee high, but unevenly trimmed. On the right was a grand, sprawling oak tree, but on the left were the remains of another oak that looked like it had been hit by lightning years and years ago. The top was clipped off and the branches were all dead and knuckled. The bark was a sickly gray. Why anyone would keep it there was a mystery. Perhaps it served as some sort of reminder and warning about the power of nature.

Once, the unique house had a dark brown wood cladding with what must have been nearly milk white trim, porch railings and shutters. It looked like it hadn't been repainted since it had been built. Most of it was chipped and faded, and one of the windows on the second floor had been broken and covered with a sheet of plywood.

"Did you say your father told you he was a house painter?" I asked.

"Yeah," Harley said.

"I guess this is a case of the shoemaker without shoes."

"I guess."

He took a deep breath and drove us up the driveway. There was no garage. We saw a truck parked in the rear that probably belonged to his father. It was a battered panel truck with a rear bumper that had been tied with rope and some wire to keep it from falling off. I noticed a doghouse, but no signs of any dog. We could see that the grass was even higher behind the house. Off to the left there was a vegetable garden with some homemade scarecrows comprised of aluminum tins, cans and old rusted strips of metal. I recognized tomato plants and zucchini. There were stalks of corn and what looked like pea vines as well. It was a rather ambitious home garden.

The house itself looked dark. Curtains were closed on all the windows. When Harley turned off the engine, we sat there, listening and looking at the front door, over which was hung some chimes. Their musical clang and the occasional distant sound of a car horn was all we heard.

"Maybe nobody's home," Harley muttered.

"He knew you would be here today, right?"

Harley nodded, but still didn't move.

"What should we do?" I asked.

"I guess we should just go up and knock and see," he said. He dismounted and helped me. "Careful," he said as we headed down the narrow walk. I tried keeping the tip of the crutch on the rocks.

We walked up the steps and to the front door. Our footsteps rattled the loose slats on the porch floor. Looking through the window on the right, I could see a dimly lit lamp on a side table in what was surely the living room. There was no buzzer on the door and no knocker. Harley shrugged and then tapped the door with his knuckles gently. He waited a moment and rapped it harder.

A good thirty or forty seconds went by before we heard a latch undone. As the door opened, a tall, very dark-skinned woman — with her hair pulled up in a twist so tightly it stretched the skin on her temples and forehead — looked out at us.

She wore a dark purple dress with sleeves that came to her elbows. Even though her skin had only barely discernible wrinkles, her hair was streaked with gray. I had never seen such piercing ebony eyes. They were set above very high cheekbones. Her jawbone was sharp, giving her a narrow, harsh chin, but her lips were full, soft and when they lifted, they revealed bone white perfect teeth.

"Oui?" she said.

Harley looked at me to see if I knew what that meant. I shook my head.

"I'm Harley," he said. "I've come to see Fletcher Victor."

She shifted her eyes from him to me and then she turned and, leaving the door opened, walked back to what I thought was the doorway to the living room.

She mumbled something and a moment later, the man who I imagined to be Harley's real father appeared beside her. He looked like she had just woken him. His thick head of black and gray hair was as messed as it would be if someone had run his or her fingers through it for ten minutes. He wore a pair of coveralls, stained with blue, white, red and green paint as well as a very faded T-shirt beneath. He was barefoot, the toenail on his right foot's big toe bruised black.

Both Harley and I could only stare. It was natural for us to look for resemblances. Harley and he had similar noses and both had hazel eyes. I thought their mouths were different, Harley's being softer with thinner lips, but they had the same jaw and identically shaped ears. Like Harley, his father stood over six feet, but he had a stouter build and a thicker neck. His shoulders, however, were somewhat stooped.

What was most surprising of all, I guess, was how old he looked. Did time and hard living age him this quickly? Or was he much older than we imagined when he had met Harley's mother?

He scrubbed his cheeks vigorously to wash out the sleep and then smiled.

"Well now," he said. "Well, here you are. This is my boy," he told the tall, black lady.

She stared as if she were deaf. There was no reaction or interest in her face.

His father stepped forward.

"Come in, come in. Let me look you over, boy."

He reached out, his hands jetting at Harley's shoulders, grasping them firmly and holding him for a moment while he drank him in and nodded.

"Just look at this kid, Suze. Is this a chip off the old block or what? Huh?" he said turning to her and being more demanding for a reaction.

"*Oui,*" she said. So that's her way of saying yes, I immediately concluded. "*Bon,*" she added.

"So," Harley's father continued, still holding him at the shoulders, "you made it pretty good, huh?"

"Yes," Harley said. Then he glanced at me. "Well, maybe not so good. We had an accident just outside Centerville. Two guys in a pickup harassed us and I spilled trying to get away from them. Summer hurt her ankle," he continued, so nervous he had to keep talking. "I brought her right to the doctor here, and he treated her foot and gave her that crutch to use while we were here."

"No kidding?" He released Harley and turned to me, his hands on his hips. "What he call you — Summer?"

"Yes sir," I said.

"Who is she?" he asked Harley.

"She's my best friend," he said quickly. "We kind of grew up together," he added.

"Oh. I see. Well, we'll have plenty of time to get acquainted. Suze made one of her special dishes in anticipation of your arrival. She knew you'd be here in time." He leaned toward us. "She's got special powers," he whispered and winked. "Where's your things?"

"Oh, I left it all on the cycle," Harley said.

"Well, you go get it. Suze will show you places to sleep. You want two rooms, I imagine," he added with a tight, impish smile.

"Yes," Harley said immediately. "If that's okay."

"Sure. Right, Suze?"

"*Pas de problème*," she replied.

"What?" Harley said, smiling.

"Oh, that's her way of saying no problem. I told you, she's Haitian. She can speak pretty good English when she wants," he added, giving her a mild look of reprimand. "She's got to get to know you a little before she does though," he added. "Go on, get your things. C'mon into the living room, meanwhile, Summer. Suze's got to fix the other room anyway."

She nodded and headed for the short stairway. Harley glanced at me as his father started to return to the living room.

"I'll be right back," he said. I nodded and followed his father.

"Have a seat, have a seat," he said nodding at the well-worn sofa, the arms of which were scratched and stained. It looked like it had been left outside for years.

Everything about the room was old, tired and faded. The area rug over the dark, hardwood floors was shredded on its edges, and there looked to be small holes that resembled burns from cigarette ashes in it as well. The walls were a light brown, but here and there some white showed through where the paint looked thin. A half-dozen very inexpensive prints of countryside scenes in cheap frames were hung above the fieldstone fireplace and between the two front windows. There was a pile of newspapers and some magazines on the floor beside the oversized cushion chair Harley's father sank into across from me. He put his bare feet up on the footstool and reached over to get his white meerschaum pipe from the side table. I could see some tobacco had fallen over the table and imagined that was the reason for some of the burns in the rug.

"So where are you from?" he asked, packing his pipe with tobacco.

"Harley and I live on the same estate," I said.

"Estate?" He scrunched his mouth and nodded. "Back in Virginia?"

"Yes sir."

Harley came rushing back into the house.

"C'mon in, c'mon in. Give Suze a chance. She'll want those rooms looking as clean as a hospital room. The house may not look it because of the mess I make, but she's a stickler when it comes to cleanliness. Sit down," he instructed Harley and nodded at the sofa, too.

Harley dropped our bags and sat next to me.

"So you two live on an estate," he said. Harley looked at me.

"He asked where I lived."

"Oh. Yes, it's Summer's family's property. When my mother married Roy, they built a house there."

"Your mother was quite a good-looking woman. I bet she was pretty right to the end, huh?"

Harley swallowed hard.

"Yes," he said.

"We got a lot to catch up on," his father said, bringing a match to his pipe bowl. He puffed hard, his neck moving in and out, reminding me of a thick snake. Then he sat back and just looked at the two of us for a long moment as he smoked.

"I'm real glad you called, Harley, real glad. I often wondered what Glenda had done. Glad she told you about me," he said. "I was surprised to hear she kept track of my comings and goings and knew where I was."

"She didn't," Harley replied. "When I discovered your name and stuff, I found out about you another way."

"Oh? How's that?" he asked, freezing.

"On the Internet. Computers," Harley added.

"Oh, yeah, yeah. I gotta confess I don't know diddly when it comes to that. Just an old-fashioned guy is all I am. So, you're what, seventeen?"

"Yes," Harley said. I could hear the disappointment in his voice. A father should at least know how old his son is.

"Right, right. Seems like yesterday," his father continued, blowing smoke off to his right. He paused as though he just realized something. "You had no pictures of me then, nothing like that?"

"No, sir. My mother didn't like talking about you much. I always asked," he added to show how interested he had been.

"Yeah, yeah, I'm sure," his father said and looked very thoughtful. "Real sorry about Glenda. The world is a bowl of troubles, not cherries. For most of us, that is," he added, glancing at me.

Harley nodded and looked down for a moment.

"This is an interesting house," he said. "How did you come to own it?"

"Oh, it's been in my family for a long time. About ten years ago, the county historian got it put on some special list and as a result, I don't pay real estate taxes. Big savings as long as I don't change it. Actually, now it's illegal to change it."

"Can't you even paint it?" I blurted.

Harley's father laughed.

"Yeah, I can restore it to its original colors and such, but I've just been lazy about it. You know how it is. You get work and you concentrate on that because someone's paying you and you forget your own place. One of these days, I'll get around to it. It's a nice size property, too."

"There aren't too many octagons, original ones like this," Harley continued.

"Right. You know about that stuff?" his father asked, surprised.

"Harley knows a lot about architecture," I bragged for him. "He's going to become an architect himself someday."

"That so?"

"I guess so," Harley said smiling at me. "Or else I'll be in big trouble."

"Right, right, know what you mean. It's in the Victor blood to have to have someone pushing you all the time. We don't have what some people refer to as much ambition on our own. Trouble with us is we're too easily contented. But we live long lives because of that," he declared.

"When the doctor asked us where we were going, we told him your name, but he said he knew you only as Buzz."

"Oh, he did, huh? Yeah, that's right. I've been going by that nickname since I was knee-high to a grasshopper. One of the first things I saw was a bee, I guess. At least, that's what they told me, because I used to go around making a buzzing sound. So . . . there's why I got the nickname. Of course, I never told your mother," he added quickly.

We were quiet for a moment. I nearly jumped when Suze appeared. She appeared suddenly in the doorway as if she had simply materialized out of thin air. She must walk on air, I thought. I never heard her coming down the stairs or walking in the hallway.

"Everything set already, Suze?" Harley's father asked.

"*Oui,*" she said. "I show you," she told us. "Come."

"Get settled in. We'll have some dinner and talk until we all pass out," Harley's father said. He looked at me. "How else do you catch up on seventeen years, huh?"

I smiled.

How else? I thought. You don't run off and lose complete contact with your own child. That's how else. Of course, I didn't say a syllable of that. I simply nodded and rose with Harley to follow Suze up the stairs.

The rooms were small, but they did look tidy, each with a simple double bed, no headboard or footboard. Each room had a dresser and a pair of nightstands. The overhead fixtures in both rooms did not work, but there were standing pole lamps that did.

I saw a pink cloth with a string tied around it forming a ball set on my pillow.

293

"What's this?" I asked.

"That be good *gris-gris,* magic bag give you sweet dreams," she explained.

"What's in it?"

"Charms, herbs, some nail clippings."

"Nail clippings?" I looked at Harley and he raised his eyebrows and shook his head.

"You see, it will work," Suze insisted. "We gotcha a bathroom right across the hall," she continued. It sounded like they had just made it. "You share, all right?"

"Oh yes," I said. Harley put my suitcase down beside the bed and then took his to the room next door.

"Towels and such are in the hallway closet," Suze continued, standing in the doorway and nodding at a door in the hallway. *"La,"* she said. "There. You got soap and shampoo in the bathroom."

"Thank you," I said.

"Merité," she replied and nearly smiled. "That means you're welcome."

"Merité," I repeated. That brought a smile to her face. "How do you say thank you then?"

"I say *merci.*"

"Merci."

"What's all that?" Harley asked, returning.

"Haitian talk," I said. The constant pain in my ankle made me grimace.

"Your foot, it hurts a lot?" Suze asked.

"Yes."

"I fix something for you," she said.

294

"Oh, I've got medicine the doctor gave me."
She smiled with confidence.

"I give you medicine that works faster," she insisted.

Harley raised his eyebrows and widened his eyes as he shrugged.

"I must look after supper now," Suze said. "Be ready in ten more minutes."

She turned and went down the stairs. Harley and I watched her and then looked at each other and smiled.

"She put one of those magic bags on my pillow, too."

"I hope they work," I said.

"What do you think of my father?" he asked.

"He looks older than I expected."

"Me too."

"He seems nice though."

"We'll see," Harley said cautiously. "Something does smell good, doesn't it?" he remarked, picking up the aromas coming from the kitchen.

"I'll freshen up and change into the best thing I brought," I said.

"I'm okay. I'll just go back downstairs and talk to him."

"Okay. Tell them I have to call home, too."

"Right," he said. "Your ankle does hurt a lot. I can see it in your face," he said.

"It hurts, but I'd rather hold off on taking the pain pills until I go to sleep."

He grimaced. I knew he was still feeling guilty.

"It wasn't your fault, Harley. You did the best

you could, and you might have just saved our lives."

He nodded and then smiled.

"Maybe Suze does have a magic medicine."

"Oh, I wouldn't take anything from her, Harley."

"I know. See you downstairs," he said.

Now that we had stopped moving and my attention went fully to myself, the pain in my ankle began to sing its song louder and louder. I hopped about, pulled out my dress and took my makeup kit into the bathroom. When I looked at myself in the mirror, I realized how the ride and our ordeal with the men in the pickup truck had taken its toll. My hair looked like it had been through a shredder. I should have put on some sunscreen before we started on this trip, too. My cheeks were red. Even my chin was scarlet. Was it from the sun or the wind? I set to work, rubbing in my creams and fixing my hair as best I could without washing it.

Harley had to come back up to call me to dinner.

"It's ready," he said. "They're waiting for you."

"Okay, okay," I cried and hurried as fast as I could. The pain was thumping in my leg, and I wondered if I should at least take one of my pills now. I didn't want to bring any unhappiness to the table, not for this first and important dinner with Harley's father.

"I guess I'll just take one of the pills," I reluctantly decided.

I did so and then Harley helped me go down the stairs to the dining room. He looked a lot happier.

"Guess what he wants me to do tomorrow," he whispered as we went along.

"What?"

"He wants me to go on a job with him. He says I could be a great help since he lost his assistant this week."

"How?"

"He said he was a big drinker and got arrested for his fourth or fifth DWI. He's in jail."

"Oh."

"Best way to get to know someone is to work with him," Harley said, "especially if he's the father you've never known."

The dining room table was a hard cherry wood that once must have been a beautiful piece of furniture, I thought. Now it was stained and badly scratched. The chair legs were so loose, I was afraid that mine might just fall apart. I never sat so still. Suze hadn't put a tablecloth on the table, but she had a thick candle burning at the center.

Whether we liked it or not, we were in for a Haitian dinner. Harley's father explained each dish Suze brought out from the kitchen. We began with a pumpkin soup. I thought it was quite spicy, and so did Harley from the look on his face. Our main dish was something called griots, which I gathered from Suze's broken English explanation was pork first boiled and then fried. She served it with what she referred to as *riz pois colles,* which looked to be nothing more than rice cooked in with red kidney beans.

For dessert, we had *pain patate,* which was a cake she had made with sweet potatoes, coconut and raisins. It was delicious. Most of the flavors were true discoveries for both of us. Harley scraped his plate clean.

"I guess I was really hungry and this was all so good," he explained.

Throughout the dinner, I noticed how intently Harley's father stared at him. It's only natural, I thought. He was looking for resemblances, re-calling memories of Aunt Glenda, perhaps feeling proud of the good-looking young man who now sat at his table.

Harley did a great deal of the talking, more than I had ever heard from him. He talked about our property, the lake, working with Roy, his interest in architecture. It was as if he were trying to get seventeen years of life summarized quickly so that he and his father could have a fresh beginning, move on from this moment as if they had never been apart. It was a hope I could see in his eyes as he spoke.

For his part, his father listened, asked an occa-sional question, glanced at Suze and smiled, and ate. He told surprisingly little more about himself. I tried to get more out of him for Harley's sake.

"How long have you been living here?" I asked.

"Oh, a while," he said.

When Suze went back into the kitchen, I remarked at how unusual it must be for someone from Haiti to be living here. I was hoping he would explain how they had met, but all he did was agree.

Suze gave us a juice drink with our meal. It was a little too sweet, but when Harley's father bragged about how hard she worked to make it, I thought I had better drink it all. Just before we finished our dessert, she looked at me and nodded.

"That be helping you now," she said.

"Pardon?"

"Suze means she gave you something for your pain."

"Gave me something? When?" I asked nervously.

"In your drink," Harley's father said laughing. "Don't worry about it. She's kept me alive for years, and the way I neglect myself and abuse myself, it's truly a miracle. Her mother was the equivalent of what we might call a witch doctor or something. Hell, I ain't been to a regular doctor for nearly ten years now. I haven't even been to a dentist!" he bragged.

"Maybe she shouldn't have done that," Harley said cautiously. "Summer already took one of her pills before we began to eat."

"Naw, nothing to worry about. Everything she uses comes from nature," his father assured us.

Maybe it was the power of suggestion, but my stomach suddenly took a spin and then rumbled. I felt myself go a little white in the face.

"You all right?" Harley asked.

I shook my head.

"I think I have to go to the bathroom," I said. I rose and reached for my crutch.

"There's one off the kitchen," Harley's father said.

I looked at Harley.

"Maybe I better use the one upstairs."

"Suit yourself," his father said and sat back to light his pipe while Suze began to clear the table.

"I'm sorry I can't help with the dinner dishes, but . . ."

"That's okay. I'll help her," Harley told me.

I moved quickly up the stairs, found the bathroom and went in almost too late. Everything I had just eaten seemed to run right through me. Taking the pill before such a spicy dinner was probably a bad idea, I thought — or else what she had given me in that drink had brought this about, too.

I was in the bathroom so long, Harley came by to see if I was all right.

"Summer?"

"I'm sorry, Harley. I got sick so fast!"

"It's okay. Let me know if you need anything."

"I'll be out soon," I promised. When I did finally step out of the bathroom, I felt myself spin so badly, I nearly toppled. I guess I hit the wall hard enough for Harley to hear and come running, his father beside him.

"I feel a little weak," I said.

Harley rushed to my side and put his arm around my waist.

"Just let her lay down for a while," his father suggested. "She'll be fine in an hour or so, for sure."

"Yes, I'll be fine," I said. My eyes felt so heavy, I thought they might roll out of my head.

Harley practically carried me to the room. He guided me to the bed and I lay back. He took off my shoes and pulled the blanket up to my neck.

"How you doing, Summer?"

"Tired," I said.

"Just rest a while. I'll check on you in a few minutes or so," he promised.

I nodded, but I didn't speak or open my eyes.

The next time I did open them, I was greeted by the light of morning. For a few moments, my mind was so clouded with confusion I didn't move. It was as if my most recent memories had been washed away. Where was I? How did I get here? Why was my ankle bandaged? The struggle for these answers put me into a terrible panic. I started to cry. Finally, I sat up and concentrated until it all began to flood back in and over me.

"Harley!" I cried.

I listened. All I heard was the sound of water running through a pipe somewhere in the house.

"Harley!"

The water stopped running and I called again, louder. Then, I heard footsteps coming up the stairway. I looked to the door of my room. It opened and Suze came walking in. She had another juice drink and what looked like a slice of some kind of fruit and nut bread.

"*Bon jour!* I bring you something for *matin* . . . breakfast. *Comment ça va?*"

"What?"

"How are you?"

"I feel terrible," I said.

She nodded.

"You drink and eat this. It is good for your stomach," she declared. She handed me the glass.

I shook my head.

"Where's Harley?"

"He be gone to work."

"Gone to work? What time is it?"

"Ten-thirty," she replied.

"Ten-thirty! I slept until ten-thirty!"

I tried to stand up, but the room spun. I sat back quickly, gasping for air.

"Drink," she said, pumping the glass at me. "It give you strength."

"What is it?"

"Just combination of herbs and juices," she said. "Take," she said with more insistence.

Reluctantly, I took the glass and brought it to my lips. It didn't have much of an aroma, but when I tasted it, I thought there was a lot of banana and coconut in it.

"Drink," she urged. "You feel better. You see."

I drank some more and then she handed me the plate with the slice of bread.

"Something solid now. Go."

I nibbled on the slice. It didn't taste bad and

maybe she was right. Maybe I did need something in my stomach. I ate as much as I could. She stood there watching me as if she was afraid I might throw it away and pretend I had eaten it. Her hair was exactly how it had been yesterday, but today she wore a light brown dress and sandals. I noticed she had a chain around her neck that looked like it was made of bone with some crystals at the center.

Suddenly, I realized I had fallen asleep before I had called Mommy and Daddy to let them know I was all right. It put such a panic in me, my face got hot with fear. Suze's eyes widened. I imagined she thought I was having another reaction to the food and medicines.

"I forgot to call my parents!" I cried. "I've got to call them right away. Is there a phone upstairs?"

She shook her head and picked up my tray.

"Well, where is the phone?"

"Kitchen," she said and started away. "Oh," she said, stopping. She reached into a pocket of her dress and pulled out a slip of paper. "He give me this for you when you wake up." She stepped back to hand it to me.

"Thank you," I said. *"Merci."*

"Merci," she repeated, nodding and smiling.

I opened the note.

Dear Summer,

I had to leave with my father early to get to his job site. I checked on you all night, but you were sleeping so soundly, I didn't want to wake you.

Same this morning. We should be back by four. I know you are going to call your parents today. I'd like to ask a favor. Please don't tell them exactly where we are just yet. I need this day with my dad and I know if they find out where we are, your mother will tell Roy for sure and they'll either come get us or call the police to come get us and ruin it all. I know it's mean of me to ask you to do this but it would be just for another day. If you can't, you can't. I'll understand.

Love,
Harley

I expected Harley was right about what Mommy would do and certainly what Roy might do, but it wasn't going to be easy to keep such information from her. I hoped I could make her understand. If she wasn't so angry at me, that is, I thought and got myself moving. I dabbed my face in cold water and after going to the bathroom, started down the stairs. I heard Suze humming some Haitian melody as she cleaned the house. Going directly into the kitchen, I picked up the receiver and dialed for an operator. I listened, but I didn't hear any ringing, so I tried again and listened. I pressed the hook up and down and dialed and listened. Still, all I heard was silence so I went to find Suze.

She was dusting in the living room.

"Excuse me," I said and she stopped humming and working and turned to me.

"The phone doesn't seem to work. Is there something wrong with it?"

She pressed her lips together and walked to the kitchen. I hobbled behind her and watched her lift the receiver and listen after she had dialed the operator, too. Then she cradled it and shook her head.

"It be dead again. Out of order," she recited. "Thunderstorm last night probably do it down."

"Well, when will it be fixed?"

"Soon, maybe. Maybe not so soon," she replied. She started back to the living room.

"Well, is there any place else nearby with a phone that would work?"

"The grocery store on the corner has a phone," she said. "Pay phone."

"Okay."

I took a deep breath and started for the front door.

"You need rest," she advised.

"As soon as I do this," I said. *"Merci."*

She shook her head and returned to her work. I opened the door and went out. The sky was quite overcast now. The break in the clouds that we had earlier had completely disappeared and there was a stronger breeze. I could almost feel the rain coming. It was a typical summer thunderstorm day where it would rain in isolated areas for a while and then move on to another area. I might get caught in it, I thought, but I have to call Mommy. I can't let her worry another minute.

I moved as quickly as I could while still keeping

off my left foot. If I did put it down too hard, my ankle immediately complained. Thankfully, it wasn't that far to the grocery store. I could see the pay phone on the outside wall near the door. The moment I lifted the receiver and dialed for the operator, I knew this phone was out of order, too. My heart sank. I had to get in touch with my parents. I had to.

I entered the grocery store. There was only a short fat man sitting behind the deli counter. He had a round, pockmarked face with thinning light brown hair, but thick sideburns. He looked up at me through thick-lensed glasses, which made his eyes look like they bulged, resembling fish eyes.

"Can I help you?" he asked with a face of curiosity. After all, how many strangers on a crutch came into his store? I thought.

"I need to make an important phone call and the phone in the house I'm in doesn't work and your pay phone doesn't work," I explained.

He smirked.

"Oh. Well, we had a bad electric storm early this morning and the lines are dead."

"When will they be fixed?"

"I don't know. Sometimes it takes hours and hours."

"There isn't a phone here that works?"

"I don't know," he said. "Probably not," he added. "Where are you staying?"

"At Mr. Victor's house," I replied.

"Oh," he said. Then he grimaced and added, "Maybe he just didn't pay his phone bill again.

I'm tired of taking calls for him. You can tell him Stuart said so."

"If your phone's dead, too, then his isn't dead because he didn't pay his bill," I pointed out.

"Maybe," he said. "How long has it been dead?"

"Well, it was working a few days ago. I know that," I said feeling a pain through my temples. Why was I standing here arguing with him? There was something so irritating about his tone of voice that his arrogant manner made me want to defeat him.

"You said it yourself. A few days ago. Between then and now, they might have turned off his phone. Once, he had his electric turned off, too. What are you, a relative?" he asked, turning the corner of his mouth down with disgust.

"I'm a friend of a relative," I said.

"Lucky for you," he quipped and looked down at whatever he was reading. From what I could see of it, it looked like either *Playboy* or something close to it.

"Thanks. Sorry to have interrupted you," I said and left to the sound of his grunt.

When I stepped out, I felt some raindrops and hurried back toward the house. I got caught in a sprinkle just as I was turning down the walk. However, the sprinkle turned into a regular cloudburst before I reached the steps. I gasped and cried out, swinging my crutch ahead of me. One of the stones was already slick and the bottom of the crutch slipped off, causing me to lose my balance when it shot out. I fell into the bushes and then sat hard on my rear. The rain got even heavier.

Gasping, I shouted for help and worked myself to my feet. By the time I got up the steps and under the porch roof, which leaked, I was soaked to the skin. I practically lunged for the door, but it was locked. I pounded hard and finally Suze came to it.

"Look you now. I said so," she remarked. "You need to get clothes off quickly and not track in all that mud, too. I just done washing the floor."

She shut the door.

"Wait," she said and rushed down the hallway. Moments later, she was back with a towel and started to rub my hair vigorously. I had to stop her because she was so rough. Then she started to help me take off my clothes.

"I get these dry," she said as she gathered my jeans and my blouse. My bra and panties were wet as well. She waited, beckoning me to give my undergarments to her. I did so quickly and wrapped the towel around me. Then I moved as quickly as I could to the stairway and went up to my room. I got out some new clothes: another pair of jeans and a sweatshirt along with another pair of panties. Then I went into the bathroom to clean up.

I considered taking a warm bath and stripped off my Ace bandage so I could use it again. Then I started to fill the tub. What a mess I was in, I thought. Everything I do to try to make it better, just makes it worse. However, once I lowered myself into the warm water, I immediately relaxed. It was so soothing. It even helped my ankle. I closed my eyes and just enjoyed the soak, imagining I was back home, back in my own luxurious bathroom. Soon I would go downstairs to one of Mrs. Geary's wonderful lunches. If you pretend hard enough, I thought, maybe you could make it happen.

Of course, it didn't, but I did feel better. The rain would stop. The phone line would be fixed, and I'd be able to call Mommy and Daddy. They'd understand. They'd be happy to hear from me. Harley would get to know his father and all would be well.

Why, I wondered, did that sound so much like someone's fairy-tale hope?

It wouldn't be all that much longer before I would find out.

12

The Shrine

It suddenly occurred to me that here I was in some strange house daydreaming in a bathtub, but daydreams were really no more than cobwebs easily tearing under us and dropping us back into reality, and the reality was that I was in a place so different from my home, I could be on Mars!

The water was warm enough and clean enough, but the tub was old and chipped and stained with rust. The faucet dripped no matter how hard I tightened the handles. The linoleum on the floor was torn and cracked as well as faded. The walls around me were crying out for a coat of paint like some naked child in a snowstorm crying for clothes and warmth, but mostly crying for loving concern.

Harley's father lived here with his Haitian woman. However, they didn't treat this home with love and respect. They weren't half as proud of it as Harley was, and Harley had just seen it for the first time yesterday.

All of these thoughts left me cold, even in the tepid bath. I had seen and heard enough to start a small drip of ice down my spine. Harley won't be happy here, I concluded. He won't find the father he's never had or the family he thought was just waiting to embrace him as soon as he showed up on their doorstep. There wasn't really much of a doorstep, and no one had put out the welcome mat the way I would have wanted it put out for me. If they had, it would probably have been a shredded, torn and faded thing anyway, I concluded.

Hopefully, Harley would realize all this for himself, and when he returned from work with his father, he would come to me and almost apologetically say, "Let's go home, Summer. Let's go now."

Surely it was too weird here to stay much longer. His father had only vague memories of his mother, and Suze was truly from another world, spoke another language and lived with a much different set of ideas and beliefs. Harley would feel like a stranger in this house.

I was sure I'd soon be calling Mommy from the road to tell her we were on our way back.

"We just had to see for ourselves," I would say. "You understand, Mommy. I know you do. Now it will be easier for Harley to go on."

When I arrived home, I knew she would welcome me proudly, proud that I had helped Harley.

"You frightened us," she would say, "but you

did a nice thing for someone you care about, and I guess I can't fault you for that."

Was I daydreaming again, imagining it all and wishing too hard?

My reverie ended when I heard Suze in the up-stairs hallway. What she hummed wasn't exactly a song so much as it was a chant. Unexpectedly, she opened the bathroom door and stopped the moment she saw me.

"*Excusez-moi,*" she muttered. "Excuse. *Pardonnez-moi,* but me need to get water."

She held up her pail and mop.

"I'm sorry," I said. "I'll get out now. I'm finished anyway."

She didn't step out. She stood in the doorway and waited, watching me lift myself up and out of the tub as carefully as I could. I reached quickly for my towel and wrapped it around myself. I didn't consider myself an overly bashful person, but I still had modesty, especially in front of someone who had such searching eyes. She looked like she was judging every bone in my body.

"You not be one to have many children," she remarked, shaking her head.

"Why not?" I asked.

With her free hand, she made a gesture over her hip bone and across her abdomen.

"Not good for many children."

"I don't want many children anyway. Just two."

"*Bon,*" she said nodding.

She wasn't going to leave so I started to dry myself, glancing at her furtively.

"What about you?" I fired back at her. "Have you any children?"

"*Oui.*"

"You do? How many?"

She held up one finger.

"A boy or a girl?"

"Boy," she said.

"Well, where is he?" I asked, clipping on my bra and slipping my arms through the sleeves of my blouse.

"Downstairs," she replied.

"Downstairs?" Obviously, she wasn't understanding me, I thought. I shook my head.

"No, where does he live now?"

"Downstairs," she repeated.

I paused.

"Downstairs? Where, downstairs?"

"In my holy room," she said. "I'll show you when you are ready."

She stepped farther into the bathroom. I sat on the closed toilet seat, refitted my bandage over my ankle and slipped on my sneakers while she emptied the tub and then stuck her pail under the faucet to fill it with warm water.

Holy room? What was she talking about?

When I was completely dressed, I reached for my crutch. She went out, set the pail on the floor and nodded at the stairway. Nervously, I started down.

Why had I even asked her about children?

When I reached the bottom, she moved past

me, into the kitchen, beckoning for me to follow. We went through the kitchen to what I had thought was the pantry, but turned out to be another room.

What I saw made my skin crinkle up and down my body. A half-dozen large black candles provided the only light. The room wasn't very big, but it was crowded with charms and bones, dolls, and bunches of feathers and hair and what I was positive were snakeskins. There was a human skull on a center table and beside it was a chair upon which sat a large jug. On the floor beside the chair were two sets of crossed brooms. There were candles on the floor as well, lighting the ends of a strange design drawn in some sort of bone-colored chalk.

"I don't understand," I managed to say.

"My son be gone. His soul be in there."

"Where?"

"The jug. We must bring back the souls of our loved ones and safeguard them. The chair on which the jug sits belongs to Legba, the god of the crossroads, who controls passing between the living world and the world of the dead."

"Your son is in the jug?" I muttered.

She nodded.

"That's not his . . . not . . . his skull, is it?" I asked nearly gulping in fear of her response.

She shook her head.

"It be the skull of an ancestor who guards and protects, too."

"How did your son die?"

"His lungs go bad," she said putting her hand over her breast.

"How old was he?"

"Five."

"Five? How terrible. I'm sorry."

She nodded.

"I've got to do the floors upstairs now," she told me and closed the door.

I watched her walk away and looked at the door to the holy room. What was really in that jug? It gave me the shivers to think about it, about everything in that room. I got myself a glass of water and tried the telephone again, hoping to speak to Mommy. It was still dead and the rain had turned into a steady downpour. It beat against the windows and on the roof now, sounding more like hail. How even more dreary and dark the house itself appeared when it rained. I wandered through it, looking at the other rooms, each of which was as drab as the one before, the furniture as worn as that in the living room and the dining room.

The television set was not working either. That line was down, too. In this out-of-the-way place, everything seemed to fall apart so easily, I thought. Still nervous, I searched for ways to distract myself. It would still be hours before Harley returned, unless the weather where they were was just as bad and made it impossible to work. I was hoping for that.

On my way back through the hallway to sit in the living room and wait, I realized there was a door beside the scratched and chipped dark walnut cabinet. The door was so narrow and the paint so faded on both the wall and the door that it was easy to walk right by and not notice it. I imagined it was just a closet, but I opened it anyway and was surprised to see a short stairway down. Perhaps it was a wine cellar, I thought.

Just before I closed the door, I saw the light switch and flipped it. A very low wattage overhead bulb threw dim illumination over the half-dozen steps. I was about to turn the light off and close the door when I noticed a picture on the wall directly opposite the short stairway at the base. It was in a pearl oval frame and the young man in the picture so resembled Harley, I couldn't ignore it.

I paused, listened and heard Suze still upstairs, chanting and working, so I edged myself carefully down the stairway to look more closely at the picture. What a remarkable resemblance, I thought. Was this Harley's father at a young age? He had his hair short, almost military style and wore a shirt and a tie. Yet, as I studied the picture longer, I thought the face in it was too handsome for the man I had met. The man in this picture had Harley's mouth as well as his jaw and his ears. In short, there was a much closer resemblance.

Do people's features change so much as they grow older? I wondered. What difference does it make anyway? I thought. It doesn't change my feelings about his father and this place.

As I turned to go back up, I saw a half-dozen

cartons on the floor. They were open, some of their contents overflowing. Most of it was old papers, legal-looking documents, but I saw more pictures on another carton. I knelt down and started to sift through them.

There were many pictures of a young couple enjoying a vacation to what looked like Disney World. In most of the pictures a little boy held onto the hand of a woman I imagined to be his mother. The little boy looked like he could have been Harley. That's how close the resemblance was. Of course, I didn't recognize the woman, but I thought she had a soft beauty. In other pictures, she looked more troubled and in none of them did she look directly at the camera. Her eyes were always shifted in another direction. In some pictures, she seemed to be covering her face deliberately by raising her arm or twisting her shoulder.

There was, however, one good head shot that revealed she had hazel eyes, light brown hair and almost perfectly symmetrical diminutive features. She wasn't smiling in this one either. She looked almost hypnotized, staring without expression.

The house in the background in most of the pictures of the young men, young woman and little boy was different from this one. There were pictures of other people, some alongside the man, woman and child, and then there were pictures of the child at what was obviously his birthday party.

They weren't taking very good care of these photographs, I thought. Some were already torn or bent and many were fading from the dampness.

Even the carton itself looked like it was about to collapse. I put it all back, stacking the pictures more carefully than they had been, and then I glanced at the carton on the right. It wasn't as full and it looked like it contained old newspapers. Were they of some historic value? I wondered and glanced at the issue on the top. The date was only twelve years back. Why save this?

I perused the front page and almost put it back before I noticed a short column on the lower left. The headline read: **Local Boy Dies in Police Chase**.

Fletcher Victor, 37-year-old son of Ed "Buzz" Victor and Francine Marie Victor, was killed today when his car veered out of control off Highway 70 out of Sandburg during a police pursuit. Mr. Victor had just committed an armed robbery of the Sandburg Farmers' Credit Union when his vehicle careened down an embankment and into the Sandburg Creek, where it sunk in twenty feet of water. State police divers retrieved Mr. Victor's body and the stolen funds late in the day.

The story was continued on page 15, where there was a picture as well. There was no mistaking who he was. The man in this story was Harley's father.

That meant that the man living in this house was Harley's grandfather!

I spun around and looked up the short stairway at the open door as if I expected him to be standing there. The chill that ran through my body was so cold to the bone, I felt like I couldn't move.

Why? Why would he pretend to be his son? Why didn't he tell Harley the truth about his father?

Thinking I heard Suze coming down from her cleaning work upstairs, I put everything back quickly and went back up the short stairway. I closed the door softly behind me just as she turned to come through the hallway. She looked at me a moment, her eyes small and suspicious. Perhaps she did have some sort of mystical power and knew what was in my mind and what I had done. I avoided her and went into the living room.

My body was trembling. I was torn between just walking out and running off or waiting for Harley. There shouldn't be any danger here, I thought. After all, the man was still his grandfather. Maybe there was some sensible explanation. Maybe he was ashamed of his son and didn't want Harley to know about his father. Should I be the one to tell him?

A short while later, Suze came to the doorway and interrupted my thoughts.

"I go to shop," she said. "I put out some cheese, crackers, bread and fruit in the kitchen. You want lunch, you eat."

"Thank you. *Merci,*" I said quickly. She nodded and left the house.

I was a little hungry, so I went in and made a plate for myself. Even though I still had pain, I decided not to take any more of my pills. I didn't want to be sleepy, especially now. As I sat there nibbling on some cheese and crackers, I stared at the door to the so-called holy room. Did Harley know about this room, too? Had Suze told him this morning before he had left for work?

My curiosity about the jug was growing. What could possibly be in it? Had her son been cremated? Were his remains in the jug? Bones? I rose and went to the door, opening it slowly to peek back inside. The candles were all still lit. The skull seemed to glow under the soft light, and the flickering flames made the eye sockets look like they had eyes that blinked at me. I listened. The house was quiet except for the sound of the light rain falling now.

Courageous or foolish, I continued into the room and approached the jug. Just as I reached for the cover, the holy room's door snapped shut. My heart began to pound. Was it the wind seeping through the cracks and under the windows that had blown it closed? Or was it some spirit of the dead? Anyone would get spooked in this room, I thought, glancing at the snakeskins.

The skull seemed to be looking up at me, waiting. My hand froze inches from the lid of the jug. I could see my fingers trembling. Then I heard what sounded like a squeaking to my right and looked down to see a large rat slinking along the wall and the floor. It paused and looked up at me, its nose twitching. I couldn't breathe or swallow. When I lifted my crutch, it scurried under the table and disappeared in the corner.

I felt nauseous from the sight of it and decided to forget about the holy room and the jug and whatever was in it. What difference did it make now anyway? What we had to do was leave and leave as soon as we could. The door didn't open at first, but it was just jammed because of the way it fit in the frame. A little jiggling of the handle got it to open. I closed it quickly behind me and returned to the living room.

My ankle was throbbing so badly now, it brought tears to my eyes. Maybe I would have to take a pill. Desperately, I fought off the need. I tried to concentrate on happy things and put it out of my mind. Fortunately, I fell asleep finally and didn't wake up until I heard laughter and noise and opened my eyes to see Harley and the man I now knew to be his grandfather coming into the house. They both paused in the doorway to look in on me.

"Hi," Harley said. "How are you doing?"

I tried to smile and sat up.

"You're in a lot of pain, huh?"

"Those things always hurt more the day after," his grandfather said. "Suze give you something else today? She cures all my aches and pains."

"No," I quickly replied.

"Where is she?" he asked, listening for sounds of her working or moving about.

"I don't know. Last I remember she told me she

was going to shop. I fell asleep so I'm not sure whether or not she has returned."

"Oh. Probably going to fix us another one of those special Haitian meals." He smiled, his eyes brightening with anticipation. "Maybe she's going to do *lambi en sauce*."

"What's that?" Harley asked.

"Conch in a thick sauce. It's my favorite. She's like that, very quiet, but always planning, plotting, thinking. I'll go look for her," he said. "She might be saying her evening prayers," he added and left us.

Harley stepped farther into the living room.

"We had a great day together," he said. "Neither of us shut up for more than a minute. He had so many questions to ask me, and he's really impressed with my knowledge of architecture. He said he really didn't know how valuable this house was until I explained it so well. The work went so fast, probably because we were both babbling constantly," he recited, spooling his words like a line off a fishing pole.

"I thought with the rain and all, you might not be able to do any work."

"Probably not if it was outside work, but he had a job to paint this apartment. He said it would have been a two-day job without me. I saved him a lot of time and money," he told me proudly.

"Did he tell you any more about himself?" I asked cautiously.

"Oh yeah, yeah, lots of stuff. He was in the navy, you know. On a destroyer like President

Kennedy! And he's seen a lot of the world. That's what I'd like to do, too, travel, see stuff. He's got so many great stories. Once, he and his buddies had a brawl in a tavern in Hong Kong. It was them against these drug dealers, and they ended up wrecking the place and having to spend a night in the jail there.

"And then he told me about this sailboat race he was in off of Gibralter. He misses the sea, but he says he's not upset because he's got lots of great experiences to remember. That's more valuable than money in the bank, he says. You store them here," Harley declared, pointing to his temple, "and no one but you can make a withdrawal. Funny way to put it, but when you think about it, it's true.

"I learned a lot about painting today, too, Summer. Most people think you just dip a brush into a can and slop it on as evenly as you can, but there are lots of little tricks, especially when you get down to the detail work. He did most of that, but he let me try a few frames once I got the hang of it. He said I was a chip off the old block."

He smiled like a conspirator, pulling his shoulders up with manly pride.

"We had a couple of beers together. He said age shouldn't matter when it comes to a few beers, especially if you're doing a man's job.

"Oh, and I asked him about Suze," he continued, barely pausing for a breath, "where they met and all. They met when he was working in New York City. She was living in an apartment next to the one he was using. It was a friend's and he used to hear her chanting and doing other strange things through the walls. So one day he asked her about it. He said they hit it off right away, and he started to look after her, but she really looked after him, fixing all sorts of medicines for him, bringing him good luck and such. When his father died, they just moved up here to take over the house so it wouldn't fall into disrepair."

"Disrepair? This isn't disrepair?"

"Well, more so than it has," he added laughing. Then he stopped smiling and looked at me. "Did you get to talk to your parents?"

"No. The phone's been out of order all day and when I went down to the corner to use the pay phone, that was out of order, too. It's terrible, Harley. I've got to reach them. I'm sure they're frantic with worry."

"Sure. We'll do something about that right away," he said. "The rain's finally stopped. Maybe the phones are working again here. You get my note? I hope you understand why I asked you not to tell too much detail."

"Yes, I understood, but Harley, we've got to go home," I said.

"Well, I was thinking about that, Summer. I'm sorry I put you through all this. I shouldn't have dragged you into something."

"You didn't drag me, Harley. I came along because I wanted to, and I'm not unhappy about that, even with the accident and all."

"I appreciate that. But what I'd like to do is get

you on a bus or on a plane and send you back. I want to stay a while. We're just getting to know each other and I wouldn't want to stop it abruptly."

"Harley, listen, you don't understand it all. Today, I had a chance to look around and . . ."

"Well, I was right," we heard. His grandfather came into the living room. "That's exactly what she went out and done. She got the ingredients she needed for *lambi en sauce*. You guys are in for a treat. Say, you want to see that '82 Honda Hawk cycle I have in the shed?" he asked Harley. "We've got a few minutes before we need to wash up for dinner. We can't be late for dinner," he warned. "Suze is a stickler when it comes to her dinners, especially if she makes a big effort like she's done for us tonight."

"Yeah," Harley replied with excitement. "I'd love to see that cycle."

"Maybe you can tinker with it from time to time and get it running again," his grandfather told him.

Harley smiled at me, but I didn't change my expression of worry. With my eyes, I tried to tell him to stay and talk to me, but he could only hear his own happiness. He misread my look of concern as being only for myself.

"Oh," he said, "Summer needs to call her parents right away."

"Sure. Phone's in the kitchen," his grandfather said.

"It wasn't working all day."

"That so. Well, try it now," he advised, "while I show Harley this old motorcycle of mine. Antique, I should say."

"Great," Harley said heading for the door with him. "We'll be right back, Summer."

I heard them leave, and then I got myself up. I had to get Harley alone soon and tell him what I found, I thought. It was obvious his grandfather wasn't going to tell him. He had plenty of opportunity to do so today and hadn't. I decided it wasn't right no matter what his reasons. Harley had to know the truth even though it would be painful to him. Learning about it later would be even more unpleasant, I thought.

I made my way back to the kitchen and to the phone. Suze was working on dinner, but didn't pay much attention to me. I lifted the receiver and dialed for the operator, but still I heard nothing.

"Why isn't the phone working already?" I asked in desperation.

Suze paused and thought a moment.

She shook her head.

"Sometimes, he forget to pay the bill," she revealed.

"What? The bill. You mean it's not just the storm?" I asked. I thought about the man in the grocery store and what he had said. "Why doesn't he pay his bills?" I hung up before she could reply.

"He do what he has to when he has to," she replied casually as if the problems and worries of this world were not very important in her scheme of things. She probably makes her phone calls on spiritual wires and doesn't care, I thought. Angrily, I headed for the front door again. I had to find Harley now and tell him. I wasn't going to keep Mommy in limbo a moment longer.

It took me a while to make my way around the house. I heard them talking in the shed and called for Harley. I had to shout loud for him to hear me over his and his grandfather's voices and the noise they were making tinkering with the motorcycle engine. Finally, he peered out of the door.

"Hey, what's wrong?"

"The phone's still dead, Harley. Suze says they might not have paid the phone bill."

"Naw, I paid that bill," his grandfather asserted coming up beside him to look out at me. "It's just the aftermath of the storm. Hell, once it took two days to get the phones working in this town again."

"Maybe the pay phone at the grocery works now," I said.

"If it doesn't work here, it doesn't there. We're on the same line," his grandfather insisted. "Tell you what. After dinner, I'll drive you over to Hurleyville. They have a different system and theirs might be working."

"I need to call right away," I cried.

"Only be a few hours, the most, and maybe our line will be back on by then anyway," he added, raising his arms.

Suddenly another sprinkle of rain began, quickly growing harder.

"Another cloudburst," Harley's grandfather

shouted. "Let's get inside before we all get soaked."

He charged out with Harley.

The two of them scooped me up and, laughing, carried me to the front of the house. We got under the porch not a second too soon because it did become another downpour.

"I hate this weather!" I screamed.

His grandfather laughed.

"Farmers need it," he said. "It's been dry up until now. C'mon, let's wash up for chow."

He opened the door and waited for us to follow. I glanced at Harley.

"I'm sorry, Summer," he said, "but I promise I'll get you to a phone tonight."

"Sure. Don't worry about it," his grandfather commented.

Upstairs, I thought, upstairs, I'll tell Harley everything I know.

Harley went directly up to shower and change. I followed and when I was positive we were out of earshot, I began.

"Harley, I had time today to do nothing but explore the house," I said.

"It's an amazing construction, isn't it?" he interrupted quickly. "I'm surprised more modern-day builders don't use some of the innovations here," he said taking out a fresh shirt, underwear and socks from his bag. He was kneeling on the floor, his back to me.

"I'm not talking about the house, Harley. I'm

328

talking about what's in it."

"Oh," he said standing. He nodded, thinking he knew exactly what was on my mind. "Well, he doesn't have much money. He's really laid back about material things. We talked about that today. He says at his age, he likes to do only what he has to and enjoy his relaxation."

"Did he talk about his age, explain how a man his age would have had your mother for a girl-friend?" I asked pointedly.

"No," he said shaking his head. "I didn't want to make too much of that. Lots of older men have younger girlfriends, Summer. Some women like more mature men. They're looking for a father figure."

"Oh, suddenly you're an expert on what women like and female psychology?" I asked.

He smiled.

"Hardly."

"I wasn't talking about the furniture in this house, Harley, or the worn rugs or anything like that. I found a door that led down a short stair-way to a basement room where old things are kept."

"Oh?" He paused now, holding his clothes. "I'd better get washed up," he whispered. "You heard what he said about being on time for dinner."

He kept walking.

"Harley!"

"Don't take too long, you guys," I heard his grandfather call up the stairway.

"Just let me wash up first, Summer. We've got

all night to talk about it."

"Harley, wait."

He went into the bathroom and closed the door.

Frustrated, I stood there listening to the shower start. I was going to stand there and wait for him to come out of the bathroom, but his grandfather came up the stairs to get something in another room so I had to move down the hallway and pretend I was doing things to get ready for dinner, too. He saw me and began to talk about the food.

"I bet you never ate nothing like it," he said. "First time Suze cooked for me, I thought her food was more than just food. It makes you feel good inside, like magic. I know that sounds silly, but maybe you'll see. Your mother a good cook?"

"She doesn't cook much anymore," I said. "We have an Irishwoman who's been with us forever and she's a wonderful cook."

"Oh," he said, nodding thoughtfully.

Harley emerged, his hair brushed neatly, his face cleanly shaven.

"You look real handsome, son," his grandfather said. He turned to me. "And despite your bad ankle, Summer, you look very nice too."

"Let's eat," Harley cried, slapping his hands together. His grandfather laughed. They looked at me, waiting like gentlemen for me to go ahead. Reluctantly, I started down the stairs ahead of them, listening to them babble on and on about the work they had done today.

At dinner their conversation was about other

jobs his grandfather had held in his life. I listened carefully, waiting to hear something that would make Harley question who he really was. From the way he spoke, he seemed to have worked his way around the world, doing everything from being an electrician to a waiter. When could he even have had a chance to meet Aunt Glenda? I thought, and hoped Harley had the same question in his mind.

"You did so many interesting things," Harley said instead.

"When you're hungry, you're innovative," his grandfather declared. "You learn how to survive, and that, my son, is the best sort of education. It prepares you for every hardship and every disappointment in life. Kids today have it too easy. Everything's done for them," he said, glancing at me. "Parents think if they give them more, they'll love them more and be better people for it. Don't believe it. Something you earn with your own sweat and effort has more value to you."

"I believe that," Harley said. He looked at me and smiled. "Neither of us is spoiled, if that's what you might think."

"Oh no, no. One look tells me that you both have some grit, and that comes from self-confidence. Ain't this just the most delicious meal you ever had," he declared.

"It's different. I'm finding brand new flavors and tastes," Harley said. "Right, Summer?"

"Different," I said.

Suze had been staring at me throughout the

meal. It made me very nervous and I tried to avoid her eyes, which I guess only confirmed suspicions. His grandfather appeared to notice.

"I guess Suze showed you her holy room today, eh, Summer?" he asked.

I looked at Harley.

"Yes, she did."

"She showed it to me this morning," Harley said, winking.

"Her beliefs seem strange to you, I'm sure, but your beliefs would probably seem just as strange to someone from her land. It all depends on where you're standing when you see something," he declared. "I learned that from being on the sea."

Harley smiled at him. He was becoming so charmed, even bewitched, with his grandfather and every word out of his mouth with every passing minute would make it more difficult for him when he learned the truth, I thought. I almost felt like keeping it a secret and just leaving, hoping he would make his own discoveries and learn to accept them. It confused me. I really didn't know what to do.

When I offered to help clean up, Harley's grandfather insisted I go into the living room and relax.

"As soon as I help her, I'll drive you over to Hurleyville to make that phone call," he promised.

"Great," Harley said. "Thanks." He looked at me and then turned back to him and said, "Dad."

His grandfather beamed. I had to look away quickly.

"You don't have to help me," Suze told him. She looked at me hard. "You take her to call."

"Okay. You heard her." He leaned toward us. "You don't fool around with a woman who knows Voodun and could put a wicked spell on you," he whispered with an impish smile.

Harley laughed, but I felt a lump stop my swallowing. I was hoping for a private moment with Harley before we left, but his grandfather was on top of us constantly, helping me navigate the porch steps and getting me into the truck. They put my crutch in the back, but we were all still squeezed close together in the cab.

As we rode along what seemed to me to be rather bumpy roads, his grandfather talked about the area, pointing out different buildings and houses in which he had worked.

"About five years ago, they started this custom home development and I took on more work than I wanted. Suze bawled me out for it and eventually I got myself out of some contracts. She really looks after me. Nothing better than having a good woman look after you," he lectured.

He glanced at me after he made a turn onto a better road.

"Harley says you're about the best friend he's got now. Nothing wrong with a man having a woman as a best friend. There's trust and that's important. He knows you won't do anything to hurt him and vice versa," he added.

When I looked at him, I thought his eyes were fixed more firmly on me. Was he trying to tell me something? My nerves were frazzled as it was. Now they felt like they were snapping like strained wires. My heart pounded. I felt Harley slide his hand into mine and squeeze. When I looked at him, he was smiling. I didn't think I had ever seen him as happy as he was these past hours, and on the tip of my tongue were the words that would wipe that happiness out of his mind and heart as quickly as someone erasing the words *I love you* from a blackboard.

I stared ahead, thinking only of Mommy and what I would say.

We stopped at a garage and Harley's father pointed to the pay phone.

"If that one don't work, none of 'em work here," he remarked.

Harley jumped out to see if there was a dial tone and waved me on, smiling.

His grandfather came around to help me get out of the truck. He handed me the crutch and smiled.

"Thank you."

"No problem," he said. I went to the phone. Harley handed the receiver to me and our eyes locked for a moment.

"I want to go home tomorrow, Harley," I said.

He nodded. "Fine," he said. "Just don't tell them where I am until I say so, okay? Please," he begged.

My heart felt so heavy. I glanced back at his

334

grandfather, who stood by his truck, watching us. I could blurt it out right here and now, I thought, but what would it be like afterward? I was afraid for both of us.

I nodded and dialed the operator to place a collect call. Moments later, I heard Daddy's voice.

"Summer, where are you? What's going on?"

"I'm fine, Daddy. I really am. We're with . . . Harley's family," I said quickly, "but I'm coming home tomorrow. I'll fly to Richmond," I said.

"Your mother's beside herself here. This was just crazy, just crazy."

"I'll explain it all better when I'm home, Daddy."

"You're sure you're all right?"

"Yes, Daddy."

I thought it would be easier to explain my ankle when I was there.

"Your mother has to speak to you," Daddy said, and a second later, I heard Mommy say my name.

"I'm okay, Mommy. Please don't cry," I begged. "We didn't want to hurt anyone. It was something I had to do for Harley and now it's over and I'll be on my way home."

"Where are you?"

"I'll tell you everything, tomorrow," I said.

"Your uncle Roy is very, very upset, honey. He's worried and just beside himself. He hasn't worked. He sits by the phone. Can you get Harley to call him?"

"I don't know, Mommy."

"He really cares for him, honey. He is sick over

this and after all his sadness, too."

"I know, Mommy," I said, tears burning my eyes. "I'll talk to him about it. I promise."

"What time will you be home?"

"I'll call you from the airport in the morning, Mommy."

"I don't know what to think about all this. I just don't know," she said, her voice cracking with disappointment. It made me sick inside.

"I'll see you tomorrow, Mommy. Tell Daddy I love him and I love you."

"Summer, hurry back," she cried.

I hung up, the tears now fleeing my eyes like tiny fugitives frantic for a quick escape from my burning cheeks.

Harley put his arm around my shoulders.

"Thanks," he said. "I'll get you to the airport first thing. I promise."

I couldn't talk. I just nodded and he led me back to the truck.

"Summer's going home tomorrow, Dad," Harley told his grandfather.

"Oh. Well, that's okay. She's welcome to stay as long as she wants, of course."

"I'll have to take her to the airport before joining you at the job."

"No problem," his grandfather said. He smiled. "With all we got done today, I could take a whole day off and it wouldn't hurt the schedule. Might even do that," he declared.

Harley laughed. He held my hand and stared at me and then, when his grandfather wasn't looking, he leaned over to kiss my cheek and whisper "thank you," one more time.

How do you tell someone who thinks he is standing on top of the world that he's standing on a bubble of lies?

And it could be a long and painful way down to the truth.

13

The Secret Room

Suze was standing before us in the hallway when we returned. She was crouched, her eyes beady, looking like she had been prowling through the house to find signs of something evil. She waited for us all to enter, her gaze fixed mostly on me.

"Anything wrong, Suze?" Harley's grandfather asked.

I heard her close the basement door.

"You left the light on downstairs," she told him.

My heart almost did a full flip-flop in my chest. In my haste to leave after making my shocking discoveries, I had left it on.

"Me? I don't think so," he replied. "What's the difference if I did? It don't burn much electricity. Well, what do you think, Suze? The phones over in Hurleyville were working after all."

She smirked, her dark eyes still turned on me.

"They all leaving then?" she asked.

"Just Summer," Harley's grandfather said. "My

boy's going to stick around a while and help his old man get through some of this work, right, Harley?"

"Yes sir," Harley said.

"Hear that, Suze? 'Yes, sir.' That's my boy. That's what I'd expect. Well, we're all taking some time off tomorrow to take Summer here over to the airport. You want to go for a ride with us?"

Where would he put her? I wondered, in the back?

"No. I got some work," she said. "I don't take days off at the drop of a pin."

Harley's grandfather roared and shook his head as she turned and went back to the kitchen or her holy room.

"Let's see if the television's back on at least," his grandfather suggested.

"I'm tired, Harley," I said.

"Maybe you should take another pill, Summer. You need the sleep tonight."

I nodded. I was hoping he would come up so we could talk, but he lingered, obviously wanting to sit around with the man he thought was his father. He cherished every moment.

"Maybe I will," I said.

"Good night there, Summer. We'll make sure you're at the airport early," his grandfather called to me.

"We don't even know what times the planes leave for where I need to go," I said.

"We'll find all that out in due time. No sense worrying about it tonight. I never worry today over stuff I can put off till tomorrow," he added with a laugh. Harley laughed too.

That's irresponsibility, I thought. It's not something to admire in someone. Uncle Roy would never say something like that. He would have everything planned and prepared. Couldn't Harley see the difference? Was the need for someone to love and someone to love him so great that it didn't matter if he was real or not?

It made me angry, but then I thought I shouldn't be so condemning. After all, Harley's the one who had lost his mother recently. He's the one who feels like an orphan, and the one who has come here looking for love.

"Okay," I said and started toward the stairs. When I reached them, Suze came out of the kitchen and glared at me as she wiped a pan with a dishtowel. Her eyes were fixed on me and piercingly scrutinizing.

"Anything wrong?" I asked, my very bones in a tremble.

"Who sent you here?" she asked in a whisper. Her eyes widened in expectation of the answer.

"What? Sent me? No one sent me. I came with Harley."

"Why you come?" she followed quickly.

"You know why," I said.

She continued to stare. I fought down a scream and continued up the stairway, fleeing from her. Maybe I shouldn't wait until tomorrow morning, I thought. Maybe I should have Harley take me to the airport on his motorcycle or get myself a taxi.

I sat on the bed, thinking about it. Would it be right to just leave him behind in all this though? I wondered. Later, would he be angry that I had left without telling him about my discoveries?

My mind was in such turmoil, I didn't know whether it was that or the pain radiating up my leg from my ankle that made me feel as nauseous and dizzy as I was. I had to lie back. Through the floor, I could hear the murmur of Suze's chanting. I imagined it came from her holy room. How was I supposed to fall asleep with all this going on anyway? I should have remained downstairs with Harley.

I closed my eyes and tried to think what Mommy would do. She wouldn't leave without telling Harley everything, I decided. She would say the truth might be a hard thing to swallow, but swallow you must if you wanted to be free of deception, especially when the person you're deceiving is you, yourself.

"I've got to tell him," I muttered to myself. "I've got to."

Why were my eyelids so heavy? I fought to keep them open. I wanted to hear Harley come up the stairs and call him to my room as soon as I had. I would stay fully dressed and wait, I thought.

I'll just rest a little, but I'll continue to listen for him. I did try to stay awake, but I was like a mountain climber on a hill of pure ice, my feet slipping until I lost my hold completely and slid rapidly down, down into the darkness of a tunnel that dropped me into a pool of nightmares.

Suze's face oozed out of the blackness. Her eyes glittered like tinfoil, the ebony pupils spinning and spinning until tiny drills extended toward me. I heard myself scream and she popped like a soap bubble, only to be replaced by that horrible rat in the holy room. Its body swelled until its head receded under the folds of gray and it turned into a dark gray ball that began to roll toward me.

I felt myself running, limping as my foot touched the ground and the pain was triggered, shooting darts up inside my leg, darts that entered my stomach. I groaned. The ground beneath me turned into softer and softer mud. I sank deeper and deeper until I disappeared, gagging as the muck sank into my mouth and then my nose.

My eyes snapped open. I looked about quickly. Was I awake or still in my nightmares? I held my breath and listened. There was no more chanting. It was very quiet and very dark. I glanced at my watch in the soft shaft of moonlight now coming through the window and saw I had been sleeping for hours. Oh no, I thought, Harley has already gone to bed. I was in too deep of a sleep to have heard him.

I sat up, feeling just horrible. My lower back ached, my leg felt like it had gone numb from the pain and my stomach continued to rumble. Why had I eaten Suze's rich food? I found my crutch and rose. There was no light on in the hallway, but my eyes were used to the darkness enough for me to safely make my way to the bathroom.

Afterward, I felt weaker and sicker. I thought I

342

was going to vomit, too, but I held it down and returned to my room. I lay there, curled up, moaning softly and chastising myself for having been so stupid. Once I had learned about the lies, I should have screamed them aloud and not permitted this madness to continue. Who knew what else that woman had put into my food?

I was hoping Harley had heard me moving about and would come to see how I was, but he must have fallen into so deep a sleep that he could hear nothing. Perhaps his grandfather had given him more beer to drink and maybe he had drunk too much.

I couldn't fall asleep again. I was worried I wouldn't have an opportunity in the morning to tell Harley what I had discovered. I hated my stomach for still being in such turmoil. Every time I tried to sit up, a ribbon of pain snapped across it and around my sides, down my back. Sometimes, it took my breath away. There was nothing to do but rest and wait for it all to pass.

Seconds became minutes; minutes became hours. Despite my fears, I fell asleep for a while and woke with a shudder. Carefully, I lifted my head from the pillow and edged myself into a sitting position. My stomach was still sore, but at least it wasn't forecasting storm after storm of pain anymore. Blinking my eyes and trying to pull myself back into focus, I lowered my feet to the floor, grabbed my crutch and started out again. I tried to be as quiet as I could in the hallway.

Harley's door was closed. I opened it slowly and

peered in to see his head on the pillow, bathed in the soft moonlight. He looked so contented, perhaps sleeping comfortably for the first time in a long time. I thought I even detected a tiny smile on his lips and imagined he was dreaming about all the things he would be doing in the days to come with the man he thought was his real father. Just for a moment it made me hesitant. I knew that often the person bringing bad news is hated as much as the news, but I wasn't the one doing the terrible wrong thing here.

If his grandfather really did care for him, he wouldn't be layering one coat of lies over another, dipping his paintbrush into a can of illusion and smearing gobs and gobs of deception over Harley in hopes he would never know the truth. I didn't care what his reasons were, even if they were noble. If I had learned anything from my parents and the stories Mommy had told me about her troubled childhood, it was that lies have a way of spinning out of control and weaving a web of confusion and pain so tightly around you that it would take forever sometimes to break free.

I moved quickly to his bedside and touched his shoulder. He moaned, but his eyes didn't open.

"Harley," I whispered. "Harley." I shook his shoulder harder this time and his eyes snapped open.

"Whaaa? What?" He turned toward me. "Summer! What's wrong?"

"Everything," I said.

"You're feeling bad?"

"Yes, but that's not half of what's wrong."

I heard what sounded like a loud creak, the kind of noise you might hear if someone was tiptoeing in the hallway.

"What?" he asked louder.

"Wait," I whispered and listened hard.

"Summer, what are you doing?" Harley questioned, sitting up quickly.

I didn't hear any more sounds so I turned back to him.

"I have something to tell you, Harley, something that is going to make you very unhappy, but I couldn't permit myself to leave here tomorrow without you knowing it all."

"What is it?" he demanded, his face becoming fully awake now, his eyes widening.

I took a deep breath and sat beside him on the bed.

"When you were away, I had nothing to do but explore the house," I began.

"And you found Suze's holy room, I know."

"No, she showed me that, but that's not it, even though it's plenty weird."

"What then?" he pursued with some impatience.

"I found this door in the hallway and opened it thinking it was just a closet, but it was a door to a small basement room. I went down the stairs to look around."

"Oh, so you were the one who left the light on," he said, remembering Suze's accusation.

"Yes."

"Well, why didn't you say so?"

"Let me finish, Harley."

"I'm waiting for you to finish," he said, his impatience growing. "It's late and I can hardly think. So what did you find, some voodoo doll or something?"

"Worse, Harley. I found a newspaper article about your father. It told about his being chased after committing an armed robbery."

"My father?" He started to smile.

"And his death," I added. "He had an accident fleeing from the police."

His smile held a moment and then evaporated as he shook his head.

"What are you talking about, Summer? You sound crazy. You having a bad dream or what?"

"I wish it was only a bad dream. I'd be very happy, Harley."

"I don't understand. How can my father be dead and be here in the house at the same time? Is he a ghost, someone Suze brought back from the dead?" he asked with a smile.

"No, Harley. The man in this house is not your father. He's your grandfather," I told him. "The newspaper article makes that perfectly clear."

He stared without speaking. Then he looked away for a moment as if he hoped that when he looked back at me, I'd be gone and all this was just his dream.

"You've got to be mistaken," he said finally. "You just didn't read it right. Maybe it was a cousin or someone with a similar name or . . ."

"I did read it right, Harley, and there are pictures down there, too, pictures of your grandfather and your grandmother and your father when he was a little boy. There's a picture I believe is your father on the wall as well. Don't you see? It explains why he's so old now."

"No," Harley said, shaking his head vigorously. "You're wrong, Summer. You've got to be wrong. He talked about my mother. He knew all about her."

"Whatever he knew, he knew from listening to your father talk about her."

"Why would he do this? It doesn't make any sense, Summer," he insisted.

"I don't know his reasons. Maybe he's ashamed of it all. Maybe what happened left him so empty inside, he grabbed onto the opportunity to have you. Maybe Suze told him some mystical reason and performed some voodoo ritual. Who knows? The thing is it's all so strange and I didn't want to leave you without you knowing."

"I still can't believe it," he said shaking his head, but not as vigorously.

"Perhaps he means to tell you the truth someday, but I didn't want to take the chance of his never telling you. I couldn't leave here like that. I'd be thinking about it all the time, worrying about you."

He glared angrily into the darkness. Then he threw off his blanket.

"I want you to show me this stuff right now," he said. "I'm sure it's a mistake. I'm sure."

"All right," I said. "I will."

He got up, found his pants and slipped them on. He didn't put on his shoes and socks, however, or a shirt.

"Let's go," he said, "and very quietly. I don't want us waking them up if we can help it."

"I don't want us waking them up either," I said, but not because I would feel bad about disturbing their rest.

We left his room and moved very quietly down the hallway to the stairs. At the top, we stood and listened to be sure they were asleep. The house seemed very quiet, but a house like this was never completely quiet. Its shutters tapped in the wind. Its ceilings and floors creaked and the pipes moaned in the walls. Things scurried about in the shadows.

A thick candle burned on a table in the kitchen and the glow of that threw shadows over the walls, shadows that moved and trembled with the flickering flame. I felt every muscle in my body tighten. When I looked at Harley, I saw how anger had filled his eyes and tightened his jaw. I knew that for now most of that anger was directed toward me. With all his heart, he wanted me to be wrong. Seeing such fury in his eyes made me almost wish I had left without telling him.

"I'm better off without the crutch," I told him. "I'll use the banister and just limp."

He nodded and we started down. The steps became little tattletales moaning and groaning under our careful footsteps. After one in particular sounded as if it might give way completely, we both paused to listen and see if we had been heard.

Harley nodded and we continued to the bottom of the stairs and then down the hallway to the basement door. He looked at me and then he opened it and I showed him the light switch. He flicked it and the light, as poor as it was, made us squint for a moment.

"It's all right there in those cartons at the bottom," I said softly.

He started down and I followed. He stopped to look at the picture on the wall.

"I think that really is your father," I said.

He glanced at me and back at the picture.

"I don't see much difference."

"Okay, Harley." He would see what he wanted to, I thought, until he was forced to see the truth. "Look in the second carton on the right. I left it all on top," I said.

He went to it and squatted. I joined him, making myself as comfortable as I could under the circumstances and watched as he read the news clipping. His eyebrows lifted and fell with the revelations. Then he shook his head.

"I don't understand this," he muttered. "Why pretend to be my father?"

"Like I said, maybe he's ashamed of it all. Maybe he thought he could do something nice. Maybe . . ."

We heard the door above slam closed and both looked up the stairway.

"What was that?" he asked.

He stood up and helped me to my feet. We heard a loud scraping noise and a bang against the wall and the door.

"What's going on?"

He hurried ahead of me up the stairs and tried the door. It didn't budge an inch.

"It's locked or blocked," he reported as I came up behind him.

"Bang on it. Maybe Suze found it open and just closed it," I said.

He nodded and pounded on the door.

"Hey," he called. "We're down here. Open the door. Hey!"

We waited and listened. There were some footsteps in the hallway and then, silence.

Harley tried the door again, pushing with all his strength.

"It feels like that cabinet was slid in front of it," he said.

"She must have done it. She's crazy, Harley, really weird. She thinks she has her dead son's soul in a jug!"

He nodded and started to shout louder. He stopped and we listened; again, we heard nothing.

"He couldn't sleep through all this," Harley remarked angrily. He pounded the door with his closed fist. It was a thick door, like all of them in the house. His thumping seemed easily absorbed and smothered.

"Why isn't he waking up and coming to let us out?" Harley cried. He pounded and pounded.

"Harley," I said, now growing more terrified. "What are they doing to us?"

He looked at me a moment, his own face filling with shock and fear. Then he shook his head.

"I don't know. This is crazy. You're right," he said.

He continued to pound and pound until his hands were red. I sat on a step and waited.

"Why would they do this?" Harley muttered. "Why?" he shouted at the door.

I looked up at him. He not only looked betrayed and frightened. He looked terribly guilty when he turned his eyes to me.

"What did I get you into?" he asked, shaking his head.

"It's my fault, Harley. I should have told you about all this earlier."

"Why didn't you?" he asked, suddenly realizing and wondering, too.

"You were so happy here. Everything was going the way you wanted. I felt horrible even thinking about it, and then I told myself I would tell you everything before I left, but I got so sick from that food and whatever else she put in mine that I missed a chance to do so earlier.

"I was also hoping you might go back with me and I could tell you everything once we had left. I'm sorry," I said. "This is my fault, my fault."

"No, no, don't blame yourself. That's silly. They have no right to lock us in here. And what for? Why? Why?" he screamed at the door.

Then he looked at me and we stared at each other, both of us feeling that cold overwhelming fear that came with the question lingering above us like a storm cloud. The answer could be more horrible than we could even imagine, and yet we had to know, we had to ask.

Why?

It was madness, all of it, the impersonation, the holy room, being locked down here.

And we were trapped in it.

"He probably thinks he's teaching us some kind of a lesson," Harley decided.

He sat beside me on the next to bottom step. I nodded, willing to accept anything that was short of the horrors running through my mind.

"I had such a good time with him today," he continued, shaking his head with a soft, dazed smile on his lips. "When he showed me stuff, he was so patient and interested, and when I did it right, he looked so proud and happy.

"Roy's shown me stuff too, and he looks satisfied when I do it right, but this was different. It was important to him. It was like something of him had found a place in me. I felt very good about it, too," he said, turning to me. "I felt a good family feeling."

"He's probably a very confused man, Harley. What his son did must have had a very big effect on him and then there's that Suze. Who knows what strange ideas she's been putting in his head? Before, when I went up to sleep, she stopped to ask me who had sent me?"

"Who had sent you?"

"Yes, like it was part of some evil conspiracy, like I had come from the devil, maybe to steal her dead son's soul out of that jug. Who knows?"

I gazed about the small room.

"We've got to get out of here. That's all I do know," I said.

Harley nodded and stood up.

"This is too small to be the entire basement for a house like this," he said. "It was probably built to be some sort of storage area."

He started to inspect the walls and paused on the far right.

"This part was built relatively recently."

He gazed around and then returned to the cartons, taking everything out of every one of them, finally holding up a pair of scissors. He looked at me, quickly becoming concerned.

"You're very tired, aren't you?"

"Yes," I had to admit. "I got sick from the dinner before, and it's left me feeling weak."

"You've got to rest," he said.

He found a few empty potato sacks and then formed a makeshift pillow with all the newspapers. He spread out one of the sacks.

"Lie down here for a while," he suggested. "It's not very comfortable, but you can get a little rest while I try to figure out a way to get us out of here, Summer."

"Maybe they'll let us out in the morning," I said. "They've got to. We could die down here if they don't. They wouldn't let that happen, would they?"

"Don't make yourself sick with worry. Just rest. I got us into this situation. I'm going to get us out of it," he vowed.

"I'm all right."

"Please, rest, Summer," he begged.

I rose and went to the makeshift bed. I sprawled on my good side and lowered my head to his improvised pillow. Then he drew another one of the potato sacks over me to serve as a blanket.

"You all right?"

"Yes," I said and closed my eyes.

Was this a dream? Would I wake up any moment and laugh about it?

I felt Harley's lips on my cheek and opened my eyes with surprise.

"Thanks for worrying so much about me and caring so much about my happiness that you kept all this to yourself, Summer. It's nice to know someone is that concerned about me and my happiness."

"Then you're not mad at me?"

"Are you kidding? I can't imagine ever being mad at you. Well, maybe for a split second," he admitted.

I smiled and he kissed me again, this time on the lips. Even at this horrible time, I could stare into his face and see he really did love me.

"Sleep," he whispered kissing my eyes. I kept them closed, and he returned to the walls to find a way out of the trap I had put us in. It was all my fault, whether he wanted to say it or not.

The combination of the pain from my ankle, my having an upset stomach and the terror I felt after our being locked in this basement room was enough to make me sleep, despite my great effort to stay awake for Harley. I guess I passed out more than just slept. All I know was I closed my eyes and when I opened them again, Harley, exhausted himself, was seated on the floor across from me, his back to the wall, some of the wood pulled away, exposing what looked like an opening.

I glanced at my watch. Because there were no windows in this room, there was no way to tell if it was morning. My watch told me it was just a little past six a.m. The sun should be up, I thought. Maybe they would wake soon, realize what they had done, and open that door.

I licked my lips. They felt so dry. Being down here in this cool, damp room made my muscles ache, too, especially after having fallen asleep in so awkward a position and on so hard a surface. I moaned with the effort to sit up. Harley was so still, his lips barely trembling with each regular breath. I rose to my feet and gazed up the stairway.

There was something at the top, something that hadn't been there before.

I went up the stairs and looked at what was a new carton. Opening the top, I gazed down to see two bottles of water and some of Suze's home-made bread rolls, cheeses, and some sticks of what looked like beef jerky. Included with it all was a sheet of paper. I read what was written.

I know you're angry right now. I'm angry, too. You shouldn't have gone snooping about. Suze has read the signs and told me Fletcher's bad spirit had awoken in you and might take control. I don't believe everything she says, of course, but she's been right most of the time.

Suze says you've got to stay down there until the evil spirit is out of you. It won't be long. She's working on it.

I don't know why you couldn't have let things be. We were doing so well.

Perhaps Suze is right and it's not your fault. You can't help what's happened any more than I could help it.

I guess you know who I am now, so I might as well just write it.

Grandpa

This really is madness, I thought, pure madness. They want to keep us down here until his voodoo lady thinks it's all right for us to come up?

"Summer?"

Harley stirred, wiped his eyes and stood up.

"What's happening? Did they unlock the door? Are they letting us out?"

"No. It's worse," I said. "They shoved some food in here in a carton and your grandfather has written you a letter. At least he admits who he really is," I said.

Harley came up the stairs, looked into the carton and then took the letter and read it, smirking and shaking his head.

"Evil spirit is out of us?"

He lunged at the door, pushing against it with his shoulder and then pounding on it.

"Grandpa! Get this door open now! You hear me!"

We waited and listened, but heard nothing.

"Do you think it's safe to drink this water?" I asked. "I'm very, very thirsty."

Harley studied it and shook his head.

"I don't know."

"Maybe I should wait a little longer," I said.

"There's something behind that wall. I think there was once a door there and it has been covered. It might be another way out of here."

He hurried back down the stairs and started pulling at the wood, prying what he could with the scissors and ripping some away with his bare hands. He worked frantically, madly, frightening me with his wild efforts.

"Take it easy, Harley," I said. "You'll hurt yourself."

He ignored me or didn't hear me. He was in a frenzy by now, kicking and pulling on the wood with the side of his foot, tearing off only a few inches at a time sometimes, but gnawing away at it like some underground creature. I stepped up beside him and put my hand on his shoulder, which finally brought him to a pause. The sweat was running down his temples and his face and neck were crimson, flushed. His right palm was bleeding.

"You have hurt yourself and you'll exhaust yourself quickly, Harley. You hardly slept and you haven't eaten or drunk anything either."

"I've got to get us out of here," he moaned, his eyes glassy with tears of anger and frustration. "You've got to go home. We both have to go home," he said.

"We will, Harley. We will," I said softly.

He calmed some more and looked at the opening he had torn.

"Can you see anything in there?" I asked.

"No. It's very dark. Obviously no windows on that side either. Still, there might be another door or a door that goes directly outside. Many of these old houses had doors on the basements and stairways up with a metal door over them. I'll work slower," he promised and went at it more methodically.

While he worked, I searched the small room for something else that might be of some use as a tool. Just under the stairs, I saw a thick piece of wood and pulled it out — a yard-long two-by-four.

"Harley?"

He turned and smiled.

"Yeah, that's good. Good work," he said, and took it from me. He used it to pry away more of the wall, and soon he had torn enough for him to slip through.

"Be careful," I said as he started. "Don't scratch

yourself or step on anything sharp."

He didn't have a shirt on or any shoes or socks.

"Okay, okay," he said, anxious, and worked himself through the opening onto the other side.

He was so quiet for a while, I became very nervous.

"Harley?"

"It's all right," he said. "This is very strange. I'm looking for some kind of light, but it looks like I'm in an old living room or something. Wait."

There was a flicker and then some light.

"Electricity works," he cried.

I poked my head through the opening and gazed around. It did look like an old living room. There was a thick-cushioned light brown sofa and a matching settee across from it with a table in between. Beside the sofa was a pole lamp with a flowery shade, and on the far right of the settee was the small lamp Harley had lit.

"It's more than just a living room," Harley called back from behind another wall. "There's a kitchenette back here and a bathroom, too.

"The water runs!" he cried. "I'll let it run a while and we can drink this without worrying."

I decided to slip through the opening, too, and did so. I tried to keep off my bad ankle as I hopped to the sofa. It was very dusty. Our movement stirred up the layers of dust on the concrete floor, making the air even more murky. There was a very musty odor. Water had seeped in around the foundation from time to time, staining the walls and the floor.

Someone had once tried to turn this into some kind of a retreat, I thought. There were some weak attempts to give the room warmth. Although there were no windows, a curtain had been hung to make it seem as if there was a window. Half of the curtain drooped. It was once white and blue, but now looked gray and very dirty. Here and there were framed prints of rustic scenes: farmhouses, woods and fields. There was a clock lodged in what was a hand-carved Swiss house with figures of milkmaids and farmers on a small platform in front. The little door looked like it opened on the hour. I touched the chimes and to my surprise, they began swinging steadily back and forth, the clock beginning to tick as if it had never stopped.

On the table next to the sofa were the remnants of someone's efforts to knit what looked like a dark blue sweater. There was a bag of wool, more knitting needles and some more completed knitting beside it. On the wall behind the settee, I saw a table upon which was an old phonograph and a pile of what looked like antiques to me . . . the large, 33 rpm records I had seen in our house, records once collected by my great-grandparents.

Harley had crossed the room and turned on another lamp. It was beside a convertible bed pulled from another sofa. There was still a blanket, pillows and a sheet on the bed. At the foot of it was a trunk. He lifted the lid and peered down.

"More bedding," he said, "and another pillow."

Over to the right of the bed was an armoire. I

limped over to it, opened it and saw the clothes. They were all women's clothes. There were about a half-dozen or so pairs of shoes at the bottom, too.

"Who lived here?" I asked Harley.

He shook his head.

"No one said anything to me." He remembered the running water and went back to the kitchenette to get me a glass. "Cold," he said handing it to me. "It comes from a submersible well. Good water." He drank a glass himself.

I couldn't believe how thirsty I was. He returned to get me another glass while I continued to explore the room, looking at the contents. I found a stack of old books and some very faded, sepia photographs of a woman and a man. The man looked very serious, almost angry, but the woman was pleasant looking, pretty with an enigmatic smile, one that could mean happiness or could mean a deep sadness.

"There's no door out of here," Harley reported with disappointment after inspecting every inch of the room. "The entrance and the exit must have been that short stairway. The foundation of the house is deep, which explains why there are no windows."

"It must have always been damp and dark here then, Harley. Why would anyone want to stay here?"

"I don't know," he said. "A hideaway of sorts, I guess."

The clock that I had started suddenly struck

the hour and the doors opened to release a couple of dancers, a man and a woman, who spun for a few moments and then retreated back into the clock.

Harley laughed. He had his arms folded across his naked chest.

"You're going to get sick with all this dampness and no shirt and shoes on, Harley," I said.

I returned to the armoire and searched through the clothes until I found a light blue cotton pull-over sweater. I held it up.

"It'll be tight, but it's something," I said.

"I'm not putting that on. That's a woman's sweater."

"Harley Arnold, I'm not going to let you get sick down here. Put it on."

Reluctantly, he took it from me and shook it and then pulled it over his head. It was so tight, he could barely move his arms. He looked at me and smirked and then he took the scissors out of his back pocket and cut off the sleeves.

"At least I can breathe," he declared. "Now don't ask me to put on a pair of those shoes. I couldn't fit my feet in them anyway."

"At least put on these socks," I said holding up a pair I had found. Reluctantly, he obeyed.

"Let's see what else of value we can find," he suggested.

We both returned to exploring the room.

"I wish there was a telephone down here," he called from the side of the bed while I went through the cabinets in the small kitchenette.

"It wouldn't do us any good. Your grandfather probably didn't pay the bill."

"Right. Hey," he called, "there's a carton of stuff shoved under the bed."

I came out and watched him take out more pictures, books, and then what looked like a little girl's rag doll.

"Strange. I didn't think a kid was down here," he said turning the doll in his hands.

"It's someone's childhood memory, Harley. Women often keep the dolls they had as little girls."

"Yeah," he said thoughtfully. "I guess. So who lived here?" he asked.

I studied the room more carefully until my eyes settled on a smaller box below the table upon which the phonograph and records were. Opening the box, I found what looked like an old composition notebook, the edges of the pages yellow with age. While Harley tapped on the walls, looking for another possible entryway that had been covered, I sat on the sofa, opened the notebook and began reading.

"Harley!" I called.

"What?"

"I know who was down here."

"Who?" he asked starting toward me.

"Your grandmother," I said. "The sad-looking pretty woman in the photographs we found out in the other room. This," I said, holding up the notebook, "is her diary. She must have written it while she was down here."

"How can you be so sure she wrote it down here?" he asked.

"From the very first sentence," I replied. He waited and I looked back at the notebook and read.

After Fletcher died, I told Ed that the only place I didn't hear the voices in our house was down in the basement. In the beginning, I only heard the voices at night, but after a while, I could hear the whispering even in the daytime, so he fixed up the basement for me so I would have a safe place whenever I needed it. He even put a little kitchen in for me.

I paused and looked at Harley. His lips were turned into his cheek, his eyes full of astonishment. I looked back at the diary.

He said, "Come up whenever you want, Francine."
I smiled at him and shook my head. He knew. He knew very well.
I'd never come up again.

Harley and I looked at each other.
Would it be the same for us?

14

Grandmother's Diary

"Are you hungry?" Harley asked me.

After what my stomach had gone through the night before, I didn't feel like putting anything more than water in it, but I had found some tea and thought I might make a cup. The small electric stove range worked.

"For the time being, I think I had better give my stomach a little rest, Harley. I'm feeling much better, and I don't want to take any chances, especially under the circumstances," I emphasized.

"I can't help it. I'm hungry. I guess the beef jerky can't be poisoned. It's in a wrapper. I'll go back and get that and see if they've come to their senses and opened the door yet," Harley said and went while I boiled some water.

He returned with the carton they had left.

"Rolls aren't bad," he said, chewing on one. "They can't mean to poison us. You really need to put something in your stomach, Summer," he insisted. "You can't go all day on just some tea."

"Okay," I said. I nibbled on a piece and then sipped some tea.

"The door's still locked," he said. "I listened, but I didn't hear a thing. For all I know, he might have gone back to work and left us with her. I tried banging and calling, but no one responded."

I nodded and looked at the diary again.

"Would you like to hear some of this?" I asked.

"Might as well. There's not much else to do until I figure something else out," he said, and sat beside me on the sofa.

I glanced at him and saw he was relaxed and ready. Then I opened the notebook and began.

Ed is becoming increasingly angry at me, I know. He cannot understand why I want to avoid going out. He is constantly telling me about people asking after me, but I know he's making that up. None of the people he refers to now really ever cared to ask after me before I stopped going out.

I let him go on and on about it. He needs to pretend. He's always needed to pretend more than I have. For years he told people Fletcher was doing so well. He made up so many stories about him, I had trouble keeping up with them and sometimes would be dumbfounded by the questions and comments people had.

Once he told people that Fletcher was working on constructing telephone communications in Saudi Arabia and that's why he was never here anymore. Then he told them he was working for the army and he was in Brazil. I think most of the stories came from Ed's own secret fantasies.

The truth was Fletcher wasn't doing anything as exciting and glamorous as anything Ed described. If Fletcher ever called, it was always from someplace on the road, just out of some Midwestern city or Eastern town where he had held down a job for a few months and either had gotten bored or fired and was on his way to someplace else. His future was always just 'someplace else.'

I know Fletcher was the way he was because Ed had pumped him up so much he made him think he should always be the one in charge, made him think he knew more than anyone. It was why he got into so much trouble in school and had to leave.

Ed's a good talker. He can spin words and weave them like silk. For years and years, he's been doing that to me and to Fletcher. Fletcher left, but I remained behind, living in the cocoon of illusions Ed spun. For a long time, it didn't matter. No one bothered me and Ed seemed content, too.

But the dreams and the make-believe began to wear thin. I could feel it happening, feel the world around me begin to collapse and holes start to form, holes through which the ugly, dark creatures I call Realies crawled. I'll never forget the first time I saw one.

We had finished dinner. Ed was tired. He had been working a job fifty miles away and the work and the travel were wearing on him. He began to look tired, gaunt, the circles around his eyes darkening. After dinner he went into the living room to watch television as usual and quickly fell asleep. I cleaned up and came in to sit with him, but he had slumped down on the sofa and had his eyes closed, so I picked up my knitting needles and continued to work on the afghan.

The television droned on. I had gotten so I rarely looked at it or heard anything, but I didn't mind the constant music and talk. It kept me company, kept me from feeling as lonely as I was. Hundreds and hundreds of faces moved through the glow, one merging into another, and the same was true of the voices. They became my electronic family, I suppose. They had no names, just different shades of light and color and different sounding voices.

Sometimes, Ed would complain about the soft, silly smile on my face as I worked.

"What's so funny?" he would ask. "It's the news you're watching and it's horrible."

"What? Oh. I wasn't watching or listening to that," I told him.

"Then why are you smiling, Francine?"

I put down my work and thought. Was I smiling?

"I don't know, Ed. I didn't realize I was smiling."

"Damn," he would say with disgust.

I know I was beginning to annoy him more and more. He was very angry when I made him go out for our groceries, but I couldn't do it anymore. The last time I went to the supermarket, I froze in an aisle and forgot my whole list. I left with nothing.

"I work all day and then I have to go and do our

shopping because you won't leave the damn house!" he yelled.

I didn't cry or argue. I just stared and he would give up and just do the shopping, furious the whole time. I didn't even feel guilty about it, although I knew it was unfair for him to have the added burden.

"I'm sorry, Ed," was all I could say.

"Sorry does me no good," he would reply, but he swallowed it like bad-tasting medicine and after a while, he stopped complaining and just picked up my list and either got what we needed in a separate trip or on the way home from work.

In the beginning I did get a phone call or two from other women I knew, but after a while, they stopped calling altogether. I suppose that was because I stopped answering the phone or if I did answer, I just listened and said, "Yes" or "no," but nothing more. I didn't even say goodbye sometimes. They did and then I hung up.

So I knew he was doing another one of those pretends when he would come home and tell me about the people he had met who all asked after me. No one asked after me.

Anyway, I remember going into the living room and sitting and starting my knitting and looking at Ed from time to time as he snored or muttered in his sleep, and then, suddenly, there it was: a Realie, sitting at his feet, all crumpled like a decrepit old man, its shoulders caved inward, its arms and legs as thin as spider legs, its head very big, but very, very wrinkled with large black, accusing eyes and lips made of two thick, blood filled veins, smirking at me.

He or I should say it didn't speak. It didn't have to. Its eyes said it all. It said you know all he says is a lie and you know your son is no hero, no young man blazing trails in foreign lands. You know it's cold and dark outside and people don't really care about you, don't have the slightest interest in whether or not you're even alive. Then it laughed.

I screamed, of course. It was the first time, so I was very frightened.

Ed woke, blinked and sat up.

"What the hell you screaming for?" he asked.

The Realie looked at him and then popped like a bubble and was gone. Later, it appeared in the hallway outside our bedroom, still smirking at me.

I told Ed and he stared at me and then shook his head and lowered himself to the sofa. He was asleep again in minutes.

Sometimes, there were two or three Realies at a time. They usually came in when the door was opened, so I stopped opening it and I kept the windows shut tight. I couldn't help it when Ed came home. If he left the door open while he carried in packages, I would scream and run to shut it, but it was always too late.

More and more of them streamed in, each with another ugly truth to tell or remind me about, like the one about my father hitting my mother or the one about Aunt Elsie dying from a burst appendix when it should have been easily treated. Her mother distrusted doctors and nurses and wouldn't call for *help. She put a hot water bottle on her stomach. She was only twenty-nine years old, and I couldn't believe she was in that coffin and being put in the ground. I was just nine at the time.*

Who needed to be reminded, especially reminded by something as ugly as a Realie?

It got so my living room was filled with Realies and when I walked by, I could hear them all chatting away. They often laughed, but it was more like a cackle than a laugh. Some of my earliest childhood nightmares were in there with them, ready to be run on the television screen like a rerun of an old movie if I glanced through the door.

I walked through the house with my head down. Whenever I went up to my bedroom, they followed. They even followed me into the bathroom. It got worse after Fletcher's death. More of them entered the house, each with a story to tell about him, about some of the other bad things he had done. They loved to describe his death, all the gory details, such as how the truck burst into flames before it hit the water and how he was screaming for me.

Finally, I went down into the basement one day to get away and discovered they couldn't follow. They couldn't go down. They couldn't go below. I was safe here.

In those days, all we had was a storage area. I put a chair down here and spent my whole day here in the dank, dark place. Ed discovered that and when I told him why, he sighed, shook his head and then, one day, he started to build all this for me. He moved things down for me and some-

times, he stayed with me.

Eventually, he did that less and less. There were times he left so early, I would only find some food at the door in a carton. There were times he was away for days. I could tell the passage of time with my cuckoo clock, but I really didn't care what day it was. The only thing that vaguely interested me was how long Ed was gone.

One day he admitted something.

"No one's asking about you anymore," he said, and I knew the Realies were still upstairs and now making him stop pretending, too.

"I should take you to see a doctor," he told me on more than one occasion, but he didn't. The Realies made him say it, but that was as far as it went. I wouldn't have gone anyway and he knew that.

Many things happened to me down here and I should have gone up and out to see a doctor and a dentist. I had a terrible toothache one day. It didn't stop no matter what I did, so I asked Ed to pull the tooth out of my mouth. He refused and went upstairs, but not more than ten minutes or so later, one of the Realies sent him back down with a pliers and he did it.

I passed out, but when I woke up, I began to feel better.

"Let that be a lesson to you," I told Ed. "Never pretend something you know has to be done doesn't have to be done."

He shook his head at me just like he always did and left me. He was gone almost a week this time, and I ran out of many things. It was then that I re-

alized as long as he stayed away from the house, he could stay away from the truth. Out there, on his jobs, away from this village and these people, he could be whoever he wanted again and he could continue to make up stories about Fletcher, even though Fletcher was dead and buried.

Then, one day, I heard more than one pair of footsteps above and Ed came down with a dark-skinned woman he called Suze. He said she was going to be our housekeeper and she would look after me and maybe, she would be able to help me come back upstairs.

"Wait a minute," Harley said. He had been sitting so still and had been so attentive that I almost forgot he was there. "That's not the story he told me. He told me he met her in New York City."

"That was all probably part of the deception, Harley. Maybe it was something he imagined happened to your father or something. I'm sure you noticed that reference she made to food left in a carton?"

He nodded.

"Go on," he urged.

"You sure?"

"Yes."

"Okay," I said, but I knew I wouldn't be so eager to hear such bizarre things about my grandparents. It would frighten me, I thought.

I didn't like Suze from the beginning. She had something evil in her eyes. It took me a while to re-

alize what it was. One of the Realies had entered her and was using her to get down to me. I told Ed and he told me I was wrong. Suze would help me. Where she came from, she was considered the same as we consider doctors, doctors of the body, but more important, doctors of the soul. He claimed she had already helped him to feel much better about Fletcher, much better about everything, even me.

She made all sorts of different things for me to eat and she cooked and cleaned upstairs. Before long, Ed stopped coming down very much.

I continued to read and knit and listen to my music, but one day I noticed I was getting thinner and thinner. Even though I was eating more, I was losing weight. Suze always had something else for me to eat and some of it did taste good, so I was confused.

I'm disappearing, I realized one day. Suze is making me disappear. That's how she's getting me back upstairs. If the Realies can't see me, they can't bother me. I don't have to hear any more ugly truths.

So, I didn't complain. In fact, I haven't complained about anything since I've been here.

Today, I decided I would make a list of all the things I've liked in my life and all the things that have brought me happiness. I'll add to the list all the time as I remember things.

One thing I have to put down right away is Fletcher's first cry. Nothing compares to that for a woman. She hears the first note of life that came from her and her heart is as full of joy as it will ever *be. I can close my eyes and see his face and I can see and feel his tiny fingers and I can sense the wonder that was going on inside him.*

That was so powerful a happy moment, remembering it is enough to keep me smiling for days on end, although it's hard to see my smile anymore. My face is so thin, the bones have taken over and bones don't smile. But I know it's there. The smile is there.

What I've discovered now is I get very tired often. I'm tired soon after I wake up. Some days I've nearly spent the whole time in bed.

It's getting worse. I know it, but I don't complain. After all, I'm still safe.

"What?" Harley asked the instant I stopped reading. "Don't stop. What happened to her next?"

"I don't know," I said turning the pages. "These pages are all empty. Wait, here's something, but it's hard to read it. It looks like just some scribble." I squinted. "It looks like she was trying to write your father's name," I said. "Maybe."

"Let me see."

Harley studied it and nodded.

"What do you think happened? She sounded like she started to get sicker and sicker after Suze came."

"Yes." I looked at the rolls left in the carton. "Something in the food she gave her, perhaps. Some religious thing full of some magic herbs that was meant to drive the evil out of her, but slowly poisoned her instead."

"Just like she means to do to us," Harley muttered. He looked at the carton, too; then he kicked it away from us. "We're getting out of here," he vowed.

He stood and perused the room, thought a moment and then went into the kitchenette. He returned with a bread knife, holding it like a dagger.

"What are you going to do?" I asked.

"I'm going to dig out that door, even if I have to do it inch by inch. I'll try to cut off its hinges," he said and went back through the opening and up the small stairs where he began to work, now with a methodical desperation.

It was slow, painstaking work. Even though the door was old, it was constructed out of a hard wood. When the knife blade snapped, he had to find another knife. There wasn't any as big or as sharp. He worked for hours. I sat on the stairs and watched him and talked to him and tried to help, but he was afraid I would slip and cut myself. He had a few times when he nearly lost his temper.

After hours and hours, he paused, exhausted, the sweat rolling down his reddened cheeks. When he inspected his results so far, he was not happy.

"The bolt's in deep," he said. "This is going to take a while. Especially with only a butter knife and a pair of old scissors as tools."

"Let's take a break, Harley," I said. "Neither of us has eaten much and we'll need to reserve our strength."

He nodded.

"I wish one of my grandmother's Realies would come by and scare the hell out of that Suze."

I smiled.

"Maybe it will," I said.

We returned to what was now our hideaway and prison and had some water while we sat on the sofa.

"My stomach's grumbling," he said. "I guess I'll have some more of that beef jerky. How about you?"

"I'm okay."

"Women can go much longer without food," he said as if it was a fault. "I can't even imagine going on a diet, but some of the girls I know at school live on air. If they gain an ounce, they go into a panic."

"I get hungry. I'm still just recuperating from last night," I said.

"Yeah." He bit into the beef jerky and then looked ravenously at the rolls. "I can't imagine her putting anything poisonous into those rolls. Wouldn't the baking burn it out anyway?"

"I don't know, Harley."

"They tasted pretty good. And that cheese seemed all right. I'll take a chance," he decided and tore a roll in two, stuffed a piece of cheese in it and gobbled it quickly. He offered some to me and I shook my head.

"I'll have some more tea in a while," I said.

"You're going to get sick."

"I'm all right, Harley. We're not going to be

trapped here much longer," I predicted optimistically.

"Yeah, right," he said.

"He's still your grandfather," I said. "He's got to be a little worried." Harley looked at me as if I was crazy.

"She was his wife," he said, nodding at the old composition notebook that had been his grandmother's diary. "Look what he did to her."

"Maybe he didn't realize what was happening," I said. "Maybe he was sorry."

We had to have hope, didn't we? I couldn't let go of that.

He nodded.

"I can't imagine how she lived down here all that time," Harley said, gazing around the basement. "Never seeing sunlight or stars and the moon. Never breathing fresh air. Never smelling grass and flowers and tree blossoms or hearing birds sing. Hell, not even hearing the sound of a car horn. These old foundation walls are as thick as in bomb shelters."

"I know," I said. "It's unimaginable."

And yet, I thought, here we were still trapped for nearly twenty-four hours and maybe even more.

"I don't think I can be that alone either. I mean, I'm a loner, I know, but once in a while, you need to talk to someone, see some television, hear a radio, just watch people walk and talk. Something," he cried. "But to sit here and live in your own mind day after day after day. I guess she was crazy."

"Or just very imaginative, Harley. Perhaps she looked at the room and thought it was beautiful. Maybe she used her memories of a sunset and a sunrise and that was enough."

"You know that can't be enough. I'm already going bonkers down here. I can feel my insides tearing apart with anger and frustration."

"Yes, but you're forgetting she felt safer here. She wanted to be here."

He thought a moment and nodded.

"I guess so," he said. His eyes wandered and then settled on the phonograph. "You want to hear one of those old records?" he asked.

"Yes, I would like that," I said. If we got our minds off our predicament for a little while, we would surely feel better, I thought.

He rose and picked out a record. The melody was sweet, comforting, but the singer's voice was so high-pitched, I smiled.

"Music was sure different in those days," Harley said.

"The words were nice though."

He put on another and we listened. It was a song in French. Neither of us could understand it, but we knew whatever it was about was sad.

"Who's the singer on that one, Harley?" I asked when it ended.

He read the label.

"Edith Piaf."

"Play it again," I said. He shrugged and did so. Then he came to sit beside me to listen. He put his arm around my shoulders and I leaned into his chest and closed my eyes. He kissed me on the forehead and I looked up at him. Maybe it was because of the music or because of what had happened to us, but his eyes were two dark pools of deep sorrow and pain. I hated to see him so sad.

I reached up and with the tips of my fingers touched his lips. He took my hand in his and held it there and then kissed my fingers. The tingle traveled down my arm to my breast and curled over my heart.

"You're so lovely, Summer, even now, even here, even after all that's happened. When I look at you, I feel so happy inside that I forget everything terrible around me. It's always been like that for me."

"Harley," I whispered.

He lifted me gently and turned me so he could lower his lips to mine. It was a soft kiss, a kiss that was more like turning a key that opened the lock to my heart and soul. He shifted and lowered me to the sofa.

"This itches," he complained, referring to the sweater, and pulled it off.

I smiled up at him, my heart starting to tap faster. He sprawled out beside me and kissed me again, a little harder, a little longer. I turned into him and put my arm over his shoulder, holding him to me. He kissed my eyes, my nose and my neck.

"Our love is so strong," he whispered, "it protects us."

I was thinking that, too. For a few minutes, at

least, I could submerge myself in him and, like lowering myself into a warm bath after being in a cold rain, feel soothed, comforted, protected.

I kept my eyes closed as he unbuttoned my blouse and took it off and then unfastened my bra and slipped it away. His lips were on my breasts, the tip of his tongue grazing each nipple. Every move he made was slow, deliberate, gentle, soothing. I moaned softly and he pressed his lips to mine, touching my tongue with his and then kissing me harder, faster everywhere. I felt my heart thumping, my blood racing.

"Tell me to stop, Summer. Tell me to stop," he whispered, but brought his fingers to the button on my jeans and undid it.

I should, I thought, but I didn't want him to. At least, not just yet. Just a little more, just a little longer. It all felt so good and I had been terrified ever since the date rape that loving would never be good for me again.

His hand moved in and around my waist to my rear. He pressed, pushing me toward him. Then he brought his lips to my exposed stomach, lowering the jeans just a few inches at a time to clear the way for his lips. Soon, they were down to my knees.

"I love you so much, Summer," he said.

"I love you, too, Harley."

"Tell me to stop," he repeated, but moved my jeans down to my ankles. I lifted my leg so he could gently get them off and then he pulled back and took off his jeans, too.

"We're going too far," he said more in the tone of a voiced thought. He sounded like he was warning himself more than he was warning me.

"I know," I whispered. I felt drunk, my mind spinning, the warmth traveling up and twirling in my stomach and then under my breasts, moving inside me like invisible hands, soft fingers touching me in places I touched myself in dreams.

There's a point of no return, I told myself. You're reaching it. You're almost there. My panties were off. He was naked, too. We held each other, gasping, hesitant, but knowing there was a flood of passion about to overwhelm us.

"Tell me to stop," he practically begged as he brought his hardness to me.

Maybe I really did want to prove to myself that I hadn't been ruined for life by Duncan. Maybe my love for Harley was so strong that all restraint and caution was trampled beneath its marching feet. Maybe I had simply lost control and was at the mercy of the winds of my own unleashed animal desire. Whatever the reason, I did not say stop. Instead, I lifted myself to bring my lips to his and he entered me and held me, and we moved in a slow rhythm to bring ourselves higher and higher, to lift ourselves out of our pain and fear, to reach the clouds and float away on a magic carpet of love.

However long it lasted was far too short. I clung to him afterward, refusing to surrender to any aftermath, refusing to retreat. His heavy breathing slowed against my cheek and as the world around us began to reappear, the realization of what we had done settled over both of us like a cold, wet blanket.

He lifted himself away and sat for a moment. Then he began to put on his underwear and his jeans. I turned over on my stomach and buried my face in the cushion. Neither of us had heard the phonograph needle going round and round at the end of the record until now. He went over and lifted the arm away and then he went into the small bathroom.

I caught my breath, sat up and dressed. Harley moved about silently for a few moments and then said he was going back to the door to work. He face was masked in guilt.

"Harley," I called to him. He shook his head and kept walking.

I rose and went to the little mirror to look at myself and finger my hair. I found a hair brush and washed it out and moved a few strokes down my strands. Then I heard him call to me and came out of the small bathroom. He was holding another carton.

"More of her food," he said, "and water and what looks like a dessert. I don't know how she opens that door and shuts it without me hearing her move that damn cabinet away. She has to have him helping her for that, don't you think?"

I nodded.

He placed the carton on the table and we both looked down at the contents.

"We can't eat any of that, Harley."

"I know," he said. "Got to tell you though. It

smells good," he said.

"Like a trap," I muttered.

He nodded, but I could see he was still thinking about it.

"If she was going to poison us, she would have done it in the first carton of food, don't you think, Summer?"

"I don't know. I'm afraid," I said.

"Okay."

He returned to the door.

Hours went by. I fell asleep and when I woke, he was at my side. He looked very guilty again, but this time, it was for different reasons.

My eyes went to the carton.

He had eaten.

"All that effort made me hungry," he said shrugging. "I'm not feeling bad, Summer. It's okay. I was your food tester," he quipped.

"I'm still not hungry, Harley," I said even though I was starting to get some pangs.

"Whatever that cake is, it's good," he said. He smiled. "Our jailer is a gourmet cook."

"It's not funny."

"I know. I'm just trying not to crack up," he said, wiping the smile from his face.

I stared at him a moment and then nodded, realizing he was right.

"Daddy always says a branch that won't bend will break," I told him.

"Good advice. We'll roll with this until we get an opportunity to change it. Maybe, if I keep myself awake, I'll hear them move that cabinet out of the way to put out another carton of food and then I'll rush the door," he planned aloud. "I'm going to sit at the foot of the stairs out there."

He rose.

"I'll come with you then," I said.

"No, Summer. It's very uncomfortable. It's almost decent in here. There's no sense in both of us being up all night, is there?"

He looked at the bed.

"Why don't you dig out the bedding from that trunk and fix the bed for yourself. We don't want both of us to be exhausted, okay?"

"No," I said. "I want to be with you, Harley."

He shook his head.

"I'm not going to let you get sick."

"All right, here's what we'll do," I said as a compromise. "You'll take the first shift out there and then I'll come out and wake you and you'll come back here to sleep. We'll take turns at guard duty. If I hear them, I'll come and get you quickly."

"You'd have to, Summer. You couldn't do it without me," he warned.

"Don't you think I know that, Harley? I'd be too frightened anyway."

He studied me a moment to be sure I was sincere and then he nodded.

"What about your ankle?"

"It's okay. It won't be a problem now, Harley."

"Right. Okay, let's say in four hours, you come out and then four hours later, which will be closer to the morning, I'll come out and you'll go to sleep. Is that all right with you, Wonder Woman?"

"Yes," I said smiling.

He kissed me.

"We're going to be all right," he said. "This is almost over. I promise."

"I know it is, Harley."

He squeezed my hand gently and then went to the outer room to listen and wait for his opportunity.

I fixed the bed as he had suggested and then I lay down and closed my eyes. It took me longer to fall asleep than I had expected. I kept imagining I heard Harley out there rushing up the steps, but it was only the sounds from above.

What are they doing? I wondered. How can they continue to do this to us? Was his grandfather that insane, really that confident in Suze and her powers? How does someone come to believe in such things and believe in them so strongly that he would even risk hurting other people, hurting his own flesh and blood, and getting himself into serious trouble?

The extent to which people would go to avoid facing the truth and avoid accepting guilt and responsibility was truly incredible, I thought. They went so far as to create their own world and then move into it, treating this world and the rest of us as if we were the illusion.

What was real? What was not? It didn't seem to matter what age you were. The answers to those questions were always the most difficult.

Finally, I drifted into sleep, but it was a restless repose. I tossed and turned, fretting in and out of dark dreams, running through tunnels, fleeing in such a panic that when I woke after imagining hands grasping the back of my neck, I was actually gasping for breath and in a sweat.

I sat up and pressed my hand to my pounding heart to quiet it down. Slowly, my breathing became regular again and I was able to swallow. I glanced at my watch. I had slept a good half hour past my turn to listen for them, and Harley hadn't come in to wake me. I knew he wouldn't. I chastised myself for failing him and rose as quickly as I could.

It was very quiet above now. They're probably asleep, comfortable in their beds, comfortable in their damned insanity, I thought. Strengthened and energized by my anger, I started for the outer room. When I reached the entryway, I called for Harley, but he didn't call back.

I looked in and saw him sprawled at the foot of the stairs, his body curled up, his head on the hard surface.

He can't be too comfortable like that, I thought. He's going to wake up sore all over.

"Harley!" I cried and passed myself through. He didn't stir. I hurried over to him. "Harley."

I knelt down and shook him. His eyes fluttered, but they didn't open.

"Harley!"

I turned him over on his back and shook him as hard as I could, calling his name. Still, he didn't open his eyes. I saw his eyeballs move, but the lids didn't separate.

"Harley! What's wrong? Harley!"

My heart did a flip-flop. I felt a cold wave of air wash over me with the realization that Suze must have put something stronger into the food. Harley had eaten too much of it. It sent a quick chill down my spine.

"Help!" I screamed. "Help us! Something's happened to Harley! Help! Help!"

I shook him and cried and shook him and he didn't wake. The tears streamed down my cheeks.

"Harley," I muttered. I lifted him to embrace him to me and I rocked with him, calling him.

I listened hard, but heard nothing from above. They surely heard me, I thought. They surely heard me but didn't care or didn't believe me.

What would I do?

I didn't want to leave him lying here so I scooped my arms under his and lifted him as best I could. Then I started to drag him back. With my ankle still very sensitive, it was hard, painstaking work. I kept hoping he would wake and be all right, but even after all this, he still had his eyes closed, his lips just slightly open.

The most difficult part was getting him through the opening without hurting him. I don't know where I found the strength, but I lifted him and then dropped him gently to the floor. I brought him to the bed and managed to get him up and on it, putting his head on the pillow. Then I hurried to get a cold cloth to put on his forehead.

"Harley, please wake up. Harley," I cried. I

shook him and his eyelids fluttered again, but didn't open.

I crawled up beside him and held him and rocked with him on the bed.

"Mommy," I muttered. "Daddy. Please, help us. Someone, help us."

The cuckoo clock struck the hour and the dancers emerged. They twirled about and retreated.

Then all was silent again.

All I heard was my own moans, my own soft prayers.

15

Darkness Rushes In

A groan slipped through Harley's lips. I shook him gently and repeated his name. His eyelids fluttered harder, but he didn't open them, though his eyeballs were moving frantically beneath. It was as if his lids had been glued shut and he couldn't open them no matter how he tried.

When I brought my lips to his cheek, I felt how warm his skin had become. He was running a high fever. I thought for a moment and then quickly went to get him a glass of cold water. Lifting his head gently, I brought the glass to his lips and poured a little into his mouth. Some ran out and down his chin, but I got enough in so he could swallow. He groaned again and I poured some more water until he coughed and his eyelids began to open.

He had such a dazed look. It was as if he didn't know who I was or where he was. He just gazed at me.

"Harley, what's wrong? Harley?"

"Momma," he muttered. "Momma, I don't feel so good."

"Harley, it's me, Summer. What's wrong?"

"Momma, my stomach feels like I swallowed a barbecue coal. I didn't mean it. I ate my hotdog too fast again. Roy's mad, I bet."

He was hallucinating. Was it the fever or something Suze had put into the food that was doing this to him? I wondered.

"Momma, hold me, hold me," he begged. "Don't be mad. Please. I won't do it again. I promise."

I crawled beside him on the bed and put my arm around his shoulders, pressing his face gently against my breast. He was so hot, I could feel the heat through my blouse and bra.

"It's all right, Harley," I said kissing his forehead. It was like pressing my lips to a car window after it had been left a while in the noonday sun. I rocked him gently. "No one's mad at you."

"Momma . . . Momma . . ." he muttered, his eyes closing. "Don't be mad at me for being sick."

I knew that after Latisha had died, Aunt Glenda was always very nervous whenever Harley got sick, even if it was just a cold. That was understandable, no matter how frantic she would become. However, his high fever was making me just as nervous right now.

I remembered how many times my mother had suffered fevers in her life, sometimes hallucinating, too. Daddy told me her condition made her more susceptible to certain infections. The doctors tried not to pump her so full of antibiotics in fear of her body developing resistant strains, because they would then be forced to use stronger and stronger medications to cure her each time and eventually, they wouldn't work. Often, Daddy would try to break her fevers by lowering her into an ice-cold bath and sponging her down.

Recalling that, I returned to the kitchenette, found a large pot and filled it with water, running it until I got it as cold as it could be. Then I cleaned a sponge and returned to the bed. Harley looked like he was in a deep sleep again. I carefully peeled off the sweater and took off his pants. He didn't open his eyes or moan. He seemed more like someone in a coma now. I started to sponge him, talking softly to comfort him as I did so. I was frightened. I needed to hear his voice.

His eyes finally opened again and he cried out for more cold water. I helped him sip some, and he fell back to sleep almost instantly. He called repeatedly for his mother in his sleep and surprised me by even calling out for Roy. I continued to sponge him and replaced the water in the pot with fresh, colder water and did it again. His breathing finally seemed to get less labored so I stopped and watched him sleep peacefully for a while.

How often, I thought, had I tiptoed into Mommy's room when she was sick and watched her sleep. I was always so afraid I would lose her. Her being in a wheelchair always made her seem so vulnerable to every illness, every kind of pain, no matter how brave a face she wore for my benefit.

If she woke and saw me sitting there, she would smile and struggle to sit up. I'd run to her bed and she would embrace me and hold me and assure me she was going to be all right.

"I'm fine," she would tell me. "This is nothing, Summer. I just need a little rest."

No matter how many times she did that or how well and confident she sounded, I couldn't erase the memories of waking in the middle of the night and hearing Daddy with a note of panic in his voice call the doctor. Lights would go on. Mrs. Geary would be running up and down the stairs. Sometimes, the doctor would arrive and sometimes, Mommy would be taken to the hospital in an ambulance. I was too afraid to come out of my room. I'd stand by my door and peek out. When I saw her being carried out of her room and down the stairs on a stretcher, my heart would turn to ice.

After a day or so, Daddy would bring me to the hospital to see her. Even there, even under the milk white sheets, surrounded by all sorts of intimidating medical machinery, she was able to put on a bright, happy smile for me. Nothing was as important to her as my being relieved of fear.

"With your father looking over me as he does," she told me once as she held me to her, "I'll always be all right, Summer, so don't you worry. He watches me so closely, he knows exactly how many breaths I take a minute," she said.

It was almost not an exaggeration. Daddy often looked like he was a doctor examining her, watching her move, studying her eyes, listening very closely to her voice. His devotion to her and her well-being was the greatest testimony to his love for her and it did comfort me. No one was as strong and as capable of doing these things as Daddy was in my eyes. He never panicked in front of me, if he ever panicked at all. He was always as in control as he was that day he saved Aunt Alison from drowning. There was no one better in a crisis.

I tried to think of what else he would do for Harley, but most of all, I tried to be as strong as he would be if he was trapped down here, too. If I panicked and cried and ranted, I would be less likely to be able to help Harley, I told myself.

I dozed for a few minutes and woke to the sound of his groaning again, only now it was accompanied by the chattering of his teeth.

"Cold," he said. "Mommy, I'm cold."

I quickly put the sweater back on him and put his pants on as well. Then I located another blanket in the trunk at the foot of the bed and spread it over him as well. Still, he trembled and moaned, so I crawled under the blankets with him and held him to my body, hoping my heat would ease his terrible turmoil. I kissed him and stroked his face and held him as tightly as I could against me. It seemed to help. His trembling got less and less and he fell asleep again.

But what was happening to him? I wondered.

Why was he going from being hot to cold to hot so quickly? Had he caught a terrible flu or did it have something to do with what he had eaten? I had eaten a little of that roll, but I didn't feel any worse for it.

I slipped out of the bed and returned to the stairway. At the door, I began to plead.

"Please help us. Harley is very sick. He's running a high fever and I'm afraid. We need to get him to the doctor and get him medicine. Please," I begged.

I waited and listened and then suddenly, I heard Suze chanting. She sounded like she was just on the other side of the door.

"Help us!" I screamed. I pounded on the door with my open hand until my hand grew red and stung.

Her chanting grew louder and louder as I raised my own voice to scream for help, and then I had to jump back quickly because some black liquid slime oozed through the small space between the bottom of the door and the floor. More and more of it poured through.

"Stop it!" I shouted. "Stop doing this. Help us. You'll be in big trouble if you don't. Our parents know where we are. They're going to come looking for us," I cried, hoping to bluff them. I waited. They did nothing. The door remained shut tight. "Help us! Please! Harley's not well! He has trouble breathing. He could die!"

The chanting stopped and the murky liquid stopped flowing. I held my breath hopefully, but minutes went by and still the door was not opened. I closed my hand and pounded on it and cajoled and pleaded until my voice grew hoarse. Then I retreated to our room and sat beside the bed, watching Harley moan and turn in his sleep. His fever seemed to have gone down, but I put a cold wet cloth over his forehead anyway. He looked so sick, his skin turning the color of old newspaper.

The cuckoo clock ticked on. Feeling exhausted myself from the struggle and the tension, I lowered my head to the bed and closed my eyes. In moments I was asleep. I had a terrible nightmare about a rat scurrying through my hair, sniffing my scalp and scratching at me. It became more and more vivid until I woke with a cry.

Harley's eyes were wide open. He had put his hand on my head, moving his fingers trying to get me to wake, too.

"Harley, how do you feel?"

"Hurts," he said.

"What hurts?"

"Every muscle in my body aches. My throat is very dry, too. I'm so nauseous. My stomach keeps cramping up."

"I'll get you some water," I said and hurried to do so.

Why were his muscles aching? Was that a flu? If only I had something to give him besides water, I thought.

He drank it slowly, but I could see that even swallowing was painful.

"Thanks," he said and closed his eyes.

"Harley, we've got to get you out of here. We've got to," I moaned. "Please help me think of something. I've been screaming at the door, but she's performing some other ritual and she won't listen."

I waited to see if he had heard and understood, but he didn't open his eyes. His body had become so still and his skin so clammy in fact that it put a terrible panic in me, despite my grand effort to be like my father.

"Harley!" I shook him. "Harley, stay awake. Harley! Please try to think of something. Harley!"

He didn't open his eyes. I felt for his pulse. It was light, low.

He's going to die. Harley's really going to die! I concluded and finally, the dam I had built to stay in control shattered. I screamed at the top of my lungs. Hurrying as quickly as I could to get back to the stairway, I put too much pressure on my bad foot as I charged across the room and my ankle sent needles into my heart. I had to stop to gasp for breath. When I reached the stairway, I smelled a terrible stench. Climbing up slowly toward the door, I could see where the slime had been poured until it had reached the top step. The area looked charred. Whatever it was it had been ignited and it filled the area with a stink that made me choke and dry heave. The stench was that putrid. Despite my panic and urgency, I had to retreat.

She's even keeping me from begging for help, I

thought. Enraged, I stepped back and then picked up the piece of lumber Harley had used to rip through the wall to the back room, and I heaved it with all my strength at the door to the stairway. It slammed with a loud clunk and then bounced back down the steps and fell to the floor.

I waited and listened, but no one upstairs acknowledged it. There was just a heavy silence, so deep and so complete, the beating of my own heart sounded like parade drums.

They won't help us, I thought. They just don't care. We'll surely die down here.

Defeated and lost, I made my way back and returned to Harley's bedside. His face looked flushed again. I touched his cheek. His fever had returned, only it was worse. Desperate, I got the cold water and started to sponge him down, working as quickly as I could. I felt like someone trying to bail water out of the *Titanic*. Tragedy was rushing in on us. Soon, we would drown in it.

Mommy, I thought, I made such a terrible mistake. You can forgive me for anything, but you can't forgive me for leaving you and Daddy like this.

You can't forgive me because I can't forgive myself. Maybe if I hadn't agreed to go, Harley wouldn't have gone. We wouldn't be here. This wouldn't be happening to us, to all of us.

Exhausted myself, my arms and shoulders now joining my ankle in a chorus of aches and pains, I crawled beside Harley and brought his head to my bosom.

"Harley, what are we going to do? Oh Harley," I cried. My tears were so hot. They were coming fast and furious. I wiped them away and closed my eyes.

We lay there, quiet, like two souls waiting to be called home.

I didn't know whether it was just my imagination or sympathy pains, but suddenly, I felt the tiniest string of needlelike pain shooting through my lower stomach. It grew stronger and stronger until I had to gasp for a breath and sit up. The moment I did so, I doubled up and groaned. The pain began to rise in waves toward my chest. As it climbed, my legs began to grow numb. It was like being lowered into the lake back home when a sheet of ice covered it. My arms became limp. I fell back on the bed beside Harley and turned my face toward his. His eyes fluttered, his lips parted just a little.

"Harley," I thought I shouted. It was merely a weak whisper. I edged closer to him until my lips touched his cheek. And then I closed my eyes.

We were children again. All of us were on the lawn behind my house. Daddy had set up a croquet game. We had picnicked and there was a soft Chopin melody flowing from a speaker near the rear windows. Harley and I were trying to hammer our red and green balls through the hoops, and our attempts brought ribbons of laughter from the adults. Harley paid no attention to them. He was intent, his concentration determined. He took a swing and sent his ball through beautifully. There was applause.

Roy was laughing loudly. Daddy was patting Harley on the back. I tried harder now and managed finally to get my ball through, and there was applause again. I looked at Mommy. She seemed to have sunshine coming from her face. Her smile glowed so warmly. I felt like I could rise and float to her.

We were all angels then, a family of angels on a warm spring afternoon with a sky as blue as Mommy's precious teacups, forgetting everything but our own joy in each other. Latisha was still alive, but Aunt Glenda held her tightly against her breasts, holding her just like someone who knew there were evil demons out there anxious to pluck her out of her arms the moment they had the opportunity.

The memory of all of us so happy brought a smile to my face. I could feel it settling on my lips. How easy it was to just let go and float back to joyful times. This way there would be no more pain, no more tears.

Can't we start again, all of us? Can't we have a second chance? Can't we keep the doors of the cuckoo clock closed and stop time from moving us forward, the hands on the face frozen? The hardest thing about leaving the ones you love was knowing how terrible they would feel, how crushed they would be. Please don't drag us another second into the future that waited hungrily to gulp us down, I prayed.

A very deep and heavy groan rumbled through Harley's body. He, too, was struggling to come back, to pull himself up from the dark pool that waited below. I pressed my fingers against his and curled them around his so we were holding on to each other now, holding on like two shipwrecked travelers desperately clinging to a life raft.

I fell asleep again. I don't know how long we both slept. My eyes were so full of haze that whenever I opened them and looked around the room, it seemed we were floating in the center of some cloud and trying to see the world around us. I couldn't even make out the numbers on my watch, but I suddenly didn't care. What difference did time make? Time was only a reminder that soon we would be saying goodbye, I thought.

Sleep, I told myself. Sleep and forget.

And then suddenly there was a great explosion of sound. It was as if the entire house was crashing down around us. I lifted my head and gazed toward the doorway. Everything was out of focus, but I could see someone tall and big was coming at us, moving in slow motion and growling like a bear. His long, thick arms slipped around us. He lifted me with only his left arm and seconds later lifted Harley with only his right. He held the two of us with such ease it was as if we were infants. Then he lumbered back toward the door, his growl rolling like a stream of smoke trailing behind us.

I closed my eyes and felt myself being carried. I could hear his footsteps beneath us slamming down with each step so hard he surely shattered the very floor. In moments we were going up the stairway. I saw light and when I looked to the right, I saw the door had been driven in and hung from its bottom hinge. Without a pause, we were turned and carried down the hallway toward the front door. There was more growling.

It wasn't until we were outside and the fresh air washed over me that I could open my eyes completely. The lids felt like they had been sewn together and I was tearing threads to get them to pull apart, but I did and then I turned my head and I looked at the giant.

It was Uncle Roy.

He had come full of his famous rage and power.

And I was never so happy to see him and feel it as I was at that moment.

Comforted, relieved and once again filled with a sense of security, I allowed my eyes to close. I wasn't afraid to fall asleep now.

Even though I didn't remember any of it, he got us both to the hospital. I woke first and saw him sitting by my bedside, his head bowed, his thick, powerful neck bulging.

"Uncle Roy," I whispered. "Uncle Roy?"

He lifted his head slowly and smiled.

"Hey, Princess, how ya doin'?" he asked.

I gazed around.

"Where am I?"

"In the hospital."

"Where's Harley?" I asked desperately, holding my breath, terrified of his response.

He stared at me a moment and then he jerked his head slightly to the right.

"He's in the next room. He was a lot worse off than you. He's still in a coma," he said.

"What did they do to us?"

"Doctor said something about poison mushrooms in something you two must've ate. Another day or so and I would most likely have been too late."

"Is he going to be all right?"

"Yeah, they think so. They hope so," he added, to be a little more honest.

"How did you find us?" I asked.

"I searched Harley's room after you told Rain you were coming home and didn't. I found this guy's name and address and just set out. When I got there, I saw Harley's cycle behind the house. I spotted it before I knocked on the door. Good reconnaissance. My army training, I guess," he continued with a quick smile.

"Anyway, when that man told me Harley and you had left, I pushed my way in. Some weird woman was running a lit candle up and down this door in the hallway as if she was burning something away. I looked back at him and then at her. Something in his face told me I had better move quickly.

" 'Where are they?' I demanded. He looked like he was going to cry. I turned to the woman and repeated the question and she said, 'They're with the devil.'

"I tried the door and saw it was locked. I demanded the key and no one moved, so I stepped back and kicked it in. The old man just went into the living room and sat in a chair as if it was all no big deal. Just another day in hell or something.

"The rest you know now. Of course, I told it all to the police and they got them. That guy was Harley's grandfather," he said shaking his head. "His grandfather! Can you believe it?"

"We know who he was. At first, he pretended to be his father. His father was killed running from the police after he had committed a robbery."

"Yeah, the police filled me in on some of the family history."

"What about my mother and father, Uncle Roy?"

"They're on their way here. Should be here in a few hours."

"I've made such a mess of things."

"You? Why you?"

"I shouldn't have agreed to go along," I said. "Then he might not have gone."

"Wrong," he declared with the tone of a gong. "He would have gone without you. I was no help to him in his grief. And then he would have been up here all by himself and no one would have come in time to save him, Summer. You don't blame yourself. If anything, you kept him alive," he said.

I wanted to believe Uncle Roy. I knew he was telling me all of it to make me feel better, but maybe, just maybe there was some truth to it, too.

Later in the day, Daddy and Mommy arrived. I cried and kept telling them how sorry I was for making all this trouble, but they were just so happy to see me, they wouldn't listen to anything. Daddy went off to confer with the doctors and Mommy remained with me.

They checked into a motel nearby and came to the hospital every day for the next two days. On the second day, Harley woke. He was very weak but slowly he was able to realize where he was and remember all that had happened.

The night of day two, after Mommy and Daddy had left to get some rest, I got out of my bed. I wasn't supposed to, but I wanted to see Harley. I waited until there was no one in the hallway and then I went to his room, but I didn't go in. I stood inside the doorway, frozen, silent, hardly breathing.

Uncle Roy had his head resting against his palms, his elbows on his knees. He was still there, sitting at Harley's bedside.

He was crying.

Uncle Roy — the gruff, powerful giant who lumbered across our property and his, who ruled with firmness over his work crews, who didn't ever seem to offer Harley any comfort or warmth — was sobbing at Harley's bedside.

Harley woke and turned to him. Then he reached out and touched Uncle Roy's head and Uncle Roy lifted his eyes and they looked at each other.

"Thanks for coming for us," Harley said.

"Hell, boy, you did a dumb thing."

"I know."

"Your momma would have hated me for eternity," Uncle Roy said. And then he paused and said, "You don't need to go running all over the country looking for a daddy, Harley. I'll be there for you. We both lost a lot, but we still got each other if you want," he said.

Harley was weak, but he managed a bright, strong smile.

Then Roy rose to hug him and hold him.

I was crying so hard, I didn't think I could remain quiet a moment longer so I quickly retreated and returned to my room.

There were rainbows, I thought. There were still rainbows.

We both grew stronger. Daddy told me that the poisonous mushroom was the kind that could do a great deal of damage to liver and kidneys, but we were rescued in time for the effects of the poison to be reversed. He had learned from the police that Suze believed it would drive the evil spirit from us. Her mad beliefs, her paranoia about the demons coming to steal her dead son's soul was almost understandable, but Harley's grandfather's need to avoid all reality was not.

"He was selfish," Daddy said. "He was willing to sacrifice his own flesh and blood to satisfy that need. From what I've learned, he most likely drove his wife to her death as well. It's all going to be particularly hard for Harley. No one wants to think he's inherited all this craziness."

"He hasn't, Daddy. Harley's not anything like that," I insisted.

"I know. We're just going to have to help him see that, too," he said wisely.

Uncle Roy had already begun to do that, lecturing Harley about his mother's good qualities and telling him that's the side of his family he's inherited.

We had some time together alone before I was finally discharged by our doctors. I sat in his room and watched him sip tea and try to hold down some toast and jam. He paused and with narrow eyes, turned to me.

"Roy told me how you were still blaming yourself for all this, Summer. He's right. If it wasn't for you, I'd probably be history. You might never even have known what happened to me. I'd just have disappeared, forever. Don't you dare blame yourself for anything."

I smiled at him.

"Okay, Harley."

"Stop making us feel we're just saying it to make you feel better, too," he ordered.

"Okay."

"So," he said smiling, "where do you want to go next? I'll shine up the cycle."

I laughed and held his hand. He was tired again and had to nap. I kissed him before I returned to my room, promising to return in a few hours. When I did, I read to him from the newspapers or we watched some television together.

Another day passed and the doctors decided I was well enough to be discharged. They wanted to keep Harley a few more days to observe and be sure he was free of any internal damage.

"Hurry and get well," I told him.

Roy remained behind with him, and Daddy and Mommy and I returned home.

It had never been so wonderful to set foot in my own house, my own room, to breathe the air, to see the flowers and the lake and hear Mrs. Geary's lecture about being foolish. I even enjoyed her pressure to make me eat everything, every single drop. Of course, I couldn't. It took a while for my appetite to return, but I had no doubts that it would.

Mommy hovered around me even more than usual. It was funny, I thought, how now she was the one nervous about my health, my illnesses, my every cough and sneeze. Roles had been reversed, at least for a while.

My grandparents came to visit. Even Aunt Alison showed up and looked genuinely impressed. When everyone left us, however, she told me she was impressed for different reasons.

"I never thought you had the guts to do something like that. I always thought you were a Daddy's little girl."

"It doesn't take guts to do something stupid, Aunt Alison."

"Just think of it as an adventure," she said. "That's what I do."

"Are you happier because of that?" I shot back at her.

She glared at me for a moment.

"You know, you're just like your mother," she said.

"Thank you."

"Oh forget it," she cried, throwing her hands up and changing the subject to tell me about this young doctor she had met and begun to date.

When I asked her if she loved him, she thought a moment and said, "I wouldn't know if I did."

She looked very sad and for the first time, I think I truly felt sorry for her. It was almost like never being able to taste anything or hear beautiful music or smell the flowers in spring. She was incapable of being truly, deeply happy. She was being honest. She wouldn't recognize love. Something was missing and she knew it and mourned it and was bitter because of it.

Mommy had lost the use of her legs, but she wasn't nearly as bitter or unhappy, I thought.

Yes, thank you. Thank you for comparing me to her, I concluded.

When Harley returned, he was supposed to take it easy, but he was restless and didn't sit still or relax.

"I did enough of that in the hospital," he complained when everyone chastised him.

Uncle Roy tried to be gruff again, but his confessions and his revelation of love seemed to have taken the hardness out of him and Harley knew it. All he would do is smile at him.

"The boy's stubborn through and through," Uncle Roy told Mommy. "Headstrong, even after all this. He didn't learn a thing."

"He's more like you than you care to admit, Roy Arnold," Mommy told him. "There is something stronger than blood."

He looked at her.

"And what's that, Rain?"

"Love," she said. "Love."

Their eyes locked. How many, many memories flowed between them — good ones as well as all the bad, all the struggles, all the tears and yet all the smiles, for there had to be happy times. The way they spoke about Momma Arnold clearly made me think that was so.

The last days of summer were upon us quickly. Harley had been granted admittance to another college, one in Rhode Island. It was a four-year school and it had the program in architecture he wanted. He and Uncle Roy asked Daddy's advice and together they all agreed Harley would attend.

My heart was asked to be so many things the day Harley left for school. It was asked to be full of pride for him, to be happy for him and his opportunity, but it couldn't help thumping with sadness. We wouldn't see each other for a long time.

"I'll be back for Thanksgiving," he promised. "And I'll call and write you. Don't fall in love with someone new as soon as you start school," he warned.

"What about you and all those college girls you're going to meet?"

"I won't have time."

"Right," I said.

We both stood on the dock and looked out at the lake. A blackbird lifted from a thick tree branch and glided over the water before soaring up and away.

"Quickly, Harley, make a wish," I cried.

He laughed.

I closed my eyes and did so.

"Did you wish?"

"I can't tell you or it won't come true," he said.

"I don't need you to tell me. I heard you," I said.

He smiled and kissed me. Then Uncle Roy came out of our house.

Mommy and Daddy came out after him. Daddy stood next to her on the portico. Harley ran up to kiss Mommy goodbye and shake Daddy's hand. Then he got into the car. I stood there, watching and thinking, Aunt Glenda's watching too. She's standing right beside me. I can feel her.

They started away and then stopped and Harley got out.

"Hey," he called to me.

"What?"

"I heard your wish, too. After the blackbird. We'll make it happen," he said and got back into the car.

It slipped slowly out of sight below the hill and was gone. I looked up at Mommy and Daddy. They were holding hands and looking after the car. Then they turned toward me, concern in their eyes.

I took a deep breath and smiled to myself.
I'm all right, I thought. Don't worry.
There are no goodbyes.
Not really.
Not for people like us.

Epilogue

I suppose all my life I've been afraid of promises. A promise is a way of exposing your heart, whether you're the one giving it or the one accepting it. "Let's not make any promises and we'll never be disappointed in each other." That's what I told the boys I dated.

Harley and I kept up our correspondence and our relationship while I attended and finished high school. My grandfather in England wanted me to attend college in London. Mommy, Daddy and I talked about it at length, and Mommy told me about all her wonderful experiences there when she had studied at the school of drama.

It did sound exciting and my grandfather Larry was so anxious for me to come and live with him.

"Even if it's only for a year or two," Mommy told me, "it's a worthwhile experience for you, Summer."

I knew how hard it would be for her to be so far

away from me, so I knew she meant every word. She wanted the good things for me. She wanted me to taste what I had never tasted, see what I had never seen, hear what I had never heard. Experience, wide and wonderful, was so very important.

Maybe it was because her opportunities had been cut off so early in her life. Maybe she wanted to live them through me. Whatever her reasons, she was very convincing and in the end, I decided to do it.

Harley was a junior in college, already deep in his major. We corresponded while I was away, of course, but suddenly, his letters stopped coming. I thought he had found someone else. I wrote him a few times and then I stopped, too.

We drifted apart and when we saw each other the following summer, we were both embarrassed by it, fumbling for excuses. Toward the end of my school year, I did meet a very nice young man from London. His father was a member of Parliament and because of that, I got to see many royal events I would never have experienced.

However, our relationship thinned when I left to spend the summer at home. He met someone new and was practically engaged the next time I saw him. I didn't feel bad. I felt it was meant to be. No promises. No heartbreaks. No tears.

I was able to return early enough the following year to go with everyone to Harley's college graduation. He had done very well and won some awards in architecture. The result was he landed a

"Busy. I'm building a mall in Richmond."

"Wow."

"I hardly have enough time to eat these days," he said.

"But you're enjoying every moment, right?"

"Every moment," he said smiling. "Well, almost," he added after a beat.

"Oh?"

"All work and no play makes Harley a dull boy."

"Don't you play?"

"Not enough, not these days. I woke up this morning and stared at the ceiling and thought, look at me. I'm chasing the great American dream."

"So? What's wrong with that?"

"Nothing," he said. He plucked a blade of grass. "A long time ago, it seems, you and I stood by this lake and made a wish neither of us revealed. Remember?"

"Yes."

"We've traveled a long, winding road. At least I have, and here I am, back at the spot," he said looking around.

"So?" I said laughing.

"I never told you why I stopped writing you, calling you, that year."

"You didn't have to, Harley. We didn't owe each other anything."

"Yes we did, and that's why I stopped."

"I don't understand," I said closing my book and turning to him.

"I thought to myself, Harley Arnold, you have

no right to write her, to call her, to cause her to believe you can take care of her and be the man she needs, so stop the game, stop pretending, stop daydreaming and go to work.

"Then, time passed. You saw other boys. I had dates, but I couldn't shake it, Summer."

"Shake what, Harley?"

"Your face from their faces," he replied.

My heart seemed to lift as if it had been sleeping in my bosom, waiting to be nudged for real, to be touched for real.

"What are you saying, Harley?"

"I'm saying I feel confident now, confident and competent and worthy enough to hope you might remember our wish. I know you're not really involved with anyone else," he added with a smile. "Roy's been my spy."

"Is that right? No wonder he's always around whenever I go anywhere with anyone these days."

Harley laughed.

"Of course, he'd never admit that. He told me to do my own romantic dirty work, but he couldn't help telling me things every time we spoke on the phone or he came by to see me."

"I'll have to bawl him out," I said.

Harley nodded, looked down, took a deep breath and reached into his sports jacket pocket.

"It's not out of the blue," he said. "It's not something I just decided. It's not any sort of last minute idea. This has been burning a hole in my pocket for some time."

"What?"

He opened his palm and held out an engagement ring.

"It was my mother's," he said. "Roy gave it to me and said, when the time comes . . ."

I thought the breeze had died, the world had stopped turning, all the clouds had frozen against the blue sky. I know I was holding my breath.

"We belong together, Summer. We're meant to be. I can't love anyone else. I hope it's the same for you. Is it?" he asked, his eyes full of anxiety.

I looked away for a moment. Everything was right. Everything was suddenly so right.

"Yes," I said. "It's the same. It's always been."

He took my hand and put the ring on my finger and we kissed. Then we stood up, neither of us able to speak. We would go into the house to tell my parents. Uncle Roy surely already knew.

As we started up the path, I heard the familiar call of the blackbird and we both turned.

That was the only promise that counted, I thought.

The promise in our wish.

The promise that came true.

We hope you have enjoyed this Large Print book. Other G.K. Hall & Co. or Chivers Press Large Print books are available at your library or directly from the publishers.

For more information about current and upcoming titles, please call or write, without obligation, to:

G.K. Hall & Co.
295 Kennedy Memorial Drive
Waterville, ME 04901 USA
Tel. (800) 223-1244
        (800) 223-6121

OR

Chivers Press Limited
Windsor Bridge Road
Bath BA2 3AX
England
Tel. (0225) 335336

All our Large Print titles are designed for easy reading, and all our books are made to last.